"Don...

"I . . . . more apprehensive now than when she'd first awakened in Senecca's presence—which now seemed like hours ago—yet somehow she believed his words.

A small smile of recognition spread over his face. "I've already seen you without your clothes, so I won't be shocked."

"You won't be shocked!"

"Not at all. So don't worry about me."

Lila sensed his attempt at a bit of humor, but it didn't lessen the tension hanging heavily in the air between them. "I wasn't worrying about you."

"That can only mean you're worried about yourself. No need to be."

"No need?" Lila thought that was a strange comment.

"None. I must take care of your wound, or you may become infected. I can't let that happen." He set the lantern down on the floor near the bed. "Just think of me as a doctor. Turn on your side so I can see."

"You're not a doctor."

"I'm the closest thing you've got to one. Will a medicine man do?"

He smiled and took hold of the blanket. Lila held it tightly to her. She searched Seneca's face and, seeing no threat in his eyes, she turned slightly. He pulled the blanket away just enough to uncover the wound, and she felt a shaft of cold air slither down her spine. Whether it was from the air in the cabin or the thrill whirling crazily inside her, she didn't know . . .

PRAISE FOR GARDA PARKER'S BOOKS

"Breathtaking, exciting, thought provoking, and . . . emotion-packed."

—*Rendezvous* on SCARLET LADY

"A different outlook on life in the Old West . . . tender, loving, suspenseful, and humorous."

—*The Paperback Trader* on SCARLET LADY

GARDA PARKER
BLUE MOUNTAIN MAGIC

ZEBRA BOOKS
KENSINGTON PUBLISHING CORP.

ZEBRA BOOKS are published by

Kensington Publishing Corp.
475 Park Avenue South
New York, NY 10016

First Printing: June, 1994

Printed in the United States of America

With deepest thanks to all those who generously gave me their time when I requested assistance in writing this book. Among them are Richard S. Weiner of Escargot Books in Brielle, New Jersey; Sagamore Institute, Racquette Lake, New York; the Adirondack Railway Preservation Society, Eagle Bay, New York; the Adirondack Museum, Blue Mountain Lake, New York; Shibley Pixley, Hamilton Central School Library; dear friends Charlene Jeffris and Mary Lynch; and to Bob Milner for his good-natured trips with me poking around old cemeteries, ghostly empty mountain villages, rusty railroad tracks and shells of former stations, and abandoned lodge and hotel sites; for waiting patiently while I asked questions of every friendly Adirondacker I met; and for his extensive Adirondack map collection—but mostly for his love and support.

GP/93

One

New York City, winter, 1882

The tension fluttering through her was so charged, Lila believed she could cut it with one of the gracefully curved knives that rested to the right of her dinner plate. She couldn't sit still. Tonight something was going to happen that would change her life. She knew it as well as she knew her own name.

Lila let her nervous gaze sweep around the elegant dining room of the home she'd known all of her life, the stately Stockdale mansion in Gramercy Park. Eleven people chatted at a Queen Anne table. She noted with curiosity that the table had been set for twelve, and the twelfth chair was conspicuously empty. She couldn't imagine who had been invited to fill it, but it mattered not. One more cigar-smoking crony of her father's would only blend in with the others, and she'd be forced to make small talk with him and be ever the charming hostess.

Absently she ran a finger around a brilliant gold-rimmed white china dinner plate. The set had been specially designed with a flourished gold *S* in the middle of the plates and as usual was flanked by the family-crested gold-plated tableware. Gold-rimmed crystal glasses, three to a setting, shimmered against a background of blush-hued linen napery beneath a gaslit crystal chandelier. Two youthful male servants in matching black jackets, their pomaded hair catching the flickering light, glided swiftly along both sides of the table pouring champagne for each guest. When all crystal flutes were filled, Garrett Stockdale, presiding at the head of the table, rose and raised his glass. All eyes swung toward him, gazes filled with expectation.

"Ladies and gentlemen, I'd like your attention." Stockdale's voice glanced off the black walnut wood wainscoting and resounded around the gathering. A short rotund man with a head of thick gunmetal gray hair, Stockdale commanded a presence his stature belied. His face was so heavily jowled, his neck was not visible above his stiff white shirt collar. Lila thanked her lucky stars she'd been blessed with her mother's fine-boned features.

At the opposite end of the long table Lila felt her father's gaze skim over her and alight upon the young man seated at her right.

"I am pleased to announce the betrothal of my daughter, Lila Catherine, to Harrison Mayne," Garrett continued with a smugly proud tilt that jutted the point of his chin out of its shroud of jowls. "It is my pleasure to accept Harrison into my family. I have always regarded him as the son I never had. This marriage will make it legal."

"Hear, hear!" came the chorus of guests, all business associates of Garrett's. They followed their cheers with a murmuring of congratulations and best wishes, offered more to Garrett than they were to the newly betrothed couple.

Lila showed outwardly none of the turmoil of emotions she felt inside. *Her betrothal!* Garrett's words echoed in her mind. She should feel outraged at her father's surprise announcement, especially since he hadn't bothered to consult her about it, but she didn't. It was her place to accept it. She knew it was coming sooner or later. All things considered, she would have preferred later. Much later. Never.

The pairing of Lila and Harrison had not been of their own choosing. An understanding between Garrett Stockdale and Stewart Mayne regarding the marriage of their children had developed during the formation of their partnership in the construction of the Union Pacific Railroad. She'd grown up hearing about it, but somehow Lila had believed it would never come to this—the actual announcement of her engagement to Harrison Mayne. Though, considering how well she believed she knew her father, how she could have ever even hoped he would abandon the idea astounded her now.

Lila turned toward the fleshy-faced bespectacled Harrison. He didn't look at her once. His gaze was fastened firmly on her father. He seemed caught up in Garrett's words and basked in the attention bestowed upon him.

Garrett was right in thinking of the young man as the son he'd never had, for Harrison was more like Stockdale than he was his own father. Lila knew Harrison would display more devotion to her father than he ever would to her. Perhaps a more accurate term would be allegiance. Not that she'd ever done anything to encourage Harrison to become devoted to her. She felt absolutely nothing for Harrison Mayne. Never had. Never would.

"Thank you, sir," Harrison replied. His eyes never shifted toward Lila. "I'm honored by your acceptance. I won't let you down."

In all fairness Lila couldn't say Harrison actually felt anything for her either. But she believed he welcomed this announcement because she represented the irrevocable connection to her father he sought. She sensed Harrison's father was less inclined toward ruthlessness than Garrett, and Harrison admired ruthlessness. Certainly the partnership of their fathers had brought more gain to Stockdale than it had to Mayne. But, of course, she shouldn't know about those things. Business was much too important and complicated for a mere female to be interested in or, heaven forfend, understand.

"I hope you'll be very happy, my dear Cat," a frail voice whispered from Lila's left.

Lila shifted her gaze and let it rest lovingly on her aunt Maddie, a petite, reed-thin woman in her midsixties. Madeline Christopher Allgood, her mother's only sister, had called her niece Kitten as a child and then Cat as she'd grown up.

"Lila Catherine!" Lila's closest friend, Evalina Madison, seated on the other side of Maddie, leaned forward, pouting. "I'm shocked!" she whispered over the buzz of voices. "Why didn't you tell me you and Harrison were officially engaged?"

"I didn't know it myself until this moment," Lila whispered back.

Evalina's eyebrows shot up in surprise. "I don't know how to react," she said, giggling into her champagne. "I won't say I hope you'll be happy. I don't see how you could be with . . ." She lifted her gaze toward Harrison.

"It's easy once it's been drummed into you," Lila responded with irony. She lifted her glass and tapped her eyebrow in mock salute toward Garrett Stockdale.

"Now dear, don't do anything impetuous in front of the guests," Aunt Maddie warned. "You know how your father feels about propriety. You know what he expects of you, of us both."

Lila lowered her glass. As she drew in a steadying

breath, her heart filled with love for the dear old lady. She would do nothing to cause Aunt Maddie anxiety.

The other guests around the table politely drank to the health of the newly engaged pair. Lila had met the other couple, Clyde and Harriett Brigham, on Ladies Evening at her father's exclusive Amsterdam Club. Of course she knew Evalina's parents, Joseph Madison, who'd been Garrett's business partner for years, and his wife, Iris. As they beamed their practiced smiles upon her, Lila concentrated on forcing an appropriate one in return. *Stuffy and mindless women, just as I'll grow to be as Harrison's wife.* She sighed. *Perfect wives. Chattel. Just as Mother said.*

Harrison's father, Stewart, sat at his son's right, a grim expression tightening his spare features. He stood with some effort. A tall man with hunched shoulders and long thin arms and hands, he carried the pasty-faced look of one with a nutritional disorder. He raised his champagne flute and managed a small smile. "Mrs. Mayne and I are most pleased to welcome Lila into our family. Harrison is our only child, last in line of the Maynes, for the moment. We look forward to many grandsons."

Lila winced. Then she lifted a napkin to her lips, hoping no one had caught her reaction to Stewart Mayne's reference to future grandchildren. She couldn't picture them married, let alone Harrison as a father.

She barely could picture herself as a mother. She'd been thinking, lately more than ever, that mothers should know themselves first before they could give all that's necessary to a child. Lila possessed a wonder about herself, questions she couldn't answer, and knew she should not even be asking. How could she ever answer a child's questions, provide for its every need, if she couldn't do it for herself first?

Peering at him even now through champagne and crystal, Lila found nothing attractive about Harrison. In fact, she was repelled by the doughiness of his body and his thick stubby hands. It was impossible for her to accept the idea of him as her husband, claiming his conjugal rights in the marriage bed. She shivered. Her dreams of her wedding night had always been cloaked in perfume and lace and sweet gentle awakening. In those dreams her husband was tall, lean muscled, with the hands of an artist. Those dreams did not include Harrison. Now she narrowed her gaze through the effervescent liquid. His fleshy round face appeared softer, as jowly as her father's, as pliable as was Harrison's personality in the hands of Garrett Stockdale.

Seated next to Stewart Mayne, his buxom, round-hipped wife, Rosamund, whose application of exaggerated makeup and false beauty marks gave an almost polka-dotted appearance to her countenance, pruned her lips and offered nothing in addition to her husband's welcome. Lila took it to mean she had no intention of releasing her maternal grip on her only son. She'd seen Rosamund's possessive nature at several social functions.

She needn't feel threatened by me, Lila thought. *I'm not going to take him away from her.*

Harrison strongly resembled his mother. Lila watched the vacuous expression on her full-cheeked face and had a mental flash of what Harrison would look like when he reached that age. She wondered if someday they'd be seated at such a gathering as this, coldly discussing the betrothal of their own daughter. *If* they had a daughter. In order for that remote possibility to occur, she knew what she'd be forced to do. She controlled a shudder. The thought of Harrison's hands on her made her stomach clutch and her skin recoil as it had when she'd seen a green garden snake slither through the backyard flowers last spring.

"Bring on the food," Garrett boomed toward the doors that led to the kitchen, breaking Lila's reverie. "We've railroad building to discuss." As was typical of Garrett Stockdale, further dwelling on anything so frivolous as his daughter's engagement was foregone for discussion of business.

A formally dressed aging houseman, who went only by the name of Martin, held open the swinging oak door to the kitchen to allow two women servants in matching starched white aprons and caps to bustle through. He scrutinized their performance like a taskmaster as they efficiently arranged trays of gold-plated platters and bowls on the Queen Anne sideboard. They lifted the covers on glass plates of chilled shrimp in a piquant lemon and dill sauce. To admiring oohs and ahs all around, they presented each guest with a crystal bowl of the plump pink curls nestled among leaves of crispy deep green endive.

"Shouldn't we wait for our other guest?" Lila's gaze indicated the empty chair to Garrett's left. Despite her conviction that she cared not a whit who the guest might be, as a young woman well schooled in the ways of a gracious hostess, she was simply being polite by inquiring.

"Perhaps your future father-in-law might advise us." Garrett shoveled three shrimp into his cavernous mouth and spoke again as he chewed. "He has invited a mystery person."

Lila wondered silently how it was Garrett had allowed someone else to control anything at all, especially an extended dinner invitation to a mystery guest to his home, the place he considered his well-guarded castle. All who visited here were usually known to him or they did not gain entrance.

"Apparently he's been detained," Stewart said.

"Who is he, Mr. Mayne? Is he one of your business—"

"Don't be impertinent, Lila," Garrett cut in. "It's none of your affair."

Just as this betrothal is none of my affair, Lila thought.

Mayne frowned in Garrett's direction. "It won't matter anyway if he doesn't make an appearance."

"Whatever." Garrett stuffed the endive into his mouth and chewed broadly. He washed it down with a large gulp of champagne. "It's settled then. We shall all depart for a holiday in the Adirondack Mountains late May."

Evalina sent Lila a wrinkled-nose glance that spoke volumes about how much she was not looking forward to a rustic mountain holiday. Lila shrugged. They both knew they'd have no choice in the matter. They were treated as if they were children, regardless of their age. Evalina didn't seem to mind, but Lila had grown resentful. There was so much in her life she longed to change, longed to escape from. Still, she felt powerless to change anything.

Lila leaned behind Aunt Maddie and whispered, "These Adirondack Mountains could be the most exciting place we've ever visited."

"How?" Evalina whispered back. "I hear there are flies as big as blackbirds. And mud. And underbrush so thick it hides animals and vermin. Not to mention the—"

"Wild men, thrilling men!" Lila raised her eyes heavenward, baiting Evalina by showing her relish for such an adventure.

"Savages," Evalina hissed. "No one really knows what kind of people live up there in that wilderness, if any. I, for one, purely hate the whole idea."

"And I, for another, cannot wait to go," Lila whispered with excitement. "I'd love to meet a savage, as you call them."

"You are engaged to Harrison!" Evalina whispered the reminder.

Lila leaned lower behind her aunt's back. "All the more reason to—"

"Shush!" Aunt Maddie warned again. "Your father's glaring in this direction."

"Are you saying you don't want to marry Harrison?" Evalina whispered, ignoring Maddie's reprimand.

She licked her lips, and Lila knew just how delicious Evalina would find the whole thing if she broke the engagement on the spot. Everyone in this room would be mortified if she were to flat out refuse to marry Harrison, or any man not of her own choosing. It would be the talk of the club, to be sure, and Evalina would revel in the gossip and carry it all back to Lila. And Lila wouldn't care.

Friends since they were children, Evalina was as plump, bubbly, and lackadaisical as Lila was slim, calm, and controlled. Evalina had been left to her own devices, allowed to express herself freely. She could exhibit the tendencies of a spoiled child if not for her incredibly open and loving nature. Lila, on the other hand, was ruled by the stern hand of Garrett Stockdale, more so since the moment of her mother's death. She'd been groomed to act as the gracious wealthy hostess, at once a decorous and ever-silent support to her father and eventually to her future husband.

Lila sent Evalina a look she knew her friend would understand, a look that said she'd tell her everything later. She sat up straight and concentrated on the ongoing conversation.

"It's hardly going to be a holiday for me," Stewart Mayne was saying, a heaviness in his voice.

"A working holiday, if you prefer then," Garrett returned. "We can secure the rest of the land and survey our railroad before the others know what hit them."

"Where shall we take rooms?" Iris Madison whined, directing the question toward her husband. "It's so . . . *primitive* up there."

"I've chosen Prospect House on Blue Mountain Lake." As usual, Garrett answered for his partner. "It utilizes all the latest conveniences."

"Thank heavens for that," Iris whispered. "I thought you expected us to camp out-of-doors in those rustic sheds I've heard more than enough about."

"Lean-tos," her husband told her.

"I've heard it's the latest thing in outdoor sporting," Harriett Brigham said in her meek voice.

"I do wish we could wait until civilization reaches there," Rosamund Mayne said. "Who knows what might befall an unsuspecting party of genteel people? What about the safety of the ladies?" She dabbed at the corners of her mouth with more energy than was necessary. The other ladies nodded polite agreement.

"I certainly hope you don't expect us to be transported in a wagon to this place," Iris Madison sniffed.

Garrett let out a harsh breath from his nostrils and set his jaw. "We'll take the night boat to Albany. From there we'll board the Delaware and Hudson train and travel to North Creek."

"That doesn't sound too awful, Mother," Evalina said. "We do so enjoy rail travel."

"From North Creek Station," Garrett continued, ignoring Evalina, "we'll board Prospect House's own stagecoach, which will take us directly to its door at Blue Mountain Lake."

"A stagecoach? Well, I don't know about that," Rosamund Mayne said. "It sounds so like the frontier. I don't think my heart will take another episode like that trip across those treacherous plains. And all just to see another nail driven."

"Rosamund," Garrett snapped, "that was history in the making. The driving of the Golden Spike at Promontory Point united the first transcontinental railroad. It's making this country a major world trade force. It was a beginning for great things."

Stewart Mayne patted his wife's hand, comforting her from Garrett's stinging reply. "And it was the tragic end of some great people."

"That was almost fifteen years ago, Stewart. I wish you'd forget that unfortunate accident." Garrett looked anxiously toward the kitchen door.

"Accident," Stewart said dully.

"Father, do hush up," Harrison admonished. "I'm certain Mr. Stockdale and the rest of his guests would prefer to keep this occasion free from unpleasant discussions in honor of the ladies." He sent a conspiratorial glance toward his future father-in-law.

The servants emerged through the swinging doors, breaking into the tension. The omnipresent Martin took up his post at the sideboard and watched them clear away the first course plate, then followed his staff into the kitchen.

"It's the right time to be in the railroad business," Garrett said.

Lila felt more than heard the collective sighs of the women around the table. Whenever the men were together, all they talked about was railroad building. Their wives found it tiresome at best. But Lila found it thrilling, wishing she could be a part of the transportation expansion.

"The Canadian Pacific has been laying down record

lengths of track for the last two years," Garrett continued. "The Northern Pacific is complete."

"President Arthur expects the railroads to make the United States the trade power of the world," Lila said without thinking. She caught her father's silent reprimand at her outburst. She returned her concentration to what she was expected to know most about—dinner.

Garrett pounded the side of his hand on the table as he spoke. Crystal glasses tinkled against each other. "Mark my words, gentlemen, the Adirondacks will become a suburb of New York City precisely as the *Times* reported."

"You can't always believe everything you read in the *Times*," Brigham put in.

Garrett ignored him. "In less than a decade, as many as a hundred track lines will mesh those mountains. The sports will be drawn there by great hunting and fishing. The wealthy will flock there for respite from the trials of business. They'll need comfortable transportation into the wilds. We'll provide it for them. Our railroads will take their money to the mountains—and ultimately to us."

"I'm not so certain it can be done," Clyde Brigham said.

"It can't be done." Joseph Madison's voice was unemotional.

Stewart Mayne cleared his throat. "The Delaware and Hudson Railroad Company has for the last seven years monopolized rail traffic to Adirondack points with its Albany to Montreal line," he said with studied calm. "They have railheads at Ausable Forks and Saranac Lake, running trains from Plattsburgh. Even the Central Vermont and the Rome, Watertown, and Ogdensburg Railroad can't compete with them for traffic to Canada."

"Ah, but the Adirondack Railroad is a force to be reckoned with," Garrett averred.

"How do you suppose?" Joseph Madison asked.

"That's an unfinished line. And for good reason," Stewart added. "It's owned by the Lake Ontario and Hudson River Railroad. Their financial problems go too deep for us to get involved. Their investors have been ruined. They're millions in debt."

Lila sensed that Stewart was making every kind of excuse for not talking about railroad building. She wondered about that and about the great tragedy he'd spoken of earlier. She didn't remember any talk of it as she was growing up.

Garrett nodded. "Exactly. They're ripe to get rid of that unfinished line. It's been nothing but trouble for them. As I see it, we can acquire the Adirondack Railroad and build an extension line from North Creek to the Saint Lawrence River with access to Lake Ontario. The trade possibilities will be limitless."

Before anyone could respond, Martin returned to the dining room followed once again by his team of servants who, with great flourish, presented platters of succulent sea bass. Ada VanSchyler, the Stockdale's longtime cook, had personally selected the bass from the fishmonger at the Fulton Market, then steamed them in wine with fresh ginger and tiny white onions from the Chinese grocer. The aroma was heavenly, and Lila might have been carried away by it for a lovely moment if it hadn't been for Garrett's fist connecting with the table to make yet another point.

"And when we open lumber mills, hotels, and the like, we'll stand to make millions more in the bargain. You will have plenty of time to vacation later when you are wealthier than you ever dreamed. Think of the luxurious camps you will build for yourselves. Mine is already under way."

Lila raised her eyes momentarily, wanting to question

her father about the mountain camp he'd just mentioned. Just as quickly she returned them to her plate where a servant had placed a slice of sea bass. *This fish will never open its mouth again,* she thought. The fact that it was now laying inert on a dinner table, never to swim or blow bubbles again, might be a lesson for some people who opened their mouths more often than they should, or dreamed dreams they knew better than to even fantasize about. She'd been prone to those unhappy circumstances more often than not of late, and to let her mind wander more than it should.

As so often before, she had to work at paying attention to the evening's function. This one was no different than any of the others, except for the announcement of her engagement, of course. As usual she let her mind travel to lovelier destinations when her father and his associates spoke business. That's what society ladies did, didn't they?

Her father was pontificating as usual. *Pontificating.* Lila had loved that word ever since she'd discovered its meaning while studying at Miss Bolton's Boarding School for Girls. The moment she'd heard it, a picture of her father had flashed into her mind. Now he was pontificating once again about building a railroad through the Adirondacks.

Lila's gaze wandered down the long table toward the empty chair once more. Her eyes traced the fan-shaped detail of its back. Her curiosity escalated about who would occupy it this evening. Whoever it was, she admired the sheer effrontery of this guest's behavior by arriving at a Garrett Stockdale dinner much later than was fashionable—or worse, not appearing at all.

Savoring a luscious bite of sweet potatoes whipped with Gruyère cheese, Lila allowed a bit of mischievousness to take over. She leaned behind her aunt and tapped Evalina on the shoulder. "The Prince of Transylvania," she whispered, shifting her eyes toward the empty chair.

Evalina leaned back, nodding her head in understanding. "You've announced him before, and he has never appeared," she whispered, pushing up the point of her dainty nose with an index finger. Her soft brown eyes danced with merriment.

Lila laughed lightly. Aunt Maddie cleared her throat, and Lila knew she was enjoying the exchange as she always had when she and Evalina were little. It was a guessing game they'd played often as children when they'd overheard their parents speak of important guests who would attend one of their snooty and oh-so-correct soirees. Dressed in their nightgowns, the girls would perch in the butler's pantry, believing those to be the most perfect events on earth, where they might catch a glimpse of someone whose photograph had recently appeared in the newspapers. Like all young ladies, they'd scoured the society pages, whispering over this debutante's latest event or that young rogue's escapade.

When the two girls went off together to Miss Bolton's School, they continued the game when faced with disagreeable lectures or boring parties. The object of the game was to meet the men of their dreams in the most unpredictable of ways. They'd been much more precise then in their descriptions of their dream men of the moment, always hoping one or the other would meet her heart's desire. It never mattered which of them it was, for the other would be ecstatic if one of them fell in love and was swept off her feet by a dashing man of wealth and breeding.

Now Lila toyed with a cluster of steamed brussels sprouts arranged in a half circle on her plate. She'd hated brussels sprouts all her life. Swallowing an emotional moment, she recalled how her mother had always spirited them away from her daughter's plate. Concealing them in her napkin, Catherine would discreetly pass them to Maddie, who'd whisk them into the kitchen and drop them into the bowl belonging to Mrs. VanSchyler's mangy dog. Later Maddie would gleefully report that the dog had rejected them as well, and she'd gone off on another disposal mission.

Even now the hateful faded green things kept appearing on Lila's plate over protestations to her father that, as an adult, she had the right in her own home to forego food she found disagreeable. Garrett Stockdale had not seen it her way. She was building character, he'd say, by eating food and performing duties of a female of her station. *Her station.* She hated that term.

She slid a glance toward Harrison, who seemed to be relishing the brussels sprouts on his plate. Harrison had never liked the vegetable either. Lila had the distinct impression he was making a show of enjoying them simply to ally himself with her father.

Evalina winked at her when she caught Lila toying with the vegetables. She leaned behind Aunt Maddie again and whispered, "The Earl of Brussels."

Lila swallowed a laugh and leaned back. "Too green for experienced women such as ourselves." She returned to close examination of the brussels sprouts on her plate, rearranging them to resemble a rather lumpy green worm.

Aunt Maddie choked daintily on a brussels sprout while stifling a giggle herself. Lila covered an uncontrollable grin with her napkin.

Garrett sent an admonishing frown toward his sister-in-law, and Maddie immediately responded by fixing him with an interested stare.

"What makes you think you can build a railroad in that

wilderness?" Brigham asked. The light from the chandelier glistened off his bald head. "And how will you know the terrain is agreeable to construction?"

"You've seen Stewart's drawings. He has secured the services of an excellent surveyor," Garrett answered. "And then there are mountain guides—hermits and trappers who know the land well. They've lived all their lives among the trees and animals in the mountains. I'm told they're excellent guides."

"Mountain hermits?" Harriett Brigham asked timidly.

"Barbarians. I'm told some of them are not human through and through," Rosamund Mayne added.

"Now what does that mean?" Stewart Mayne said wearily.

"Frieda Woolworth told me there are men in the Adirondacks who are half human and half mountain lion, or something."

"For heaven's sake, Rosamund, use your head. That defies the laws of decency. Just how do you think something can be born which is half human and half animal?"

It was obvious Stewart Mayne realized the impropriety of his question the moment it had passed his lips, for he fidgeted then with the brussels sprouts on his plate. The ladies around the table made great performance of accepting a second helping from the servants, while the gentlemen barely stifled amused snickers. Maybe her least favorite vegetable was useful for something after all, Lila mused.

When the others seemed preoccupied, Lila leaned in back of Aunt Maddie again and tapped Evalina's shoulder. "What would you think of that?" she whispered. "A wild mountain man who will bear you away to his cave and make passionate love to you for days. I think it would be thrilling."

Evalina blushed and shivered. "Scares me to death. As your best and true friend, I can do nothing but relinquish him to you," she whispered.

Lila whispered back, "Think of what it would be like with a primitive man."

Evalina patted her chest to indicate a fluttering heart. "You are the one who has always talked of meeting a man who wasn't a gentleman."

Lila sucked in the corner of her bottom lip. "I just wondered about it, that's all. You are the one who can get away with behavior beneath our station."

"You are of fainter heart than I supposed, my friend."

Lila nodded acquiescence. "Dreams are just that. It's expected that I—" She caught her father's frown of reprimand and went back to her dinner plate.

"What about Indians?" Iris Madison asked.

Lila leaned back to catch Evalina's eyes. She mouthed the word "Indians" and raised her eyebrows in approval. Evalina gave a mock shudder.

Martin had entered the dining room from the front hall archway and for a time stood erect and imperious, waiting for the moment Garrett Stockdale would notice him. Lila marveled at how rigid he could remain, how patient—patience being not one of her strongest virtues.

"What about Indians?" Garrett's voice carried a measure of irritation.

"Are they friendly?" Iris returned, seemingly undaunted by Garrett's tone. She leaned forward in anticipation of his answer.

Garrett dropped his fork and chewed rapidly on a large brussels sprout. "What few there are have no choice but to be hospitable. They know their place." He looked up and caught Martin still standing at attention. "What is it, Martin?" Garrett's irritation spread to the houseman.

Martin sniffed. "A Mr. Pierce has arrived, sir." His face registered the disdain he felt for the newly arrived guest. "He's waiting in the front parlor."

Evalina shot a quick glance toward Lila, who nodded her head. This was perhaps the moment when the mystery guest would enter the dining room and their lives.

A frown pleated the space between Garrett's eyebrows. "Pierce, did you say?"

"Yes, sir. Not the sort I would think you would . . . that is, he doesn't appear to be altogether a gentleman, sir."

"Ah, he's arrived then," Stewart Mayne said, rising and turning toward the houseman. "Show him in, Martin." When Martin didn't move, Mayne added quickly with a slight bow to his head, "With Mr. Stockdale's permission, of course."

"This is your invited guest?" Stockdale demanded. When Mayne nodded, he added, "Why—?"

"He is our Adirondack surveyor," Mayne told him.

Garrett frowned. "I should have been informed of that. The least he could have done was to arrive on time. Don't ever assume again that you have free rein to invite someone to my table, Mayne. Especially someone named Pierce." Stockdale narrowed his eyes and set his jaw.

Lila and Evalina exchanged questioning looks. Lila sensed there was more to her father's antipathy toward this guest than merely his tardiness. She turned toward Aunt Maddie, who slightly raised a hand to quell the possibility of her openly expressing curiosity.

"Shall I show him out, sir?" Martin clearly enjoyed the exchange between Garrett and his partner.

"No." Garrett raised his arm and flapped his fingers, indicating just the opposite.

"Very well," Martin complied and turned around smartly, heading down the hall. He returned only a moment later, his white-gloved hands pressed smartly against his black trousers, his chin raised enough to effect an air of superiority. "Mr. Seneca Pierce," he announced and stepped aside.

A chorus of shocked gasps came from the women. Lila's breath caught and hung heavy in her chest. The pointed black walnut archway framed a man such as she had never before seen nor even conjured in a dream.

Tall and imposing as an oak, the strength of Seneca Pierce's broad shoulders was evident under the cocoa-brown coat and white tucked-front shirt. He'd omitted the stiff collar worn by the other men. Instead a wide necklace of varicolored wooden beads, strung intermittently with what appeared to be seed pods, encircled his neck and dropped gracefully down the front to end in a flat circle of brown animal hide, below which dark leather fringe disappeared into his coat.

His coal-black long hair was swept back, the coil of it caught at his nape by a beaded thong, the thick tail falling below the back of his neck. Lila marveled at how his hair shone under the gaslight, which flickered a blue sheen over the top of his head.

But it was his eyes that captured her gaze, and finally all of her attention, and held them fast. They were blue as a clear summer sky and as penetrating as a bolt of lightning that could slice through it at whim. He stood erect, commanding, brilliant—paling in her vision every other presence in the room. The gathered guests were frozen with shock, simply by his imposing appearance.

Lila was stunned.

Without breaking his gaze on Lila, Seneca Pierce strode soundlessly to the empty chair at the end of the table near her father. He placed both long-fingered bronze hands over the curve in the chair back.

"This place must be reserved for me." The rich and soft voice penetrated the tension in the room like a cool breeze through the lull before a thunderstorm.

Martin nodded in his imperious fashion.

Seneca Pierce's clear gaze swept over the gathering, returning once again to linger on Lila. When he spoke, his controlled voice held the attention of everyone but connected most completely with the pulse roaring in her ears.

"Then Mr. Stockdale is correct. We Indians do know our place."

Two

Seneca Pierce pulled out the empty chair at the elaborate Stockdale dinner table. He had to admit he enjoyed this reaction every time it happened. These prune-faced ladies and gentlemen of polite society held one view of Indians—one view only—based on stories from the wars or out of the West. Indians were always filthy, half-dressed drunken savages. These people never reckoned to see a sober one, freshly bathed, and even more incongruous, wearing trousers and coat.

Seneca opted out of wearing the requisite vest every time, feeling it was a symbol of gluttony and greed. Inside, a vest held a thickening waist and middle bulging from the many indulgences in food and drink and the inactivity of the idle rich. Outside, it carried the rich man's pocket watch and gold ornamental fob. The watch's only function, as far as he could ascertain, was to tell the man it was time to get something more, take something more from someone else, whether it was material possessions or a life.

Seneca's eyes scanned the dinner guests. He saw in them disdain, ignorance, and more. There was hatred in Stockdale's eyes. Or was it fear? Seneca suspected Stockdale might be justified in the latter. In the face of the giggly plump young female with fussy hair near the end of the table, he saw open curiosity. At least that was honest. Next to her a frail old lady smiled a welcome. That was pleasant.

Next to the old lady a pair of green eyes blazed out of the face of a young woman so beautiful, so still, Seneca wondered if she were real, or the rich man's latest lifelike ornamentation. Her eyes were so exquisite, so sparkling in the room's light, they were all his senses could take in at once. Her gaze was frank, direct—equal to the intensity with which he leveled his own on her. Her eyes radiated countless questions and sent statements of their own that he could not read but was compelled to know.

"Ladies and gentlemen," Stewart Mayne said as he ambled toward Seneca's chair, "I present Mr. Seneca Pierce." He placed a hand warmly on Seneca's shoulders. "Mr. Pierce, your host, Garrett Stockdale." He opened his other arm and directed it toward Stockdale.

"Pierce," Stockdale said evenly, his voice taking on a distinct edge of wariness.

Seneca's gaze shifted momentarily to his host. "Mr. Stockdale, we meet at last. Thank you for the invitation to your home."

Seneca knew that response would rankle him. Stockdale would not relish seeing him. And he hadn't invited him. Stewart Mayne had. Seneca did not extend his right hand in greeting. That was the white man's way. Since he was only half white, he gladly let his Indian half take over in this instance.

Mayne continued his introductions all around. Seneca was met with stilted greetings or none. Most of the women in the group lowered their eyes, raised them quickly, then lowered them again. He smiled wryly, figuring they thought by doing that—if they ignored him—then he truly wasn't there. It was always one way or the other. Ignore

Indians as if they didn't exist, or wipe them out because they were in the way.

"Miss Evalina Madison," Mayne continued his introductions, gesturing toward the still giggling young woman.

"A pleasure, Miss Madison," Seneca replied, smiling.

Evalina tittered behind her napkin.

"Madeline Allgood, Mr. Stockdale's sister-in-law."

Maddie nodded her head, smiling faintly. "Mr. Pierce, how lovely to meet you."

"Thank you, Miss Madeline. I'm honored. You're very gracious."

Seneca winked at her and enjoyed the hint of a saucy tilt to the lady's gray head in response. He let his gaze fall on each one of them for the brief moment of introduction before letting it return to the end of the table and the stunning woman with the green eyes he found so fascinating. Her gaze was still intent upon him. Mayne passed over her and motioned toward a doughy-looking young man at her right.

"My son, Harrison Mayne."

Seneca reluctantly dragged his gaze away from the green one and nodded his head toward the younger Mayne, who abruptly turned away. *Not even the politeness of a cool greeting,* Seneca thought. He'd seen many of his type when he'd attended college.

"My wife, Rosamund." Mayne tapped her on the shoulder and she jumped as if bitten by an insect.

"Mrs. Mayne." Seneca watched her nod faintly while staring at her plate.

"And I've saved the best for last," Mayne said, puffing out his chest and gesturing toward the end of the table. "May I present Miss Lila Catherine Stockdale, daughter of Garrett and soon to be my daughter-in-law."

Seneca creased his brow briefly at the mention of her future status. She spoke before he had time to greet her.

"Mr. Pierce, welcome to our home." Her voice was low, smoky, and sweet like fresh hot maple syrup, a complement to the blaze in her eyes, which she never lowered from his face.

"Thank you, Miss Stockdale." He let his gaze slip momentarily from her face to young Mayne's, then back to hers again. "May I offer my congratulations on your impending marriage."

"Thank you. Our engagement was announced only this evening. The wedding date is quite far into the future." She was so still, so calm, not at all like that fidgeting young friend of hers. Yet that smoky voice told him all was not perfect in the supposedly perfect world in which she lived.

"I hope we don't have to wait too long, my dear," Stewart Mayne said, smiling benignly.

Harrison Mayne came alive then. He'd watched the exchange between Seneca and his newly betrothed, and Seneca sensed he hadn't liked what he saw. "Actually I expect we won't put the wedding off for very long at all. Since we'll have just a simple garden ceremony, I think early this spring will be time enough to wait."

Miss Madeline's mouth drooped sadly, Seneca observed. It would seem this recent announcement was not the happy event the Maynes purported it to be.

Still, Lila Stockdale didn't move. "Weddings take time to plan and prepare," she said quietly, her eyes still on Seneca.

"Indeed they do," Miss Madeline concurred, brightening. "And I'm afraid I don't move as quickly as I used to. Just try to bear with me in the preparations, Mr. Mayne.

It may take me months to make all the arrangements. Perhaps more than a year."

"That will be enough, Madeline," Stockdale cut in, and the older woman shrank back into her mouselike self.

Seneca sensed the tension on both sides of the table surrounding this wedding. No matter. The marriage of two spoiled society children shouldn't—didn't—interest him.

Lila Stockdale sat serenely erect and still in a high-necked forest-green velvet gown adorned in simple elegance by one exquisite emerald mounted in an intricately detailed gold brooch. Her burnished golden hair was swept up in loose shining coils, with wispy tendrils framing her lovely oval face and skin, which reminded him of the first peaches of the season. One long thick ringlet from her nape draped softly over her left shoulder.

Mayne hadn't told him about this—when he'd invited him to Stockdale's dinner, Seneca had expected it would be the usual gathering of men of finance and commerce. He could take these dinners or leave them, whatever suited his mood. But the name Stockdale was a big draw for him. It was more than due time he should see Garrett Stockdale in the flesh. Yet he hadn't expected a dinner also attended by women, one so personal as a betrothal celebration.

Stockdale's daughter. Who would think so loathsome a man could have such a thoroughly lovely offspring? The seeds of the plans he had been forming regarding Garrett Stockdale had been planted without knowledge of a daughter. Her presence complicated everything, and he sensed in more ways than he could ever have imagined. For the first time since he'd learned where Stockdale was, he felt threatened.

"Be seated," Stockdale commanded.

Without lifting his gaze from Lila, Seneca lowered into

the chair and slid it closer to the table. He heard the audible sighs that traveled around the room and the nervous clearing of Stockdale's throat.

Two servants scurried out of the kitchen under Martin's watchful eye and set about serving the newly arrived guest. He let his gaze drift momentarily to smile and murmur thanks to them, before settling into dining while the other guests resumed eating or accepted additional helpings.

Seneca lifted his eyes and focused more closely on Lila. Her head was tipped slightly toward the old lady and she whispered only a word. Her hair glowed copper and gold like maple leaves under autumn sun. Her narrow shoulders barely moved as her delicate hands gestured almost imperceptibly. Fascinated, Seneca watched those hands.

What was she doing with her napkin over the edge of her plate? His vision was usually acute enough to spot a rabbit in decayed underbrush in the forest. Here in the elegant dining room, it was sharp enough to see society daughter, Lila Stockdale, cover a number of brussels sprouts on her plate and spirit them away in a napkin pouch. Seneca controlled the twitch of a knowing grin as he saw the pouch being passed under the table to Miss Madeline, who subtly stashed it away, no doubt, in a pocket in her skirt.

"More brussels sprouts, Miss Lila?" A woman servant bent toward her holding a serving dish over which she poised a gold-plated spoon.

Lila's attention had been fastened upon Seneca Pierce until he'd been distracted by the servants offering him dinner. She'd seized that moment to smuggle away the nasty brussels sprouts into Aunt Maddie's waiting hand. But now her father's eyes were on her with a questioning glare. She knew he would reprimand her later, and not for her act of brussels sprouts rustling. He would chastise her for being so bold as to stare at the new guest—and worse to allow him to stare at her without lowering her eyes demurely.

"Yes, of course," she said absently to the servant. Then she noticed Harrison watching her with the smug expression on his face that she so detested. She smiled sweetly at him. "On second thought, no. I won't be selfish. Give all of them to Harrison. I know how much he *adores* brussels sprouts." She peered around the servant's rotund hip. "Don't you . . . *dear?*"

Harrison's face went to dull ashen. The servant nodded and obligingly emptied the bowl of the remaining brussels sprouts onto his plate.

There—may you choke on them, Lila thought, none too charitably.

She shifted her gaze when she felt another's eyes on her. Seneca Pierce was watching her, chewing thoughtfully, an enigmatic smile upon his lips, before he spoke. She knew he had observed the whole scene, and against what she knew to be the proper thing to feel, she enjoyed the surreptitious deception she shared with him.

"You're a better man than I, Mayne," Seneca said. "Never could stand brussels sprouts myself. Won't eat them. Not even just to be polite." He lifted his eyebrows toward Lila for the briefest of moments, then went back to the fish.

Lila stifled a small laugh, but Madeline was not so fortunate in her attempt. A little giggle escaped her lips, caught by the ever-vigilant ears of her brother-in-law. Garrett gave her his usual admonishing glance.

Harrison coughed lightly. "Of course, brussels sprouts are an acquired taste that only those with discerning appetite—Mr. Stockdale as an example—can truly enjoy.

I'm sure you're more used to things like fish bait and meadow weeds." He sniffed.

"If you mean fresh-caught trout from a mountain stream with a plate of virgin fiddlehead ferns, well, then, you're right." Another gasp from the older ladies. Seneca continued as if he hadn't heard it. "I must say this fish is elegantly prepared. Rivals that served at Delmonico's. My compliments to your chef, Miss Stockdale." He made a slight dip with his head as if to salute her. An amused smile played at the corner of his mouth as Seneca spoke to Lila.

A beautifully shaped mouth with a full bottom lip, she thought. When he dipped his head, the flickering light caught the deep ebony of his hair, making those disconcerting blue-black glints move over it. Lila's hand trembled as she lifted it to smooth a stray lock of her own hair that had fallen over her eye.

"How gracious of you, Mr. Pierce. And do you dine at Delmonico's often?" She caught her father's admonishing look, yet surprised herself by avoiding acknowledgment of it, holding her composure and defending her normal nature to withdraw from the conversation.

The gazes of the gathered guests shifted toward Lila.

"Only occasionally," Seneca replied. "I find the atmosphere rather constricting. Having to maintain stiff manners is not at all good for the digestion."

The gazes shifted toward Pierce, back to Garrett whose chins pleated as he glared at his daughter, then swung to Lila.

"I hadn't thought of an evening at Delmonico's in quite that way. Do you have a favorite haunt?"

"I much prefer the hunt. I always say there's nothing like the taste of leg of a turkey shot with your own arrow and roasted over your own fire ring. Ever tried that, Miss Stockdale?"

Seneca held his full gaze on her. Below her chest Lila felt her insides squirming, and she enjoyed the challenge of maintaining a calm exterior for the other guests while trading spirited conversation with the fascinating Seneca Pierce. There was the twinge of a bittersweet thrill knowing her father would most certainly favor her with one of his lectures on feminine propriety—but these moments were, as Evalina would say, too delicious to pass up.

Harriett Brigham sucked in an audible sharp breath. "Oh, dear, do you shoot turkeys, too, Mr. Pierce?"

"You mean in addition to white settlers, Mrs. Brigham?" A twitter of hushed nervous laughter traveled around the table while Seneca paused, an amused smile tilting the corner of his mouth as he watched her fan her reddening face with her napkin. "Well, yes, I do. That is, when I can't get pheasant or quail." He shifted attention back to Lila. "What about you, Miss Stockdale?"

Lila took a moment to sip water and slowly replace her glass next to her plate. "I can assure you, Mr. Pierce," she said, a like smile in return, "I've never once shot a white settler."

Seneca raised his water glass in a silent toast toward her.

Evalina burst into gales of bubbly laughter. Aunt Maddie's practiced elbow connected with Lila's hip. Garrett cleared his throat rather loudly, while Stewart Mayne didn't lift his napkin to his mouth quickly enough to cover a grin.

Lila could hold no longer Seneca's intense gaze nor her own half of their surprising conversation. Her father's lack of attempt to control Seneca Pierce, as he usually did anyone who graced his dinner table, did not go unnoticed by his daughter or by anyone else there. Lila knew she'd pushed the boundaries of his tolerance and would suffer the consequences later, but she held the profound sense that she would secretly believe the last few minutes with Seneca Pierce would be worth any punishment her father could administer.

Although dinner passed subsequently amid the usual polite—although at moments strained—exchanges, Lila had never felt quite so unnerved in her life, quite so devoid of her usual collected demeanor. Even the surprise of her father's announcement of her engagement to Harrison hadn't managed to shake her so deeply. Letting the idea slip into her mind now, she considered that she must believe the marriage would never occur. Fantasy, perhaps, but she knew she'd performed well in the moment of the announcement under the watchful eyes of the gathered guests. She would handle the matter with her father later, privately.

Now under the penetrating and disturbing scrutiny of Seneca Pierce, she marveled at the strength she could summon to hold her senses under control. What did it mean? Why was she having such a physical and emotional reaction to his presence?

She couldn't keep from watching him, entranced by the movement of his hands as he consumed his dinner with the deportment of a lord of the manor. But she was most fascinated by Seneca's eyes. She anticipated—no . . . *hoped* he would lift them and look at her every time she looked at him. He did just then, and her breath caught in her chest. In those eyes she could see the sky: clear, blue, cloudless. Eyes as perfectly open as the sky had been when she'd once stood at the shore of the Atlantic Ocean and watched a blackbird soar high and free while she wished she could wear its wings for just one day.

At the exactly correct moment, the servants descended again and cleared away the dinner dishes. They returned with small baskets and pale bristled brushes for the removal of crumbs. Martin had trained them well, Lila noted. They were so experienced in being unobtrusive that their swift work did not intrude upon the proceedings.

"What brings you here, Mr. Pierce?" Clyde Brigham asked with exaggerated politeness.

"An invitation to dinner," Seneca answered immediately.

"No, not here. I meant to New York . . . State."

Seneca regarded him openly. "I live in New York State."

"Where might that be in New York State?" Harriett Brigham ventured.

"The mountains. The Adirondacks."

Iris Madison's wineglass slipped from her fingers. "The Adirondacks did you say?"

Seneca did not immediately respond. Lila saw the look on Iris's face when she shot a glance toward Garrett and knew exactly what was going through her mind. Here— sitting at the same dinner table with her—was one of the savages of whom they'd been speaking prior to his arrival. *Iris must be squirming with fear inside her corset,* she thought with returning amusement.

"I'm not a plains native. I was born in New York State."

"And . . . do you favor your parents in looks?" Rosamund Mayne inquired.

Lila began to feel uncomfortable at this line of questioning. These people whom she'd been taught to respect, even to emulate, were asking insulting personal questions of a stranger, a guest in their home. The worst thing was, she sensed they felt in their right to do it because he *wasn't one of them.*

Martin pushed open the swinging door. As always, Lila

knew he understood the exact moment in the evening when dessert and coffee should be presented. He listened to the discussion briefly, then discreetly slipped back into the kitchen hall, letting the door close with nary a whisper. This was not the moment.

Seneca took his time wiping his hands on a white linen napkin, then set it carefully on the table. "What exactly are you asking me, Mrs. Mayne? Why don't you come right out and ask if my parents were heathen Indians?"

Rosamund flushed, and her shoulders jerked. "Mr. Pierce, I do hope you don't think I'm prying. I wouldn't dream of—"

"Yes, Mrs. Mayne, I do think you're prying. You know what people say about curiosity and cats." She sucked in her breath, and he appeared to wait long enough to let the resultant memory of the old saying have its impact. "However, since it's clear to me I won't be left to finish this delicious meal unless you know the information you so insistently seek, I'll tell you this much. My father was half Iroquois, my mother full-blooded."

"Oh, a half-breed," Rosamund said haughtily, her eyes shifting over the faces of the other guests.

Lila froze, her gaze fastened to Seneca.

"Your term," he said, eyes hard and blazing. "Derogatory, of course, and one I detest. My heritage makes me three-quarters Iroquois. Or one-quarter white, if that will ease at least one quarter of your mind."

Well done, Lila thought. That should put Harrison's meddling mother in her rightful place.

But his retort was not enough to silence Rosamund Mayne. "And your hair and dark skin, is that from your mother or father?"

Lila was stunned that Mr. Mayne did not quietly admonish his wife to stop this interrogation. Both he and

Harrison gave the impression they weren't listening to the conversation, but she could tell they were very aware of what was being said.

Seneca did not waver in his forthright response. "Fortunately I 'favor' both my parents in looks and in integrity. I was educated at Saint Lawrence University. I've been in this city teaching a class at New York University. I am here at this dinner at the invitation of your husband. I trust that information will satisfy you for the time being?"

"Are . . . are your parents with you?" Rosamund Mayne asked with a measure of trepidation covered by her usual cutting tone.

"My parents are dead," Seneca replied.

"Were they killed, or . . . ?"

Seneca turned his head slowly and gave her a penetrating stare. "You mean in a raid when the settlers came to wipe out the buffalo and the teepees?"

Rosamund swallowed hard and silently dropped both hands heavily into her lap, for once undone by her own air of superiority.

"If you must know, my father took his own life." Seneca shifted his hard gaze toward Garrett Stockdale. "I believe he was driven to it. And in that case I believe he was killed—murdered as surely as if someone had put a gun to his head and pulled the trigger."

Lila gasped with the horror of Seneca's words. "How utterly devastating," she breathed.

Garrett Stockdale moved uncomfortably. He sent Seneca a narrow-eyed glance, then studiously straightened the napkin in his lap. Lila sensed tension between the two men. What was that about? Did they know each other? Seneca's gaze shifted for only a moment to Lila's face, then back to linger steadily on Garrett's. She saw rage in his eyes—in a burning blue fire—and instinctively knew she would never want to be on the receiving end of that anger.

"And your mother?" Clyde Brigham pressed.

Seneca lowered his eyes toward his plate. "My mother died of a terrible sickness." His voice was quiet, thick.

Lila felt a lump form in her throat. Nervously the other guests began chatting among themselves. Unable to keep from looking at him, she watched Seneca Pierce finish his dinner. She wondered more than ever why he'd been invited this evening, but she was certainly not going to ask outright. She'd already contributed more than her fair share of tension to the evening.

Evalina leaned behind Aunt Maddie to tap Lila's shoulder. Lila bent to meet her. "It's delicious, just too delicious," Evalina whispered. "No one *ever* puts Mrs. Mayne in her place, not even Mr. Mayne. Mother says Harrison won't even try it. He sides with her." She looked over her shoulder at the last guest, then back to Lila. "Isn't Seneca Pierce frightening?"

"Fascinating," Lila whispered back. "Seneca Pierce is utterly fascinating."

Evalina frowned at her friend's response. "Lila! This isn't a game. You know he's strange."

"Different, yes."

Maddie gave her a gentle cautioning nudge with her pointed elbow, and Lila sat up straight. Seneca Pierce wasn't strange at all. He truly was fascinating, or rather he fascinated her. And he was frightening, too—Evalina was right about that. There was something wild about him under his civilized clothing. He smoldered under it. Lila felt it. And she was drawn to him involuntarily, like a moth hypnotized by a flame.

"I, for one, think Mr. Pierce can be of enormous assistance to us, what with his knowledge of the Adirondacks and all," Joseph Madison said, ignoring the resultant sighs of the women. "We should enlist his opinion on the probability of appropriate ground for tracklaying."

"Indeed. That's why I invited him this evening," Stewart Mayne said. "What do you think, Seneca, of the future of commercial development in the Adirondacks?"

Seneca's shoulders settled. "You know, of course, that the Durant family has huge holdings in the mountains," he told them. "Whole townships, businesses, their own extensive camps."

"Yes, we know all that," Garrett Stockdale returned impatiently. "Ever since Dr. Durant's involvement with the transcontinental railroad, his family thinks they can do anything they want. This is one time they won't control everything they see."

"Developing the forests and lakes of the Adirondacks into a playground for the rich should not be turned into a chess game played by former railroad partners still smarting from their losses and the scandal," Seneca said darkly, leveling his penetrating gaze on Garrett.

Garrett flushed red. "What difference could that possibly make to me in this instance?"

"There are those in the mountains who strongly oppose what the Durants are doing. They will oppose just as strongly the intrusion of others like them. And there will come a time—whether of their own self-destruction or from the powers of nature—when the vision of these developers will be swept away."

"There are ways," Garrett said, "to make people see things the right way. I intend to do just that."

Seneca lifted his strong angled jaw. "The Iroquois have an old saying: 'The deed must serve all the people well to serve best for one.' "

Lila watched her father and Seneca Pierce square off

while the others remained silent. Her sense of an underlying current between them had grown stronger with every word they'd spoken. The way Stewart Mayne was squirming in his chair, she knew he felt it, too. Or perhaps he knew something she didn't. He'd been part of the Union Pacific organization as well. He'd gone down with her father at the same time the company was blown wide open by embezzlement and scandal. She didn't know the facts, but she did know the results.

Again Martin came to the swinging door. Again he retreated. Lila looked around at the gathered guests and understood their discomfort. The women were rigid in their chairs, benign expressions on their faces as they strove to remain uninterested and uninvolved in male conversation as they'd been taught. She took in a deep breath as she broke her father's stern command that she conduct herself as beautiful, lacking opinion, silent.

"Father, perhaps we should consider dropping this subject for the moment. Martin is anxious to serve dessert."

"Lila, hold your tongue. You've said just about enough this evening. This is none of your affair."

Once again her father had pronounced whatever was being discussed as none of her affair. But wasn't she supposed to be hostess in this house? That being the case, she would very well take command of the correct presentation of the rest of this dinner. Once again the penetrating gaze of Seneca Pierce settled upon her. Lila pulled her posture erect and lifted her chin.

"Then I suggest we allow Martin to serve dessert and coffee," she said calmly. "After which you gentlemen may then retire to the library for brandy and cigars and resume this business discussion, while the ladies engage in conversation in the front parlor. Martin, you may present dessert."

Followed by the servants bearing trays of vanilla crème molds covered with caramel sauce, Martin came through the door more quickly than Lila had ever seen him move. She knew Mrs. VanSchyler must have been stewing in the kitchen over the molds melting and the sauce crystallizing.

A chorus of ahs around the table spelled the break in tension as each guest exclaimed over the lovely dessert. Lila noticed that Seneca politely refused the sweet concoction. He did accept coffee which he did not lace with cream or sugar.

For the next half hour the guests partook of sweet tastes and subdued conversation. And Lila enjoyed a moment of triumph she knew she would pay for later with one of her father's tonguelashings.

Garrett flared again at Seneca once the men had gathered in the library. "Durant's in hot water and you know it, Pierce. His investors have already lost millions of dollars. He intended to make connection with the Adirondack Ironworks. He hasn't. He planned for track to go to Blue Mountain Lake, Long Lake, Tupper Lake, and skirt the shores of the Eckford lakes. It hasn't. He planned . . . well, it doesn't matter what else he planned. What he cannot achieve, I can. I could have proved that with the Union Pacific if he, and . . . others hadn't thwarted me. I will show him and everyone else this time just what Garrett Stockdale is made of."

He strode to the breakfront on the far wall and took out a crystal decanter of brandy and a tray of glasses. He poured and distributed all around, avoiding Seneca's eyes when he offered a brandy, which was refused. Harrison Mayne downed his in one gulp and took the glass Seneca left on the tray.

"Is this how the rest of you feel, gentlemen?" Seneca scanned the faces of the others around the room.

"These gentlemen will do and think as I tell them," Garrett cut in. "That's the way our partnership operates. Mark my words, Pierce," he pointed a warning finger, "the Adirondacks will be open to development and tourism, to building, to clubs, to hotels. Trade will open with northwest Canada and beyond. Nothing can stop progress."

"Stewart Mayne invited me here," Seneca continued, untouched by Stockdale's admonition. "I've been asked for my opinion and I'll give it. It is in the best interests of the Adirondacks that railroads stay on the perimeter. Adirondack land holds significance for the future far more than you will ever know or understand. Trade can be achieved by other means. Progress cannot be stopped, I agree. But progress can be deterred or it can be guided. I suggest you pick the latter or abandon this idea of a spiderweb railroad. For your own good, Mr. Stockdale."

Stockdale's face went ashen as his jaw dropped. "I don't take threats lightly," he managed after a tortured moment, glaring at his opponent.

After another difficult hour in the library with the gentlemen guests, and soon after the departure of the grumbling Harrison, Seneca decided to take his own leave. He'd had enough of pompous, strained conversation and the smell of cigars. He'd refused the brandy and did not partake of the toast Stockdale raised in honor of his future empire in the Adirondacks. For his part, the faster Seneca could get out of the city and back to the mountains the better. This damnable white man's suit was stifling him.

He managed to elude the ubiquitous Martin and was passing what he presumed was the smaller family parlor, when he heard voices coming through the door which stood slightly ajar.

"Stop it, Harrison!" Lila's voice shot out over the sounds of a scuffle.

"Why? You're about to become my wife. You won't have the right to refuse me then. Might as well get used to it starting now." Harrison sounded a bit worse for the wear from wine and brandy.

"If you hadn't been drinking, I'd like to think you wouldn't speak that way to me. We both know we can barely tolerate each other, let alone—"

"I don't have to like you to take advantage of my conjugal rights. And believe me, I will, as often as I please. And you won't say a thing about it."

"You disgust me, Harrison. You're right. I won't say a thing about it because I won't do it. I won't marry you. Now we can forget about this conversation. Please leave."

Lila attempted to sound strong, but Seneca heard the tremor in her voice. The sound of a decanter being opened and the contents being poured reached him as well. He stepped carefully to where he could see into the room without being observed.

"You'll marry me. You have no choice, Miss High-and-Mighty. And I'll enjoy bringing you down off your pristine pedestal." Harrison strutted across the oriental carpet, raising his brandy snifter and examining the contents in the light from the wall sconces.

"When I tell Father how you've spoken to me, that you put your hands on me, he'll denounce you and call off the engagement." Lila's voice was stronger, full of conviction. Seneca observed that she stood very straight, almost regal in the dark green velvet gown that flowed over her, throat to hem, skimming her soft bosom, curving in then hugging her hips. Her hands were clasped below her waist.

"I don't think so."

"I hate that smug tone."

"You'll learn to live with it. Your father will not call off the engagement, and you *will* marry me." Harrison downed the contents of the snifter in one swallow.

"I won't!"

"You will to save your father." Harrison walked out of Seneca's view.

The sound of the decanter opening again.

"What . . . what do you mean, save my father?" Lila's voice trembled now and had lost its superior edge.

"Despite his display of wealth and his big talk, he's practically penniless, thanks to his double-dealing in the Union Pacific scandal."

"I . . . I don't believe you."

Harrison strutted as if he believed he was now the superior one. He closed the distance between them, and he lowered his voice to a dangerous pitch. "My father has the money your father needs, but he's weak. Fortunately my mother and I are not. And your father has the gall and the fame we need. I'm in control now. My father will allow his money to go into the railroad only if you and I are married. He clings to some stupid idea that you—and what he perceives to be your gentility—can restore the Mayne name. Of course, he doesn't expect *me* to make anything of myself on my own, so why should I go to all the trouble of working? So, dutiful child that you are, you'll want your father to realize his only dream, and you'll do exactly as I say."

Seneca saw Lila move to a chair and slump into it. "This can't be true. You're lying."

"You know I'm not." Harrison followed her and stood with legs apart in front of her. He bent down and lifted the hem of her gown. "You will marry me and I'll have what's under your skirts whenever and however I want it."

Lila slapped his hand away. She let out a harsh breath, and her voice was thick in her throat. "I may be forced to marry you, but I'll never submit to you. I despise you now more than I ever knew I could."

"I don't care if you submit or not. In fact, I want you to fight me every time. I'd like that," Harrison growled. "I saw the way you looked at that savage at the table tonight. You'd open up for him if he laid his filthy hands on you, wouldn't you? You think you're too good for me, but I could see the lust in your face when you looked at him. I know your kind. Lady on the outside and whore on the inside."

Seneca knew he'd stayed outside the door longer than he ever should have. What was he doing eavesdropping on their conversation? He'd never cared about the meaningless emotional games the idle rich played, and listening to this exchange proved why. The lady was being threatened by a highbred lowlife, but it was none of his business. His departure was long overdue. He started toward the front vestibule where his overcoat hung.

"You disgust me," Lila hissed. "Get away from me."

"In due time," Harrison drawled with a sinister intonation. "I intend to get a taste right now of what I will have the whole platter of later."

"No!"

A scuffle ensued and Seneca snapped around. Damn it—he was going to have to interfere now. He pushed open the parlor door and was inside the room in one long stride.

Harrison had one arm around Lila's waist and had her crushed to the center of his body. His other hand grasped her breast and he was forcing his tongue into her mouth.

She kicked and fought him with a fury her slim frame belied.

"Get out of here, Mayne, now!"

At the sound of Seneca's voice, Harrison froze.

"I said get out of here. Let the lady go." Seneca stood tall, his feet apart, hands on hips.

Harrison stared at him, then a sneer crossed his mouth. "Why, Injun? So you can do this yourself?" He squeezed Lila's breast harder. "You're hot to spread her legs yourself, aren't you?"

"That's enough, Mayne. You're drunk, and it's time you went home to sleep it off." Seneca started toward them.

Harrison released his grip slightly. "Who do you think you're talking to, you filthy—"

Lila surprised all three of them by jerking her knee up and ramming it hard into the center of Harrison's body. He let out a groan on an expulsion of air. She slammed her fists against his chest and broke his grip.

"Why—you little bitch! I'll teach you a lesson right now!" Harrison lifted his hand to slap Lila's face.

Seneca caught Harrison's wrist in a bear-trap grip and snapped his arm back so hard the crack of Mayne's shoulder resounded in the room. Harrison doubled over in pain.

"I told you to let the lady go. Now that you have, I'm telling you to leave."

Grasping his shoulder, his face contorted with pain, Harrison shot a venomous look at Lila. She didn't let it touch her. She heard only the controlled power in Seneca Pierce's voice, and it filled her with a strength she drew on. She sucked in a deep breath and squared her shoulders, then turned her back on the two men.

"This is not the end of it, Lila," Harrison snarled. "I'll see you in church *and* in bed, and it won't matter to me which comes first." He slammed out of the room, then stopped and stepped back inside with a last threat. "And I'll see you dead, Pierce!"

Three

Seneca went to Lila and lifted his hands to place them on her shoulders. Before they contacted with her, he withdrew them.

"Are you all right?" he asked, his voice husky, almost a whisper.

Lila breathed deeply and turned around to face him. She tilted her head back and lifted her eyes to behold his face. His blue eyes were intent yet soft. The high cheekbones and chiseled jaw flexed. The blue-black hair gleamed where the thong-wrapped tail of it grazed a broad shoulder. She swayed toward him, feeling the strength emanating from him and drawing her into its powerful embrace.

And then his arms were around her, hard muscled yet gentle. Her hands rested at his waist, her cheek against the smooth beads and napped leather of his neckpiece. She leaned against him and felt the hardness of his thighs through her skirt and petticoats. Beneath his cotton shirt she heard the pounding of his heart like encroaching thunder in stormy air. Inside her, prickling impulses touched her nerve endings like flashes of heat lightning in a summer night sky.

"Should I call for your aunt?" Seneca whispered against her hair.

She lifted her head and looked up at his face. "No. I

don't want her to know about this. I'll be fine. Thank you."

He nodded. "I'll go, then." But he didn't move. His burning gaze bored into her, reaching dark places in her soul and igniting them.

Lila stood very still. His arms were still around her, her hands remained at his waist. Their chests pressed closer as their breaths rose and fell together. She should break from him, she knew that. But she didn't. She couldn't.

He closed his eyes for not more than a second, then released her. "If you're certain I can do nothing more for you, I'll bid you good evening . . . Miss Stockdale." He stepped back, holding her gaze for a moment. He lifted her hands from where they still rested at his waist and kissed the backs of them. And then he left the parlor.

Lila swayed, then caught her balance. She followed him out into the vestibule and watched as he shrugged into a long brown hide overcoat with a deep fur collar. She noticed that he carried soft moccasins in his hand and had pulled on heavy boots such as she'd never before seen.

He opened the door and stepped out onto the snow-covered landing and pulled the door softly closed behind him.

Lila reached quickly for the handle and pulled the heavy door open. She stepped out onto the landing. The air was cold and heavy with the full silence that falling snow provided. He stood very still. She stood next to him, very still. She could feel the sleeve of his coat against the sleeve of her dress, feel a pulsing current pass between them. She knew why she'd stepped outside, knew what she wanted. She didn't know how to say it, but did know she shouldn't say it, shouldn't even feel what she wanted. She shivered.

Seneca waited. He should walk down the steps now and not look back. He knew what he wanted, and knew it was the last thing he should do. Close to him he felt Lila—Lila *Stockdale,* he reminded himself—felt her warmth, felt her shiver, felt the pressure of her arm on his.

He turned abruptly and swept her into his arms, enveloping her inside his bearskin coat. Her arms went around him and clasped his back. Her face was upturned to him, eyes heavy lidded, veiling the glittering emerald of her gaze. His lips hovered above hers. The mists from their breaths mingled in the cold air, caught in the falling snowflakes, and floated away together, over and over. And then he caught her lips lightly, released them, caught them again and held them softly.

Her lips quivered against his, triggering a violent response inside him. He took her whole mouth then, pushing his tongue into the sweet recesses, devouring her as if it would be his last, his only taste of her. Her first reaction was to go stark still, but her next was one he would never have expected. She melted against him, opened to him, offered her own tongue inexpertly but freely. They kissed thoroughly, knowingly, as if they'd both expected it.

And then he let her go and rapidly descended the stone stairs. He turned at the bottom step and looked up at her.

Snowflakes drifted heavily between them.

She watched them settle on his hair and face, saw his bronze skin shimmer in the light from the streetlamp like frosted copper. She shivered and hugged herself against the cold . . . and more.

And then he turned and strode away, enveloped by the night and the falling snow.

* * *

Spring, 1883

Seneca floated across the glassy smooth mountain lake in the canoe he'd spent several months building. He'd created another after the custom of his mother's people, with a white birchbark skin so smoothly fitted that the craft slipped through the water soundlessly. But this one he'd built in the lapstrake practice in white cedar, slippery elm, spruce, and red and white pines, all steam bent and formed in a shed at the back of his cabin. He'd spent hours consumed by the work of constructing and polishing until the fifteen-foot-long craft had absorbed the sweat from his brow and the painful memories from his spirit. It was sleek as the back of a wet beaver and weighed not much over fifty pounds.

Now he paddled the canoe within a few inches short of and parallel to the finely pebbled shoreline. He stepped out and carefully lifted the craft so as not to damage the keel, then pulled the bow onto dry land. Then he bent down and grasped the thwarts, lifting it and turning his body, stepping under the overturned craft. Settling the yoke over his shoulders and bracing the thwarts for support, he portaged his canoe into a hiding place among the trees.

For a moment he turned back and looked out over the water to the island where his cabin stood. He never ceased to feel distinctly the conflict of emotions that warred inside him whenever he left the island—and whenever he returned to it. It was as if the two worlds in which he lived could be bridged with his canoe between his island and the mainland. He could feel the change in himself halfway across the water between the two, whether he was arriving or leaving.

He took one last look at the dense evergreens that

masked his cabin from view at any point on the mainland, breathed deeply, then turned and started into the forest.

His soft footfalls over the thick duff blended with the early morning sounds of nesting and feeding birds. Spring was awakening in the Adirondack Mountains. Blue jays squawked overhead as they flitted among the tall pines, tamaracks, and larch trees, while black-capped chickadees and goldfinches, still in their late winter olive plumage, fluttered among the branches. He listened to their song and responded with his own soft whistles that mimicked each bird.

At a mound of smooth round rocks in a protected area, he lifted a glove from the pocket of his wool jacket and flicked away dead pine boughs and dust. Tenderly he touched a pink granite rock at the top of the mound.

"It's spring again," he spoke to his mother's spirit. "Your favorite time of the year." He raised his eyes overhead and peered through pine branches dappled with warming sun. "Looks like the jays are building nearby again. I saw a fox as I climbed up the hill this morning. You'll have a lot of company."

Like his mother had, Seneca loved spring, loved the way the earth renewed itself. He could smell it in the fragrant soil and ancient duff under his boots and in the crisp air laden with the scent of pines. He heard it as a soft wind rustled through the cedars and low ferns, shaking their branches and fronds until they reached for the sun. Trillium and fiddleheads poked above their protective covering and dotted the hills and meadows up the mountains with bright yellow-green infant stems and buds. Seneca had always believed in the promise of spring, for the season brought so much that was new and renewed his faith again in what had always been and would ever be.

He picked up a small winter-dry branch near his feet

and methodically stripped its bark. That hopeful contemplation might be in jeopardy now. This spring, and those to come, could mean a threat to Seneca's world—the world he preferred of the two into which he'd been born. And after the winter months he'd spent in the city, he knew which of the two worlds he preferred to avoid. He wanted none of the entanglements that wealth and associations brought. The evening he'd spent in the home of Garrett Stockdale underscored his conviction.

Garrett Stockdale. The brackish taste of old hatred boiled from his depths and lingered in Seneca's mouth. Somehow he would see Stockdale brought down once and for all. He would pay dearly for what he'd done to Seneca's family. Garrett Stockdale was the cause for all Seneca detested about wealth and power.

He snapped the branch in two.

Then why could he still see the vision of Lila Stockdale in velvet the color of balsam pines, with an emerald brooch rivaling her eyes in clarity and light? Why did he still taste the sweetness of her lips, feel the heat of her kiss, feel the surging fire of his own desire?

His reaction to her had been unexpected. His desire to see her again was difficult to control. His continuing memory of her was even more disturbing.

For the rest of his residency at the university, he did not return to the Stockdale home. He never spoke to Lila Stockdale again, and that was just as he preferred. Once he saw her on the street across from the university in the late afternoon, but he'd purposely stayed in his lecture hall until after dark when he knew any respectable lady would be safe inside her own parlor. Remembering the scene between her and Harrison Mayne that evening, he wondered now if Lila Stockdale's own parlor was indeed safe for her.

Stewart Mayne had tried to draw him back to dinner there once more, but Seneca had managed to evade the invitation. He'd been offered employment with the company and accepted for his own reasons after much introspection and soul-searching. He'd fulfilled Mayne's request for topographical renderings of the Adirondack area Stockdale and his partners planned to develop. That area included this sacred place right where he now stood. Mayne and his partners deemed Seneca the most knowledgeable of guides in the region, knew him to be expert in the lay of the land, with the education to interpret it with accurate survey maps. Even Stockdale had been forced to admit that, albeit grudgingly.

Seneca sensed the old man felt a certain satisfaction in using the son of Eli Pierce as a means to achieve his next development scheme. That was all right with Seneca.

For the time being.

With the submission of his drawings and maps, which included his addition of nonexistent precipitous ledges and thick rock formations, Seneca had managed to discourage them from using this tract of land.

For the time being.

He knew in his heart it was only a matter of time before the railroad—whether Stockdale's or some other company's—reached like a long hand of greedy fingers across these mountains, this wilderness he called home, the place where his mother and her family rested in their final home. Only a matter of time before the feet of thousands of people, their buildings, their playgrounds, spread over this land. He'd saved his family's sacred place with a lie, and he would continue to lie as much and for as long as was necessary.

And Seneca would feel not one shred of remorse over

lying to Garrett Stockdale, to thwarting him, to destroying him by any means.

If only he hadn't met Lila Stockdale.

He dropped down next to the mound that had been his mother's grave for almost fifteen years. Beyond her burial place, higher up on the hillside lay those of her father and beside him her mother. His sister's tinier mound was behind his mother's. His father's remains lay scattered somewhere on the plains. It was to this clearing—past which a full stream rushed—that Seneca came often to meditate, to speak among his ancestors, and wait for their wisdom to fill his heart and mind.

He slanted his bow against his leg and slipped the ash pack basket containing arrows from his back. He touched the arrow shafts, ran his fingers over the perfectly mounted end feathers. They were exactly as his grandfather had taught him to mount them when he was a boy. "You have your great-grandfather's gift for making perfect arrows each time," his grandfather had told him softly. "This gift among many was given to you at birth. You must take care of your gifts, use them wisely, teach your sons."

Seneca closed his eyes and leaned back against the stone mound. "They keep coming, Mother. We've managed to keep them at a safe distance, but I don't know how long we can hold out. You know I will die defending my family, your family. They build their hotels, their rich houses. Every year they find new ways to extend the railroad tracks. It is spring. They are coming again now. And every spring I know I've lost another season of our ancestral tradition. And now my father's honor is once again at stake."

Above him the jays squawked, and the trees rustled as the wind floated through them. Pebbles loosened from somewhere and rolled toward the stream. Seneca rose, stretched in the warming morning air, and easily reached for his bow. Flexing the bowstring, he ambled toward a stand of tall pines away from the mound and leaned against a tree, running his fingers over the smooth curve in the wooden bow.

In an instant he was around the tree and had slammed a body against it, holding the curve of the bow under a straining neck.

"You're slipping, Bear. Your long winter's sleep has made you dull-witted like your namesakes." Slowly Seneca released the bow.

A wool-and-canvas-covered trapper slumped to the base of the tree. "And you," the trapper's husky thickly accented voice rasped, "are much too like the rabbit, *mon ami*. Too long sleeping in the city. *Mon Dieu!* I fear for my own hide." He held up a hand.

Seneca laughed, set the bow down, and pulled his old friend to his feet. "Just using my mountain senses so you won't think I've let the big city and civilization change me." He threw his arms around him and gave him a hug befitting his name.

Robert LaDoque, a French-Canadian trapper, had tried to teach the residents of the below-mountain hamlets to say his name the way it should sound. He would tell them, "Row-bear Law-dock," and they would usually reply, "Bear Duck." Bear had given up, grateful only that they didn't think of him as a naked bird.

"And you tramp through the forest like you lost your hunting sense and intuition. I heard you from half mile down the mountain." He pounded Seneca on the back, and a pair of oily black crows flew out of the thicket behind them and took to the skies. Bear laughed heartily. " 'Tis good you're home, *mon ami*. Too long gone."

"You're right," Seneca said, bending for his bow. "Six

months was too long." His gaze drifted over the burial ground, then down the mountain.

"Regarde," Bear said, peering up into Seneca's eyes. He stroked his full rust-red beard and swiped a knitted cap from his bushy head. "I must see." He squinted his small brown eyes and scrutinized his friend for a long thoughtful moment. *"Oui.* You are changed."

Seneca grabbed Bear's cap and pulled it down over the trapper's head and eyes. "I am not," he said wearily. "It was just a long and tiring time away. I'll not do it again."

Bear resettled his cap. "The teaching? Not good?"

"The teaching was fine."

"The university not want you?"

"They want me more than ever, but I don't want them."

"Stockdale and the railroad people. You were not successful with surveys?"

"I was successful. I just wish I knew how long I can manage to keep them hanging." Seneca turned toward his friend. "Did you know Stockdale had a daughter?"

"Voila! I know everything now!" Bear's laughter resounded around the forest.

"Just what do you think you know now?"

" 'Tis a woman! *Oui!* A fair mademoiselle has a keener arrow than Seneca's own! Aha!"

Seneca stared down into the face of the closest friend he'd ever known and nodded his head, then quickly shook it. "A fair mademoiselle . . . your brain is still foggy."

"Aha! I knew it, I knew it! Robert LaDoque is never wrong!"

"What is true is that Bear Duck has been sleeping in a winter cave too long."

"May-be-e-e." Bear stroked his beard again.

Seneca turned and started back toward his mother's burial ground to retrieve his pack basket. "We've had this discussion before," he said over his shoulder. "You know how I feel about women."

"*Oui, oui,* just as I do." Bear brought his thumb and four fingers together and tapped them against his lips, making a smacking sound. "Kees, kees, kees, then *au revoir.*"

"Only one 'kees' and then a definite goodbye," Seneca said distantly.

"Old grandfather wanted sons. You'll never get them that way," Bear said wisely.

"Grandfather's time has gone. What is in its place is a time I don't want to be part of. Grandfather's time rests forever with my mother and sister. It is no more, not for me. And what is now is not for me. So . . . there will be no sons for any time."

"So . . . there will be no mademoiselle? Only many mademoiselles and perhaps a madame or two, eh, *mon ami?*" Bear let out a low suggestive laugh.

Seneca laughed in kind, then said, "I think it might be good to be a priest."

"*Mon Dieu!* No women! Aaach! No, no, no! I could not live without my women." Bear shook his head vehemently.

They started down the mountain together. Seneca clapped Bear on the shoulder. "But could you live with just one? Or more to the point, could she live with you?"

The laughter of the two friends echoed through the forest.

Three miles short of North Creek Railroad Station, a train including the custom-fitted Stockdale parlor car rattled along the track. It had been stalled twice from spring washouts, but the engineer treated the delays as everyday occurrences. Lila sat with Evalina on a red velvet settee in her father's private parlor car. Aunt Maddie dozed intermittently in a matching side chair, her head nodding to the movement of the car, her black hat tilting forward, its circle of matching feather plumes trembling. They watched the rugged scenery pass outside their red-draped and gold-corded windows.

"Oh, it is breathtaking!" Lila sighed, running her hand up and down over the sleeve of the soft deerskin riding coat her father had given her for the trip. In the lap of her dark green wool skirt rested a fashionable brown fur hat with warm ear muffs. "If we weren't rolling along this railroad track, one would think no man had ever stepped foot here in these mountains before now."

Aunt Maddie roused and said dreamily, "This is quite an adventure, isn't it?"

Lila saw how weary Aunt Maddie had become from the almost twenty-four hours spent traveling. Beneath the wool dove-gray traveling suit, her slight frame seemed even thinner than ever. They'd taken the night boat to Albany at six the previous evening and had boarded the train from that city at seven this morning. They'd been due in North Creek at noon, but owing to mechanical and now weather delays, it was already past two. And there would be more travel to come once they reached North Creek Station. Lila looked forward excitedly to the next part of the trip. Stagecoach travel would be a new experience for her. In recent months she'd been eager for new experiences, open to them as she'd never been before.

Before Seneca Pierce.

Her own energy flagged now. She leaned her head against the window, closed her eyes, and let the clunk-clunk of the rails rolling beneath them lull her into a reverie. She knew much of her fatigue was the result of the difficult winter months she'd spent deep in the turmoil of new emotions. She hadn't passed one day or night without thought of Seneca Pierce.

"There's snow out there!" Evalina shrieked, making Lila jump. "It's almost June and there's snow out there!"

"Isn't it wonderful?" Lila sat up. "I love snow."

"I don't think it's so wonderful. It's supposed to be spring, isn't it? I hate to be cold. I wonder if I've brought enough clothes."

"You have plenty of clothes, Evie." Lila noted the many petticoats under her friend's brown wool skirt and assessed she must have three camisoles under her brown plaid wool jacket and white waistcoat. "You have four cases with you now, plus all that you sent on ahead with the campsite provisions."

"Campsite." Evalina shuddered. "I do wish we didn't have to go on to there."

"It will be delightful sleeping in a tent under the stars," Lila came back.

"Yes," Maddie put in. "Five years ago when I went up to Saranac Lake with the Smithfields, we arrived at our campsite via steamboat. John Philip Sousa's band was aboard. Fancy that! Sousa on a steamboat in the Adirondacks. Oh, it was delightful, and then so cozy later in the tents."

"How can it be cozy in a tent? It's made of . . . *cloth*. And no conveniences." Evalina pouted.

"Evalina!" Lila patted her friend's arm. "You'll have all the conveniences of home. Father thought of everything when he chartered that special train car to send all our belongings ahead."

Lila had gone with Garrett crosstown to Forty-second Street and watched as the car was loaded with five tents, fifteen mattresses, various crates of china and cooking utensils from all the family households represented, plus ten carpets, twenty-five trunks, and food and wine for the month. Martin and a servant for each family had gone ahead with the car.

"Cost a hundred dollars," Maddie concurred. "Extravagant for a month's holiday, I'd say, but Garrett was determined to do it."

"Well, it would be perfectly dreadful if he hadn't," Evalina sputtered. "Heaven knows it will be dreadful enough. I was barely able to pack enough dresses."

"Evalina! You have more dresses with you than all of the ladies put together," Lila returned. "And your mother even insisted upon bringing her laundress."

Evalina folded her arms stiffly over her ample chest. "Well, I'm certainly not going to do up the linens and my clothes every day. Nor will you."

Lila knew that was so and dropped the subject. That would be a new experience she'd not relish. She craned her neck upward as she peered through the window. "The trees are so tall I can't see the tops. I do wish Father would let us go out on the platform."

"He's concerned for our safety, dear Cat," Aunt Maddie told her. "There will be plenty of time for you to see the tops of the trees."

"Yes, but rolling along under them like this . . . it must be thrilling to see the tips pass against the clear blue sky. I've been studying about the trees and animals in the Adirondack Mountains. I do wish I could get out and touch them. The trees at least. And I would love a breath of fresh air." The smells of cleaning ammonia and brass polish in the closed car had made her head ache.

"Since when did you become so interested in nature?" Evalina asked.

"I've always been generally interested in nature. You

knew that," Lila said with an offhanded air she wasn't very good at effecting.

"I'm not certain I did know that, generally. Why are you so interested in the Adirondack Mountains, in particular, all of a sudden?" Evalina pressed with a teasing tone.

Lila escaped a response. She drew up straight. "Oh, look at that huge black bird at the side of the track!" She strained her face against the window.

"Where?" Evalina pressed into the glass as well. "Oh, dear Lord!" She turned back, clutched her chest, and sank against the settee.

"What is it, child?" Aunt Maddie asked without turning away from her own window.

"That huge ugly bird was eating a poor little rabbit. Why would it do such a cruel thing?"

"I believe it could be called dinner up here in the wilderness," Lila said, poking Evalina's ribs.

"You are disgusting." Evalina pouted. "Daddy always gave me baby bunnies at Easter. They were so cuddly and soft."

"And what did you do with them when Easter was over?"

"Why, I . . . they left home, I think."

"To be eaten, no doubt, by an alley cat or a tramp." Lila lifted both hands to explain. "Dinner."

"Really, Lila, that's a horrible thing to say."

"No, my dear, it isn't," Aunt Maddie said gently. "It is called survival. But if I may say, I think it's a bit more cruel to have brought the bunnies home and then to simply discard them in the city."

Evalina blanched. "I don't know why we had to come up to this awful place anyway."

"It won't be so awful, Evie," Lila told her. "Think of it as an adventure. Think of who you may meet up here."

"Up here? Surely you can't mean the man of my dreams? I sincerely doubt that," Evalina said, sticking her bottom lip out. "Not unless he is one of those half human and half animal creatures I've heard about. And that would be more of a nightmare than a dream."

"Really, Evalina. Your imagination is working too hard."

"Well, what about you meeting the man of your dreams, Lila? What about that? Don't have the temerity to sit there and tell me you expect to meet him up *here*." Evalina folded her arms across her chest.

Lila turned and stared thoughtfully out the window again. "Those were girlhood dreams," she said distantly, knowing she hadn't let go of those dreams—especially since Seneca Pierce. She'd dreamed of meeting him again in the mountains. But she'd been afraid to dream of anything beyond a meeting.

Evalina was at once contrite. "Oh, Lila, I'm so sorry. Of course, there's Harrison. I simply forgot for the moment that you are betrothed to him. I didn't mean anything. Please forgive me."

Of course—Harrison. There was always Harrison. Lila turned back and hugged her friend. "Don't think about it. There's nothing to forgive."

If the truth be known, Lila would have liked to have forgotten about the betrothal. Harrison had traveled to the mountains several days before their departure, and Lila had been relieved to have the time to herself without wondering if he would come to call and make those insinuating remarks. She wished he would disappear from her life forever.

Evalina hugged Lila. "How have you managed thus far

to keep him at bay? Last winter I thought he might fairly drag you to the altar within the fortnight. Remember that strange dinner at your house? The night of your father's announcement?"

"I remember." Lila slumped back against the settee.

"Oh, and that Indian was there. Remember?"

Lila sighed. "Oh, yes, I remember."

"Well, I must say, between that Indian and the fun over the brussels sprouts, and Harrison's practically drooling over your father's every word—well, it was a dinner to remember, wasn't it?"

Lila nodded, at once taken into the memory of the night she'd never forgotten. The night she'd met Seneca Pierce. The night Harrison attacked her. She'd managed to keep that incident a secret and to keep Harrison away to a certain extent by threatening to tell her father. But that wasn't the memory that had presented her the most difficulty.

Her greatest struggle was with the memory of Seneca Pierce. When she closed her eyes she could still picture the moment he appeared, filling and being framed by the archway as if he were a costly painting of a frontier hero. And she remembered vividly how he'd intervened between her and Harrison, throwing him out of the parlor, and then holding her until her fears subsided.

And his kiss in the falling snow. A kiss such as she could never have dreamed or imagined on her own. Such a kiss took two people. She believed that.

The evening had happened over three months ago. Yet every night since, just before drifting off to sleep, she could still feel his arms, his chest, the beads, his lean waist. She could see his sky-blue eyes, his bronze skin. She could still feel his warm, sensual lips. She knew she would never forget that kiss, not for as long as she lived or to whom she was married.

She'd thrilled when she'd overheard Seneca was working for her father's company. And she was surprised he'd agreed to do it. He'd seemed so against the development of the Adirondacks. She'd wished it was because of her, because he wanted to see her again, that he'd done it. But he never returned to her home.

At a later dinner Stewart Mayne had displayed several maps that Seneca had drawn and, when they'd been rolled back into cylinders once more, Lila had wished she could snap them open again and frame one to hang in her dressing room. Her wish had made her cheeks burn, and she'd had to excuse herself from the dinner table to rush to the parlor to regain her composure.

Later she'd sneaked a look at a drawing while her father was away from his study. While she'd had no understanding of what she was seeing, she'd run her fingers over the finely drawn black lines, the numbers indicating altitudes, the swirls of rock formations, and the lines of trees and terrain, just to touch the paper where his hands had lain.

Her worst moment had been when she'd taken a walk in the late winter bitter cold to New York University and stood across the street, watching for him to emerge. She'd waited in vain, shivering in the cutting wind, until the lateness of the afternoon's hour waned almost beyond a lady's discretion before she'd reluctantly turned for home. Thankfully Father had not noticed she'd been missing. Martin had caught her coming in, but to her knowledge he hadn't said anything to Garrett. She'd managed to keep the incident her secret. And later she'd felt the silly fool for engaging in such a desperate act. Seneca Pierce had probably forgotten she existed.

"So how have you managed it?" Evalina pressed, breaking into Lila's thoughts.

Lila lolled her head toward her friend and emerged from her reverie. "Managed what?"

"To postpone the wedding this far, of course."

"Oh, that."

"Yes, that! We're all waiting, you know. It will be the wedding of the season! Of course, we always promised to be each other's honor attendants in our weddings. You haven't forgotten about that, have you?"

"No, Evie, I haven't forgotten our promise."

"Well, then . . . when? I know you practically loathe Harrison, but that's always how it is with married people, isn't it? I mean, my parents can barely abide each other. Wouldn't a summer wedding be lovely?"

Evalina was growing more giggly and excited by the moment, much to Lila's irritation. She sat up and thought of a hundred reasons why she would put off this wedding until she was six feet under. She started to say them when Aunt Maddie interrupted offering a plausible excuse.

"I fear it's been all my fault that you haven't been given permission to shop for a bridesmaid's dress, Evalina."

"You, Mrs. Allgood? Why?" Evalina leaned her elbows on her knees and dropped her chin into her cupped hands.

"My health. It's been precarious at best these past few months. And you know, a wedding is such a monumental task to arrange. My darling Cat is so precious to me. I want to be at my strongest and sharpest to do for her what her mother would have wanted. Perhaps in the autumn I will be rested enough. You will simply have to be patient, Evalina." Her gray eyes darted conspiratorially to Lila, then back to Evalina.

"Oh, all right." Evalina brightened and fixed her gaze on Lila. "But what if you meet the man of your dreams up here this summer? What will you do about Harrison?"

Lila swallowed hard, then patted her friend's hand.

"Didn't you point out a few moments ago that there's no danger of meeting the man of anyone's dreams up here?" *Besides, I've already met a man I'm dreaming too much about.*

"If you could pick out a husband on your own, what would he be like?" Evalina had started a new game, Lila could tell. She turned toward Maddie. "Mrs. Allgood, what do you think makes the best husband?"

"Oh, no, you young people talk about it." Aunt Maddie touched her cheek with one delicate hand.

"Go ahead, Aunt Maddie," Lila said softly. "I think it would be good for you to talk about him and good for Evalina to hear your story."

"You have a story?" Evalina breathed. "Oh, please, Mrs. Allgood, do tell."

Aunt Maddie grew dreamy eyed. Even though Lila had heard the story often over the years, she never tired of hearing it. She adored her mother's sister, and felt the heartache the frail old lady still carried inside. And now she wondered about herself. Would she grow old alone, carrying in her heart the painful memory of the one man who had stirred every emotion, touched every nerve inside her with one look and one kiss?

At that moment Lila believed she would rather be alone forever than to be with a man she didn't love.

Four

Madeline Christopher Allgood looked at the two young women who watched her in rapt attention. How she loved listening to their games, observing their growth into young women with so much to look forward to, so much already in their lives. She wished Lila, her dear little Cat, could be happy. Even with all her wealth, the opportunities available to ordinary girls had seemed unavailable to her. Lila and Evalina talked about their dreams, love, marriage, but she believed they knew nothing about romance. Madeline had once been touched by real romance—true love, the only love of a lifetime—and the memory of it now was at once as joyful as it was painful.

She turned and leaned her head against the window of the rocking train car. "His name was David. I was sixteen. We met at a church picnic. He was twenty, more worldly than I. And oh, he was so handsome in his army uniform. We fell in love over a bowl of blueberry ice cream."

Evalina giggled. "How romantic."

"Yes, indeed, especially since he was terribly allergic to blueberries. He broke out in a hideous rash." Madeline laughed lightly.

"He must have been mortified."

"Yes, a little. But I extracted a small pot of zinc oxide ointment and a bit of cotton from my bag. I carried it to use against the mosquitoes. I couldn't bear the itching, and the nasty things were forever finding me and getting into my clothes no matter how much I covered myself."

Evalina leaned forward. "Did he let you apply the ointment?"

"Oh, he most certainly did." Madeline smiled at the recollection. "He couldn't stand the itching under his coat and shirt, so he simply removed them."

"Oh, my! Was your family simply scandalized?"

"They didn't see. We'd taken our ice-cream bowls down by the creek."

"However did you . . . ?"

Madeline sat up straight and faced the two young women. "I simply took my wad of cotton and dabbed him all over his back and arms . . . *and* . . . his chest. A manly chest it was, too, with smooth muscles and dark hair and—" She flushed and looked down at her hands. She could still see the pot of ointment and wad of sticky cotton.

"I'd swoon, I'd simply swoon. It's so delicious!" Evalina fairly squirmed on the settee. "What happened then?"

Madeline looked out the window. Tears moistened her eyes. "He kissed my lips very softly."

"Dead away. I'd faint dead away, I just know it."

Lila laughed. "I doubt it. You'd probably run directly to me and tell me how delicious was his kiss, leaving him there pondering your disappearance."

"I would not! Really, Lila." She turned back to Madeline, breathless for more of the story. "Did he propose to you on the spot?"

"Indeed he did. We were married in Mother's front parlor a month later." She held up her left hand where a tiny gold ring, worn thin from years of use, shone in the light. She opened the top two buttons on the snug neck of her dress and lifted out a gold chain at the end of which was suspended a large gold band. "He wore a wedding ring. Most men don't like to wear them, but David wanted to." Her eyes misted. "He was so wonderful. They gave me this ring when they buried him. I didn't know they were going to take it off his finger. I wanted him to wear it for all eternity."

"What . . . happened to him?" Evalina urged.

Madeline's heart still fluttered at the thought of her beloved David, and she thought of him every day. It was still difficult, almost fifty years afterward, to talk about his accident—how she and her father had found him buried under the crushing weight of a collapsed grain bin on their farm—but she managed it. She grieved even now for her beloved dead husband and for the stillborn daughter lost the week of his passing.

A widow at eighteen, Maddie had not remarried. In later years when Lila's mother had taken sick, Madeline had moved in to care for her and had stayed on after Catherine's early death to watch after twelve-year-old Lila. Madeline was penniless, thus the opportunity to remain among her sister's family held twofold importance.

But more, she and Lila took solace in one another's company. They became mother and daughter, and Madeline could not bear to think of Lila marrying a man as distasteful as Harrison Mayne. She wished fervently in her heart for a man as beautiful as David to come into her dear Cat's life and give her as precious a love as she had once held. Even if it weren't to last, it was better than a loveless marriage with a man who did not truly love and care. Madeline closed her eyes and said a small prayer, asking God that if she could help in any way to bring that love to Lila, to show her how. She would do anything to make her baby happy.

"Oh, how utterly tragic," Evalina said when Madeline had stopped talking. She sniffed into her handkerchief.

"Yes," Madeline said after a time, "but I know what true love is. And it comes but once in a woman's life."

Lila placed a comforting hand on her aunt's shoulder. *Is it better to have loved and lost him than to have never had one true love?* Feeling the emotion pooling in Aunt Maddie, she quickly took the focus away from her and turned with studied interest toward Evalina. "What about you, Evie? Have you changed your mind about what you always said you wanted in a husband?"

Evalina brightened. "No, I haven't changed my mind at all. My husband must be handsome, worldly, a true gentleman." She giggled into her hand. "And he must sweep me off my feet and make my head swoon."

Lila laughed warmly. "I'm not certain it's possible to have a true gentleman together with a dashing swain all in one man. But just in case I'm wrong, what business will he be engaged in? You must think now of your welfare. A house costs dear these days."

"Yes, I know. And all the parties. Mama says she has to double a week's household money just to provide for one party. It is a problem I suppose, but I've never given it that much thought."

"Don't you tire of the parties?"

"Only sometimes. What else is there to do to break up the monotony?" Evalina shrugged.

"Sometimes I wish I could take meaningful work," Lila said. "Father says it isn't seemly for a woman of my station to work. My mother studied medicine. She dreamed of becoming a doctor."

"Fancy that," Evalina said. "In my family it would have been deemed scandalous if the women thought of going into medicine."

"It is in the Stockdale family as well," Lila said, thinking of how her mother had given up her study of medicine when Garrett Stockdale rescued her from near poverty. He'd told her in no uncertain terms that it was unseemly for a woman to practice as a physician. The medical profession did not enjoy social recognition, and social recognition in the world of finance and commerce was the only area where a man could achieve the highest. To do that, he needed the services—*services* is what he'd said—of an appropriate wife.

"When Mother married Father he expected her to give up her dream. As he would expect of me. He thinks I have no dreams." She turned and peered out the window at the passing pines, her thoughts taking her away.

Her father had instructed her well, and Lila had dutifully learned. Soon she'd been capable of taking Catherine Stockdale's place at Garrett's social functions. His business associates had often spoken about how remarkable she was, how adroit for one so young. "Yes, indeed, she'll make the right man a perfect wife someday," Garrett had responded often as she was growing up.

She never told him the sentiment that stayed with her through a lonely decade. It arose from something in her mother's dying words. She'd held Lila's hand between her two weak ones and whispered in a frail voice, "Follow your heart, my precious daughter. A wife is nothing more than chattel to her husband. I knew early in our marriage that being a wife was not enough for me. I had nothing of me, nothing to feel passionate about, until you were born. You must escape that fate."

But Lila hadn't escaped, had she? She'd remained under Garrett's roof because that's where he'd told her she belonged. As a child she could do nothing but obey him. But what had lived in her heart was most likely not something her mother would have urged her to follow. She longed to live on her own and study the science of healing herbs and perhaps midwifery. She knew several women who went to herbalists for special potions to ease their monthly discomfort. And some women had learned of plants that would prevent pregnancy or bring on miscarriage.

"Well?" Evalina tapped Lila on the shoulder, breaking into her reverie.

"What?"

"You haven't spoken in just ages about your dream husband. What would he be like? Harrison exempted from this discussion, of course."

"Of course." Lila stood at the parlor car door. The rumble of the rails reverberated through her. "If I could dream up any man on the face of the earth who would be willing to marry me right now, I would do it in a trice. Then I could exempt Harrison from any future conversations we might have on marriage and husbands forever, and even Father could do nothing about it."

Aunt Maddie gasped. "Oh, Cat, dear—you know you don't mean such a scandalous thing. You mustn't even think those thoughts."

"I think those thoughts constantly, Aunt Maddie."

Evalina giggled and clapped her hands. "Delicious! Simply delicious! But it's very unlikely you'll find such a man. They are all so skittish about marriage. Except for Harrison. He's positively eager."

"I know," Lila said with resignation.

"So then, you'll marry him, don't you think? After all, you do need a husband."

Lila leaned her head back against the door. "I don't see what for. I think it's quite possible I could go through life without any husband whatsoever."

Evalina's eyes widened as she scrutinized Lila's face.

"You don't mean that," she breathed. "You can't wish to be a spinster."

Lila dropped her head back against the door's frosted window glass upon which was etched the Stockdale monogram. "I don't know what I wish."

"But Lila, you were the one who always knew. I was the one who couldn't make up my mind."

"At least it was your own mind."

Evalina fell silent but not for long. Lila could tell Evie didn't believe what she'd just said, and Lila didn't wish to pursue the path of the conversation.

"All right. Just pretend then," Evalina pushed. "What would your dream husband—if you should ever dream such a thing again—what would your dream husband be like?"

Lila saw she wasn't going to get out of the game this time. Since there was nowhere else to go but in the train car, she gave in to Evalina's eagerness.

"I've always fancied my husband to be strong jawed and strong willed, a man with his own principles and convictions, a man unafraid to voice his opinions. He would be right, of course, and my father wrong, always wrong."

Evalina gasped, then giggled. "Dear Lila, you are scandalous!"

"Yes, I suppose I am. Would you think I'm scandalous, Aunt Maddie?" Lila reached out and placed a hand on her aunt's shoulder.

Aunt Maddie patted Lila's hand and smiled up at her beloved niece. "I couldn't say, dear."

"What else?" Evalina pressed. "Tell us more."

"Well, I would link my own strong arm through my husband's strong one, and concur with him, adding my own knowledgeable discourse on the subject at hand. Then we'd smile into one another's eyes, showing our impenetrable unity to Father and everyone else." Lila lifted her chin and licked her lips.

"That could never be Harrison, I fear," Evalina said.

"No, most definitely not." Lila shook her head.

"This isn't about a husband," Aunt Maddie added. "It's about you, darling Cat."

Lila dropped her head toward her aunt and said dreamily, "Most definitely yes."

"You truly are scandalous! As I see it, you can only forget this fantasy and get on with things as they are," Evalina said.

Lila bit her lower lip.

"Not necessarily," Aunt Maddie said enigmatically. Both young women turned toward her. "You girls are the new generation. It's up to you to change things."

"We can't change anything," Evalina responded. "How could we? We are powerless. But isn't it all right to be that way? My mother is. Shouldn't I be, too?"

"Not all women are powerless, dear," Aunt Maddie said.

"That's true. Just look at Harrison's mother. She rules both of the men in her life." Lila dropped down to the settee.

"And they're both a mess." Maddie giggled.

"Aunt Maddie!" Lila laughed. "You do surprise me at times!"

"I think a woman should always be a little bit surprising, a lot unpredictable," Maddie said.

"I don't think men would care for that," Evalina said.

"Doubtless they would abhor it," Lila said.

The three were silent for a few moments before Evalina pressed again. "What does he look like, Lila, your dream husband?"

Lila turned toward the window again, not seeing through it, but rather seeing into it like a crystal ball.

"He's tall, strong. His hair is dark, his eyes as blue as the sky." Her voice drifted into dreamy timbre. "He possesses a quiet, thoughtful nature. He's still, like a lake in summer but with a powerful undercurrent. He respects the ancient laws of nature and the changing force of the future. And he respects me as much." She leaned her forehead against the cool glass.

"I believe you now," Evalina said thoughtfully. "You must not want a husband. What you have described could never exist in a man. What will you do? What can any of us do?" she moaned.

"Keep dreaming," Aunt Maddie said. "Picture it always in your mind how you want your life to be. Picture who it is you want to be with." She leaned over, touched a hand of each young woman and whispered, "And every now and then make a wish on the evening star just for insurance."

For the last quarter mile, the three sat with hands clasped all around.

North Creek Station bustled with the incoming mountain guests and outgoing passengers waiting to board for the trip back to Albany. As the servants were busy counting every piece of baggage, Lila heard the stationmaster tell her father that the Bradley stage to Prospect House had left promptly at 12:25, true to their advertising. Mr. Bradley prided himself on getting his stage to Prospect House at exactly 8:00 P.M., as promised. He would then pull out the next morning at exactly 7:30 for the shorter trek, owing to the downhill roll, to North Creek. Never mind that he'd left this time with nary a customer.

Lila made Aunt Maddie comfortable and left the grumbling Evalina and Iris Madison with her. They were all suffering from hunger, having expected to arrive in North Creek at noon, move promptly out on the coach, and take lunch five miles out at the North River Hotel. She went to her father's side to learn what they would do next.

"Then rent me one of those horsecars over there," Garrett demanded of the stationmaster, snapping his head to a covered shed where three open-sided conveyances stood empty.

"Those are three-seated buckboards. Anyway I can't do that," said the dark blue-clad lanky man of about forty years.

"Why not?" Garrett asked.

"Well, as I see it, you ain't exactly fit to drive four mules and a buckboard thirty miles to Blue Mountain Lake. 'Sides, Hank Bradley takes care of his own business, and since he ain't here . . ." The stationmaster shrugged.

"Well, what do you expect me to do with ten stranded people, six of whom are women?" Garrett's frustration mounted visibly.

"Well, let me see now . . ." The stationmaster tipped up his billed navy blue cap and with the same hand scratched a wiry thatch of gray hair. "Guess you'll just have to stand over there with that other party and wait for the next stage."

"And when will that be?"

Suddenly a shriek punctured the air. Lila whirled and saw Evalina streaking toward them, hands waving frantically over her head. Thinking something had happened to Aunt Maddie, Lila ran toward her.

"It's true! It's true!" Evalina shrieked.

Lila grabbed Evalina's arm and stopped her. "What's the matter? Is it Aunt Maddie?"

"It's true what they said. It is. I saw one!"

"Saw one what?"

"A . . . a *thing.*" Evalina clutched the lace on her bodice and gasped for breath.

"What thing? Evalina, stop this and tell me what you saw."

"Half man, half animal. Oh, it was hideous." Evalina shuddered.

Lila shook her head. "Is Aunt Maddie all right? Everyone else?"

"Yes, I think my father scared him away."

Lila linked her arm through Evalina's and hurried toward the others waiting on the train platform. As they turned the corner, Evalina screamed again.

"There! See?"

Lila did see. A big hulk of a man in a dark cotton shirt and canvas vest stood apart from the group. His baggy canvas pants bloused over heavy laced brown boots. His thick mass of rust-red hair and full beard of the same color glistened in the sun. The hulk would have appeared menacing—towering over the others as he did—if it hadn't been for the sudden planting of his hands on his hips, the tipping back of his head until the green knit cap he wore fell off, and the spate of rich laughter that pealed out of him.

"We have a deal, then?" Stewart Mayne said.

"*Oui,* deal," the bearded one responded, nodding his head vigorously. Just then he caught sight of Lila and Evalina as they drew near. "Ah, the lovely mademoiselle has returned and brought another with her."

The other women in the group had flattened themselves

against the station wall, while Mayne, Joseph Madison, and the other men clustered together.

"My daughter's a bit flighty at times," Joseph Madison explained. "I'm certain she's recovered now."

The bearded man bent to retrieve his cap and spoke to Evalina. "Ah, mademoiselle, I am so sorry I frightened you. Allow me. I am Robert LaDoque at your service." He bowed toward the two young women, and Evalina stepped back as the shaggy head lowered toward her. "I am called Bear."

Lila nodded. "Hello, Bear. Are you a real mountain man?"

Bear laughed heartily. *"Oui,* that I am, that I am."

"Bear," Evalina said weakly, eyeing him from head to boots. "How appropriate."

"Whatever I am, mademoiselle," the big man said gently, "I appreciate the beauty of a delicate flower."

Evalina giggled almost giddily. Lila saw her blush and was certain the color reached to her toes.

"Mr. Bear, here, says he can drive us in a coach to Prospect House," Joseph said to Garrett when he approached.

"When?"

"Soon as I hitch up mules. Going to take eight to haul this load," Bear said, sweeping his arm over the crowd.

"No, no," Garrett told him. "Just ten people in our party."

"Eleven in theirs." Bear pointed to the other group.

"Let them get their own coach," Garrett demanded.

"Can't. There isn't one," Bear said and took long strides toward the mule barn.

Lila went to Aunt Maddie, Evalina close at her skirts.

"Lovely man, isn't he?" Maddie said, smiling. "And how kind of him to offer to drive us to the hotel."

"Ooh," Evalina said. "He frightened me out of my wits. He's beastly."

"I thought he had kind eyes," Lila said. "Big and brown like a Saint Bernard's."

"I want to go home," Evalina wailed.

Lila would not know how to explain this to anyone in New York City, but by the time she crawled inside the coach to take the remaining floor space, Bear had managed to place all twenty-one people and most of their luggage on the swaying Concord coach. They were on top, on the back, on the driver's box, and inside. All the ladies were to remain strapped down tightly for the duration of the journey. It was so decreed on the passenger ticket.

"How long before we get there?" Garrett called out as Bear climbed up to the driver's box.

"Take about ten hours," Bear replied.

"Ten hours!"

"So sorry. That's with twenty-four passengers. With twenty-two, can make it in eight or nine maybe. Gee haw!" Bear cracked a whip over the mules and they lurched away from the train station.

True to his word, Bear got them to Blue Mountain Lake in just under nine hours. The stop at a tiny hotel for a late lunch and leg stretch had taken almost an hour, but that and one stop at water barrels along the way to refresh the mules and again unkink the backs of the passengers were necessary and welcome delays. It was pitch dark as the coach rumbled over the dirt drive and pulled to a stop at the front door of the famous Prospect House.

"I feel shaken to death," Evalina said from her seat above Lila.

"No wonder they call it a corduroy road," Lila observed, trying to reach around and rub the base of her sore spine. The rocking and pitching of the Concord had slammed her back and shoulders repeatedly against the coach door. She was stiff from holding her body away from it.

The men climbed off the top and back. Lila heard their feet hit the dirt, felt the coach sway again. She stifled a groan.

"Opening door!" Bear yelled a warning.

Lila leaned forward. Bear opened the door and Garrett slipped his arms under hers and lifted her out, then assisted the others.

Lila stood up, unkinking each vertebra as she did. She shifted her ribcage and walked around the coach on wobbly legs. When she faced the main piazza of Prospect House, she sucked in her breath. "Oh, look at that!"

She tipped her head back and raised her eyes level by level until she reached the top, the sixth story. It seemed that every window on every floor was lit with a bright light. Evalina came around beside her and stared up in awe. Garrett and the Maynes joined their daughters.

"Edison electric light in every room," Garrett said. "The first hotel in the entire world to equip its sleeping rooms with this luxury. Running water and steam heat in every room as well. I think you'll find it comfortable."

"It's incredible," Lila breathed, starting up the steps.

Evalina followed her. "Do we have to move into the tents?"

At breakfast in the vast dining room, Lila felt like a child for the first time in a long, long while. Her fascination the night before with the Edison electric light, an uncanny wonder in the wilderness, lasted as long as it took for her eyes to grow heavy and close with much needed sleep. Aunt Maddie was already snoring in the next bed when Lila turned off the light.

Prospect House was more than she could have ever expected, even in so sophisticated a city as New York. But the surprise—the veritable shock—of finding such a fabulous establishment in the wild Adirondack Mountains was staggering. She and Evalina and Maddie had ridden down from the second floor in a steam elevator. They'd enjoyed the ride so much they'd promptly gone right back up and down again. And imagine a two-story privy with covered entrance walkways and accommodations for twenty-four at one time!

"Three hundred rooms, just think of it!" Aunt Maddie exclaimed over a breakfast of fried trout, fresh fruit cup, and fluffy biscuits.

"And all full. It's a city in itself," Rosamund Mayne added. She scanned the room. "The men were out early this morning. Something about meeting a survey team. I do wonder where Harrison is. I imagine you're anxious to see him as well, aren't you, Lila?"

"Don't worry about him, Mrs. Mayne," Lila said without looking up from her plate. "Harrison is very resourceful." *Unfortunately, he probably won't even get lost.* She turned to Evalina. "Let's do explore everything today, want to?"

"Yes, and I want to sit in a woven chair upon one of the piazzas, or maybe on all six of them, and read."

"I plan to do that, too," Aunt Maddie said, "but I shan't take a rocker. I am all rocked out from that coach ride."

"Don't forget tea this afternoon," Harriett Brigham reminded them. "Everybody who is absolutely anybody is here this week. I think there will be a great deal of talk about development."

"Tea will be lovely," Rosamund Mayne said. "Stewart has instructed me to spend time with Mrs. Huntington. I've heard she'll be trotting out her famous diamonds. It will take me hours just to decide what I can wear that won't embarrass me." She lowered her fork. "As I understand it, Lila, you are to seek out Mrs. Whitney and Mrs. Vanderbilt and ask them to join us. You are capable of that, aren't you, my dear?" she asked snidely.

"Yes, of course," Lila answered dutifully.

"Did you see the notice in the office?" Evalina asked with excitement. "There's to be a masquerade ball tonight! Isn't that just too delicious for words?"

"It would be if we had known in advance to bring costumes," her mother said. "I don't see how we can possibly attend."

"The hotel provides masks for everyone," Evalina said. "We'll think of something to wear, won't we, Lila?"

Lila watched the eagerness in her friend's eyes. She couldn't think of going to a ball. Harrison would definitely be back by this evening, and she wanted to hold one more day to herself without his interference. The thought of sitting on a high piazza and looking out over the most beautiful lake she'd ever seen was luring her to devise excuses.

"Oh, Evie, I know I won't feel up to a ball this evening. I'm tired, and I'll just keep Aunt Maddie company in our room."

"Now, Cat darling, don't worry about me. I won't want to stay in my room tonight." Aunt Maddie patted her hand. "I'd like nothing better than to attend a masquerade ball, with or without a mask. I think the gaiety will be beneficial to my health."

"Of course, Aunt Maddie." Lila considered she'd have time enough to create a plan to avoid the ball at the last moment.

"I want to stay here for the whole month," Evalina gushed.

"Well, we can't do that," her mother told her. "The tents will be ready for our arrival by the end of the week."

"Perhaps I should go out there, too, and be of some help," Lila offered, trying out her first excuse. Shaking rugs and making up cots seemed a welcome activity and diversion from the continuing round of society parties that had apparently accompanied them into the mountains.

"Nonsense," Rosamund said, glaring. "It's not fitting for a woman of your station. Do I have to remind you that you are Harrison's future wife?"

Her station. That word again. Lila needed no reminders of her father's expectations. "Excuse me," she said, rising. "I think I see Mrs. Vanderbilt going outside. I should try to catch her." She hurried out of the dining room so the others would not catch her in a lie.

Lila stepped off the piazza and walked quickly down the long lawn toward the extensive boathouse. The sunny morning air was clear and crisp, and she breathed deeply to ease the stifling tightness in her chest. She stopped halfway and watched the clear lake flowing past Prospect Point. The gently lapping water seemed to kiss the shore lovingly. All around, paperbark birch and maple trees provided cooling shade, and birds sang among their branches. She waded through knee-high ferns and wildflowers in showy splashes of golden yellow and brilliant scarlet. Scattered over the grounds were boulders so immense in size and weight, they might have been thrown like so many marbles by the hand of Atlas. And all around were the dark blue-green rolling tips of the mountains beyond.

Breathtaking—that was the scene in front of and around her. Breathtaking. Thrilling. Menacing.

Inviting.

She gazed into the dense blue of the mountain towering above the lake. "Is it atop a mountain much like that one where Seneca Pierce lives?" she asked into the air. That was the first time since they'd met that she'd said his name aloud. She imagined he would have a glorious house high in the sky, where he could turn in every direction and see the thrilling mountains and lakes of his Adirondacks.

The Blue Mountain breeze swept her words away over the lake and offered no response.

"I need you, *mon ami,* to do this one thing for me," Bear pleaded.

"You always ask me for one thing," Seneca responded, scraping the hide of a fox he'd killed. The two stood outside his cabin at a log-constructed workbench. "Then I always end up doing 'one thing' over and over."

"*Oui,* it's true. So we have a deal?"

"We do not have a deal. The 'one thing' I will not do is go to a masquerade ball at Prospect House. Dressing up like some society boy and tripping around the room while some tittering debutante bats her eyelashes and waves a fan in my face is not what I care to spend my time doing."

"*Oui.* That is why I must go. *We* must go."

Seneca scraped harder, his knife whipping over the hide like a stormy wind. "I know you understand English, my friend, but *no* is the same in French as well."

"Ah, I need you, *mon ami,*" Bear pleaded. "There's a girl. She's *très féminin,* bee-you-tee-full. With hair like a grizzly and a voice like sleigh bells."

Seneca stopped scraping and raised his eyes toward his friend. "Hair like a grizzly bear? Only you could find a grizzly bear attractive." He went back to his work.

"*Oui.* And I could tell she liked me, too. But it will be difficult. She is rich. I can see her only if I go to this ball.

Do you not see why I need you? Who will let me in to Prospect House? But you, *mon ami,* if you were to go with me, they would think this is a costume!" Bear swept his hands over his beard and clothes and laughed heartily.

Seneca slowly set down his knife. He regarded his friend a long time and saw the honest emotion behind his entreaty. He gave Bear a beleaguered stare. "I know I'll regret this, but all right, I'll go." Bear jumped around in a circle letting out a whoop. Seneca grabbed his arm to restrain him. "But you will be in my debt, my friend, until your dying day. That is, if you don't ask something else that will make me hurry the process along myself."

In the anteroom of the Prospect House ballroom, Seneca, dressed in his own deerskin pants and jacket, allowed the greeter to fit him with a black mask that covered his forehead, eyes, and the top of his nose. His hair flowed freely to his shoulders. Around his own head Bear had tied a red bandanna cut with two eye-holes. Seneca thought he rather looked more like a derelict pirate than a society dandy in an authentic costume.

Seneca scanned the crowd of whirling dancers. Music came from a full orchestra in formal dress. Waiters scurried by bearing trays loaded with champagne flutes and whiskey glasses. "All right, where is this beautiful girl that has turned your head enough to find us both looking like fools at a dance?"

Bear stepped beside Seneca, stood with his booted feet wide, and planted his thick fists on his hips. "I shall know her when I see her. Have no fear of that."

"With hair like a grizzly and a voice that clanks like sleigh bells, I have the feeling I'll know her immediately as well. But thank you for the warning." At the opposite end of the cavernous room, Seneca spotted a long table laden with food and decorated with an elaborate ice sculpture. "Might as well take supper, long as we have to be here." He led Bear around the dancing couples, grabbed two glasses of whiskey off a passing tray, then waded into the crowd.

"Isn't it just delicious?" Evalina gushed, tapping a pleated paper fan against her lips. She adjusted her pink sequined mask.

Lila dropped down into a tufted side chair and flexed her feet under her royal-blue silk gown. "Who would think so many inexperienced dancing boys could be found in one place on one evening? My slippers are ruined and my feet along with them. Then there is the permanent stain on the shoulder of my dress from their nervous sweating."

"I do admit our partners have been awkward at best," Evalina allowed. "But the ball is exciting, isn't it? I simply had no idea that such a fabulous event could be found in this wilderness." She giggled, and her plump hips shook under the weight of her many petticoats. She wore a gown of so many colors in panels down the skirt that it reminded Lila of a Maypole.

"I'll grant you that is a surprise. Whatever made me think I might find solitude on a mountain holiday?" Lila yawned. "Have you seen Aunt Maddie?"

"Only a moment ago. She was dancing with a young man in a military academy uniform and thoroughly enjoying his attention, I might add. I think that's so lovely, don't you?"

"As long as it's Aunt Maddie and not me. As soon as I am able to move I shall take leave of this. I abhor crowds. You will want to stay, no doubt."

"Oh, absolutely. I have the feeling I shall meet *him* tonight." Evalina giggled again.

"Evie, you've met scores of *hims* tonight, and I'll wager not one of them would you want to appear in your dreams, let alone be a part of the rest of your life."

"True. But I still have two more hours before the ball is over. Anything can happen."

"That's what I'm afraid of." Lila had been quietly glad that Harrison had failed to make an appearance at the ball thus far. She hoped she might scurry away and be safely in her room before that changed. Evalina was distracted, and Lila chose the opportunity to push herself up from the chair. "Make my excuses, will you? I'm going now."

Lila picked her way through the crowd toward a door to the veranda. The jostling dancers reminded her of the coach ride, and it was not a pleasant recollection. Near the far end of the room, an exuberant dancing couple whirled around and collided with her. Oblivious they danced away in a spate of laughter, unaware that Lila had lost her balance and was starting to fall.

A pair of arms caught her and saved her from crashing to the floor in an embarrassing heap. They lifted and steadied her.

"Are you all right?" a rich male voice said near her ear.

Lila was breathless. "Yes. I'm terribly sorry."

"Not your fault. They didn't see you." His voice was muffled by the escalating music from the orchestra.

Lila frowned. The voice reminded her of someone she'd heard before. She turned and looked up into the face of a very tall man in a black mask. He wore a fawn-colored deerskin jacket and pants, as soft as the jacket her father had presented her for this trip. Above his mask, thick strands of dark hair curved around, then down the side of his bronze face, long enough to graze his shoulders and below. Lila peered hard before she regained the sense to stop staring. Was it the subdued lighting of the ballroom, or did he possess sky-blue eyes almost as perfect as the ones invading her dreams? She was hypnotized by them, drawn inside of them.

And then the most unseemly words spoken by a lady tumbled from her lips. "May I have this dance?"

The blue eyes behind the mask darkened. His gaze locked to hers, he spoke not a word. Almost reluctantly it seemed, he slipped his arm around her trim waist. She lay her right hand in his left one, and they glided onto the floor amid the dancers. Her left hand slipped up and rested against his upper arm where it met his shoulder. The jacket was soft, velvety, and she felt his muscle move under it as their bodies swayed together.

Lila barely heard the music or the voices of the people around them. It was as if a cloud had descended and engulfed them both, muffling any other sounds except that of their own shallow breathing. This was a dream, it must be a dream, for the cloud swirled around their feet and seemed to lift them above the dance floor. She looked down and saw her own ivory satin slippers. And . . . *brown moccasins.*

Seneca could not take his eyes from the emerald-green ones that shone in rivalry with the golden glittering mask over what he knew was the beautiful face of the woman who floated in his arms. Her hips swayed provocatively below his hand where it rested at the back of her waist. Her dark gold hair was piled loosely atop and around her head. Her blue gown dipped in a low décolletage, revealing a creamy expanse of smooth skin fragrant with a soft yet spicy scent. His senses reeled from the sight, scent, and feel of her.

Was he leading her or was she guiding him? He couldn't

tell, but it didn't matter. Together they left the ballroom and stepped out onto a moonlit veranda. A finger wisp of cloud over the moon, a soft breeze, and raindrops gathering in the air signaled an approaching rain shower. Beyond the veranda stretched a carefully landscaped garden with a deserted arbor at the far end. Without speaking and now without touching, the two strolled toward that arbor.

Under the protective canopy of vines, they stopped and turned toward one another. Seneca saw the waning moonlight, filtered by the leaves, reflected in her eyes. And then all he could see was her lips, soft, quivering, inviting.

In her hypnotic spell Lila raised on tiptoe and kissed the well-defined lips below the black mask. Nothing in her youthful training would have given her permission to perform such a bold act, but everything in her feminine dreams propelled her toward it. She pulled back slightly. He dipped his head and caught her lips again, softly, then more insistently.

She leaned into the kiss, and then with a mighty force they were in each other's arms, straining against each other, devouring lips, exploring mouths, clinging and holding. They parted slowly, each desperately needing to breathe, but reluctant to release the kiss.

Then in an instant Lila turned and ran.

From a secluded bench in the arbor, Madeline Allgood watched her niece with the tall man. She saw his stunned reaction when Lila fled, saw him remove the mask from his face. She smiled to herself. So her many wishes upon the magic evening stars had been granted in a roundabout manner.

Madeline rose when the man left the arbor. There was a bit of work to do now, and she hoped she could weave a little magic of her own.

Five

Seneca stepped inside the ballroom and readjusted his mask. He felt dazed, as if he'd been hit over the head and been unconscious for a time.

"There you are, *mon ami*." Bear caught up with him. "I have been looking all over for you. I've found her! My little grizzly bear, I've found her! Come, you must help me now."

"I don't think I'm in any condition to help anyone right now."

Seneca let his gaze drift around the ballroom, but he could not focus on anyone. He could still taste the sweetness of his mystery woman's kisses in the arbor. Ever since he'd returned from the city he'd been spending a lot of time alone, perhaps too often brooding at the graves of his family. As the mountain guides often said, the lonesomeness in the mountains could play tricks on a man's mind. And try as hard as he had, he couldn't forget Lila Stockdale, nor the taste of her kiss. In his heart he believed it wasn't possible that two women in all the world could possess the same magnetism, the same jewel depth in their eyes. Where was the mystery woman now? When he found her, she wouldn't remain a mystery for long.

"What has happened? You look like you have seen a ghost." Bear shook his friend by the shoulder.

"Perhaps," Seneca replied distantly.

"I have never seen you so . . . what is it? Present in the body, away in the mind."

Seneca shook his head. "I wonder what was in that whiskey." A peal of tinkling giggles broke around them, startling Seneca. "What was that?"

"Ah, that is my little grizzly. See? There." Bear pointed to a knot of bedecked, feathered, and masked women. "With the brown hair and dress like a rainbow."

Seneca located her, a bouncy brunette with thick curls and a plumpish form under an enormous dress. "That's your . . . ? Yes, I see what you mean."

"Come help me."

"You don't need my help. Simply go over and ask her to dance."

"You think?" When Seneca nodded, Bear started to walk slowly away. "You watch me. See that I do good job."

Seneca watched his big friend push through the crowd, oblivious to the frowns and startled stares as he passed. Bear approached the woman in the colorful dress from the side and tapped her on the shoulder. Seneca could see his lips forming the request for a dance. The woman turned, shrieked, and tried to run. Bear caught her around the waist and before any of the other women could do anything, he'd dragged her onto the dance floor and was maneuvering her toward Seneca.

Oh no! Seneca thought. He was in no mood to make small talk with a silly rich woman. And he wanted to rip the mask off his face once and for all and fling it into the nearest potted tree. He started to back away.

"Wait, wait!" Bear shouted from the dance floor, and Seneca froze.

The woman was no longer struggling with Bear. In fact

she was looking up at him as if he were some kind of god who'd stepped out of the sky in a clap of thunder. Bear was hurrying her toward Seneca so quickly her feet seemed to touch the floor only every third or fourth step.

"See? See?" Bear was as excited as a child with a new toy. "Is she not perfect?" He pushed the woman in front of him and presented her to Seneca. She giggled loudly.

The woman from the Stockdale dinner! This had to be her! Evalina something. Seneca could barely speak. "Perfect, yes, indeed. How do you do?" He bowed slightly toward the giggling woman, who responded with more giggles.

The orchestra broke into a fanfare and the crowd quieted. A man in a stiff collar and formal suit stepped up onto the orchestra platform. "Ladies and gentlemen!" he shouted. "It is time to crown the king and queen of the Prospect House masquerade ball! Please form two lines down each side of the room. My assistants will walk through your midst and tap you on the shoulder, then escort you to our thrones."

Four young men brought out two highbacked chairs decorated with ribbons and flowers. Two equally formally dressed young men started down the center of the ballroom. One headed straight for Bear and his giggling grizzly. Seneca could not imagine how Bear was going to react to this! He could just picture him with a crown tilting precariously over his thick hair.

But the man moved past them and stepped toward Seneca. Seneca felt his smile fade. They wouldn't. . . . The man veered past Seneca's side and down several feet from him, to Seneca's extreme relief.

"Our queen!" he announced.

As a round of applause swelled from guests, Seneca turned and saw him take the hand of his mystery lady and start to lead her past. She pulled back, shaking her head. The man cajoled. Reluctantly the lady allowed him to lead her. Seneca scrutinized her in the subdued light and in his much mystified mood.

The other young man was still roaming the ballroom. He made a sudden turn and walked directly to Seneca. "Our king!" he called out. A roar of applause went up once again.

"No!" Seneca growled to the young man. "Select someone else."

The young man only smiled and tugged on Seneca's arm. Over his protests, Bear stepped in and dragged his friend toward the orchestra platform and the two thrones. He heard Evalina giggling as she followed behind. Seneca was pushed onto the throne, a golden paper crown set upon his head, and a wooden scepter presented. Next to him the newly crowned queen sat rigid, cradling a large bouquet of flowers in her arms, and staring straight ahead.

The lights came up full. "Ladies and gentlemen, we will now unmask our king and queen and present them in their first royal dance!"

A lavishly gowned woman, decorated by a sparkling array of diamonds, sashayed out and stood before them. Seneca gritted his teeth. Bear would pay for this embarrassment for months to come. The woman removed first his mask and then the queen's. The two looked toward each other as she moved away.

Seneca's chest tightened. *Lila Stockdale.* He felt no real surprise, no shock, but he did sense an air of foreboding.

He watched her emerald eyes widen and her hand tremble as she brought it to her hair at the side of her face. "Mr. Pierce," she breathed.

"And now our king and queen will take the dance floor alone. Please welcome them!"

A roar went up from the crowd, and the orchestra struck up a waltz. Thinking that perhaps he should be the one paying Bear for unwittingly placing him in a situation he would never have chosen for himself, Seneca stood and held out his hand to his queen. Slowly she lifted hers and stood. He led her to the dance floor, pulled her gently into his arms, then swept her away on the strains of the music. As they whirled down the line of smiling guests, Seneca caught sight of Miss Madeline Allgood talking to the host. He was patting her hand, and they were speaking conspiratorially as they watched the dance.

Seneca winked at the old lady as he danced Lila near them. Perhaps it wasn't Bear he should be paying after all.

Lila's heart pounded so hard she barely heard the music or felt her own feet moving across the dance floor. She was dancing in a dream, she must be. What other explanation could there be for what was happening? Had Aunt Maddie been right? Could it be so that if one pictured it long enough, a dream or a wish could come true?

As the other dancers joined them on the floor, she leaned back in the circle of his arm and gazed up into the sky-blue eyes of Seneca Pierce. He held her gaze and tightened his arm around her waist.

Bear and Evalina came to them. "Can you believe it? He did not want to come to this dance tonight!" Bear laughed uproariously.

"Neither did Lila." Evalina giggled. "And look now. Oh, Mr. Pierce, I was just so very surprised to see you here."

"Not half as surprised as I am, Miss." Seneca gave her a warm smile.

"Oh, Lila, isn't it just simply delicious? Isn't it just as you dreamed?"

Embarrassed, Lila was flustered so profoundly she could barely speak. "We can talk later, Evie," she managed.

Yes, the evening truly was delicious. If she were still in a dream, then she didn't want to wake up. This was the most thrilling time she'd ever experienced. She didn't feel like the Lila Stockdale she'd grown up with. She was different now. She was someone else. And she was floating in that woman's aura.

Again she felt the soft deerskin that covered Seneca's shoulders and arms. It felt wild yet tame all at once. A chill coursed over her skin as she sensed the same elements about Seneca. His hair moved as they waltzed, and she watched the light catch it again as it had the night they'd first met. She whirled in the dream of his arms.

And then she saw her father. Garrett was glaring at her as she passed.

Beside him stood her betrothed, Harrison Mayne, a murderous gleam emanating from his eyes.

Dressed in boots, a dark woolen skirt, a stiff cotton shirt with a high collar, and the deerskin jacket Garrett had given her, Lila walked through the tall pines early the first morning of their camping holiday. She carried an ancient textbook on dendrology and was lost in identifying the white and yellow pines, balsam, paperbark birch, and tamaracks.

The move out from Prospect House had been made more difficult than it might have been, what with Harrison's snappishness and the grumbling of Harriett Brigham and Iris Madison. Lila and Aunt Maddie had looked forward to moving to camp, but now Lila was concerned about the real lack of privacy and the further lack of the hotel's six floors of rooms that she'd utilized to evade Harrison.

Her father had strongly reprimanded her for her behavior at the masquerade ball three weeks earlier. Worse, he'd done it in the presence of Harrison, who'd gloated over her dressing down. It wasn't seemly, Garrett had said, for a woman of her station to leave her betrothed standing awkwardly and humiliated at the sideline while she waltzed across the floor with another man. And of all men, Seneca Pierce!

Her station! Lila was sick to death of it, hearing it, *being* it. If Harrison had chosen to remain at the sideline, awkward, humiliated, then it wasn't her fault. There were any number of unattached women in that ballroom with whom he could have requested a dance. Lila wouldn't have cared one whit. In fact, she would have been more than a little glad to see him working his oily charm on another woman who may have welcomed his advances.

Birds flitted overhead among the trees. Lila tilted her head back and peered up through the needles and lace of the pine branches that went from deep green to black the higher her gaze traveled toward the sun.

"It's magic," she whispered into the crisp morning air. "Like being in a mystical kingdom." She laughed a childlike laugh. "Or queendom."

That's what she'd prefer, she suddenly thought. A place where everything in life didn't revolve around the male head of the clan. Her favorite times growing up had been when her father was away on business and she and her mother were alone in the house with only the servants. And later, after her mother's death, when she and Aunt Maddie would read to each other and play Parcheesi or dominoes.

No, on second thought, she wouldn't want to be in any place that revolved around one person, whether male or female. How lovely if two could be at the center of her universe: a man and a woman, herself, together. That was the real dream, one that could never come true. She sighed and wandered among trees, touching with wonder rough bark here and smooth bark there.

She came upon a mound of smooth rocks that overlooked a deep ravine and a narrow outlet from the lake. In back of it lay a smaller mound. With piqued curiosity she walked around the mounds. At the top of the larger one was a glistening rock of pink granite. If nature had simply dropped the rocks in the mud slides or blow downs she'd heard about, then the handiwork was very neat and artistic. If not nature, then what? Or whom? She sensed the mounds had meaning, perhaps like Stonehenge in England. Wouldn't it be fun for her and Evalina to fabricate intriguing tales of ancient mountain dwellers?

She walked around the mounds. Beyond the site she could see a small island, dense with spike-tipped trees. She dropped down onto a large rock overlooking the ravine and stretched her legs out in front of her, surveying that part of the lake that looked like a huge dark jewel in the rising morning sun. She opened her jacket and pulled out the printed silk scarf she'd looped around her neck as a barrier against the scratchy shirt collar. She smiled as she smoothed the fabric over her hand. Evalina had given her the scarf for her birthday because it incorporated her favorite shades of blue, from bright to muted.

In the susurrus in the air and the swirls of the scarf's colors, Lila saw the twirls of silks and rustling taffeta on the ladies at the masquerade ball. How glorious the evening had been! It had started out as the usual ball—like so many she'd attended before—but had turned to a flight of fantasy as she'd danced with a mystery man in a black mask. She hadn't allowed herself to admit it then, but she could now—she'd known who he was or who she desperately wanted him to be. Seneca Pierce.

And . . . she'd shamelessly danced out to the veranda with him. And . . . they'd kissed. It hadn't been at all like before when she'd *let* one of her suitors kiss her, or even in her dreams when she'd visualized herself kissing a prince because she'd simply wanted to.

This time the two had kissed, together. She could still feel it, taste his lips, feel his moist warm tongue part her teeth gently and explore for the merest moment the slickness in her mouth. For the fleetest of instants, she'd thought about trying the same with her tongue, but fortunately hadn't the courage. What she'd done was shameless enough.

And then to see—in front of the entire gathering—that her mystery man was indeed Seneca Pierce! Her stomach fluttered at the memory. Shameless, that's what she was. More shameless than she'd thought possible. She'd fantasized over and over about their first kiss that night at home, reliving it in her mind and on her lips. And she'd wanted more. Kissing him in the Prospect House arbor was a dream come true, and she hadn't wanted to miss it. She'd wanted him to kiss her, wanted to kiss him with more of herself. Now she wanted more of everything.

What in the world was wrong with her? A lady wasn't supposed to have these feelings. *She* shouldn't have these feelings, should she?

She lifted her eyes and gazed back toward the island. She owned nothing but clothes and jewelry. If she were to possess anything that was hers and hers alone, she would wish for an island. She couldn't live isolated all the time, she knew that—but to know she could retreat to her own secret piece of earth where no one else could find her, even for only a few blessed hours of exquisite solitude, would make everything else more palatable. She could dream her dreams to her heart's content, and no one could tarnish their brilliance.

Lila sat still for an immeasurable time in the warming sun, listening, seeing, feeling the sensitivity of her own rhythms in harmony with nature. She knew this sense of touching her own deepest emotions was happening even though she hadn't experienced such sensations ever before in her life.

She'd been born in the city, grown up in the city, and in the city she would live and die. It had all been arranged by her father. And by Harrison.

She swatted aimlessly at an annoying blackfly that persisted in landing at the back of her ear. Harrison. The intruding thought of him and his derisive sneer as her father scolded her for her actions at the ball brought her out of the expanse of morning light and air and back into the darkness in her mind. She'd suffered her father's punishing silence, Harrison's accusing glares on the trip to camp, and the smug glances of his mother since their arrival. How could she go through with marrying Harrison, with living with his family? He'd told her she'd have no choice in the matter. She'd accepted that, albeit with reluctance. Even with her declarations that she would not marry him, she knew the event was inevitable.

Yet, now, up here in these wild mountains, in the clarifying air, she questioned whether she did indeed have a choice. Even with her father's command—that was the only way she could think of it—that she marry Harrison, she felt driven to find a way out of it. But a foreboding sense remained that something was very wrong. Something about her father's behavior disturbed her more than just his insistence that she marry Harrison.

Lately Garrett seemed edgy whenever she was out of his sight for very long. Even while he pushed her toward Harrison, it was as if he were almost *afraid* she would leave him. He had summoned the men the evening before when she'd wandered off just before dusk for a look around their newly set-up camp. She hadn't been gone ten minutes, she was certain of that, but Garrett had reacted violently when he'd found her missing. She'd felt constricted, suffocated. This morning's jaunt she'd planned for when he'd gone off before breakfast with Stewart and the others to look at a parcel of land. He would be back for breakfast at any moment. She'd best return to the campsite. She would watch his movements carefully and at the best possible moment try for a walk by herself again in afternoon.

Unwillingly Lila rose from the rock and turned away from the lake and the island to head back to camp.

When she stepped into the clearing—around which were arranged on wooden pallets canvas tents large enough to accommodate the Stockdale entourage, their servants, their belongings, and their kitchen—she was positive no one had missed her. Everyone was up and the camp was bustling. Most likely they assumed she'd gone off to take care of her morning ritual. Breakfast was being prepared by Martin and his none-too-happy staff. Their heads were covered in green canvas helmetlike affairs fitted with green netting all around, which protected their faces, chests, and the backs of their necks from the ubiquitous Adirondack blackflies. She ignored the helmet Martin offered her and found she was barely bothered by them.

The lovely morning outside passed dismally inside with

the women staying within the confines of the dining tent, the better to avoid the bites of flies and other insects. She wondered, too, if the confinement were a way of enforcing a watch over her by Rosamund Mayne. Lila felt trapped by the pairs of eyes that settled on her often and by the endless discussion of parties, dinners, gowns, and who was doing what with whom and when. She was relieved when the servants laid out the noonday meal. At least it was something to do.

After lunch Lila sat on a blanket on the tent floor with Evalina reading poetry. She grew restless after a bit. She'd chosen Elizabeth Barrett Browning, and the lovely sentiments of a lady's aching heart plunged her into melancholy.

"I so wish we could take walks alone," she said sadly, closing the volume of poetry. "I'm feeling sluggish from eating and resting all the time. I've read about the restorative air of the Adirondacks, but so far we've had to breathe it inside of tents and through fly netting. I feel what a bird on display in a zoo must feel peering at freedom through wires and knowing there is no escape."

"You had your walk alone this morning," Evalina said, with a hint of smugness. "Don't think you weren't noticed. Your aunt and I spied you disappearing through the trees."

"I just have to get away from"—she passed her hand through the air in the shape of the tent—"all this now and again. I've been wondering what it would be like to take a camping holiday on my own, or perhaps with you or Aunt Maddie, and take care of all our own needs without a corps of servants milling sullenly about. I do hope Aunt Maddie wasn't too upset to see me leave."

"She wasn't. I believe she would go off on a walk herself if she didn't think your father would be horribly displeased. She does worry about you. And you must be careful. Who knows what, or *who* is lurking in the forest?" Evalina giggled behind her hand.

"Evalina, I'd sooner have fear of a possible mountain lion than from what you are hinting about."

"Wouldn't it be delicious if Mr. Pierce were to come upon you and—"

Lila reached over and placed two fingers over her friend's mouth. "Shush. You must not mention his name. You know how Harrison and my father feel."

Evalina frowned. "I know," she whispered. "They certainly did seem to overreact at your merely dancing with him at the ball. I mean, how could you know you'd be crowned queen, and he, of all people, crowned king? Oh, but it was delicious, wasn't it?" She giggled.

"Yes," Lila whispered, "it was delicious." Her thoughts again drifted back to the evening, and to the shadowy veranda.

Evalina leaned over and tapped her friend's arm. "What are you daydreaming about?" She narrowed her eyes at Lila's silence. "You're keeping something from me. I can always tell, you know."

Lila looked down at the book of poetry in her lap. She traced the gold lettering. "It's true. I haven't told you everything. But some things one must keep private."

"Well, I don't. I tell you everything. I keep no secrets from you."

"Perhaps you shouldn't, Evie. Don't you have some secrets so lovely you want to keep them to yourself?"

"I don't have any secrets like that. And if I did, I'd tell you. You're my dearest friend." Evalina pouted. "Well, all right, I'll tell you one thing. I have been fantasizing at night about—" She leaned forward and whispered the word, scarcely audibly, "Bear."

Lila let a smile spread slowly across her lips. "You

have? Oh, my, wouldn't your mother become consumptive at the very thought of her delicate daughter dreaming about a grizzly French fur trapper from Canada?"

Evalina tittered. "Wouldn't she just?" She wagged a finger at Lila. "But you can't tell."

"Don't be silly, I wouldn't say a word. Do you want to see him again?"

Evalina tapped her fingers against her lips. "I don't know. He scares me. *I* scare me when I think about him. He's so . . . so *primitive.*"

Lila laughed warmly. "A little rough around the edges, yes. But something tells me he has a heart as big as his beard and as wide as the mountain range."

Evalina twisted a handkerchief in her lap and leaned over in eager anticipation. "Now tell me your secret. I've told you mine."

Just then Iris Madison approached them. "It's time for your afternoon nap, girls. Stop your chattering now."

"Oh, Mother, please. We aren't tired. There's no reason to nap."

"Evalina, do not argue. You know why a lady must always take an afternoon rest." Iris turned and left them then.

"She has always said that, and I have never known why a lady must take an afternoon rest. Do you?"

Lila shook her head. "It's probably because her mother said the same thing."

Evalina got to her feet. "Will you tell me your secret?" She searched Lila's face.

Lila rose and sighed. "All right. I promise I'll tell you. But not just yet. Soon."

The two walked together to the ladies' sleeping tent. Evalina took to her mattress after confiding to Lila that she would dream about her wild mountain man from the masquerade ball. Aunt Maddie was already napping, and the other women were preparing for the same. Once again the men were out plotting track beds and gaming clubs.

Lila stretched out on her mattress and waited for the onslaught of even breathing. Certain the others were asleep, she grasped the opportunity to steal away for some time by herself in the woods. She shrugged into her doe-skin jacket, tied on her boots, and slipped out of the tent.

Less than half an hour later, in a tiny sun-dappled clearing, Lila stretched her arms high over her head, then spread them out in front of her in an expansive arc. How she longed to embrace the wind, hold the sun, inhale the spicy-sweet scent of balsam and cedar, and commit the bird song to memory. She whirled around in a dance of abandonment with nature. For one wild moment she wished she could throw off all the constricting clothing she wore and sail naked among the ferns and newborn wildflowers. She closed her eyes and reached her face toward the sun.

The hard grip came around her and clamped over her breasts, knocking her backward. She fell against the intruder onto the underbrush. He rolled over her and pinned her against gnarled tree roots. She shrieked and the grip slapped over her mouth.

"Waiting for your savage to come and drag you away by the hair, my beloved?" a voice growled in her ear before his teeth sank painfully into her lobe.

Lila struggled against his thick body. "Harrison! What do you think you're doing? Let me up this instant."

Harrison gripped her wrists and slammed her hands up over her head and leaned above her, grinding his pelvis into hers, shoving his knee up hard between her legs. "It's a little late to get your patrician dander up, isn't it Lila? It didn't bother you when that Indian had his filthy hands all over you. At least I know what to expect from you when I take my husbandly rights. You'll be squirming all over when I shove my hands and more in—"

Lila wrenched under him. "Shut up, Harrison—you disgust me."

"Oh, that's good, that's good," he grunted. "The lady with the heart of a whore. Just what every man wants. Squirm harder, you bitch, and know that our wedding night will be just like this."

Lila fought against the nausea that threatened at the back of her throat. "You'll never get that chance, Harrison. When I tell Father about this—"

"You won't tell him. And if you do, he'll think you seduced me."

"He'd never believe anything so ridiculous!" Lila pushed harder, trying to get away from him, but Harrison only ground his fleshy weight into her more.

"Of course he will," Harrison rasped. He slammed his head into her throat and sadistically sucked the delicate flesh at the opening of her shirt. "He knows how guilty you feel after shamelessly kissing that savage."

Lila blanched and went dead still. "What—do you mean—kissing—?"

Harrison's laugh was sinister. "Did you think you weren't seen out in the arbor? Really, my dear Lila, you underestimate the powers of your future husband. I'll tell Garrett that, as the gentleman I am, I tried to resist you, but you felt so guilty I had to make you feel better. He knows. Your mother was a cold fish. He's visited enough whores in his life to know how wily they can be, how they can make a man's blood boil. He'll be so concerned you'll become like one of them, he's likely to advance the wedding date to August as I've suggested."

"No! I'll be dead before I marry you!"

"That can be arranged if you'd like, but I'd prefer it right after the wedding ceremony. That would suit my purposes better."

Lila managed in her struggle to free one leg. She brought it up far enough to slam her boot sharply into Harrison's soft belly. It was enough to catch him off guard. He relaxed his grip slightly, and she sidled out from under him and rolled to her knees. He caught her foot and dragged her back down, tearing her skirts. She lashed out with her foot and caught his shoulder, knocking him back. He caught her again as she ran and hauled her back down. He raised her skirts and tore at her petticoats.

Fear and loathing mounted in Lila's chest. Her strength was waning. Tears burned at the back of her eyes, but she fought them as hard as she did Harrison.

And then he was on her again, trapping her beneath his weight. This time she knew she could not break free.

Seneca glided soundlessly on moccasined feet through the dense Adirondack forest. He carried his bow and a quiver of arrows slung over his shoulder, resting against his soft deerskin overshirt. The sun dappled the ground through the tree canopy, while overhead birds chattered as they flitted about the business of morning feeding and exercising their wings. Now and then he caught a glimpse of a blue wing or a yellow breast. He reveled in the momentary utter quiet when they stopped chattering long enough to gather and swallow.

His prowess with a bow and arrow had been slipping ever since he returned from his trip to New York City. He was irked about that, not having had anything substantial to eat because of it. City ways had permeated his senses in a short time. He'd been glad to get back to the mountains and let the virgin forest and clear air cleanse his Iroquois blood. His native half cried out for the solitude his white half compromised every time he returned to the city.

But the woods hadn't calmed him the way it always had in the past, hadn't filled him with the level of serenity he sought and savored. Now, every time he closed his eyes he saw a pair of glittering emerald ones and a cascade of curls the color of fresh honey from a bee tree. A cheek covered with alabaster skin as smooth and soft as a water-polished pebble clouded his concentration. His native blood boiled together with his white blood and heated his need. This intrusion interfered with the way he'd planned his life. The plan did not include a woman, especially not a spoiled wealthy city woman like Lila Stockdale.

He swatted at some blackflies which had gathered around his face and ears. They were getting thick as bird flocks. Seneca spat with vengeance into a muddy rivulet. So far this morning he'd managed to draw and let fly a swift arrow at a falling maple tree branch. Nothing he'd like to cook for dinner. And he'd missed a perfectly good rabbit and tried to blame it on the intrusion of blackflies that had destroyed his concentration. They weren't the only thing that was driving him crazy. He had to stop this or he'd starve to death like some lovesick schoolboy.

Lovesick? Seneca Pierce? No. It must be a dose of the awakening spring after a harsh winter, a long cold winter in the air as well as in his heart.

He started back to the shore and stopped near the graves of his family. Dropping down onto a nearby fallen log, he let his concentration fade from his quest for meat back to the masquerade ball at Prospect House almost three weeks previous. He'd had no intention of going back to the hotel after that night, not for any reason.

He could still hear the waltz, still feel her soft curves floating effortlessly in the circle of his arms. The whiskey he'd downed had made him too relaxed. That must have been it. How else could he have succumbed to so ludicrous an event as being crowned king of the ball? He must have known somewhere in his sixth sense that Lila would be crowned queen. Why had something so frivolous seemed important enough to make him stay? He could have walked out of there, should have right after they'd kissed. They shouldn't have kissed. He'd sensed a danger in it immediately, almost as if it were a threat to his very existence. He still could not make any logical sense out of it.

Bear told him the Stockdale party had left the hotel and moved to their campsites far up the lake and into the forest. It didn't matter to him. He had no desire to tangle with Harrison Mayne again, nor to be embroiled in any of their meaningless society dilemmas. He had more important things to consider than another chance meeting with Lila Stockdale. He hadn't been with a woman in a long while—that was probably the reason he'd been so physically and mentally unsettled by the memory of her.

"She's a beautiful woman," he said to the birds. "Who wouldn't be moved by her, even a cynical wretch like me?"

A rustle of brush and the snapping of twigs echoed through the quiet forest. The hair at the back of Seneca's neck bristled. He stood and backed against a birch tree, his every muscle and sinew taut. Steps sounded with a light crunching underfoot.

A deer.

Seneca couldn't see it, but he felt it with his native sensitivity. With controlled action, he raised his arm and reached behind his shoulder until his fingers closed over the stiff feathers at the end of an arrow protruding from the quiver. He held his breath in his throat, lifted the arrow and smoothly lowered it in front of him, fitted its slit into the bowstring and grasped two fingers around it.

The crunching sound grew louder as the footsteps neared. The animal was running. Something must have scared it.

Seneca waited. He could almost smell the venison cooking over a spit. He wouldn't miss this time. There! Through the thick pines. A flash of soft brown, a flash of white. Smoothly he lifted the bow and straightened his arm, then pulled the string back along his ear, resting the acute arrow tip between his thumb joints. He lowered his head, touched his cheek for a split moment against the arrow feathers.

The footsteps drew nearer. The crunching escalated, then stopped. And then the footsteps quickened and started away. The deer must have smelled him. Seneca's sharp vision focused at the end of the arrow tip. He stood as still as the sturdiest tree in the forest. And then another flash of golden brown passed the sight of the arrow.

Seneca lifted his head and let the arrow fly in the flash of an eyelid. He heard the arrow stop with a muffled thud as it penetrated flesh, heard the footsteps stumble, and then crash into the underbrush. He licked his lips, satisfied with his renewed prowess. He hadn't lost it after all.

Dropping his bow and quiver next to a shaggy yellow birch trunk, Seneca drew his knife from its waist sheath and ran toward his fallen prey. He could see his arrow's feathers sticking up like a flag. Dodging low branches and thick bushes, he skirted the area until he came to the clearing where his trophy lay at the mound of rocks that marked his mother's grave.

Something caught his eye—a flash of color that had

nothing to do with nature. Seneca's breath caught. He stopped. A sickening wave engulfed his stomach. He hadn't shot a deer. The crumpled form in front of him was human!

He leapt over fallen cedars and dropped down next to the still body. His arrow protruded through a jacket. *A doeskin jacket!* A dark stain spread in a ragged circle around the hole. He touched the shoulder. The neck and head were wrapped in a silk scarf printed in splashy shades of blue. Who . . . ? He reached under the head and slowly turned the body over. The scarf fell away, revealing a mass of honey-colored hair in tangled disarray.

Lila Stockdale!

Six

Seneca left the arrow in Lila's shoulder, tore the cotton shirt under his deerskin overshirt into rags, and packed it around the wound's opening. Then he lifted and carried her on a run through the forest to his canoe, beached at the lake shore, and swiftly crossed the water to his cabin. He needed his herbs, needed the chance to carefully extract the arrow and tend to the wound properly. She'd hit her head on a rock. That and the pain and shock of the arrow's penetration would take her in and out of consciousness. He had to work fast.

Inside his cabin he lowered Lila to his bed of balsam pine boughs covered with Hudson's Bay blankets. Gently he rolled her over on her stomach. He heated a basin of water, quickly took out his supply of clean cloths and bandages. With his hunting knife he cut away her deerskin jacket and cotton shirt and slipped them off. Then he cut the delicate lace straps on her camisole and gently pulled it away from the wounded area.

Deftly he removed the arrow. He'd constructed his arrows so well they could enter flesh cleanly and be removed with a minimum of tearing. He thought of a frightened doe as he looked at her lying still, her dark gold hair spread out over his blanket.

As he worked over her, Seneca knew now the dangerous

mistake he'd made. All he could see through the thick trees was a flash of deer-colored hide moving swiftly. He'd aimed and pulled the bowstring, thinking his judgment was as clear as it had always been. He hadn't bargained for the fact that in letting himself think so deeply about Lila Stockdale he'd muddled his mind to anything else. Perhaps that was a strange blessing. If he'd been performing at the peak of his acuity, it wouldn't have been her shoulder he'd hit and would have been fatal. He shuddered thinking of it.

Satisfied with his medicinal ministrations, Seneca shrugged on a clean blue cotton shirt, cleaned up his cloths and bandages, and went outside to empty the basin onto the ground beneath the trees. The water was dark with Lila's blood. A knot caught in his throat and choked his breath. Back inside the cabin he took her jacket to determine how much he could do to repair it. Her shirt was in shreds and stained with blood and was unsalvageable. He disposed of it. Her skirt was torn at the bottom and elsewhere.

She stirred and moaned. Seneca went to the pine bough bed and gently turned her over on her back. Beneath what was left of her thin camisole, the stark loveliness of her round breasts showed through. The dusky nipples seemed placed like beauty marks in the ivory softness. A tightness gripped his groin.

He dragged his eyes away. She was so vulnerable, unconscious as she was. He'd injured her and so had to minister to her. What in hell was he doing allowing a physical reaction like this? He really had sunk into some pretty awful depths since his trip to the city. He had to cover her and stop this emotional onslaught. He reached for a clean shirt of his own and carefully placed it over her breasts.

He grabbed a blanket to pull over her, then stopped

when he saw something else that made him frown. Bruises tarnished the soft skin of her wrists and upper arms. They'd spread in ugly purple-gray blotches with greenish-yellow stains at their centers. Surely she couldn't have sustained all those bruises in her fall when he'd hit her. And certainly not on both arms, around both wrists in quite that manner.

Her petticoat was torn and had blood on it—in fact the bloodstain seemed to be darker in some places, indicating that it was still wet. With hands he had to force to remain steady, Seneca raised her petticoat. Her stockings were shredded and he could see mean streaks down her thighs and more blood. What had caused that? Thorns? He didn't think that was entirely possible.

Seneca went back for more warm water. He untied the petticoat, lifted her buttocks, and slipped the petticoat carefully down. Then he stripped away her stockings and boots, leaving the cotton drawers, which were torn and bloodied as well. He had to remove them. He knew that. He could see a dark patch through the thin fabric. Forcibly he lifted his eyes from her delicate form and set about to cleanse the scratches on her legs first. He gently pressed clean water against them. Bruises had formed on her thighs. She looked as if she'd been attacked by an animal.

Could all of that have happened when she'd been running, when she fell after he'd hit her? He berated himself for the injuries he'd inflicted upon her. Yet he couldn't grasp the severity of those injuries as being the result of her flight and his strike with the arrow.

Now he had to bathe her most private place. There was no choice in this matter. He wondered for a moment if she was in the midst of her monthly. Judging by all the cuts and bruises that covered her body, Seneca had reason to consider more important questions. If she'd been injured there—and it was quite possible she had been—then those injuries had to be tended to just as quickly as the others. She was unable to take care of herself at the moment. How he wished his mother could be present now to see to this. But all he had was himself to rely on. All Lila Stockdale had was Seneca Pierce to tend to her wounds, even though he had inflicted many of them himself.

He set about the task, remembering the time when he'd come upon a doe in the throes of a painful birth. The fawn was coming breech first and the mother's tissue was tearing and she was bleeding profusely. She was losing consciousness and life in a most excruciating manner. Seneca had ministered to the doe, binding her legs with reeds, then carefully turned the fawn and delivered it. He'd taken care of the mother as best he could, suturing her tissue and cleansing it with the inside of pine bark and water. Before she'd come around he'd released her and set the fawn to nurse. From a distance he watched until she rallied and began to cleanse her infant before cleansing herself. He waited through the night to protect her from predatory mountain cats and other animals. In the morning he'd crept carefully away, certain she'd gained enough strength to protect herself and her fawn.

He prepared a basin of clean water and cloths, believing he could do as much for Lila Stockdale as he had for the wounded doe. As he was gently drying the injured delicate tissue, Lila moaned. Seneca watched her exquisite face contort with pain as she rose to greater consciousness. She was as beautiful as a mountain wildflower, seemingly fragile yet full of life.

Another thought shot as swift as his arrow through his mind. *He didn't want her in his cabin.* It was bad enough she'd haunted his mind. But he'd almost killed her. It was his duty to take care of her now, he knew that. But it didn't stop him from wanting her to go back to her family—get out of his cabin and out of his mind.

He bent down and touched her face, ran the backs of his fingers over her brow, and checked for fever. Then he ran the tips down to her throat below her jaw to gauge the rapidity of her pulse.

"No!" Lila called out in her rapidly sharpening consciousness.

"It's all right, it's all right," Seneca soothed. "I just have to be certain you're—"

"No!" She slapped at his hands and fought hard to scramble out of his bed. "Leave me alone. I'll tell Father!"

Seneca rose to his knees and straddled her. He pushed gently on her shoulders, trying to restrain her. "Shh, shh, you're all right. I'm so sorry I did this to you. I'm so sorry."

"Get away! You're . . . a monster!" She pushed at him, but her strength flagged and she sagged onto her shoulder. She moaned in pain and tears fell rapidly down her cheeks.

Gently Seneca pulled the blanket up over her. He moved to sit with his back against the cabin's wall. He gathered her into his arms and rocked her, murmuring "shh" over and over.

Lila stiffened. Her head swam, and she felt a burning and throbbing in her shoulder and down one arm. She tried to move, but her back hurt and her neck had shooting pains in it. Her hand moved along an arm. *Father? No, it couldn't be.* Her breathing quickened. *Was it Harrison? Oh, God, no!*

She opened her eyes and snapped her head back, bracing her hands against his upper arms, ignoring the pain that shot all around. It took several tortured moments before she could focus on the face above her.

Her vision cleared. She saw a strong angled jaw and black hair falling straight over a wide shoulder.

"Seneca?" she breathed weakly.

"Shh, shh," he whispered. "You're going to be all right. I'm so sorry. Just sleep."

She tried to move and in her fuzzy state realized she was locked in the circle of his arms. Her head dropped against his chest, and her heavy eyelids closed. Seneca Pierce. They'd been dancing, hadn't they? Then why did she feel so groggy? Had she been dreaming all along?

She forced her eyes open again. All she could see was a patch of blue cotton and something smooth and bronze colored. *Skin?* She pushed back. Her arms ached, her wrists throbbed. She moved her head slightly. A rolled blue sleeve and a muscular arm cradled her shoulders. *He truly was Seneca!* He was rubbing her back, murmuring soothing words, words that sounded to be in another language.

"What happened?" Lila stirred and Seneca relaxed his arms.

"I feel so terrible about this. When I think of what could have happened, how clumsy I was, I'm angry with myself."

His voice was husky yet rich. Something was strange. They weren't dancing. Lila realized they were in a bed or on a pile of something. She moved her hand and felt the blanket around her. As she smoothed her hand down her leg she winced. The skin on her thighs felt sore, and deep in her feminine depths she felt searing, throbbing pain.

"Harrison!" She sat bolt upright and instantly regretted it. Her entire body ached and her head swam.

"I know. I'll go and get him for you if that's what you really want." Seneca started to rise.

"No!" Lila clutched his arm.

Seneca turned and looked deeply into her eyes. A confused frown pleated his brows. "I wouldn't blame him for being furious. I . . . almost killed you."

Now it was Lila who felt confused. "What do you mean, *you* almost . . . killed me?"

"I was momentarily distracted. I heard running footsteps, and I thought it was a deer. I was in need of meat. I didn't think beyond that. I just raised my bow and let the arrow fly, never dreaming it was a human being. I guess it was your jacket. I'm so sorry—I honestly cannot believe I could do such a stupid thing."

Seneca raked a hand through his hair, and Lila could see how distraught he was. Had she been shot? With an arrow? Why couldn't she grasp what had happened? The last she remembered she was arguing with Harrison.

"You're hurt more than just from the arrow. You must be so . . . delicate, so fragile. The scrapes and bruises. I'm so sorry."

Lila raised her hand to stop Seneca's speech. Her thoughts were all fuzzy. And God, she ached all over, and her shoulder felt on fire. "Please, please don't say anything more," she said. She needed to think. Her head throbbed.

Seneca rose and strode on moccasined feet to a high ledge that spanned the length of the room and retrieved a black kettle. "All right, if that's what you want. I'll make some tea for you. Just rest now."

He went outside then, closing the door carefully behind him. She heard him moving about and then heard a fire crackle. She tried to focus her eyes as they drifted over her surroundings, but she couldn't see much in the dim light. The room smelled of pine and wood smoke and something else. Bacon? Vaguely she wondered what time it was.

She settled back on the soft bed and let her fingers drift over rough-napped blanket beneath her. What was under that? She lifted an edge of the blanket and felt. Some kind of tree branch it was. She felt the needles . . . long and silky and fragrant like a balsam Christmas tree she remembered having at home when her mother was alive. When she brought her hand away, she could smell the woods on her skin and she smiled to herself. One of the best things about the mountains was the scent.

As she moved, her hand came in contact with her own naked ribs. She ran her fingers over her body, her legs, her feminine place. Her skin was damp. She was entirely naked! Quickly she drew her hand out from under the blanket and touched her burning cheeks. It was a fever, she was certain of that, more than just a flushing from the embarrassment of knowing Seneca Pierce had removed all of her clothes.

She sighed and closed her eyes for a moment, resting her arm on her moist forehead. When she opened them and lowered her arm, she caught sight of the bruises on her wrist. How—?

The door opened and Seneca stepped inside. His massive build in deerskin leggings and cotton shirt filled the doorframe. Heated exhilaration coursed through Lila, a fiery fusion of fear and fascination. She watched him silently glide toward a high shelf at the back of the room. His deft hands intrigued her. She couldn't take her eyes from them.

He lifted down a teapot and set it on a cedar table supported by whole smooth logs. He opened a covered tin can, scooped out tea, and let it fall gently into the pot like leaves on an autumn breeze. Lila grew more fascinated by his artful hands. Seneca's hands that cooked, made tea, skinned animals. Hands that had shot her with bow and arrow. Hands that dressed the wound. Dreamily she ran her own hands over her body, thinking of his hands that had removed her clothes, touched her naked legs, her thighs . . . and more!

He turned around to her. "It'll be ready in a few minutes. Are you feeling any better?"

A true look of concern settled in his eyes. *Eyes that had seen her without clothes.* She dropped her gaze, no longer courageous enough to look more deeply into his.

"As soon as you feel up to it, we'd better start back to camp. Your family will be looking for you, you know," Seneca said, walking to the bed.

He placed a folded blanket behind her back so she could lean against the cabin wall without adding too much pain to her wound, then checked the bandage. Lila could tell he was satisfied with his medicinal handiwork by the look on his face. He tried to appear stoic and noncommittal, but she knew she was reading him correctly. He went back to the table and filled a tin mug with tea.

With trembling hands, Lila accepted the mug when he handed it to her. His fingers slid along hers and she almost missed gripping the handle. Once again his hands disturbed her—the look of them, the touch of them. She sipped the tea gingerly, inhaling the fragrant steam. "I know. But I don't want them to find me . . . yet."

Thoughtfully Seneca returned to prepare a mug of tea for himself. He came back to the bed, crossed his ankles and dropped easily down to the floor, resting his elbows on his bent and opened knees.

"All right."

Lila watched his face, waiting for him to ask why she'd made that announcement. He didn't. He'd simply accepted her words, and she didn't know how to respond. Whenever she resisted her father, she was always forced to provide a detailed explanation. Seneca's acceptance of her decision stopped her usual response. She should offer one anyway. Shouldn't she?

"It's . . . it's not that I actually blame you for what happened. Shooting me, I mean. It was an accident. I know that." She waited for him to say something. He didn't. "I mean, I was running. Father always says a lady shouldn't run." No response. Seneca sipped his tea. "And then the jacket . . . well, that would be easy to mistake for a . . ." A moment of disgust overtook her. "Do you actually *kill* defenseless animals?"

"I have to eat," he said evenly. "I have to wear clothes." He inclined his head and gave her a sidelong glance. "Or would you have me running around the forest in naught but a bit of loincloth I'd skinned from a tourist's shirt?" A hint of a smile played over his full bottom lip.

Lila's pulsed raced. How *savage* . . . she thrilled, then swallowed the word. "But a deer. I've seen them in a zoo. They are so beautiful, so delicate, so defenseless."

Seneca's penetrating blue gaze captured hers. "No more so than a salmon in a hatchery or a cow in a slaughterhouse."

Lila blinked against that gaze, but she could not weaken its intensity.

"And we must remember your deerskin jacket, mustn't we?" he added.

Lila squirmed under the blanket at his remark. She winced at the sharp fingers of pain that gripped her body everywhere. She suddenly felt cold. Why were they having this ridiculous conversation anyway? There was more, so much more at stake.

The tea began to warm the chill inside her, and a measure of courage returned. Timidly she raised her eyes and looked at him. The bronze planes of his face over a nose that could have been carved by a meticulous sculptor, the long angled jaw that flexed at the temple curtained by his long blue-black hair, and the expansive blue eyes that seemed to encompass all of her in one glance mesmerized her. She suddenly felt the same way she had the day she'd watched the blackbirds fly away over the ocean. She could have watched them all day, and a longing had filled her to be a part of their flock. A longing filled her now—an ache she couldn't define, an ache that couldn't be soothed in the way she'd been living her life up to now . . . up to this very moment in a cabin somewhere in the Adirondack forest, with a man born of nature and tempered by the winds of chance and change.

"Don't you want to know why I don't want them to find me?" she ventured.

"Your reasons do not concern me."

He sat so maddeningly straight and still while everything in Lila's body that could ache or throb was doing it with escalating intensity. But it was more than that, and she knew it. She just didn't know how to define the meaning of why her equally aching and throbbing heart, mind, and emotions were making it difficult to breathe.

"But aren't you the least bit curious?"

"No."

"What if they come looking for me? What if they come here?"

"That would concern me. They won't come here."

Lila lifted her chin. "Why . . . won't they come here?"

"When you can get up and look around, you'll see why. This cabin is secluded among thick pines and cedars." His rich voice was low, even. "They would have to be in a boat on the lake before they could see smoke from our fire."

Our fire. Lila let the words languish in her fogged mind.

They warmed her. Her fingers tingled. The back of her neck prickled. Her body was behaving in a most unseemly manner, not at all befitting a lady. Suddenly Lila wanted to discard the tag *lady*. The thought jolted her mind so forcefully her shoulders twitched uncontrollably and pain from her wound shot down her arm. She knew Seneca saw her physical reaction.

"That upsets you, I see," he said. "Which is it, that your father and your future husband will, or will *not*, discover your hiding place?"

He let fly with his question as swift as he had his arrow. She was coming to expect and fear his acute intuition, which went straight to the heart of her thoughts with breathtaking speed and accuracy.

"I . . . I don't know. That's not what is upsetting me . . . I think."

Seneca rose with a fluidity as graceful as a column of smoke. It wasn't until he had his hand around hers on the tea mug that she realized how tightly she'd been gripping it. Her fingers vibrated when she released the mug and he slipped it from her.

"Your father is a strong and determined man. Your future husband is his perfect choice for you. You know that. You cannot hide from them forever. Sooner or later you will have to go back to your family, your life." He turned, walked soundlessly to the table, and set the tea mugs down.

Lila bit her bottom lip. She didn't want to go back to her father and especially not to Harrison. She had to think. Now that she was alone in the company of Seneca Pierce she could not think properly, could not make sense of all that had seemed to make sense before.

Seneca turned back to her and leaned against the table.

"I wonder how my explanation of your wounds will be received by your father."

Lila knew exactly how Seneca's explanation would be received. There had to be another way. Perhaps if she didn't go back at all . . .

"The lovely Miss Madeline will worry, won't she?"

Aunt Maddie! Lila hadn't thought of the dear lady since she'd awakened. How could she have been so selfish as to think about hiding out from her father and Harrison and not think that Aunt Maddie would be sick with worry? Aunt Maddie, as delicate and sensitive as a rabbit, should not be left alone in the coarse and indifferent proximity of Garrett Stockdale without an ally.

Lila released her lip and sighed. She raised her eyes to his face. "You are right, of course. I don't know what I was thinking." True enough. Her thinking had been churning over the last few months, and now it spun like a whirlpool.

"Understandable. You've been through a shocking experience."

Lila held his gaze for a long moment, then turned her face away and could not control the flow of tears.

Seneca saw pain cross Lila's face and berated himself once more for being the one to inflict it on her. Beyond that he was angry for the intrusion upon his life of a progress he knew he could not prevent, Lila Stockdale represented everything about the opposite side of life that Seneca Pierce did not want to embrace. Society, wealth, greed, disregard for time and place past, disrespect for people. Now the material things available in the present and how to get them were all that Lila and her kind thought about. He'd witnessed it happen to his own father, had seen it through the course of his education in a white world. Inside he warred with himself for loathing what she represented—and at the same time he wanted Lila Stockdale with a heat in his blood that rivaled his fierce defense of the mountains and wilderness.

He set his strong jaw into an even stronger angle. On the souls of his ancestors, he swore not to allow her unique magnetism to weaken his resolve to preserve the land, the blessed mountains. He'd seen firsthand the change across the plains because of the advent of western settlement. He felt a decree had been sent to him from the god of his people to be the custodian of their spirits, the caretaker of this soil and seed. He was too strong, too filled with the ferocity of conviction to let a wealthy spoiled white child dilute the powerful instincts he'd known all his life.

But the sight of Lila lying wounded by his own hand, fearful, in pain, was more than he could bear at the moment. He went to her side and hunkered down next to the bed. The balsam aroma was made stronger from the heat of her body. Mingled with the light floral scent of her perfume, it drifted over him in a heady mist that muddled his thoughts. Forcibly steadying his hand, he touched her pale hand where it lay on her hip.

"As soon as you feel stronger, I'll return you to your family and your future husband," he said quietly. "Do not worry. I'll take full responsibility for your disappearance. They will not deal harshly with you. I will explain how you were hurt by my recklessness and your flight away from me, and—"

"No!" Her anguished sobs broke through.

Seneca watched her, saying nothing. She would tell him what he needed to know in her own time. A moment later he dismissed the thought. She was not Iroquois. She couldn't think like he could. He knew that. True to her people, she would alter the truth to fit her own desires. And even though his experience had taught him how to work within that framework, he simply deplored using that knowledge. It went against his Iroquois principles. Yet, looking at Lila now, he thought she was either as wily as a forest fox or as wide open as stripped tree bark. He lifted his chest and asked the question he knew would ensnare him in a manner he'd wished up to now only to avoid.

"Why don't you want me to take you back to them?" He waited a long moment for her answer.

"They . . . they'll do something terrible to you. You don't know what they're capable of."

Seneca closed his eyes and caught a fleeting glimpse of his own father. "I think I do," he whispered. He opened his eyes and watched her tortured expression. "If you're worrying about my safety, don't. I can take care of myself. I can take responsibility for your injuries."

"It's not your fault."

Seneca tilted his head at a slight angle. "I'm the one who has caused you this pain, this dilemma. I shot you."

Lila looked up at him with glistening eyes. "The pain of your arrow is nothing compared to . . . what . . . happened."

He frowned. "What do you mean? What happened?"

Lila clamped her eyes closed. "You wounded me only in the shoulder. He cut me as deeply as a man could ever hurt a woman." Her hand clutched the blanket where it lay, and she clung to it.

Seneca wanted to ask who hurt her, but this time he waited silently, if impatiently. In his heart he knew she would tell him what he needed to know . . . for now.

She pushed herself up to a sitting position against the wall. "I cannot go back to my father just yet. I have to have time to think," she whispered. She raised her eyes. "Harrison followed me on my walk."

Seneca nodded. "Then he will have told your father that you're lost somewhere in the woods."

"I wonder." She lowered her eyes and studied her hands.

"What?"

"I wonder just what he will tell them. I wonder just what I will tell them."

Lila still didn't remember being hit by Seneca's arrow. She didn't remember how she got to his cabin. But she did remember now quite clearly her struggle with Harrison. That was coming back all too sharply. She had to tell Seneca the awful truth. It was somehow of the most supreme importance that she spare him further guilt.

"You are not responsible for all of these wounds," she whispered. "Harrison caught up with me in the woods. We had words. I provoked him. Then I ran, and he chased me. He caught me and—"

Seneca's back arched. "You mean he did this to you? These bruises on your arms and wrists?"

She nodded weakly. "He grabbed me, knocked me down. I fought him, but he was very heavy. He pinned me down. He . . . he forced himself . . ."

Seneca's face contorted in pain. "Did he manage to— that is, have you further injuries?"

Lila lowered her eyes. She didn't know much about what happened physically between a man and a woman, other than what she'd read and fantasized about. And she'd never discussed something so intimate as this with anyone except her aunt, her doctor, and once in a while during speculation with Evalina. Yet she felt compelled to tell Seneca what happened.

"I believe he meant to," she said shyly, "but he didn't— that is, I don't think he . . ."

Seneca's jaw flexed, and his eyes glittered with an anger

Lila had seen only once before. "He is more savage than they ever thought I could be. He is less than an animal. I'll take care of him." He rose sharply and started for the door.

Lila sat up. "No, Seneca, please. No. Don't go. Don't tell them where I am yet. I have to have some time. Please. Except for Aunt Maddie, I don't want them to know where I am yet."

Seneca turned back to her. "Your father won't rest until he finds you."

"And then he'll be terribly angry with me and prepare for an immediate wedding."

"You don't have to marry if you don't want to."

"You don't understand. It's expected."

"Was what Mayne did to you *expected?*"

Lila swallowed. "In some ways, I guess it is. I provoked him. He . . . he's jealous of you, of what he thinks is . . . is between us."

Seneca's eyes blazed hot. "Stop blaming yourself for provoking him. You didn't deserve—no woman deserves what he subjected you to. And you can't take the blame for his thinking there's something between us when that is impossible. Harrison's weak. He needs to feel strong. And the only way he can feel strong is to hurt someone weaker than he is."

Lila watched the feral strength in Seneca's reactions. Of course, there could be nothing between them. Her reaction to him was because she'd never been around a man like him. Seneca unnerved her. She hadn't been able to move without feeling as if her limbs were hinged with wooden pegs, her breath as uncontrolled as a floating circus balloon. She wondered if anyone else had sensed her distress. Perhaps not. It was clear from his words that

Seneca had not. She could rest her mind about that, couldn't she?

This was an entirely different place for her to be. She'd been thrown into alien circumstances. Here, she couldn't smile outwardly and seethe inwardly, knowing she had no choices but those of her father's. Here, the choices rested with her and her alone. She sensed Seneca would not force her to do anything against her will. Here, she had to think for herself. If she only knew how.

"I should go back, shouldn't I?" She smoothed the blanket under her hands, studied its dark gray stripes over deep red.

"Should you?"

"Don't you want me to go back?"

"It's not my decision."

"But it's your home."

"You are welcome to rest here."

"I should go back."

Seneca waited, then nodded as if to say he knew her decision had been made.

"Shouldn't I?"

"Only you know what you want to do."

"I don't know what I want to do," Lila admitted and sniffed back a sob. "I never know what I want to do. Only what I should do. How will I know?"

Seneca looked at her for a long time. "You will learn," he said at last.

Seven

Garrett Stockdale stepped into the clearing in front of the dining tent where Rosamund Mayne and the Brighams, the Madisons, Evalina, and Madeline sat on canvas folding chairs sipping late afternoon cocktails. He walked past them without speaking.

"I say, this is rather awkward," Harriett Brigham complained, attempting to get her glass under a fly-netting helmet without letting a resourceful blackfly under with it. "If I hadn't spent so much time in that tent already, I'd retreat to it immediately and try to enjoy this fine sherry."

"I think it's a game," Evalina said. She giggled and managed a swift sip. "At times I'm almost faster than they are."

Madeline turned slowly to look at her. "I find if one remains calm they don't seem to bother."

"That's because you repel them with that disgusting lavender toilet water you use," Garrett said unkindly over his shoulder. "Where is Lila, Madeline?"

"She and Harrison stepped out for a walk some time ago," Rosamund Mayne answered.

"You know how young lovers are," Stewart concurred.

"Yes," Stockdale replied thoughtfully. "I suppose as a father I should be worried about that. But since it's Harrison, I know she'll be safe."

Madeline shifted uncomfortably in her chair. Ever since Lila had confided in her about the encounter with Harrison in the parlor after the dinner party announcing their betrothal, Madeline had viewed him with different eyes. Up to that evening she'd thought he was a rather dull young man, boring, harmless, lacking in any spirit whatever. Now she knew how well he covered his true personality, and she believed him to be dangerous to her beloved niece.

"They had some differences to discuss," Rosamund said. "It's best they come to an understanding before the marriage. It's in Lila's best interests, of course."

"Of course." Garrett waved away any further discussion. "Roll out those survey maps again, Clyde."

Brigham retreated to a tent while Garrett, refusing to wear a fly-netting helmet, took a glass of whiskey from the completely covered Martin, who even wore protective gloves. Brigham returned and spread out the maps on a long table constructed of logs sawn flat and planed smooth on one side. The men gathered around and slipped into their debate over the placement of railroad tracks.

"As I see it," Garrett said, the best route is around Blue Mountain Lake, then north to the Saranacs. As you can see, Prospect House is doing a land-office business. Even the other houses that pass for hotels are full. Just think what trains coming directly into the village could do for these mountains."

"I've heard there would be strong opposition to that route," Joseph Madison said. "Something to do with Indians, I gather."

"What Indians? They've all gone up into Canada."

"Yes, but they trap and fish on that land."

"Madison, the grant from George the Third over a hundred years ago settled that question. There are numerous tracts that can be bought from the state at attractive prices. I've a place picked out for my hotel and plan to start building by the end of next month."

"That was fast," Stewart Mayne said.

"Yes. Yes, it was, wasn't it?" Garrett smiled.

Madeline watched the exchange and saw the tense silence among the women. Rosamund was paying strict attention to the conversation, but the others were clearly occupied with the battle against the blackflies. Madeline guided them toward the dining tent, speaking of how fragrant the wood fire was at the cook tent and how the staff must be preparing a delicious feast for them.

"I'd rather go back to Prospect House," Evalina said, pouting. "Oh, it was so lovely. And I never got to participate in the bowling."

"Just as well," her mother said, "since it does not appear to be a ladylike diversion."

"But so many of the girls were doing it, and no one seemed to mind."

Iris Madison sniffed several short breaths. "Perhaps those girls had not embarrassed their parents on the night of the masquerade ball by dancing shamelessly with that disgusting mountain hermit with the hairy face."

"Oh, Mother, really." Evalina dropped down onto a long bench by the dining table. "Monsieur LaDoque was quite the gentleman. If it hadn't been for his rescuing us at the train station, we might still be lumbering over that awful road."

"Monsieur is it, now? From where I sat in the ballroom *Monsieur* LaDoque was hardly a gentleman, nor were you behaving like the well-bred Madison you are. You let him pick you up and swing you around the room like some common guttersnipe. Truly, Evalina, I can't imagine how you could possibly behave like that."

"No, Mother, I'm certain you could not. It was so delicious! And Lila being crowned queen with Mr. Pierce as her king! Oh, it was so delicious!"

"Don't use Lila as your example of behavior for a woman of breeding," Rosamund Mayne said snippily. "Without Harrison at her side, she should have refused to accept the pronouncement. Further, she should have ignored that savage instead of making a spectacle of herself waltzing with him—"

Madeline interrupted, unable to take another minute of grumbling and slander against her niece. "Rosamund, I hardly think Mr. Pierce can be considered a savage. I thought him to be a well-mannered, educated young man. And as you so rightly pointed out, he did *waltz* with Cat. Where do you suppose he learned to do that? I'll wager not around a council fire."

"Oh, you would defend him," Rosamund came back icily. "As Garrett says, you are a simple-minded romantic twit without the sense you were born with."

"Mrs. Mayne—that's so cruel!" Evalina jumped up and went directly to Madeline's side. "She doesn't mean it, Mrs. Allgood."

"Thank you, my dear, but to the contrary, I think she does mean it. Aside from the reference to my being a twit, I will take the rest of her comment as a compliment. I am a romantic, and I do not fill my head with the complicated machinations of important parties." Madeline raised her chin slightly.

Evalina giggled. "Of course." She flounced back to the bench.

Rosamund Mayne rose, her soft chin raised inside the fly netting as high above her collar as possible. "I'm going to my tent for a rest before dinner. I can't imagine what your dear niece is doing to detain Harrison," she said with sarcasm.

"I rather think it's quite the opposite where your dear son is concerned," Madeline rejoined sweetly.

Afternoon was just giving way to dusk when Harrison Mayne dragged himself into camp. He slipped into his family's tent, took a big belt of whiskey, and was stretching out on his mattress when his mother lifted the canvas flap and strode in carrying an unlit lantern.

"I saw you coming out of the forest," Rosamund said in a gravelly voice as she set the lantern down on a low wood stool. She went to where he lay and stood over him. "What have you been doing, away this long? I warn you. You keep your nose clean."

"Or you'll do what?" Harrison snapped. He rolled over and glared up at his mother through swollen eyes.

Rosamund gasped and dropped to her knees. "Oh, dear God, what happened, son?" She ran her hand over his forehead and pushed his hair up out of his eyes.

Harrison jerked and pushed her hand away. Blood streaked his wrist and forearm and stained his shirtsleeves. He felt the stinging scratches on his face where Lila's fingernails had raked him. Damn the bitch. The scratches might leave scars. She'd pay for what she did to him.

"It's nothing," he muttered.

"You're covered with blood. How did this happen?" Rosamund was fairly screeching.

"Keep your voice down. It's not important. Leave me alone, Mother."

Harrison threw his arm up over his forehead and turned toward the wall of the tent, wishing only to get his thoughts together. He needed a good explanation for what happened. Garrett Stockdale would throw him out once and for all if he didn't make this good. He could do it, if he could just have time alone to think.

"What do you mean it's not important?" Rosamund grabbed her son's arm and pulled it away. "How could you say such a thing. You're cut. You're bleeding. Have you been in a fight? What brute did this to you?"

Harrison wrenched his arm from her grip. She was always watching him, every minute. Sometimes he couldn't stand the way she suffocated him. She demanded too much of him, demanded he make something of himself, make a lot of money. The old man had become too weak to do it for her. Stewart had managed to hang on to part of his investment in that Union Pacific fiasco, but he was being frugal to the point of penury. They barely had good wine anymore, unless they were invited to Garrett Stockdale's dinners. Harrison hoped to hell he hadn't just ruined everything for himself. To hell with his mother and father. He had to save his own ass.

He felt Rosamund get up, heard her fussing with a basin and some water. Letting out a labored breath, she knelt down again next to his mattress. He heard her dip a cloth in the water and wring it out.

"Now tell me what happened. If it doesn't behoove you, we'll just come up with another explanation. Can't have Garrett suspecting you of anything untoward." She took his arm away and started to bathe his face. Lord, you look as if you've been attacked by a savage!"

Harrison stared up at her through swollen eyes. *Savage.* Of course, that was it! It was almost too easy. Harrison could barely keep his excitement in check. Lila would tell her father what had happened. That was for certain. But Harrison intended for her words to have the opposite effect on Garrett Stockdale. He could do it, he knew it!

Even the fact that she'd have a head wound from the rock he'd thrown at her when she'd run away from him could be explained if he worded it properly. It could have been an accident. Or . . . his mind whirled. He could make this story good, very good.

Who in hell did that holier-than-anybody bitch think she was, anyway? What made her think she was so smart? She acted so refined and innocent, but she sure as hell fought him off. He'd enjoyed that—her kicking and struggling against him had only made him itch all the more. If he hadn't fallen after she hit him with a rock, he'd have taught her a lesson she'd never forget. Once they were married, and he was safely ensconced in a mansion of his own, he'd make sure she put up a good fight every night. And he'd be raking in the Stockdale money in the bargain.

"Give me a drink," Harrison demanded.

Rosamund hurried about, getting a glass of whiskey for him. He drained the glass. He swallowed hard, then began his tale in the most anguished voice he could manage.

When Harrison was finished, Rosamund was outraged, as he knew she would be. She settled him in and ran to fetch Garrett so he could hear the story from Harrison's own lips.

"Don't worry about Lila," Stewart Mayne was saying when Madeline walked out of the dining tent. He and Garrett sat across from one another at a square table comparing drawings of track paths. "Harrison is with her. They've most likely simply strolled off in a world of their own. You know how impetuous young lovers can be. They'll come into camp at any moment, embarrassed because they got lost."

Madeline took a chair not far from them and settled

back, sipping her sherry, halfheartedly listening to their conversation. How she loved the crisp scent of the mountain air as the afternoon wore on toward twilight.

"Mayne, you're a fool!" Garrett boomed. "It's almost dark. Harrison hasn't the sense he was born with. He knows nothing about tracking through mountains. If they're lost, it's because of him. Lila knows better than to disobey my orders to stay close to camp. But your son thinks he knows everything better than anyone else. I warn you, Lila had best return to camp with every hair on her head unharmed."

Stewart set down his pencil and compass and lifted tired eyes to Garrett. "I thought you liked Harrison. You've certainly given him every opportunity to come into the business, with your guidance, of course. What was that all about at the engagement dinner, saying you think of him as a son? Another ploy of yours to get what you want?"

"He's got an arrogance I admire." Garrett ran a hand around his jowly chin. "Reminds me of myself at that age. Except I was focused—knew what I wanted and how to get it. He'd be a dilettante if it weren't for my direction. God knows you don't do anything to teach him about business."

"He may be my son," Stewart said wearily, leaning back in his chair, "but I don't admire him whatsoever. And I wouldn't call what you do for him 'direction.' It's manipulation, and you know it. You've got him so dazzled with what money can bring him, he thinks only of that. And you make it too easy for him to believe he should come by it any way he can. If Lila wasn't a joy to be around, I would send him packing myself. But to think of her bringing sweetness and serenity to our family, and grandchildren, gives me hope for the future—for a chance to start over and undo the mistakes I've made with Harrison."

"You've nothing to act so uppity about, Stewart. Your biggest mistake was marrying Rosamund. Everybody knows she leads you and him around by the nose. She's a shrew, but a rich one. Harrison's as much like you as he is me. You wanted into fast money years ago, and you married her. Harrison's doing the same by marrying my daughter. We both know it."

"And what does that make you, Garrett?" Stewart spat. "Selling your own daughter is what it sounds like to me. And for what?"

"You know for what, don't you?" Garrett spun around. "Where the hell are they? Martin! Martin!" His shouts echoed around the forest and brought Martin out of the cook tent. "Round up some men. Go out and search for my daughter and young Mayne. There's money in it if they're brought back safely tonight."

Madeline pushed out of her chair and scuffled over to Garrett. "What did you say? Is Cat lost?" She clutched Garrett's sleeve.

Garrett brushed her off as if she were nothing more than another annoying fly. "Don't get the vapors yet. She and Mayne haven't returned from their walk. I'm a bit concerned is all."

"They didn't go for a walk together." Madeline's voice escalated. "Cat wouldn't do that. She—"

"Will you hush up, woman? I know she's gone walking alone at least once. And you know it, too. I'll have a talk with her about that later. I guarantee she won't go out for a walk alone again when I'm through with her."

"Garrett, please, you must try a gentler hand with Cat. I fear she'll leave us if you don't—"

"Haven't I told you repeatedly that you are to call her

by her given name? I never could stand it that you called my wife, Catherine, by that disgusting nickname."

"It was . . . *is* a fitting name for both."

Rosamund Mayne rushed toward them from the direction of her tent. "Garrett! You must come with me right this minute and hear what Harrison has to say!"

Garrett rose quickly. "Harrison? Where is he? Is my daughter with him?"

"She is not. It's fortunate Harrison made it back here alive." Rosamund turned to go back to her tent, Garrett and Stewart close behind her.

"Oh, dear," Madeline wailed.

"Shut up, Maddie," Garrett admonished over his shoulder.

Madeline followed them to the Mayne tent and, from a discreet distance behind, listened to the outrageous story Harrison told.

"I tried to protect her," Harrison said weakly with a hint of a sob in his voice. "But he was like a madman attacking me."

"Who?" Garrett boomed.

"I'm sorry, Mr. Stockdale, sir," Harrison said weakly, "but I guess I should tell you everything. I wanted to spare you, but I believe it is in your—and Lila's—best interests that you know. I hope she'll forgive me for saying it."

"Tell me what! Stop babbling and get to the point. What happened when you and Lila went out for your walk?"

"We didn't go out for a walk together." Harrison moved and made a show of wincing in pain and becoming breathless for a moment.

Madeline waited. At least he was telling the truth so far. They hadn't gone out for a walk together.

Rosamund rushed to his side and bathed his scratched

face with a cool cloth, cradling him in her arms. Seeing him clinging to his mother, it was almost impossible for Madeline to believe Harrison had the strength to mistreat anyone. He seemed so much the weakling. But it was Lila who'd told her about his behavior the evening of their betrothal dinner, so there could be no mistake.

"I saw Lila go out walking alone," Harrison continued, "and I feared for her safety. I felt, as her fiancé, I should go into the woods and find her, protect her. I should have known she'd go looking for *him*."

"Who?" Garrett stood over him, fists clenched.

Harrison closed his eyes. "Seneca Pierce," he whispered.

Madeline's pulse quickened with fear. She knew her beloved niece had an adventurous streak in her which hadn't been exercised enough, but she wouldn't irresponsibly go into the forest alone looking for someone when she hadn't the remotest idea where he lived. Seneca Pierce had merely said he lived in the Adirondacks. The mountains were vast and wide. How wildly interesting to think they all might now be in the midst of his domain. But, even if Lila had gone looking for him, *and* if he'd found her, which was the more likely, she couldn't imagine him doing something terrible to her darling Cat. She had sensed some spark between them last winter. It was one of attraction, she'd been certain, and she'd had the notion confirmed at the Prospect House masquerade ball.

"And did she find him?" Garrett demanded.

"You might say they found each other," Harrison responded. In a melodramatic gesture he thrust his face toward the wall.

"What are you getting at, boy?" Garrett shouted. "Did he attack her?"

Harrison snapped his head back and weakly gestured

for Rosamund to bathe his face once more. "I thought that's what happened. They were on the ground. He was over her. I threw myself on him, fought him, dragged him off her."

"My God, man, were you in time?"

Madeline thought Harrison was going to cry, and she wished she could believe it. She was fearful of his answer.

"No. I was too late."

Madeline gasped and cried out. "You don't mean my baby is . . . is dead?" The last word was barely a whisper.

"No. But let me just say as delicately as I can that she is not the . . . innocent girl she was before she went after Pierce. The last I saw of her, he was dragging her by the hand into the forest." In a sharp theatrical gesture, Harrison clamped both hands over his eyes.

"Why didn't you shoot him, for God's sake?" Garrett shouted.

"I didn't have a gun with me. I couldn't stop him. And you know how crafty they are."

"You let him take her, you simpering fool," Garrett growled. "What's the matter with you?"

"Wait a minute—just who do you think you're talking to?" Rosamund spat. "There's no need to be so crude, Garrett, whatever you think Harrison may have—"

"Shut up, Rosamund. Your son stood by and watched my daughter being kidnapped. Now if you don't want to see him murdered in front of your eyes, I suggest you keep it to yourself."

Madeline froze. The blood left her head and a wave of dizziness overtook her. "Garrett, what's happened?" She clutched his shirtsleeve. "You can't truly mean Lila's been kidnapped!"

Garrett brushed her hand away. "Harrison says that bastard Pierce took her. And I know why. He thinks he can make me pay."

"Pay what? Do you mean ransom money?" Madeline's energy came back. If Seneca Pierce truly had Lila, she believed her niece had nothing to fear. But then why was Garrett so out of control?

"I'll kill him!" Garrett's face was red with rage and his fists clenched over and over. He stomped toward the tent flap.

"With all due respect, sir," Harrison said, struggling to sit up, "not that I wish to defend that savage, but it wasn't all Pierce's fault."

Garrett spun around. "What do you mean by that?"

"It pains me to tell you this, sir, but—well, your daughter wanted it, wanted him to . . . you know."

Garrett stomped toward the bed. "How dare you say such a thing about my daughter! It's just an excuse for your own weakness. You couldn't save her, so you—"

"No! Mr. Stockdale, I hate to have you know that Lila—well, that she wanted it to happen. She begged me to take her, and when I said I respected her too much to do that before marriage, she shouted at me that she'd get it another way. And . . . she said she wanted it from that savage. And it wouldn't be the first time, she said."

Garrett's face turned so dark red Madeline thought he might have a heart attack. "I swear it, Mayne, if you're lying I'll have your heart cut out. But I know you're not clever enough to fabricate such a disgusting story."

"I believe I know what happened, sir," Harrison said with a voice full of sympathy. "I think Lila was simply testing my love for her. And if she wants to be certain that I pledge my undying love, then I do—for what she's done hasn't changed a thing about my feelings for her. I am cut to the quick, hurt more deeply than she will ever under-

stand, but you know how headstrong she can be, how de-
fiant. I still want to marry her, sir. If she comes back, I
will marry her tonight if you wish. That way, if she be-
comes pregnant with his bastard, no one will ever have to
know what happened. Her reputation, and yours, will remain unsoiled."

Garrett let out a harsh breath through his nostrils. "I'm
going out with the others to find her. Beat Pierce at his
own game. He'll never get a cent from me."

"Garrett," Madeline said quietly, trying to inject a note
of sanity into the insane scene she'd just witnessed. "Mr.
Pierce hardly seems the sort to extort money from you."

"It isn't just money he wants!" Garrett snarled. "Where's
that goddamned wagon? Martin!"

"What do you mean?" Madeline pressed.

"Get away from me, woman!" He stormed toward the
tent opening, Madeline close and clinging to his arm.

Stewart Mayne rushed to Madeline's side and removed her from Garrett's presence. "Best to leave
him be, Maddie."

"But what is he talking about, Mr. Pierce wanting to
make him pay? Pay for what?"

"It's a long story. Right now we have to see to getting
Lila back." Stewart said to Harrison, "You best go with
them, son. You know where she was when she was taken."

"Gladly," Harrison muttered. "And if I find Pierce, you
can bet I'll see him dead before I'm through." He threw
the blanket off and groaned getting up.

"You shouldn't, you're hurt," Rosamund said, restraining him.

"Leave me alone, Mother," he said loudly enough for
everyone within twenty yards of the camp to hear. "If
Lila's hurt, I have to be with her. And I don't want Mr.
Stockdale to be alone in this. He's understandably upset.

He needs me." Harrison grabbed a coat with a grand sweep of his hand and followed Garrett out of the tent.

As he pushed by her, Madeline bit her knuckles to keep from shouting that Harrison was telling filthy lies about the precious girl who had been like a daughter to her. Lila would never do anything so base as what young Mayne was saying. There was another explanation for whatever was happening, and she had to find out what that was. She had to find Cat before it was too late. Perhaps she was hurt, lying someplace out in the forest. Perhaps it was Harrison who had hurt her. Madeline didn't trust him. Something about the way he shifted his eyes, the way he practically worshiped the carpet beneath Garrett's feet disgusted her. If Cat were injured badly, or worse, Maddie knew she'd feel it in her heart.

But she couldn't take any chances. She had to find Cat and find her soon, before Garrett got to her. And definitely before Harrison did.

Lila awoke as if from a drugged sleep. For a moment she couldn't determine where she was. She knew she was in a bed, a softer bed than she'd remembered from camp. As her eyes adjusted to the thin illumination from the shaft of moonlight slanting through a square window, she slowly felt her senses adjusting to her surroundings.

The aroma of damp balsam filled the air, a scent she was beginning to love. Where her hands rested upon her abdomen, she felt the steady rhythm of her own breathing, then realized she was touching naked skin. Her own sore naked skin. She suddenly felt very much alone as the memory of her ordeal with Harrison started to creep back into her sharpening consciousness.

And then she heard a disturbing sound quite near to

her, that of deep breathing. She turned her head to align her ear with the direction the sound was coming from. A soft breath touched her cheek. She jumped.

Something stirred next to her in the bed. Lila went rigid. Could it be . . . *him?* Fear spread over her, and she stopped breathing. Maybe it was a wild animal. What should she do? She should get away, that's what she should do. She inched to the side of the pine bough bed, her movement ever so slight, ever so minimal, ever so quiet. She moved a foot out from under the blanket and touched a wood floor. Then her leg. Next her hip, her arm, her shoulder. Where was she? The tent? Where was Aunt Maddie? And then swiftly she was out from under the blanket and up on her feet.

"Where are you going?" a sleepy voice asked.

Lila jumped and spun around, standing squarely in the shaft of moonlight. "What? Who's there?" Her heart pounded in her ears, and she felt light-headed.

"I guess they've named you right. You jumped like a cat out of a cold pond."

"S-Seneca?" Lila was only mildly soothed at hearing his voice. She was beginning to remember everything, and her head pounded with the painful memory.

"Yes, Seneca. Are you thinking of swimming across the lake and going back to your father's camp?" His voice was husky with sleep.

"No, of course not," she answered immediately.

"Well, I don't recommend you go out for a bath right now. It's cold, and you never know what might be prowling the woods this time of night."

She shivered audibly. "What? I have no intention of taking a bath."

"Oh. I thought you might."

"Why?"

"You're out of bed, and you're naked as a newborn."

"What! Oh, my God!" Lila dove back for the bed, realizing a fraction of a second too late that Seneca was in it. She landed on her wounded shoulder, and the pain shot up the back of her neck and down her spine. She groaned.

"Did you hurt yourself?" Seneca's voice held genuine concern.

Lila let out an affirmative on a shaky breath through her nostrils.

"I better check it to see if the wound reopened." He rose and lit a lantern.

Lila clamped her eyes shut. She told herself over and over in her mind that she didn't want to see him, see any man, but especially Seneca Pierce without his clothes. But her curiosity got the better of her and she lifted one eyelid. He was naked from the waist up, and his bronze skin glistened in the lantern glow. From the waist down he wore a pair of cotton long drawers. His feet were bare. She saw him pick up a clean cloth and, carrying the lantern, return to the bed. She pulled the blanket up over her breasts and tucked it tightly under her arms.

"Can you turn on your side so I can look at your wound?" he asked gently.

She bit her bottom lip and shook her head slowly.

"Don't worry. I'll do my best not to hurt you."

"I . . . know," she said, feeling more apprehensive than when she'd first awakened in Seneca's presence—which now seemed like hours ago—yet somehow she believed his words.

A small smile of recognition spread over his face. "I've already seen you without your clothes, so I won't be shocked."

"*You* won't be shocked!"

"Not at all. So don't worry about me."

Lila sensed his attempt at a bit of humor, but it didn't lessen the tension hanging heavily in the air between them. "I wasn't worrying about you."

"Then that can only mean you're worried about yourself. No need to be."

"No need?" Lila thought that was a strange comment.

"None. I must take care of your wound, or you may become infected. I can't let that happen." He set the lantern down on the floor near the bed. "Just think of me as a doctor. Turn on your side so I can see."

"You're not a doctor."

"I'm the closest thing you've got to one. Will a medicine man do?"

He smiled and took hold of the blanket. Lila held it tightly to her. She searched Seneca's face and, seeing no threat in his eyes, she turned slightly. He pulled the blanket away just enough to uncover the wound, and she felt a shaft of cold air slither down her spine. Whether it was from the air in the cabin or the thrill whirling crazily inside her, she didn't know, and she didn't want to wonder about it. She held perfectly still.

He knelt on the blanket, and she felt the pine boughs that fashioned the bed depress behind her buttocks. He unwrapped and lifted the bandage he'd applied earlier. She felt her skin pull up slightly with it. His fingers felt gently around the wound and warmed her skin, effecting another wave of sensation. Then he reached over and raised the lantern. There was a long pause, and Lila knew he was inspecting her wound closely. She wondered if he let his eyes travel to any other parts of her exposed body as she had allowed hers to do over his.

She was tired of holding herself so still, and was just about to move enough to pull the blanket up over her back, when he leaned over and set the lantern on the floor. He turned again to her and replaced the bandage. His hands were more gentle than the kindly old doctor in New York who'd once dressed a nasty scrape she'd sustained when she'd fallen down the front staircase.

"What does it look like? Is it all right?" she asked against the blankets.

"The wound is fine," Seneca said at last. "But I'm certain it's starting to throb again. I have something that will help."

He rose and retrieved a small container from a nearby shelf. When he knelt on the bed again and opened the container, she wrinkled her nose at the strong smell as he rubbed what felt like an ointment around her wound. Then he opened another container, and she smelled something that resembled strong candy. He scooped from it and began to massage her back, shoulders, and up the back of her neck. The substance was at first cold, and she shivered. But in only a few seconds the area where his hands had been massaging her felt warm, deeply warm. She relaxed. The scent of the ointment had a clearing effect on her head as she breathed it in.

"What are you using on me?" she asked dreamily. "It reminds me of peppermint tea."

"It's better than peppermint. It's called wintergreen."

"Wintergreen. A picturesque name. Where do you get it?"

"Some take it from a heath plant. I find that mashing the tender young shoots of the yellow birch produces a similar oil." Seneca closed the containers, then lifted the blanket and gently settled it over Cat's shoulder.

"Can it be made into tea and would it have the same results on an upset stomach as peppermint tea?"

"Perhaps. I haven't made tea with it, but I chew it sometimes. You're asking a lot of questions. Don't worry, I won't kill you with these particular herbs and ointments."

She sighed. "I'm not worried about that. I think I should have a notion of what you're doing to me, shouldn't I?"

"Do you ever ask your city doctor what he's doing to you?"

Lila let out a long sigh. "Doctor Merriweather patronizes me whenever I ask him anything. He says I shouldn't worry my 'pretty little head about it' for he knows what's best for me. How should he know that? He's not me. I should know what's best for me, shouldn't I?"

"I don't know, should you?"

"Well, of course I should. Father won't let me ask any questions. He says I shouldn't bother the doctor. Who else am I going to bother?"

"You're doing a pretty good job of bothering me right now."

Lila went still for a moment. "Am I bothering you by asking questions about what witchcraft you might be using on me?"

Seneca laughed. "Witchcraft? Is that what you think? I can see your conception of Indians is the same as your society friends."

"It is not!" Lila pushed her arms against the pine boughs, intending to sit up. They collapsed under her. "Ouch. That hurts."

"I don't doubt it. The wound is deep. Fortunately it's clean. We Indians are known for our perfect aim."

"So I've heard," she snapped. Then she softened. "I meant it when I said I don't hold the same conception as my father's friends do about . . . about you."

"Me in particular? Or Indians in general?"

"Both."

Seneca waited a long moment as if turning her response over in his thoughts. "You should go back to sleep now."

Lila rolled over onto her back and pulled the blanket up under her chin. "I'm not tired now." She shivered. "Did I sleep long?"

"Just a few hours. You slept very heavily, and you had some bad dreams." Seneca went to the table and returned with a tin cup of steaming liquid and one of his shirts. "Here, drink this. You'll feel better."

"What is it?"

"I think it's best I don't tell you what's in it. It's an old family recipe. I can attest to its healing properties, but I'm certain you'll suspect it's some sort of sorcerer's concoction."

She reached up to take the cup, and their gazes and fingers collided around it. The trembling in her own hand went straight to her chest, where she experienced a ripple like water after a pebble has penetrated it. He slipped his hand away first and stepped back.

"I promise I won't think that. You misunderstood. I'm not like the others, you know."

"No? What makes you say that? You were born into it, you grew up with it. You're Garrett Stockdale's daughter."

"I'm also Catherine Stockdale's daughter."

He dropped the shirt on the floor next to her and tilted his head questioningly. "Do you want to talk about her?"

Lila shook her head, then waited until he turned his back before grabbing the shirt and slipping into it. She drank the foul-tasting brew, wondering at her blind faith in his medicine man ministry. Mustering new courage, she let the liquid roll around on her tongue for a few seconds and tried to ascertain the contents. Her throat contracted as if repelled by the assault of the ingredients: vinegar for certain, a healthy dose of mustard. And perhaps something that mimicked castor oil . . . if it wasn't actually that hateful medicine.

When she was finished, Seneca took the cup and set it back on the table. When he turned around, she was struck by the magnetic presence of him filling the space. The room did not seem to be very large, but with Seneca standing in the shadowy darkness, it seemed much smaller— and she a tiny twig in the bed of pine boughs.

She lifted her head slowly. Would he walk to her now, sweep her into his powerful arms, and kiss her until she was intoxicated with the very masculine being of him? Every nerve in her body was on edge, waiting.

He started toward her. Her pulse quickened, her hands tingled. He stopped halfway between the table and the bed.

"Do you need anything else?" he asked. "A trip to the privy perhaps?"

Lila's nerves burst at once, leaving her completely exhausted. "No," she managed weakly. She was suddenly more than ready to give over to sleep and let the heaviness of her thoughts be borne away on the relief of unconsciousness. She'd been trying to force the earlier scene with Harrison out of her mind, but it hung there, reminding her she'd have to face him and her father sooner or later.

"Well, then," he said quietly and returned to the bed. He hunkered down and extinguished the lantern.

Lila waited for him to move. Her nerve endings were raw with anticipation. It seemed hours before he did, and when he did her senses again sharpened to pinpoints all at once. He slid under the blanket next to her. She pulled as taut into herself as she could.

"What . . . what are you doing?" she said in a tiny voice.

"Going to bed," he answered quickly.

"But, you can't. I mean, it's not proper."

"For whom?" He settled into the blankets.

"Why, for me, of course. My father would be outraged, to say nothing of Aunt Maddie and Evalina if they knew . . ."

"And you said you aren't like the others." He adjusted the blankets. "They aren't here at the moment, and I know I'm gentleman enough not to tell them. For my sake I hope you're lady enough not to say anything about this. Now if you don't mind, I'm very tired. I'd like to get some sleep."

"Why can't you sleep on the floor, way over by the door?"

Seneca sighed. "It's very cold tonight. I can't light a fire because if your father and Mayne are out on the lake looking for you, they might see the smoke. Further, you will be given to a fit of chills later in the night, and you're going to need the heat of my body to warm you."

"But—"

"And I don't think I need to point out that this is my bed, and I have no intention of sleeping on the floor 'way over by the door.' You have nothing to fear from me. Now, please, can we both go to sleep?" He immediately fell to even breathing.

Lila listened to him for a long time before she relaxed enough to let sleep overtake her as well.

Eight

Seneca knew when Lila finally fell asleep. He'd lied to her as much for his own benefit as for hers. She did indeed have something to fear from him. Or was it he who had something to fear from her? It was all he could do to keep from gathering her into his arms and covering her face with kisses.

He'd never been in such a position before. At college and in his travels, it had been easy to succumb to any number of dalliances with women. He didn't even try to restrain himself if the need was great enough. Those women hadn't meant anything to him. He'd felt no connection to them.

Instinctively he knew this woman was different from all the others. And he'd been different inside from the moment he'd first caught her gaze at the Stockdale mansion so many months earlier. She had seemed fearless then, engaging in conversation with him when all those around her—except for her dear old aunt—were openly shocked. He knew it hadn't been simply sport with her. She'd been honest, he could tell. He had also ascertained that she and her fiancé did not engage in that sort of spirited exchange. He'd wondered just what sort of exchange they did engage in.

An inner war had ensued, forcing him to find a new way to fight his external conflict.

When Stewart Mayne had first approached him about assisting in the survey of land tracts through the Adirondacks with an eye to the construction of railroads, Seneca had resisted vehemently. But he'd known instinctively that with or without him the railroads would be built. Those building them smelled power and wealth in trade and purchased transportation to the depth and breadth of the most remote places where tracks could reach and hold. There would be no stopping them. Not unless those who truly cared about the physical attributes of the country fought them—with no guarantee of victory—or joined them and directed the tracks in a less invasive manner than the lack of consideration sired by greed—ideally stopping them from spoiling the areas of greatest concern. He'd chosen to join them on his own terms, terms he did not share with them.

Seneca had vowed in his heart to stop the construction through the Adirondacks and to preserve something of his family's treasured place. He hadn't figured out just how he was going to bring about the halt single-handedly. But he believed he had no choice. It was for his family, their spirits, that he picked up the fight, and he knew it was as much for himself. He needed to feel something to believe in again. The death of his mother and sister, the destruction he'd witnessed of the way of life of the country's natives across the West, the greed in his father's associates, and then his death, were more than Seneca could sustain. Education had taught him much and confused him more. Now he was learning to use it for the welfare of the land and people. And himself.

He hadn't bargained that in his quest to take Stockdale down that he would find his emotions entangled with

Stockdale's daughter. When he'd returned to his mountains and his island, he hadn't bargained for this night with Lila—wounded by his arrow and hiding from her family in his cabin—sleeping in his bed.

She stirred in her sleep as if to underscore his thoughts. The shaft of moonlight had shifted and now lay across their bed like a creamy mantle. He turned his head and looked down at the tousled burnished hair that spread across his blanket. Sleep was elusive for him this night. He altered his position, moving up to lean against the cabin wall, and draped his arm over the top of the bed above her head. She moved in her sleep, instinctively taking the space his movement had provided.

Lila Stockdale in his bed. He could barely grasp the image in his mind. He looked down at her, watching her sleep in the moonlight. She was indeed stretched out next to him, content as a cat on the hearth.

Cat. That's what the lovely lady Madeline had called her. Appropriate, he mused, and tried to imagine what she'd be like were she as independent as a cat. This Cat appeared to be dependent on her family, the way of life to which she'd been accustomed. Yet Seneca sensed in her a somnolent storm of independence, a brewing of longings and desires beyond the world in which she'd been raised. The image of her secretly getting rid of the brussels sprouts from her plate was his first hint. He smiled as he recalled that incident.

And then in his mind the picture of his mother's and sister's burial mound hung sharp and clear. Garrett Stockdale would destroy them if Seneca didn't stop him. What would his action mean to his daughter? If he convinced her of the importance of keeping the mountains forever wild, could she be instrumental in persuading her father and his associates to give up their expansive plans? Could she be convinced herself?

His head had been filled with difficult images since he'd been at the Stockdale dinner party those months earlier. And his dalliances with women had stopped abruptly. Not that he hadn't needed to enjoy the purely physical actions of all humans. Seneca knew he was a child born of the earth, with all the earth's sensuality. The essences of sight, sound, smell, touch, taste—and the total release at the height of complete physical and sexual involvement were as exhilarating to him as sliding down a snow-covered mountain or being swept along a mountain river in rushing white water rapids.

Since he'd encountered Lila Cat Stockdale, Seneca Eli Pierce believed there were no more snow-covered mountains to climb or rushing waters to dive into unless she held the snowflakes in her hand or controlled the dam holding back the river. That was too much power for one person to hold over another, especially for this woman to hold over him.

Seneca closed his eyes and fell asleep to the rhythm of war drums pounding in his heart. His last image was of his own hands beating out the drums' message.

The pounding escalated so loudly that Seneca bolted from his sleep. Lila stirred at his side. Could she have heard his heart that clearly? The pounding grew incessant and was accompanied by voices.

"Seneca, *mon ami!* Are you there?"

Seneca rolled out of bed. *Bear?*

"Cat, darling, are you all right?"

Lila's aunt? Or was he dreaming? Then the familiar furry face appeared in the window. Bear. Jerkily another head popped up, framed in the window, gray hair in full topknot tumbling about her face. Madeline Allgood.

Bear clapped a hand against the log wall. *"Regarde,* Madame Madeline. He's here. Seneca, we must talk." Bear jerked his head toward the door several times indicating to Seneca that he wished to come in and that he was not alone.

"Is my girl with him?"

Seneca heard the worry in the old lady's voice. This was not a dream. He strode to the entrance and threw the long wood bolt, opening the door wide.

"Oh, thank heavens, Mr. Pierce. I do apologize for the intrusion, but—" Maddie spied Lila in the bed at the far end of the room and rushed to her. "Dear Lord, is she hurt?"

"Now, Miss Madeline, don't worry . . ." Seneca started, but his words fell on deaf ears.

Madeline gathered Lila into her arms and murmured endearing words over and over. Lila roused and, recognizing her aunt, let out a low cry and clung to her.

"It is not good, *mon ami,"* Bear said to Seneca. "Madame tells me the mademoiselle's betrothed has been telling tall tales of what you and the mademoiselle have done."

Seneca ran a hand through his rumpled hair. "What do you mean, what we've done?"

Bear leaned toward Seneca's ear and whispered the story so as not to let the ladies hear it. He clucked at the conclusion.

Seneca doubled his fists and spoke through gritted teeth. "That lying . . . they can't possibly believe him, believe that about Lila. I have no doubt of what they'd believe about me."

"Ah, it appears they do. Except for Madame Madeline,

of course. She believes you would not hurt her niece. She trusts you. But don't worry." Bear chuckled a moment. "I did not tell her that her trust was misplaced!"

Seneca clapped his old friend's shoulder. "Believe me, friend, the truth is much more interesting than Mayne's fabrications. I did hurt her, but not the way he's told it." They watched Madeline rocking Lila in her arms while Seneca relayed the story to Bear.

"Ah, *mon ami*." Bear shook his head. "It won't be easy to get you out of this one."

Lila gently extracted herself from Maddie's arms, leaned on her elbow, and peered into her aunt's worried face. "Aunt Maddie, for heaven's sake, how did you get here?"

"I don't really know," Maddie said with a wistful air. "Mr. LaDoque has me completely lost. I know we walked a good distance before we got into the boat."

"Boat? Why did you have to get into a boat?"

"To get here—to the island, of course." Maddie settled onto the bed and held Lila's hand.

"Island? I'm on an island?" Confusion whirled in Lila's mind.

"Oh, dear, is she delirious?" Maddie raised worried eyes toward Seneca.

"No. She just didn't realize we were on an island. She was unconscious when I brought her here," Seneca told her, "and she's been asleep on and off ever since."

"She must be hungry," Bear observed.

"Yes, *you* must be hungry . . . as usual," Seneca returned. He motioned for his friend to come toward the work counter in the kitchen area to talk.

Lila watched them walk away, then grasped her aunt's arm. "Don't worry, Aunt Maddie, I'm fine. Really. I'm just a little confused right now. Mr. Pierce has seen to my welfare." She gazed up into Madeline's anguished eyes. "It was an accident, his shooting me."

"Shooting you? Oh, dear God!" Madeline wailed.

"Shh, shh. With an arrow. He assures me it is a clean wound. It will heal easily."

Madeline leaned over and stroked Lila's cheek. "Ah, my darling Cat, there are too many wounds now for them to heal so easily."

"What do you mean?"

Madeline took in a deep breath and let it out on a troubled sigh. "Harrison has explained your disappearance as a kidnapping by Mr. Pierce. He told your father and his parents that he came upon you and Mr. Pierce in the woods, and that you were in a compromising position, and that Mr. Pierce was—" she closed her eyes, "—and that it was with your permission."

Lila sat bolt upright, outraged at the lies. "Harrison is despicable. It was *he* who . . . Aunt Maddie, he forced himself on me. He was an animal. He—" She broke into a tearless sob. "I managed to get away from him. I ran. He chased me. Seneca was out hunting and mistook me for a deer. He hit me with his arrow. But it was his swift action and expert doctoring that saved me. He brought me here."

Madeline nodded understanding. "And Harrison must have seen him taking you away."

"And he's used it to his advantage."

"Yes."

"Surely Father doesn't believe him?"

"I don't know what Garrett believes in his heart. He is frantic with worry and very angry that you disobeyed him. And I think he's still angry over your association with Mr. Pierce at the ball. It's almost more than anger, but I don't truly understand it. Harrison has consented to go through with the marriage, in spite of what he relates as your wild indiscretion."

"How gracious of him. I will never marry him," Lila bit out. "I will tell Father the truth. Mr. Pierce will verify it."

"I'm not certain your father will believe either one of you," Madeline said. "He does believe in the fusing of the two families with your marriage to Harrison and will not accept a mistake in his conviction. But more, I think he has a hatred for Mr. Pierce."

"I think that, too," Lila said softly. "I wonder why."

"Perhaps you should ask Mr. Pierce."

"Perhaps, but not now." She saw the two men stop talking and part.

"Don't worry, Miss Madeline," Seneca said, walking over to them. "She'll be fine. She'll need some rest and tending to, but I know you'll take very good care of her."

Madeline turned and fixed a chin-elevated glare on Seneca Pierce. He stopped still in the intensity of her gaze. Lila saw her aunt's eyes move up and down the length of him. Unnerved, Seneca looked down, then up quickly. He backed up, his hands flicking over his chest, his long drawers, the front of his drawers.

"Uh, this isn't what it looks like, ma'am. I mean, just because we slept together, doesn't mean . . . I mean, it was cold and we were forced to . . ." He backed into the table. "I apologize for how I'm dressed."

"Not dressed," Bear observed.

"I'll get dressed," Seneca responded quickly.

In the next moment his face registered the realization that his pants and shirt were on the floor next to the bed. Head down, making no eye contact with either of the two women, he hurried over and grabbed up his clothing. Then he disappeared through a rear door accompanied by the loudly laughing Bear.

Lila could not dismiss the gravity of the situation in which she found herself, but for a brief moment she allowed an element of amusement to take over. She watched the supremely strong and imperious Seneca Pierce fluster under the accusing gaze of a ninety-pound old lady whose fierce protective instinct for her niece was aroused. Aunt Maddie watched him retreat before she turned back to Lila.

"That is one beautiful man," she breathed.

"Aunt Maddie!" Lila exclaimed, feigning shock.

"Don't 'Aunt Maddie' me, young lady. I saw how you looked at him. You know it, too."

Lila nodded and looked down at her hand where it lay on his blanket. "Yes, I looked at him. You're right. He is one beautiful man. How I wish he could see me in the same way."

"Do not wish for such things, my darling. Seneca Pierce cannot be a part of your life."

Aunt Maddie spoke the few words that Lila knew meant volumes. She meant that Seneca Pierce could not be a part of the life that Garrett Stockdale had planned for his privileged daughter. She meant that a young woman who had been raised in the kind of home that Lila had could not even think about a wild mountain man such as Seneca Pierce. Even if such a remote possibility as a connection between them were to be entertained, their lives could not mesh together and become one satisfying life for the two. They were worlds apart, and when those two worlds collided, the devastation would be monumental.

"I know. I will not wish for more, Aunt Maddie. But it is too late. Seneca is already part of my life. There must be a way . . . I must find a way to . . ."

A stricken look passed over Aunt Maddie's face. With a sharp intake of breath, she drew Lila into a closer embrace.

She's frightened, Lila thought. *But I am terrified.*

The cabin door opened and Seneca returned fully clothed in fringed deerskin leggings with a shirt of the same fashion opened wide at the neck. If anything were possible, Lila mused through heavy lids and the veil of her eyelashes, Seneca Pierce was even more desirable dressed in soft deerskin than he was half naked. The pliable fabric clung to every muscle along his thighs and calves. His shirt stretched over his arm and shoulder muscles when he moved, and his bronze skin at the chest opening gleamed in the lantern light. His hair was left free to graze his shoulders.

Yes, Lila thought, *he is one beautiful man.* It was too late now for her to stop thinking, stop wishing. Definitely too late.

Bear, hot on Seneca's heels, scuffed through the door. He shrugged out of a canvas coat, revealing a green flannel shirt with the buttons straining over his ample girth. The two men went around the cabin lighting more lanterns, then Seneca rekindled the fire in the fireplace. In a matter of minutes the cabin was light and warm.

For the first time since Seneca had brought her there, Lila was awake enough to take a good look around his living quarters. The place was definitely a cabin, but solid, airy, and full of an array of eclectic artifacts that determined the resident was the enigma Lila felt him to be.

The walls were of logs so well fitted she could see no daylight between them. Windows were cut on three sides and had wooden doors fitted with strap hinges to close them against severe weather. They were open now with fly netting tacked over them. The main room was furnished with a long pine table and two benches. A copper-shaded lantern was suspended over it by a rope attached to the ceiling. A stone fireplace occupied a corner. There were two chairs made from what appeared to be small cedar logs, and there was a small table with another lantern.

On the walls were stretched skins of a fox and some kind of large cat, and antlers, one rack spiky and the other more rounded and flat but much bigger.

"Oh, my," Maddie said, viewing the cabin with an awestruck look in her eyes.

"Indeed," Lila added.

Her gaze settled on a huge brown bear hide covering the floor in front of the fireplace, which was bordered on both ends by bear paws the size of cooking pots. The enormous bear head exposed vicious teeth, and its large black eyes looked out over the cabin with a benign expression. Around the plank floor lay large squares of dark red woolenlike thick fabric with wide black stripes at each end.

The fireplace was constructed of field stones, with the keystone fashioned in an irregular dark red oval that sparkled lightly. The mantel above was forged of a highly polished dark red log and appeared to be half a tree planed on the top side, with the curved underside resting on two bark-stripped cedar logs protruding from the stone. Lila thought it a work of art.

To one side of the fireplace, a pair of snowshoes hung next to two rifles suspended on wooden pegs. Below the front square window, Lila was surprised to see a three-shelf bookcase built along the length of the wall. It was filled with books. But what surprised Lila the most was that more books seemed to be everywhere there was shelf space or a niche. She wished she could wander around the room and read the titles. *How extraordinary!* The mountain man had brought books to a log cabin in the woods.

Her surprise was rapidly replaced with easy acceptance. Seneca Pierce was an educated man, after all. Atop the bookcase were more books piled on their sides, several fat tallow candles in cedar log holders, and a wooden flute, some arrows, and what appeared to be a water canteen made from an animal's hide.

"I make stew," Bear announced. He left the cabin, slamming the heavy door behind him.

"Oh, dear, Mr. LaDoque isn't going to kill something, is he?" Maddie asked in a tremulous voice.

"No, it's already dead," Seneca said with a warm laugh. "He's just going to the icehouse for some bear meat he's prepared."

"Bear?" Lila's gaze shifted for a swift moment to the rug in front of the fireplace.

Seneca caught her look. "Don't worry, the meat never was under that particular hide. Nor under Bear's either!"

Bear pushed through the door, his arms laden with burlap-wrapped bundles, a covered tin pail, and a dark green corked bottle tucked under his arm. He set everything on the dining table and went back outside. Seconds later he returned with a basket brimming with potatoes and onions.

Maddie rose and looked down at Lila. She pushed a spare blanket behind her niece's back to make her more comfortable. "I know I should insist that these gentlemen return us to our own camp," she whispered, her eyes twinkling, "but I have a longing for bear meat stew."

"You've never had bear meat stew, Aunt Maddie, so how is it you feel this longing?" Lila whispered back.

"My darling Cat, one must always try new things," Maddie returned.

"You have to think of yourself," Lila warned. "If you go back to camp now, perhaps you won't be missed."

"Do you want to leave now?"

Lila sank back against the blanket. "I . . . I don't think I can travel just yet." In her heart she knew she didn't want to travel at all, at least not back to camp and to Harrison and her father.

"Then I'll wait until you can."

"Oh, Aunt Maddie, I don't want to put you in a more difficult situation than the one you're in. You should go back now. You can say you searched but couldn't find me."

Aunt Maddie patted Lila's hand. "And when we go back together we can say the same thing, only that I found you returning to camp on your own. Rest now. And we'll worry about our return later. All right?" She gave Lila a hopeful smile.

"All right. I guess so."

"Wonderful!" A happy smile spread over Madeline's face as she kissed the top of Lila's hair. She turned around with a springier step than Lila had noticed in her aunt in years and walked toward Bear. "Perhaps I can help you, Mr. LaDoque. I've never cooked bear stew before, but I'm willing to learn. And just look at these lovely vegetables! Wherever did you get them?"

"*Merci,* Madame Madeline. Such a lovely name for a lovely lady. Our root cellar is about empty now, but later in the season there will be more. Perhaps you might like to join me in a bit to sip while we create, no?" He took down two clear glasses from a shelf next to the cookstove.

"Oh, mercy, I don't really think I should." Maddie grew flustered, but she watched with fascination as Bear opened the tin pail and then drew the cork from the dark green bottle with his teeth.

"Ah, lady, nothing to fear." Bear nodded his head with firm conviction. "I can assure you all is well. Here we have a beer brewed by my own hand." He gestured to the pail. Maddie peered inside, sniffed, and grimaced. "And here we have a robust wine, also brewed by my own hand of the finest fruits and berries." He held the bottle under Maddie's nose for her to test.

Maddie sniffed the wine, then looked up with an expression of skepticism. "Berries? What kind of berries and fruit?"

"Mon Dieu, madame!" Bear set down the bottle and clutched his chest in the region of his heart. "I am shocked to see the disbelief in your eyes. I cannot tell you my secret recipe. But I can tell you that this wine is pure and possesses a lovely bouquet. Here. Taste for yourself." He poured a small amount into a glass and handed it to her.

Maddie sipped gingerly. Then her face broke into a wide smile. "Delicious! Mr. LaDoque, you are right."

"Please, madame, have a *soupçon* more." He poured the glass half full, and Maddie took a longer sip.

Lila was about to protest the amount, fearing for the welfare of her petite aunt, but Maddie answered before she could speak.

"Merci, monsieur. Now then, give me an apron and point me toward the flour, and I'll whip up biscuits you've only dreamed about. My own secret recipe." She rubbed her hands together and went about searching the shelves.

"Oh, no apron, madame," Bear told her. "But here is a clean flour sack to cover you." With his hunting knife he sliced a hole in the closed end and slipped it over Maddie's head. Then the two set to work cooking side by side.

Seneca watched them for a moment before going to

Lila. "Now there's a surprising pair. Who would have thought?"

"I know." She smiled lovingly at her aunt, then raised her gaze to his face. "You are surprising, too."

"Me?" He looked amused. "How am I surprising?"

"You are educated, you've been across this country and back, you've taught class at a university. You could live in a mansion as big as Father's. Yet you live here, in a cabin on an island." She tilted her head questioningly.

He stood at the end of the bed, one knee cocked, his hands lifting the hem of his shirt, his thumbs hooked in the waist of his breeches. "This isn't exactly a damp cave, you know."

"Oh, I know. I wasn't suggesting that. I just find it surprising that you choose to live here when you could live in the city or at least in a house on the mainland."

"Actually, if you knew me well, you'd know it's not surprising at all. This cabin is where I'm the most comfortable. This is where my life is, here in the mountains and lakes, on this island, in this cabin."

"But you seemed so comfortable in our home in New York. You seemed certain of yourself, not at all out of place." Lila shook her head in wonder.

"I was. I didn't mind being there, but I was very glad to get home."

Didn't mind. Lila wished he could have termed his evening in her home as something more important other than that he simply didn't mind being there. But that was another wish she should forget, and she knew it. She looked above and beyond him then, lest her eyes give away her thoughts.

She narrowed her gaze. In the low light she thought she could see a second floor at the end of the room, a very high ceiling, a railing.

"Is that a second floor I see up there?"

Seneca turned slowly back then toward her again. "Yes, it's a loft."

"A loft? I vaguely remember you telling me this was the only bed in the cabin so we had to . . . you had to sleep here."

"Well, you have to admit, it was pretty cold in here. Besides, you were in shock. I couldn't leave you alone. You might have wandered off. You'd have been in danger. It was a small lie to protect you." Seneca shrugged.

"Protect—!" Lila glared at him and folded her arms over her chest.

Bear stepped toward them quickly, holding out a tin cup. "A brew, *mon ami,* while it's cold."

"Thank you, my friend." Seneca took the cup. "Do you mean the brew or the atmosphere?"

Bear glanced at Lila and then at Seneca. *"Oui,* well, a taste of wine might warm the atmosphere." He shifted his eyes to Lila. "Will you have some, mademoiselle? Good for the blood, help you get well faster."

Lila breathed hard out of her nostrils, holding her gaze on Seneca. "Another novel way to keep away the cold." She lifted her head and smiled at Bear. "Yes, Mr. LaDoque, I'll have a taste of your wine. It seems to be affecting my aunt quite favorably."

"Ha! That it is!" Bear started back toward the dining table where Maddie, flour on her face, over her hands and up her arms to the rolled sleeves of her dress, was rolling out biscuit dough with a heavy green bottle and singing merrily to herself. Close to her floured board sat a half-empty glass of wine.

Bear brought a glass to Lila and she sipped the contents. He was right. The wine was soft and fruity, with a very pleasant taste.

"Do you have a vineyard?" she asked Bear.

"No, no, mademoiselle." He leaned over and whispered, making it obvious he did not want Aunt Maddie to hear. "Elderberries. Blueberries. Just a whisper of catnip."

Lila tilted her head. "Catnip?"

"Oui. To put the spark in a mademoiselle's eyes." Bear returned to his kitchen duties.

Lila peered around her glass at Seneca, who seemed to be lost in thought. "Did you build this cabin?" she asked.

"Yes," he answered, coming out of his reverie.

"What I can see in the light is quite lovely." She knew *lovely* was a feminine word for such a masculine dwelling, but she couldn't think of a better one at the moment. Her mind was still muddled. But it was true. The cabin was lovely, in a thoroughly wild yet civilized sort of fashion.

"Thank you," he said without scoffing at her choice of words. "It's shelter."

Lila sensed that shelter meant more to him than simply protection from the elements. "What's on the ceiling that makes it so bright?"

Seneca looked overhead. "That's paper birch bark applied and anchored with cedar logs."

Lila breathed an "Ooh." Then, "What makes that red stone in the fireplace sparkle so?"

Seneca grinned. "You do ask a lot of questions, don't you? It's garnet."

"Garnet? As in jewelry?"

Seneca nodded. "And as in sandpaper. It's all over these mountains. It was taken from a local mine in exactly the shape you see."

"It's lovely." That word again. Where was all her schooling when she needed it? There must be dozens of adjectives she could use to describe his cabin. "And the mantel? It's quite love—uh . . . smooth."

"That's red spruce. Bear spent many hours rubbing the logs with linseed oil and turpentine. They were actually once the size of giant redwoods, but he rubbed them so much they shrank."

"No!"

Lila's head filled with wonder, and she looked up sharply into his face. Then she caught the amused tremor in his bottom lip and knew he was teasing her. The idea elated her one moment, then saddened her the next. She'd always felt that when a man and woman teased in an unflirtatious manner, it was because they'd reached a different level in their relationship. She believed she and Seneca had moved to another level since their early meeting and later association. The very circumstance in which she'd arrived at his cabin only underscored that truth. She reminded herself in her next thought that she must ignore it.

"Yes. I had to keep him from polishing the whole thing with beeswax," Seneca continued.

"Beeswax," Lila replied with skepticism.

"Beeswax," he affirmed. "It's a fine protecting coat, but dirt and wood ashes are attracted to it like the original bee to flowers."

"Beeswax," Lila said again, narrowing her eyes and giving him a sidelong glance.

Seneca smiled. "I can see you've never had to polish furniture in your house."

"That's true."

"Never?"

"Never. We always had servants to perform such tasks."

"And you expect to have servants all your life, I suppose."

Lila sipped. "I've never thought about it. I suppose so."

"Have you ever wished for a different sort of life?"

Seneca's gaze and question were so very direct that Lila felt uncomfortable with them. She'd never been asked such a deeply personal serious question by anyone, not even Evalina.

"I'm still learning how dangerous it is to entertain wishes," she replied at length.

Seneca inclined his head toward her. "Why? Are you afraid of something?"

Did his directness never stop? She hadn't the answers to any of these questions, and she was afraid of looking foolish in his eyes. And she certainly couldn't tell him that some of her wishes had included him in a cursory fashion. Those were the dreams of the girl she'd once been with Evalina. She didn't know how to dream or to wish as a woman. Did women still wish and dream once they'd grown beyond girlhood? If they did, they certainly wouldn't put it into words to a *man*. Would they?

"*Are* you afraid, Cat?" Seneca urged.

His calling her by her aunt's pet name unnerved Lila. But it thrilled her more. She liked the name when it came from his lips. She wished he'd say it over and over, right now, close to her ear, close to her lips. She wished . . .

"I . . . I'm not afraid of anything." She strove to keep her voice even. "Women don't wish. At least not for things they can't have." Oh dear, was that the proper thing for her to be saying to a man?

"Women wish," Seneca said gently. "Some of them think they can't put voice to their wishes for fear they'll be forced to act on them. That's what they're afraid of, I think." He drained his mug.

He was right! Lila knew it in a flash. At least he was right about her. How did he know so much about her? Every part of her insides felt unsteady. His words, his eyes, his senses seemed to go right to her heart. She felt open, vulnerable.

"And what do men wish for? What are they most afraid of?" Perhaps if she felt he were as vulnerable as she at the moment, she would be strong enough to maintain her usual composure.

"Men wish to hold on to their freedom," Seneca said without thinking. "They are most afraid of losing it. I think women do not know how to feel that way. They've never tasted freedom the way men have."

Lila drained her glass. She lifted her chin and narrowed her eyes. "And just how is it you think you know women so well?" There. Maybe she could unnerve him for once.

"I learned very much from my mother. She was wise and understanding. She taught me that we all, men and women, rise from the power of the earth, equal one to the other. It is the external teaching that makes some people treat women differently from men. I believe your culture teaches women to ignore the passions in their hearts, and men to make women into servants and possessions. That's what I believe," he said simply.

Lila was disappointed she hadn't managed to unnerve Seneca one whit. In fact, his words resounded in her mind. *Possessions. Passions.* Her mother's words echoed over Seneca's: *A wife is nothing more than chattel to her husband.* Catherine had told her that until Lila had been born, she'd had nothing to feel passionate about since her pursuit of medicine had been taken from her. Was she to feel passionless until the birth of her own baby? *If* she were to have a baby. As her husband, Harrison would see to it that she had many babies. Enough babies to keep her shackled and weary and spiritless.

She felt tears welling at the back of her eyes. They

burned for release, but she held them in check. There was nothing more to say. They both knew it.

"We can eat now," Bear called over to them, releasing the tension. "Look what madame has done!" He swept his arm over the dining table.

"I only helped," Madeline said modestly. "Mr. LaDoque is a true culinary magician. Turning bear meat into a delicious stew!"

Lila lifted her heavy eyelids and viewed the kitchen area. Aunt Maddie had cleaned it of the flour and baking utensils and set the table with dishes and mugs. A plate piled high with her biscuits sat at one end, and a black pot steaming with Bear's thick stew occupied the middle. Lila thought the whole scene—with petite Aunt Maddie dressed in a flour sack and standing proudly at one end of the table, and the giant mountain man grinning proudly at the other end—to be homey, endearing. Satisfying.

"Can you come to the table, or would you be more comfortable if we brought the supper to you?" Seneca asked her quietly.

Lila smiled, then caught her bottom lip. "I think I'd like to be seated at the table. That is, after I've dressed."

Seneca inclined his head in understanding, then pulled a blanket strung on rope from the ceiling across her bed area, leaving Lila privacy to dress. "I'll bring you something to wear," he said through the blanket.

His selections weren't exactly appropriate, but Lila was grateful when he returned with shirt, trousers, and socks. She remembered her own clothes were torn and bloodied, and she didn't want Aunt Maddie to see them now. She never wanted to see them again either.

"Well, everything looks and smells like it was prepared by the best chefs at Delmonico's," Seneca said, rubbing his palms together loudly. "And we're just as fashionable eating at this late hour."

"Yes. I was just thinking how it's very odd that I don't feel a bit tired," Maddie said with excitement. "At home I would have retired by now and been long asleep. But tonight I feel as if I could go on for hours."

"Oh, no." Bear feigned a groan. "I fear we will bake biscuits until dawn!"

Nine

The three were laughing together when Lila emerged from behind the blanket, a bit unsteady on her feet. Seneca rushed to help her.

"I hope I haven't delayed too long and the food is cold," she said, leaning on Seneca's arm.

"Nary a chance of that," Maddie said laughing. "Look. That pot is so hot, the stew is still boiling even away from the fire!"

"I'm starving," Lila said with surprise in her voice.

"You sound as if you've never been hungry before," Seneca observed, seating her and then Madeline at the table.

Lila looked up at him, wonder floating about inside her. "I've never been hungry. I just realized that. There was never opportunity to feel so. Meals have been regulated at proper intervals all my life. I guess that was to be certain we were never to go without, like the poor."

That response gave Seneca a stab of ire, but he suppressed it. He knew Lila had no other life to which she could compare being hungry to ever-sated. That wasn't her fault. It bothered him that he was making excuses for her. But in the next moment couldn't help wondering how she might acclimate to a life in which she was required to care and fend for herself, provide the most basic of human necessities for herself instead of having them handed to her by her father or a cadre of servants. He smiled to himself, thinking how much he'd enjoy watching that happenstance should he ever be in a position to witness it.

Seneca threw up his hands in mock defeat. "Now I suppose the story will expand to include that not only did I imprison her in my cabin against her will, but I also refused to give her sustenance."

"Well, you did smear my wound with something sticky and disgusting to smell, then covered it up with wintergreen. And you forced me to drink bark juice, didn't you?" Lila chided him. She accepted a plate of stew and biscuits from Bear. "And it was utterly awful. Bitter." She made a shuddering sound that shook her shoulders.

"The salve was made of burdock root and is very soothing to the wound," Seneca defended his doctoring. "And it wasn't bark juice, exactly. It was a medicinal infusion of willow. You're healing quite well, in spite of your complaints of ill treatment," he added with equal chiding.

"Burdock?" Madeline said, smiling. "I remember my own experience with burdock while visiting at Saranac Lake some years ago. It seems Mrs. Smithfield's cook proudly presented a freshly made rhubarb pie at an elegant dinner one evening. Several of us took a first bite and knew immediately it was not rhubarb. The cook insisted that it was, and when asked to produce the plant in question she scurried back to the kitchen and returned waving a bouquet of dark green leaves with long woody red stems which she pronounced was rhubarb from a wild-growing patch she'd discovered near camp. Mrs. Smithfield became stricken on the spot."

"You mean it wasn't rhubarb?" Lila asked, caught up in her aunt's story.

"It was burdock. Unmistakably burdock. I remember how profusely it grew amid the hollyhocks near our privy at home."

Lila clutched her throat. "You did not take another bite, of course."

"Oh, but I did. I consumed the whole pie slice. I'd hoped to ease the cook's embarrassment, not to mention the sheer mortification of Mrs. Smithfield."

"Really, Aunt Maddie, I hardly think it was necessary to make yourself sick simply to soothe someone's embarrassment."

"On the contrary, I wasn't sick a bit. In fact, I had the most overwhelming feeling of well-being."

"There now," Seneca said to Lila. "You feel better now, don't you?"

Lila avoided answering Seneca with words. Instead she was busy consuming the delicious meal with gusto. Apparently the ache that he knew must still throb in her shoulder was forgotten for the moment.

"I see your niece possesses good table manners, Miss Madeline," Seneca said, making a show of cutting the meat on his plate carefully, and appearing ever the gentleman at dinner. "At least she doesn't talk with her mouth full."

"That's unacceptable behavior, of course." Madeline smiled at him.

"Really?" Bear said over a large bite of biscuit dipped in gravy. He said something more that the looks on the faces of the two women showed they did not understand.

"I rather doubt it," Seneca answered as if he'd understood every word. "I'm afraid Miss Evalina's family would find your eating habits quite disgusting, my friend," he said with humor. "You'd have to change your mountain ways if you take up with that young lady."

Bear swallowed hard. "No, *mon ami,* you can't mean that." He stared at Seneca, his hands gripped in fists holding a fork and large tablespoon upright in each, poised like sentries next to his plate. Clearly the idea of changing the way he'd always lived his life was astonishing, certainly something he'd never entertained.

"It's all a choice, a decision you come by after careful consideration," Seneca said matter-of-factly. "You can choose to remain Bear, a free-spirited mountain man. Or you can examine the alternative and decide to become Robert LaDoque, suit-wearing society husband. Simple."

"Simple," Bear said, frowning. "I don't think so."

Lila slowly lowered her fork. She stared off into space, then narrowed her eyes in deep thought. "Simple," she said absently. "Simple. Yes, of course. That's the key, isn't it? Look at all sides and decide on one course of action. Easier than one might suppose."

"Cat, dear?" Madeline searched her niece's face. "Is something wrong?"

Lila lowered her spoon. "Not any more," she answered dreamily. "I've come to a decision. A simple choice. Seneca and Bear are right."

"I am?" Bear sounded surprised.

"We are?" Seneca asked suspiciously.

Lila nodded vigorously, and her voice lost its dreamy quality. "Of course you are. It truly is simple. I've made a choice. I've decided not to go back to camp. And maybe not even New York." She resumed eating with even more enthusiasm than before.

Madeline dropped her fork. It clattered loudly against the tin plate.

Bear helped himself to another plateful of stew and biscuits. The subject of his focus—dinner—never wavered.

Seneca sat very still, one forearm resting on the table.

"Cat, dear," Madeline began timidly, "perhaps you should rest more before we—"

"I don't need more rest, Aunt Maddie," Lila said sharply. "I've rested all my life. I don't want to rest any-more." With her good arm she lifted her plate for Bear to refill.

Madeline wrung her hands in her lap. "Dear, are you quite certain you're feeling all right? What's making you speak this way? Perhaps today's ordeal has confused your mind."

"Quite right," Lila replied quickly, "it was an ordeal. But my mind is not confused any longer, and I have Seneca to thank for that and for my decision. I'm staying right here."

Madeline shifted her gaze to Seneca. "Mr. Pierce, surely you didn't tell Cat she shouldn't go back to camp, to her father, or even eventually back home. Surely you don't think—and delightful as your cabin is—that she would survive . . . here." Her voice held a hint of pleading as her eyes scanned the cabin and she searched his face.

Seneca turned a soft expression toward Madeline. "No, I did not." When Madeline let out a shaky but grateful sigh, Seneca continued over Bear's audible enjoyment of his own cooking. "And I agree with you. I don't think your niece could survive here."

"Then, I don't understand. How did you . . . ?" Madeline turned inquiring eyes on Lila.

"I was behaving quite badly and wailing that I didn't know what to do. Right before I went to sleep, Seneca told me I would learn what to do. He was right." Lila rubbed her plate clean with a chunk of biscuit just as Bear had done.

"But, dear, you know what you *should* do, don't you?"

"Yes, of course I know what I *should* do."

"Well, then . . ."

"I don't want to do that."

"But you can't stay here with Mr. Pierce."

"Why not?"

"Has he invited you?" Madeline's eyes turned hard toward Seneca.

Lila stopped chewing. She swallowed hard. "Well, no, he hasn't," Lila said tentatively, then added quickly, "but neither has he told me I have to leave."

Madeline turned her gaze back to Seneca. "Mr. Pierce, surely you know how unseemly this would look if Lila were to stay here with you in this cabin, alone. I beg you to help her come to her senses and go back with me to her father. I'm certain we can make him understand the gravity of what has happened."

"I have no say in this matter, Miss Madeline. This is not my decision." Seneca leaned back against his chair.

"Isn't it your decision to allow her to stay with you or not? Please, for Lila's sake and reputation, please tell her she can't stay with you."

"Happens all the time," Bear put in, stifling a belch with his shirtsleeve. "Men, women stay together."

Madeline raised an eyebrow at his remark, then turned pleading eyes to Lila. "Darling, I'll find a way to make Garrett understand why you don't want to marry Harrison. I'll make him believe you. We'll find a way to prove Harrison lied about everything. Garrett won't force you to marry Harrison. I'll do everything to convince him, only please, darling, come back with me."

"Aunt Maddie, thank you for being so protective of me. But you know how Father is. He won't listen to you. He listens only to himself and apparently to Harrison now. I couldn't live alone in New York. I have no money of my own, I have no employment. You have no money, either.

Only two things would prevent Father from forcing the marriage. One is if I disappeared forever. Although, it would pain me not to see you or Evalina again. And I would be sad not to see Father again, no matter how difficult he is."

Lila rubbed her temples. Seneca saw how her face suddenly lost its hopeful look and took on a weary cast.

Bear pushed his plate away, then leaned over and crossed his arms on the table, obviously very interested in the exchange. "That's only one thing, Mademoiselle Cat. What's the other thing?"

Lila sighed. "An impossibility. I shouldn't have even counted it."

"What?" Bear pressed. "Seneca can get it for you. I can help. Seneca can get anything anywhere in vast Adirondack."

Lila's small laugh was wry. "I doubt you or Seneca can help with this."

"We can, we can," Bear insisted, "can't we, *mon ami?*"

Seneca nodded, smiling slightly. "Yes, it's true. We can find everything we need here in these mountains."

Lila lowered her eyes to her lap. "I doubt you can find me a suitable husband on such short notice, no matter how vast the Adirondack Mountains."

Madeline sucked in a sharp breath and almost swooned. "Oh, my dear Lord." She sank back in her chair while Bear waved the empty biscuit plate over her face to create a strong current of air.

"There's only one perfect one like that around," Bear said over his vibrating shoulder as he kept fanning Madeline.

Lila turned her head and stared at him out of the corner of her eye. "Who would that be?" she asked skeptically.

Bear lowered the plate. "Me, of course. But, ah . . .

mademoiselle, I fear I've lost my heart to Mademoiselle Evalina, and it would pain me so to see her troubled face if I married you. I wouldn't be a good husband to you at all, not at all. *Mon Dieu!* Your fate is sealed, as you said. You will have to hide forever."

Lila let out a grateful sigh, then reached out and touched Bear's arm. "Looks like it, Bear. But I am flattered by your offer. You are a true gentleman, and Evalina is fortunate to have your affections."

"Merci. My heart is heavy for you, and for poor Mademoiselle Evalina, who does not know of my *sentiment."*

"That's probably for the best in the long run," Lila told him gently. "My dear friend Evalina, more spoiled perhaps than the rest of the girls in our circle, would be an inappropriate choice for a mountain man with as big a heart as the Adirondacks."

There was a long heavy silence.

"Well, then, that settles it," Madeline said shakily. "You'll go back to camp with me, Cat, and we'll set about to make your father see that his trust in Harrison has been sorely misplaced."

Lila shook her head. "No, Aunt Maddie. I'll think of something else."

"You are too headstrong. I knew it would happen someday. I warned Garrett." Madeline shook her head vigorously to underscore her words. "You have been under his protective thumb for far too long. He should have allowed you more freedom, more opportunity to learn and do. But no, he wouldn't hear of it. And now look. Disaster. Just disaster." She dropped her still shaking head into both hands, covering her face.

"What about me?" Seneca said gravely, breaking into the heavy atmosphere following Madeline's outburst. After the surprising words left his lips, he wondered at his response.

Lila's head snapped around, and her mouth dropped open at the moment her hand and fork fell heavily against her plate.

"You, *mon ami?*" Bear laughed. "You make a joke, no? You will never be a husband. You said so yourself, many times, have you not?"

"That I have, my friend, that I have. But these appear to be very serious circumstances."

"Marriage *is* serious circumstance," Bear said, nodding his head. "And it lasts a long time. Forever."

"Indeed it is serious. But it doesn't have to last forever, at least not in this case. Just long enough for Cat to feel safe and in a secure situation, and then go off and live her own life. What do you think, Miss Madeline?" Seneca turned a softened expression toward the old lady, who had suddenly and quite rapidly regained composure. Seneca marveled at her powers of recuperation.

"Mr. Pierce, how wonderfully gallant of you to rescue my poor niece from such a terrible fate. Yes, yes," she nodded her agreement. "I see the wisdom in your observation. By the time everyone calms down after the furor of your announcement, Cat could be very comfortable somewhere else, couldn't she? Of course, it might take a long, long time for that to happen. The marriage might have to stay intact for an extended period of time, you understand."

"Of course. I'll manage."

"Well, it's settled then." Madeline beamed.

"I don't believe it!" Bear shouted. *"Mon ami,* I'll dance at your wedding with the lovely Mademoiselle Evalina!"

"Oh dear, the wedding," Madeline said. "Yes, we will have to think of how to arrange that, won't we? Perhaps just a small quiet ceremony. A bride should have a pleasant memory of her wedding day, after all, shouldn't she?"

Lila banged her hand on the tabletop and then groaned in pain. "Just a blasted minute, all of you! Doesn't the so-called bride in this scheme you've hatched have anything to say about her choice of a husband and the size of her wedding?"

"Darling, of course you do!" Madeline reached over and patted Lila's hand. "After all, this whole thing was your idea!"

"My idea?" Lila almost choked.

"Yes, dear. You said as you saw it you had only two choices. One was to hide forever. That is unthinkable, of course. And the other was to marry so that Garrett could not force you into a marriage with a man you loathe. It is quite clever of you to think of it and of Mr. Pierce to offer the solution you seek." Madeline clapped her hands gleefully.

Lila's face colored visibly. "I can't marry Seneca."

"Of course you can, dear. It's all so simple, just as you've both described it."

"Oh, Aunt Maddie, he doesn't really mean it. It was nice of him to offer, but of course he only meant to try to help. It isn't possible."

"Why not?" Bear asked innocently.

"Yes, why not?" Seneca asked quietly. "I wouldn't have offered if I didn't mean it."

Lila turned nervously toward Seneca. "Why would you want to do such a thing?" she asked, leveling a dark gaze upon him.

She was right to ask such a question, Seneca thought. He hadn't thought about why he'd made his offer of marriage. In fact, his response was as much a surprise to himself as it was to everyone else around the table. Lila deserved an answer and a good one. They all did. He only hoped he could come out with one as solid as the situation required. This was no time to be offhanded, yet he couldn't pledge undying love to her. She'd never believe that. There was no reason she should believe it, was there?

"My mother spoke to me often about women," he started carefully. "She said I must always honor and respect them and be of the most beneficial service possible if I perceive their need to be great. She said it was a man's duty to go to the aid of a woman who was dishonored by another man, without thought of his own desires or safety. Since I honor my mother most among women, her teachings compel me—in the face of your situation—to defend your honor without thought to my own welfare."

Seneca astonished himself with his speech. There hadn't been time enough to formulate a complete response in his mind before speaking. And if he'd thought about it anyway, he most likely would have said he had no idea why he'd offered so quickly to do something so alien to him as to marry anyone, let alone a woman like Lila—Cat—Stockdale.

"Oh, Mr. Pierce," Madeline breathed. "How terribly gallant of you. Isn't he terribly gallant, Cat?"

Lila sat perfectly still, a stunned expression frozen on her lovely face. Her green eyes gave off a glint of fire, betraying her cool exterior. Seneca thought in that moment that her eyes reflected the dizzying confusion whirling around in his soul as much as it was in hers.

"Gallant, yes," Lila said at length. "And sacrificing. I wouldn't dream of letting him sacrifice his freedom, his life as he's known it, to marry me, rescue me from my own fate. And I must continue to think that—"

"It's not a sacrifice, nor is it especially gallant," Seneca interrupted. "You have presented a very difficult situation.

It follows the fact that I wounded you physically. I owe you the time to heal. I'm honoring my mother's teachings. The circumstance will be temporary—we both understand that. I will not be giving up my life nor losing my freedom. I will continue to live as I always have. And you will, I hope, manage to find your life and live it the way you wish." He paused and watched her stunned expression for a moment before he continued. "So do we have a deal?"

Lila waited, debating his words. Seneca wasn't certain which he hoped she'd do: agree or decline. By offering to help her, he'd created his own dilemma. And now he'd placed the outcome squarely in her hands.

Madeline fixed an urging gaze on her niece and nodded her head slightly to prod Lila into saying yes. Lila trembled in the throes of indecision. She bit her bottom lip. Her leg vibrated, her fingers drummed the table.

She swallowed. "We have a deal," she whispered.

Outside the cabin later, Lila walked among the trees, thinking. Tomorrow was to be her wedding day.

Her wedding day!

A single sob welled up from her depths and burst uncontrollably through her lips. None of what had just transpired in the cabin was anything like how she and Evalina had dreamed their girlish dreams together. No romantic proposal, no long engagement, no big church decorated with flowers and candles, no wedding party in gowns and formal suits, no sumptuous feast with flowing champagne.

And no Garrett Stockdale walking his glowing daughter down the aisle, their arms linked.

Lila recalled now that when she and Evalina fantasized their weddings, she'd never put a face on her dream groom. He was dressed as a groom should be dressed in

a big society wedding, but he didn't have a face. Even
after it was understood she'd marry Harrison Mayne one
day, still her wedding plans had not included a groom with
a clear face.

She closed her eyes. Seneca's chiseled face and sky-
blue eyes hung suspended in her mind. She did not visu-
alize his wedding garb—that was a blurred mist around
the edges of the mental picture—but his face was sharply
in focus. Seneca Pierce was to be her groom. Her husband.

Lila shivered. Was it from fear? Or wild anticipation?
Full of trepidation as she stood now at the shore of his
island, she knew she would not change her mind. If in
the cold light of a mountain morning the impact of her
impending act rang clear, she knew she would not run
away from the wedding. The impact would be great upon
her life and upon the lives of others, she knew that. But
nothing would prevent her from going through with this
wedding.

Except Seneca's change of mind. Lila immediately put
that fear aside.

She started to turn around and start back into the woods
toward the cabin when she heard an eerie call come out
of the mist. A lonely cry of a loon, an answering cry in
the gathering gloom.

"Lila!"

She jumped as the sound of her name rolled across the
lake and echoed among the trees. She stood frozen. That
was not a loon.

"Lila! Lila, where are you?" The anguished call of her
father over on the mainland. Lila's heartbeat pounded in
her throat.

"Father," she whispered.

She turned back toward shore. He must be frantic with
worry. She should let him know where she was, that she

was safe. She couldn't do this without his permission, couldn't go through with the wedding. He'd never forgive her. She'd hurt him. He'd done so much for her. Whatever had she been thinking? It was just another dream, her resolve to go through with this wedding no matter what, wasn't it? Just another bubble rising from her dreams to burst in the glare of the sun.

Again she heard her father's voice calling her name. She had to respond, had to let him know she was all right. He'd be so happy to see her, so glad she was safe that he wouldn't force her to do anything she didn't want to do ever again. She was his daughter, his little girl—all he had since her mother had died. How could she hurt him? She summoned the courage to yell out to him, call across the lake. She took a deep breath, enough to give her heart the courage and her voice the power.

"Lila! Lila darling, where are you? Please be safe, my precious one!" Harrison's voice. Harrison's lying voice.

Lila's own courage and power died in her throat. The truth was clear in the misty mountain night. If she went back to her father's camp, she would have to face Harrison as well. He'd fabricated a story about what happened in the forest. Her father believed him. He was angry with her now, and that came on the wings of his anger regarding Seneca, some of which she didn't understand. She did understand that he would not allow her to even see Seneca. And her trembling insides told her that she could not pass a day for the rest of her life without seeing Seneca Pierce.

"Cat?" A voice whispered from behind her in the trees.

Lila jumped. She whirled around to face the direction of the sound.

"Seneca?" she whispered.

"Yes. I heard them calling your name across the lake. They're searching for you."

He came closer to her. She could barely make him out in the shroud of dark forest, but she felt his powerful presence, the warmth emanating from him, heard his breathing.

"I know," she managed to whisper.

"Do you want to answer?"

She lowered her eyes toward the island land she knew was beneath her feet but could not see. The island. Hadn't she wished for an island? "I—"

"It's not too late. Call out if you wish. I'll take you back tonight. You'll be all right." His voice was soothing, understanding.

She waited a long moment. Again her father's voice and then Harrison's floated over the water and mingled with the cry of the loons.

"You wouldn't be all right," she said at last. "They would never forgive or forget."

"I can take care of myself. Don't let that worry you. Think only of what is right for you, then don't look back."

He waited silently, so still Lila thought he might have somehow stolen away. She lowered her head again, letting the curtain of her hair close off his image, which was becoming clearer as her eyes adjusted to the sharpening moonlight. Her mind and heart were torn in two directions—between learned duty and discovering desire. How would she ever decide? How would she know in her heart she was doing the right thing?

The right thing.

If she were to return to her father, would she always wonder what might have happened if she'd stayed with Seneca? If she stayed with Seneca, would she always chastise herself for not doing her duty to her father? Perhaps all her friends—who blindly accepted what their families dictated would be the course of their lives—were the most fortunate of all. She knew now that the way of life as she'd known it was easiest. A woman never had to make difficult decisions. They were made for her. There was no chance to be wrong, to make mistakes. She would always be correct, dutiful. How would the proper and rigidly raised Lila Catherine Stockdale respond to this dilemma, she asked herself. If she'd been thinking properly, that same proper Miss Stockdale would never have allowed herself to even be in this position of having to decide.

Seneca stepped closer to her. She felt the whisper of his arms, his chest, his thighs against hers. He raised his hands and placed them along her face, resting his thumbs below her chin. He tilted her head back, and she felt her hair fall away from her face, revealing his in a silver wash. A cool moist breeze fanned her skin in sharp contrast to the searing heat of his fingers on her face, his breath on her eyelids.

"This is a moment of truth for both of us." His voice was husky, heavy with emotion. "This moment will come and go, and nothing in our lives will be as it was before. You need not decide right now. Let your sleep and the wisdom of your inner voice give you your own truth, your own answers in the hours before dawn. That is your best truth, the foundation for you to make your decision and act upon it. I believe you understand." He closed his eyes.

"I'm trying to," she whispered, unable to keep the tremulous fragility from her voice. "I cannot help but be fearful."

He did not speak. He lowered his head and the black sheet of his hair swept forward and cloaked the outer lines of her face. He tilted her chin up, then carefully lowered one hand to slide it around her waist. He rested his splayed fingers on the small of her back, then with smooth yet tender firmness pulled the length of her soft body into

the hard planes of his own. His warm mouth captured
hers and swept her into an eddying kiss so deep, so complete, so mesmerizing she gave over every last ounce of
resistance she'd been trying to grasp.

His hand on her face slipped sharply to the back of her
neck then up under her hair. He held her head a willing
prisoner while his lips tasted, his tongue probed the inner
reaches of her mouth. Lila released every dutiful, proper,
controlling muscle, nerve, and sense in her being. She
clutched his muscular arm with one hand. Though the
other arm throbbed with its wound, she wouldn't have
pulled it away from its exquisite trap between his chest
and her breasts if it threatened to break from the pain.

She slid her other hand up over his massive shoulder
and grasped the back of his neck. With a burst of strength
and total sensual arousal, she thrust her own tongue past
his teeth until it dueled with his in a frenzy to taste and
feel all that was possible. He groaned from deep in the
back of his throat and lowered his arm quickly to below
her buttocks and lifted her off the ground. There he held
her suspended against him, burying his fingers in her hair
and controlling her head, deepening the all-consuming
kiss.

Together they clung, straining, melding every part of
each body to the other in an intense heat. There was only
one place they could go from here. Lila knew it. The memory of the pain and fear she'd experienced only hours before at the hands of her brutal fiancé dissolved in the
blazing fire now raging around her in the suspended circle
of Seneca's arms. Silently she begged for him to drop
them both to the fragrant island floor beneath them and
make her his own for all time.

The seconds were charged as her lips stilled, waiting
for his next move.

When at last he released her lips, he trailed his own, hot and wet, along the side of her throat and rested them in a searing kiss against the hollow of her throat, where she felt her own pulse slamming against his mouth. She cried out in a muffled groan of untapped primal ecstasy and anticipation, rained moist kisses over his face, then buried her face in his hair. She inhaled deeply of his masculine essence mingling with the pungent balsam- and cedar-scented night air enfolding them.

"Li-lah!" Garrett Stockdale's anguished call again stabbed the air.

Lila's body went sharply rigid. She let out a painful sob of "Oh!"

Slowly Seneca lowered her body along his until her feet rested on the ground. With one hand buried in her hair, he pulled gently but firmly back until her feverish face was raised to his.

"Open your eyes, Cat," he commanded.

She clamped her eyes tighter and tried to shake her head no. His grip on her head prevented her from completing the response.

"Look at me now," he commanded once more. "Open your eyes and look at me. Remember this moment."

At last she relaxed her face and slowly lifted her eyelids.

"I will be waiting here by the shore in the morning," he whispered huskily. "We will both know your decision then."

Lila's rapidly tear-filling eyes stared into his for one bittersweet moment. She pushed away from Seneca, turned, and ran through the forest toward the cabin.

Seneca watched Cat run away, listened until her footfalls fell silent. Slowly he raised his hand and touched his lips where the sweet dewiness of her mouth remained.

The breeze chilled the moist heated skin of his face where she'd left a trail of fevered kisses.

He turned back toward the direction of the voice on the other side of the lake. *Moment of truth.* That's what he'd called it. Stark naked truth. That's what it was. Seneca's soul rocked with it, his body screamed for it. His mind was tortured with it. He wanted this woman with every fiber in him. He should run now, disappear. It was dangerous to even entertain what he'd proposed—and more dangerous for her than she knew.

Marry Garrett Stockdale's daughter.

But he'd offered. He never went back on his word. A marriage between them would save her from a fate they both found abhorrent. He'd risked his life in the past for what he believed in, but he'd never risked his way of life with so monumental an offer.

If she decided to go back to her family, his spirit would be tormented with her loss from that day forward. Yet it would make everything else he'd planned that much easier.

If she decided to go through with the marriage, he would do it without question. If, later, when the impact of her actions subsided, she decided to end the marriage . . . he knew he would not be able to let her go without great suffering and pain. He couldn't hold her to him against her will. If she discovered what he'd been planning all along, he would suffer all the more. Yet it would make everything else that much easier for her.

A war raged within him. His vow to preserve this area of the Adirondacks, to keep it forever wild, was as clear at this moment as it had always been. Yet the means he'd been planning to use to fulfill his vow had become a confused tangle of senses, broken pictures, battered emotions. He was questioning his very reason for existing.

He should listen to his own words of wisdom, his earlier

advice to Cat. If he waited, listened to his inner voice, he would learn, would know what he should do, what he wanted to do. He shook his head—he felt as confused about her fate as she had been trying to make her decision to go back to her father's camp or not.

Seneca Pierce knew then his own fate was sealed in whatever decision Lila Cat Stockdale reached at dawn.

Ten

Lila awoke from a fitful sleep. She rolled her head to the side and took in the sight of Seneca's cabin. Dawn was barely visible outside the window. No physical remnants of the eventful supper of the night before were visible on the table or sideboard. Nothing in the room spoke of the suggestion of a marriage pact between two ill-suited people, nothing to recall that even the notion of a marriage between these two people would have a devastating effect on so many others. Had she dreamed the scene?

She sat up, starkly remembering Seneca's shattering kiss. Shamelessly she'd responded, kissing him back with a fervor she hadn't known lived within her. She'd thought then she kissed him because she believed she'd never see him again, never taste him, never know the heat and strength and power of him. Her lips burned now in their sense memory of his mouth and tongue performing their magic on her body and emotions.

A fierce yearning swept over her, punctuated by physical spasms pulsing below her abdomen and over her thighs. The sensations were shockingly new to her. Intuitively she understood the erotic power of a first physical encounter when mind, emotions, and senses were driving forces as strong as the force of natural attraction. She propped her elbows onto her knees and dropped her head into her hands. That kiss was real, made from the fabric of youthful girlhood dreams and maturing female sensuality.

In her mind she saw herself running blindly through the trees back to the cabin the night before, leaving the lake's edge and the haven of Seneca's arms, the voices of her father and Harrison echoing in the night and in her mind. Seneca had not returned, and Bear had disappeared. She'd felt completely alone inside the cabin until she'd heard the contented deep breathing of Aunt Maddie coming from the sleeping loft above. Amazing. Aunt Maddie seemed to be sleeping more peacefully than she ever had at home.

Lila had crawled into the balsam and blanket bed she'd shared with Seneca after the shooting accident. The feel of the bed reminded her of his warmth and the unsettling emotions she'd grappled with. Now she was contending with those emotions in a more intense fight than ever. Regardless of the outcome of her actions, the hours spent in this bed would haunt her forever. As unseemly as she knew it was for a lady to do so, she wished she hadn't spent those hours sleeping.

She leaned back and closed her eyes, feeling emotionally drained, exhausted. But she knew she must have slept at least part of the time, for she remembered now the clearly visible face and audible voice of her mother, smiling, saying, "Follow your heart, my darling daughter." Seneca had appeared beside her mother in the dream, saying, "I shall be waiting for you, Cat."

Over and over she played the scene and the dream in her mind. Could any man be so magnanimous as to marry a woman simply to help her out of a difficult situation? Was it possible for a woman to marry a man for the same thing? She guessed that it was more possible for a woman than it was for a man, but going into a marriage for those reasons was not how she'd dreamed marriage for herself. Where were the vows of love she longed to hear, to say? Were all marriages strictly business deals? She was beginning to think now that it had been so between her parents. And her father had certainly been perpetuating the tradition by his forcing her to marry Harrison. If what she'd observed and what Evalina had said were true, then all marriages were based purely on a form of business and survival.

Except Aunt Maddie's marriage. Lila believed the union between her beloved aunt and David Allgood had been created purely and completely out of love and desire. Couldn't that happen for every woman, for her? She let out a long sigh.

Lila stood, stiff and sore from tension and the aftereffects of her wound. She opened the door and stepped outside into the damp cool morning. The pungent aroma of balsam swept over her. She breathed deeply and started to walk.

How had Seneca come to the decision to marry her? The question nagged her. Was his answer honest? Was his desire only to aid her? Then what did that soul-searing kiss of the night before mean to him? Masculine lust? While she'd never known the depth of lust that Seneca's kiss had ignited in her—that his presence from the first moment she'd seen him had kindled—Lila believed that much between them was honest. Desire . . . basic all-consuming desire, one for the other. Why had she grown up in so naive a way as to believe that powerful desire evolved out of love?

Her father and his associates demonstrated a desire for power and wealth and control—and now and again for revenge. In that she saw just what lust could wring from life. None of that had anything to do with love either.

In her mind Lila knew she should not go into a marriage without love. In her heart she felt compelled to go through with this wedding, this union with Seneca Pierce. All clear reasoning was elusive.

A decision. Lila Cat Stockdale had to make a decision.

Madeline Allgood was a happy woman as she rose and dressed that morning. Sated with bear meat stew and a fine berry wine and a sense that all would soon be right in her world, she'd slept in the mountain air with a deep relaxing peace. Restorative—that was the only word she could think of at the moment. She heard Lila stirring and watched discreetly as she left the cabin. Wedding day jitters, no doubt. Madeline remembered having them herself. She smiled now. Back then, so long ago, her nervousness had more to do with anticipation than trepidation. She couldn't wait to be in David's arms, to make love with him. Perhaps Lila didn't feel exactly that way now, but Madeline knew she would before too long.

She descended the loft ladder and set about making coffee, a song in her heart and on her lips. It was her beloved niece's wedding day, and what a glorious day it was! Robins sang sweetly from the trees outside the cabin. It was a good omen, Madeline thought. She couldn't have constructed this perfect event herself if she'd tried. She would never have the courage to be so reckless as to arrange for Seneca and Lila to marry the perfect partner for each other: themselves. And behind her brother-in-law's back, of all things! They'd arranged it all by themselves, she marveled. She'd had nothing to do with it. Well, maybe she'd contributed just a tiny bit.

There would be certain hell to pay facing Garrett later, she knew that, too. For that she had courage. This marriage was right, even if, for the moment, she was the only one who believed it. But Madeline also knew that Seneca and Lila would have to consummate their marriage, or Garrett would force an annulment. Madeline herself would have to swear to that consummation—she knew that, too. She would do it, swear to it, whether Seneca and Lila actually consummated it or not. Observing the two of them several times, she couldn't see how they could help but consummate it once they were completely alone.

Lila returned to the cabin, breaking into Madeline's thoughts. She sat down glumly, setting a package on the table.

"Good morning, dear," Madeline greeted her. "Sleep well? Coffee's ready. Where are the men? Oh, never mind. I'm certain Seneca knows it's bad luck to see his bride on their wedding day." She bustled about getting mugs from a shelf, pouring coffee, and getting out warmed-over biscuits left from the night before.

"Thank you. I need that coffee. I feel like I hardly slept at all." Lila absently stirred the coffee.

"Cat, dear, that's just normal night-before-the-wedding nerves. You'll be fine. Just fine."

"Aunt Maddie, I'm not fine. I don't think I will be fine." Lila fingered the rawhide tie over the package.

"Of course you'll be fine. What is there to worry about?"

"Everything! What am I doing? Am I doing the right thing? What will Father say? Oh, he'll be so angry with me. And I'm feeling sick. I can't do this." She slumped back in the hard chair.

"I'm certain that nerves are the culprit for all this doubt and for your feeling sick. Although I will say I've never seen you consume such a meal as you did last night. I thought the stew was wonderful, too." Madeline kept a cheery note in her voice.

"It's not the stew, Aunt Maddie. How can I marry Seneca Pierce? I hardly know him. He doesn't know me at all."

"My dear, you both know each other better than you think. But even so, think of the fun of discovery. I think it's possible to spend a lifetime learning about each other."

"I think it's possible one lifetime would not be enough to know all there is to know about Seneca Pierce. There's something frightening about him."

Madeline watched Lila's trembling lips. She nodded knowingly. "Yes, there is."

"And yet there is something so compellingly wild about him, so commanding. And I'm not always fearful of him."

"No, you're not."

"In fact, I'm drawn to him. It's overwhelming at times." Lila's voice took on a note of desperation. "I don't understand it. It's as if he has a supreme power. It does seem that way, doesn't it, Aunt Maddie? He possesses a primal power of some kind."

"Yes, he does."

"And it's not that I'm not up to it. I mean, I'm not a shrinking flower, a weak blossom in the force of his thunderous wind. I'm truly not that, am I?"

"No, you're not."

"How I wish . . ." Lila's voice trailed away to some distant dream, her eyes traveling with it.

"Wish what, dear?"

After a moment Lila turned back to her aunt. "I wish that . . . *love* were a part of all this." She sucked in her bottom lip.

Madeline sipped her coffee thoughtfully. "Love has been known to come with marriage."

Lila raised her eyes. They brightened and were full of hope. She sat up straight. "Marrying Seneca wouldn't be a total disaster, would it? A disaster would be if I married Harrison, wouldn't it? I know Father won't see it that way, but I do, and in this case I know more than he does, don't I? Perhaps in time he'll see that I'm right. And then he'll see that I had no choice but to marry Seneca. Isn't that right, Aunt Maddie? I really have no other choice, do I?"

"No choice whatever."

"It's right that I marry Seneca."

"Completely right."

"Well, then . . ." Lila gave a sharp nod and one last hard pat to the package.

"Precisely. Come now. We have work to do in coming up with something for you to wear." Madeline patted her niece's arm and stood up. "What's in that package?"

Lila dropped her gaze. "I don't know. It was outside the door when I went out this morning. I thought perhaps Bear left it for Seneca."

Madeline smiled. "And perhaps your groom left it for his bride."

"Oh, I don't think so. He wasn't even certain last night that I was going to . . ." Lila raised her eyes to Madeline. "Could it be possible?"

"There's only one way to find out. Open it," Madeline urged.

In retrospect it wasn't much of a marriage proposal or wedding plan as that sort of thing usually went, Madeline mused as she set about preparing suitable attire for her niece's marriage ceremony, which would take place in a matter of hours. Evalina would be disappointed that the proposal lacked the usual knee-bending, ring-offering, brow-sweating elements she and Lila had talked of so often as girls. She'd be further disappointed that she hadn't gotten to wear a bridesmaid's dress. If Evalina saw what Lila was wearing, perhaps she'd be grateful she wasn't part of the wedding party. But Madeline thought her niece was the most beautiful bride since she herself had walked down the aisle to meet her beloved David.

A knock sounded at the cabin door. Instinctively Lila stepped behind the blanket curtain that Seneca had strung up for privacy the night before. Madeline opened the door to Bear.

"Are we ready?" Bear plodded into the room and scraped his cap off his head.

"Almost," Madeline replied. "And don't you look handsome this morning."

Bear sucked in his top lip and scraped his boot on the floor. "Ah, madame—you flatter." He raised his shaggy head with a proud tilt to his glistening bearded chin. "I'm to be what Seneca calls the best man. I say it must be *he* who is best man, but he says he's right that I am."

"In this case he is right, Bear. And how is the groom this morning?"

Bear leaned down to whisper in Madeline's ear. "He's behaving very strange. Pacing like a caged lynx. It's just a deal, that's all. He shouldn't be so nervous."

Madeline smiled with satisfaction. Everything she'd known intuitively about the appropriateness of this union was being proven over and over again by the couple in question. She wondered how long it would take them to know as much about themselves as she did.

"Oh, dear, I just thought of something. Is there a discreet clergyman in the vicinity?" This was no time to wonder about a most important element to this wedding, but Madeline had to be certain everything was in place.

"Oui, madame. An old friend. A hermit."

"A hermit? Bear, are you certain—?"

"Oh, *oui,* madame. Do not worry. Maurice Sender is a real preacher. Honest."

Bear nodded so guilelessly, Madeline believed him. She walked toward the blanket behind which Lila was dressing. "All right, then. Wait for us outside. We won't be long."

A few moments later Madeline stepped out into the warming morning sun to join Bear. "We're ready," she announced and turned toward the door to watch her niece emerge.

Lila was wearing both of Madeline's white lace petticoats for her wedding skirt, and a clean blue cotton shirt of Seneca's they'd found in a cupboard, buttoned to the neck with the collar lifted straight up under her hair and chin. Madeline had altered it by using her own stocking garters to push up and puff out the sleeves. She'd washed Lila's hair in rainwater from a barrel cistern outside the cabin and then had brushed it out loose and soft. It was a vast change from the more formal coiled coiffure Lila usually wore, and it was most becoming.

On Lila's feet were the contents of the package found near the cabin door. A note had accompanied a pair of high-topped white-beaded moccasins. Seneca had written that they had been worn by his mother on her wedding day. Madeline thought the gesture was most touching. She knew that Lila thought so, too, when she saw her slight smile and the tears that filled her enormous green eyes.

Bear held out a wildflower bouquet of yellow-and-white blooms and helped Lila into an arm sling for her wounded shoulder, which he'd made from his least offensive red bandanna. Even the blackflies cooperated, Madeline noticed, seeming to know enough to let up on a girl's wedding day.

"The groom, he waits by the shore," Bear announced, bowing and grinning so widely Lila thought the hairs in his beard might begin popping out at any moment.

"The shore?"

"*Oui*, mademoiselle. We take my boat to the hermit's island."

"A hermit on an island. Yes, of course." Lila whirled around to Madeline. "I'm doing the right thing, aren't I, Aunt Maddie?"

"Of course you are, dear."

"Come now," Bear urged, taking her other arm and escorting her and Madeline down the path to the lake shore. "Don't keep Seneca waiting. He's edgy as a treed bobcat."

The concept of Seneca Pierce being nervous was something Lila could not grasp. He always appeared so maddeningly calm, unruffled at anything anyone might say or do. It was his way to live and let live, she knew that. That knowledge did nothing to allay her own fears. She half-expected her father or Harrison to come barreling out of the forest and stop this sham wedding by killing the groom and dragging her back to New York. Her stomach clutched. Would they get through this without a horrible tragedy ensuing?

Was she doing the right thing? The question and doubt consumed her. Was it right to do this to Seneca? He'd volunteered. She hadn't forced him into anything. She knew no one could force Seneca into something he didn't want to do, and she admired and envied him for that. She hadn't forced him to kiss her. He hadn't forced her either. He'd wanted to kiss her. She believed that. And the heavens and all their stars and planets knew she'd wanted to kiss him. She'd been blatant. How would she ever face him this morning after her shameless behavior of the night before? Kissing him with such complete abandonment of all she'd been taught was proper! She wondered now if the proprieties of society would affect Seneca's perception of her. Ladies didn't act so brazen and definitely not before the wedding.

Before they reached the shore, Lila turned inquiring eyes on her aunt.

Madeline beamed. "Darling Cat, do not worry. You are a beautiful bride. How I wish your mother could see you now."

Lila wasn't certain she wished her mother could see her. She wondered if Catherine would forgive the extreme act she was about to engage in, taking on one kind of marriage to avoid another. Beyond that, she was too nervous to think of anything more.

When they stepped out of the forest onto the shore, Seneca was waiting by Bear's huge guideboat. At the sight of him, all of Lila's self-admonishment of her behavior the night before melted away. And that was the moment she truly wished her mother could see her now.

Aunt Maddie sucked in a breath at the same moment Lila did, for the groom was as beautiful as the bride. He wore his fringed deerskin shirt and leggings. His hair was left long and free, shining blue-black in the morning sun. He'd made a slim braid down one side, and tied it with a leather thong decorated with multicolored beads of glass and wood. Lila made a sweep of him from his head to his hands, which opened and closed repeatedly, and down his fringed leggings to his feet and the brown beaded moccasins he wore.

Seneca looked down shyly. "My mother made these

moccasins for my father for their wedding day," he said quietly. "I thought it was appropriate that I wear them."

He is nervous! Lila was secretly glad of it. If he remained calm through the most monumental event of her life, she didn't know how she'd stand to go through with it. *His father's moccasins.* Something whispered somewhere in the back of her mind that Seneca must take this wedding seriously, think enough of it to do something as touching and sensitive as to give her his mother's wedding moccasins and to wear those his mother had made for his father for their wedding. If there was no love, there was something else, something unnamed but strong.

No, she shouldn't talk herself into believing that. It was time to stop girlhood games and keep her eyes wide open to the harsh realities of womanhood. She was about to take a husband, become a man's wife. Even if this wedding were not the traditional path to a real marriage, the fact of the event held inherent expectations, didn't it? Seneca might be sentimental about his parents, but given the manner in which they were coming together, he would never be sentimental about her, Lila cautioned herself. She squared her shoulders as best she could, given the stiffness in her wounded one and the tenseness in the other.

Time to grow up.

"I've made something for you," Seneca said softly. He stepped closer to her and held out a crown fashioned of ferns and white and purple trillium blossoms. "May I?" He indicated that he wanted to place it on her head.

A nerve in Lila's neck quivered, and her heart beat faster. She nodded shyly and tilted her head down. Seneca gently placed the crown over her hair, and Aunt Maddie wove a few tresses through it all around her head to hold it securely.

"It's lovely, dear," Aunt Maddie assured her. "Would

you like to see?" She opened her pouch bag and extracted a small looking glass from a velvet sack, and held it up for Lila's inspection.

When Lila saw the crown of ferns and blossoms created by Seneca's hands—the hands she'd become so fascinated with—she let out a long breathy "Ooh." It was indeed lovely, more exquisite than any crown or veil she might have dreamed up in her musings with Evalina. It was perfect.

"It's time," Seneca said and motioned for them to step into the boat.

As they floated over the lake through the misty morning, a loon broke the silence and blue jays squawked at chickadees as if nothing unusual were happening on the lake and among the Adirondack trees.

Seneca, facing Lila, felt the rhythm of, and listened to the easy lap of Bear's paddle strokes in the water behind him as he propelled them toward the end of the lake and the narrow channel which would take them into the secluded bay where Maurice Sender's island lay. He reflected on his life up to this moment. He was about to be married, something he'd never thought he'd do. He was almost afraid to think about his reasons right now.

Far down the lake, the boat glided close to the shore, and Seneca let the shape of the lake and the forest and the mountains pass across his vision and his mind. The shapes shrouded in mist looked like textures in landscape paintings or in maps and drawings he'd made over the years. He suddenly recalled a basic course in architecture he'd taken in college. The clarity in the recollection surprised him. The external architecture of the eternal earth and humanity's presence in it reflected the texture of the internal architecture of his spirit, his essence. New shapes materialized as quickly as new towns and cities. He had to remember that and the speed with which all life was changing now.

Would Lila understand how the flow of streams, the wind currents—the effects of water, snow, and fire upon these mountains and lake shores—the death and rebirth of trees and ferns and flowers and wildlife also affected him . . . created the flow and current and elemental passion that made up the very textures of his life? And would it matter to her or to him whether she did or did not understand?

Bear pointed the prow of his boat down the narrow channel that led to the inlet and their destination for the wedding ceremony. Seneca's pulse quickened. He turned and looked at Lila's face. She avoided his eyes and kept them pinned on the shoreline. Over her shoulder he saw Miss Madeline smiling happily, her eyes as misty as the morning. Was Lila apprehensive? Or didn't this mean anything except a means to her freedom from her father and Harrison Mayne? And what about his own motives? There was more to his offer of marriage than simply coming to the aid of a woman in trouble, wasn't there?

Too late to wonder now. Bear was already out of the boat and hauling it onto the shore.

"Is this it?" Lila asked. A small frown pleated the moist skin over her eyes.

"*Regarde,* mademoiselle, soon to be madame," Bear announced with an expansive sweep of his arm. "Your wedding place."

"Enchanting," Madeline exclaimed, "simply enchanting. Like a fairy tale."

Seneca stepped lightly out of the boat and turned to assist his bride. Bear slogged into the water, leaned over and swept Madeline up in his arms, and carried her to shore. She laughed merrily. Seneca thought she and Bear were the only ones in the foursome who were completely immersed in the joy such an occasion usually elicited.

Lila let Seneca take her hand and lead her up the winding path. His grip was firm and warm and made her feel secure. At the top of a slight incline, a bark-clad shanty appeared. In front of it stood a hunched old man in flowing robes made of burlap sacks. He had a head of thick wiry gray hair and a flowing beard to match that reached below what she surmised must be his waist hidden inside burlap. On his head was a battered felt hat. Perhaps this was a guide to lead them to the church and the minister.

"Bonjour!" Bear called out.

"Duck, Duck, good to see you!" The old man's voice was scratchy, and not all of the words came out in actual sounds. Lila surmised this was from lack of use in conversation.

"Hello, Maurice," Seneca said, holding out his right hand.

"Maurice?" Lila was shocked, and her heart sank. "Not *Preacher* Maurice?"

"The same," Seneca responded.

"Oh, dear Lord," Aunt Maddie said. It was more of a prayer than a comment.

The old man withdrew a bony gnarled hand from inside his burlap robes and grasped Seneca's, shaking it more vigorously than Lila thought him capable. "Seneca Pierce. Saints preserve me!"

And they must have, Lila thought, surveying the troll-like little man. The fairy tale Aunt Maddie had exclaimed over seemed suddenly to have been fabricated by the Brothers Grimm.

"I see you passed the winter well, old friend," Seneca said.

"That I have, that I have. And you?" He peered around Seneca at the two women. "What have you brought me?"

"Does he think we're sacrificial lambs?" Aunt Maddie whispered in her ear.

"That's entirely possible," Lila whispered back.

"I've brought you my bride," Seneca said, and he was smiling as if he were truly happy about it. "Miss Lila Stockdale. She is called Cat."

"Cat. I see. Your bride. Appropriate, yes. *Your bride?* How now, Seneca Pierce?" Maurice Sender squinted and peered up first into Seneca's eyes, then Lila's, then back into Seneca's.

"It's a long tale," Bear told him. "I'll tell you over supper sometime."

"You always want a meal. You bring the food."

Bear laughed heartily.

"And may I present my bride's aunt, Madeline Allgood. Miss Madeline, this is Maurice Sender: storyteller, craftsman, builder of this church, and preacher."

"Church? This is a church?" Aunt Maddie burst out, then clamped a delicate hand over her mouth.

"The outside of anything may speak of one thing to all men, Miss Madeline," Sender said, "but it is only what is on the inside that has meaning. Come." He held out his hand to her as if to usher her through the arched door constructed of whole logs still covered with shaggy bark.

Lila followed Bear, who swiped the knitted cap from his bushy head. He trudged up the incline toward the shanty behind Aunt Maddie and the clergyman who was to perform her wedding ceremony, uniting her with Seneca Pierce. *Is this a dream?* She recalled the time on the train coming up to the mountains when she'd described her husband—the man of her dreams—to Evalina. She gave him no name then, but in her heart she knew she'd described Seneca Pierce.

She'd known all her life she'd be involved in a wedding, getting married against her will. Her father had decreed it. And while the whole short evolution of this wedding ceremony had seemed out of her hands, she knew this moment of truth, this wedding, this marriage was not against her will. Not for one second was she doing anything against her will. But she was frightened to death, frightened of so much she could not put name to the flashes of insight that illuminated her mind.

Inside the damp bark-covered shanty was a chapel Lila could never have imagined or have found to be her ideal place for her wedding to occur. At the back of the small structure was a window built in the shape of a pointed arch, the tinted red and yellow glass of which was separated into irregular-shaped panes framed by twisted tree roots. The wood and log walls were studded with small panes of clear glass set off with chunks of garnet similar to that over the fireplace opening in Seneca's cabin.

The sun was rising higher, and it beamed through the glass in shafts of light that criss-crossed the wood floor. The highest panes were angled in the walls in such a manner as to allow the sun to shine upon the garnet stones on the opposite walls and cause the facets in them to shimmer.

Maurice Sender hobbled to the tall back window. To Lila's surprise, he released a leather thong and wood hasp in the middle of it and pushed the two sides open. The room was instantly filled with the scent of a fresh mountain morning and the happy song of the birds.

Lila was imbued with a complete sense of well-being, of rightness, of newness. Slowly she turned around in a circle, taking in every part of the tiny chapel: Bear's grinning face as he twisted his cap in his burly hands, Aunt Maddie's smile and the happy tears in her eyes, and the wonderful hunched old preacher in flowing beard and burlap robes. Her gaze lighted at last upon Seneca, who stood watching her with what she could only think of was gladness.

My beautiful bridegroom. This must be a dream. She wanted to remain asleep until the ceremony was complete.

Maurice Sender, with the aid of a gnarled wood cane that was leaning against a short railing, ascended two steps to an altar made of cedar logs. The top was a large log, hollowed slightly, and polished as smoothly as Seneca's mantel. Lila believed Bear must have done this one as well. Sender lit two candles, fat with the drippings of other lightings. He turned around, then motioned with his free hand for them all to come forward.

Lila and Seneca came together at the foot of the small stairs, with Aunt Maddie and Bear on either side of them. This was the moment. Lila wondered if she would have a voice to repeat the vows. She tried to recall the words she'd heard at other weddings, but nothing came. Sender leaned his cane against the altar and raised both arms.

"We gather here now," he said in his scratchy voice which gradually grew in strength until it was almost richly resonant, "to join together this woman from one world," he touched Lila's chest over the place where her heart pounded. She stepped back instinctively, then stepped forward. She was not afraid of him. "And this man from another world." He touched Seneca's chest in the same place. Seneca did not move. "To create a new world," Sender finished.

The preacher paused for so long that Lila wondered if he'd fallen asleep standing up. It was only when she relaxed enough to breathe that she saw from the slight movement of his eyelids that he had paused for effect.

Sender peered at Aunt Maddie. "Is this marriage right and with your blessing?"

"Oh, yes. It is indeed," she responded, sniffing back a tear.

Sender peered at Bear. "Is this marriage right and with your blessing?"

"Yahoo!" Bear shouted and slapped his massive thigh.

Lila jumped.

"Is there anyone who can show just cause why these two should not be joined together?"

A cool breeze wafted through the open window, slamming one of the sides shut. Lila's heart stopped, freezing her blood in her veins. Would the voices of her father and Harrison permeate the heavy silence? Her taut nerves paralyzed her spine. She feared the next sound she heard would shatter her totally. Passing seconds moved like the building of one eternity upon another.

"The vows then," Sender said. Lila felt her blood begin to surge again. Sender peered up into both faces, scrutinizing first Lila and then Seneca.

Lila shivered. *Vows. Yes, there should be vows.* Did he expect her to recite them from the memory of other weddings?

"Say what you will," Sender said to her directly.

Apparently he did have those expectations. Perhaps he couldn't see to read from a Bible. If there was a Bible. Lila couldn't see one. Maurice Sender cleared his throat loudly, an obvious admonition for her to get on with the business of the ceremony.

Lila swallowed twice before speaking. "I, Lila Catherine, take thee, Seneca . . ." She looked up at him shyly, then down at her bouquet. She knew so little about him, even his middle name. If he had a middle name.

Seneca leaned toward her. "Eli. Seneca Eli," he whispered.

"Seneca Eli," she said in a broken voice, "I take thee, Seneca Eli, to be my—" Lila sucked in her top lip and turned a desperate silent question toward Aunt Maddie.

"Wedded husband," Aunt Maddie whispered, beaming and nodding her support, urging her niece along.

Lila hadn't completely forgotten the words. She simply craved once more some reassurance that she should go through with this wedding. Once those two supremely important words were uttered, she believed there was no turning back. Aunt Maddie offered no words of assurance, no hint that the wedding should stop. Her face shone with approval. Slowly Lila turned back toward Seneca.

"Wedded husband," she managed over the hard knot in her throat. "To have and to hold from this day . . . forward." She stopped speaking, feeling the need to take steadying breaths, fearing she would crumble upon vowing the next traditional lines. *To love and to cherish until death.* . . . But Maurice Sender did not give her the opportunity to say more.

"Say what you will," he said to Seneca directly.

Lila felt Seneca's hard shoulder soften next to hers. Was she imagining it, or was that a slight trembling she felt from him? She stole a glance at his face. His jaw flexed and the nerves rippled along it.

He's not going to say the vows! Lila felt a tide of sadness and relief flood over her as the realization hit her.

Seneca was not going to go through with the marriage pact.

Eleven

"I, Seneca . . ."

Every nerve and fiber in Lila slackened from the taut breaking point to a watery weakness that threatened to dissolve her. She barely heard Seneca's voice over the pounding pulse in her head.

". . . take you, Cat, to be my . . . wedded wife."

Seneca said the words in his mind before saying them into the air around them in the little island chapel. He was marrying. He'd believed he would never take a wife, yet here he was, saying the words that would bind Lila Stockdale to him, if not forever, than for as long as the marriage served a purpose. In his dreamer's heart this was not the ceremony he would have expected if he ever he did desire to marry. This was not the woman.

This was, however, the time.

"From this day through all the days we are obliged to be together as declared by spirits of wisdom." Ancient words, Seneca knew, but somehow for this moment, this marriage, they rang true.

Maurice Sender waited a long moment before speaking again. Seneca wondered if he expected more words from him or from Cat, but neither one of them said anything. He knew that for the moment neither of them knew of more to say that was appropriate.

"Is there a ring?" the wizened preacher asked.

Lila's emotions spun. *A ring. Of course, they should have thought of a ring. How would anyone believe they were married without a ring? There couldn't be a wedding without a wedding ring.* She despaired, believing all was lost.

"Yes," Seneca replied.

Lila turned her head slowly. Seneca reached inside his shirt to a small deerskin pouch that hung from a narrow leather strap around his neck. He opened it, and she saw that his hands shook as he did. He reached inside and withdrew a gold band set with two small red stones. Lila was stunned.

Seneca turned to her. "I hope it fits. My father had it made for my mother." His voice was thick.

Lila gave her bouquet of wildflowers to Aunt Maddie, then held out her trembling left hand. Seneca slipped the ring over her finger. It went on very easily—it was a bit too large.

"Don't worry," Aunt Maddie whispered. "I have the perfect piece of silk to tie around it to make it fit more securely."

Maurice Sender smiled upon Aunt Maddie, then brought their two hands together and placed his hand over the two joined ones. "This ring," he said, his voice filling the tiny chapel, "is a symbol of your pledge to yourself and to your own God and Great Spirit, wherever. He who gives it and she who wears it . . ."

Lila felt Aunt Maddie lean around her and tug Sender's sleeve.

"Yes? Something else?" Sender asked, opening his eyes and leaning closer to her. Aunt Maddie whispered in his ear, then pressed something into his hand. "I understand," Sender said. "Another symbol has been presented."

"What?" Bear whispered, but it might as well have been a shout.

Sender opened his hand and revealed a man's gold ring, which he handed to Lila. Lila turned quickly to Aunt Maddie, silently questioning her. Aunt Maddie lifted a long chain from around her neck. It was empty now. David's wedding ring. Tears welled in Lila's eyes, and she did not hold back the two that escaped. She leaned over and kissed the dear old lady's cheek. She turned back then and looked up into Seneca's face.

"Will you wear it?" she whispered, holding the ring in her open palm.

A shadow briefly darkened Seneca's eyes, and Lila's pulse quickened. She'd gone too far asking him to wear a ring. That was making this marriage much more real than it was supposed to be. She looked down and slowly closed her fingers over Aunt Maddie's precious ring.

Seneca's hand came over hers and gently opened her fingers. "Yes," he whispered and held out his left hand.

With hands trembling more than she ever had known, Lila lifted the ring and slipped it on Seneca's third finger. She couldn't get it over his large knuckle.

"Don't worry," Bear rasped. "A little bear grease will have that on in no time." He produced a small tin.

Sender gave him a nod of agreement. "Where was I? Oh, yes." He placed his hand over both of theirs. "The rings are symbols of . . . something. Let you both who give and wear the never-ending circles be reminded forever of why you married."

Seneca looked over at Lila's face at Sender's words, heavy with meaning for both of them. She did not return his gaze, but stared ahead toward the half-closed chapel window. Her bottom lip twitched. The thoughts in their heads might be different at this moment, but the subject was the same. When their hands parted, Seneca took the moment to push the greased ring over his knuckle. It fit his finger perfectly.

The preacher turned slowly and retrieved a black leather-bound book from the altar. With a forceful breath that belied the frailty of his stature, he blew a layer of dirt from the cover. Then with bony fingers he opened it and turned several pages, mottled with dampness and age, and stopped at one. He turned the volume and placed it in Seneca's hands. Again he turned slowly and retrieved the stub of a pencil which he handed to Lila.

"Sign," he instructed, thrusting the ledger toward her.

Seneca held the book toward Lila, and with a trembling hand he could feel vibrating through the volume, she signed her name.

"Sign." Sender nodded toward Seneca, who took the pencil and handed the register to Lila to hold, then complied with the instruction. His own hand shook as he wrote.

The bride and groom paused in a locked gaze over their two names written side by side. Sender reclaimed the volume and scratched something beside the line. He motioned for them to join hands.

Once again Sender placed his hand over the clasped hands of Lila and Seneca, closed his eyes, and tilted his head back.

"Let Cat and Seneca, who made these vows in the presence of beloved friends and family, and who wear the rings with the aid of silk and bear grease, know they are joined forever in their hearts and in the worlds that live within them. As to what exists without, should those separate worlds force their beings apart, let these two take solace in knowing their spirits are forever entwined."

No one moved. Sender's eyes did not open. He stood

so still under his layers of burlap that Lila could not be certain that he was still breathing. How would they know if he'd died on the spot, she wondered crazily.

"Have they kissed yet?" Sender gritted out, his voice reverting to its weakened hermit stage.

"No!" Aunt Maddie and Bear replied in unison.

"Are they going to?" Sender asked, clamping his eyes tighter.

"Yes! *Oui!*" said Aunt Maddie and Bear in unison, pushing Lila and Seneca at the shoulders.

The two turned toward each other. Lila's pulse throbbed so loudly in her ears that it drowned out the music of the birdsong. Seneca leaned down. Lila raised up on her toes. Their lips met for the split of a moment, parted, then returned to linger softly yet nervously. The contact was enough to make Seneca desire more. He felt the slight response in Cat. Abruptly he pulled away from the kiss. This was to be a marriage in name only he reminded himself.

"Yahoo!" Bear shouted and tossed his cap in the air.

"I'm so happy!" Aunt Maddie sobbed.

Maurice Sender sat down hard on the floor. His raspy voice filled the space around them. "I pronounce that these two have become one. Married. Sealed forever."

One. Married. *Sealed forever.* The words rang around the mountain chapel and mingled with the song of birds and the applause of tree leaves and branches in the escalating wind.

Lila Catherine Stockdale had just married Seneca Eli Pierce. They'd signed their names to the preacher's church register. She could still see in her mind their signatures on the yellowed page of the black leather-bound book. As Seneca's lips had softly held her own, she saw other variations on that name float by her stunned consciousness.

Lila Catherine Stockdale Pierce. Lila Stockdale Pierce. Lila Catherine Pierce. Lila Pierce. Cat Pierce.

Cat Pierce!

Seneca released her before she was ready for him to do so. The air that swept lightly between them was enough to restore her to her senses. Reluctantly she opened her eyes to gaze into those of her husband, to face the reality of her actions. She'd just been married *in front of God and these witnesses. For richer for poorer. To love. . . .* Now the words of other weddings came to her like the rush of a swollen stream.

She'd just been married. Not to Harrison Mayne, her fiancé. She'd just been married without her father walking her down the aisle. Without her father's blessing. A part of her heart was saddened over the last.

Then suddenly Bear was clapping Seneca on the back and hugging him in a grip true to his name. Aunt Maddie was weeping with a smile on her face, then sweeping Cat into her arms.

"Darling Cat, I'm so happy for you," she whispered. "Don't worry, it will all be fine. You'll see."

Cat let out her own stream of warm tears. "Oh, Aunt Maddie, I've never done such a rash thing in my whole life. I hope I haven't made a horrible mistake."

"Shh, darling. You've just made the first perfectly right decision in your whole life. Try to concentrate on that. Someday, years from now, you'll look back on this moment and be glad you did it."

"How long will I have to stay married to make it all work out right with Father?" Cat's insides churned with the stark knowledge of what would happen the moment her father heard of her marriage. The heat of his rage would be felt through the Adirondack Mountains.

Aunt Maddie returned the wedding bouquet to her

niece's trembling hands. "For the rest of your life, with any luck. And isn't that a fortunate thought? Shh, now, dear, your husband wishes for your attention. Be happy giving it all to him." She gently turned her around toward Seneca.

"I should have thought of a cake," Cat said, then realizing she'd uttered an inane statement. She laughed nervously with the rest of them.

"I have something to show you before we return to the cabin," Seneca said quietly.

Return to the cabin. Cat blanched. Returning to the cabin meant—

"Come back, come back again, anytime," Maurice invited, yet his scurrying behind them, patting each on the back, was more of a quick ushering out than an invitation to return.

When the wedding party was in the guideboat and floating down the lake once more, Cat sat across from Aunt Maddie, gripping her hands and feeling an overwhelming apprehension engulf her. Was it only fear of her father's reaction to the marriage or was it something else? Would she have felt this way if she'd married Harrison or anyone else? She wouldn't have this kind of trepidation if she'd married Harrison—there would be profound fear of something more sinister than her father's anger could ever elicit.

She slid a sidelong glance toward her new husband. He sat very straight and very still, his body rocking easily with the gentle motion of the guideboat, as if fused with the wood to navigate perfectly through the water. His jaw was hardened to a sharp angle, his piercing blue gaze focused straight ahead to the mountains.

He was fearless. Cat felt that immediately. Nothing seemed to touch him.

At first she thrilled at the thought that Seneca, her hus-

MORE PASSION AND ADVENTURE AWAIT... YOUR TRIP TO A BIG ADVENTUROUS WORLD BEGINS WHEN YOU ACCEPT YOUR FIRST 4 NOVELS ABSOLUTELY *FREE* (AN $18.00 VALUE)

Accept your Free gift and start to experience more of the passion and adventure you like in a historical romance novel. Each Zebra novel is filled with proud men, spirited women and tempestuous love that you'll remember long after you turn the last page.

Zebra Historical Romances are the finest novels of their kind. They are written by authors who really know how to weave tales of romance and adventure in the historical settings you love. You'll feel like you've actually gone back in time with the thrilling stories that each Zebra novel offers.

GET YOUR FREE GIFT WITH THE START OF YOUR HOME SUBSCRIPTION

Our readers tell us that these books sell out very fast in book stores and often they miss the newest titles. So Zebra has made arrangements for you to receive the four newest novels published each month.

You'll be guaranteed that you'll never miss a title, and home delivery is so convenient. And to show you just how easy it is to get Zebra Historical Romances, we'll send you your first 4 books absolutely FREE! Our gift to you just for trying our home subscription service.

BIG SAVINGS AND CONVENIENT HOME DELIVERY

Each month, you'll receive the four newest titles as soon as they are published. You'll probably receive them even before the bookstores do. What's more, you may preview these exciting novels free for 10 days. If you like them as much as we think you will, just pay the low preferred subscriber's price of $3.75 each. *You'll save $3.00 each month off the publisher's price.* (A postage and handling charge of $1.50 is added to each shipment.) Of course you can return any shipment within 10 days for full credit, no questions asked. There is no minimum number of books you must buy.

4 FREE BOOKS

TO GET YOUR 4 FREE BOOKS WORTH $18.00 — MAIL IN THE FREE BOOK CERTIFICATE T O D A Y

Fill in the Free Book Certificate below, and we'll send your FREE BOOKS to you as soon as we receive it.

If the certificate is missing below, write to: Zebra Home Subscription Service, Inc., P.O. Box 5214, 120 Brighton Road, Clifton, New Jersey 07015-5214.

FREE BOOK CERTIFICATE

4 FREE BOOKS

ZEBRA HOME SUBSCRIPTION SERVICE, INC.

YES! Please start my subscription to Zebra Historical Romances and send me my first 4 books absolutely FREE. I understand that each month I may preview four new Zebra Historical Romances free for 10 days. If I'm not satisfied with them, I may return the four books within 10 days and owe nothing. Otherwise, I will pay the low preferred subscriber's price of just $3.75 each; a total of $15.00, *a savings off the publisher's price of $3.00.* I may return any shipment and I may cancel this subscription at any time. There is no obligation to buy any shipment. (A postage and handling charge of $1.50 is added to each shipment.) Regardless of what I decide, the four free books are mine to keep.

NAME _____

ADDRESS _____ APT _____

CITY _____ STATE _____ ZIP _____

TELEPHONE ( ) _____

SIGNATURE _____ (if under 18, parent or guardian must sign)

Terms, offer and prices subject to change without notice. Subscription subject to acceptance by Zebra Books. Zebra Books reserves the right to reject any order or cancel any subscription.

ZB1694

GET
FOUR
FREE
BOOKS
(AN $18.00 VALUE)

ZEBRA HOME SUBSCRIPTION
SERVICE, INC.
120 BRIGHTON ROAD
P.O. Box 5214
CLIFTON, NEW JERSEY 07015-5214

band, appeared invincible. Perhaps in his shadow she would feel invincible as well. On second thought his complete calm nagged at her. There appeared to be none of the trepidation about marrying her that she felt about marrying him. He wasn't worried about being inside the cabin alone together—had no visible apprehension about their wedding night.

Suddenly Cat was consumed by a raw-nerved vulnerability she'd never before experienced. Even in the throes of Harrison's attacks upon her, she didn't feel this torn wide open. It was her unwelcoming physical body that was subject to her fiancé's attempt at forced invasions. She'd possessed the strength and the determination to fight him off then. Right now, with her marriage to Seneca Pierce only moments old, Cat felt everything about her was torn wide open to him. Her body, her mind, her emotions. Her heart. She possessed no strength, no determination to fight against him. She knew he was in complete control of her—but more, she was moved by knowing she willed him that control.

With a blinding flash of knowledge, Cat understood how life could change in the brief existence of a moment. She clutched her aunt's hands with childlike fear.

"Aunt Maddie, you'll stay the night, won't you?" Cat's own voice sounded desperate to her.

"Oh, my dear, no. It will be difficult enough to explain my absence last night. Although perhaps no one missed me. I heard your name echoing through the forest but not mine." Madeline sighed.

Cat rubbed her aunt's thin arm. "Father does care about you, Aunt Maddie. He just has a hard time showing his true feelings."

"On the contrary, I think he shows his feelings rather well," Madeline said. "It's perfectly fine with me," she added hastily. "I have no delusions of what I am to him, and he holds no delusions of what he is to me. We understand each other."

Seneca lifted an arm and pointed in the direction he wished Bear to direct the guideboat. Instantly Bear lifted his paddle out of the water. Seneca turned back to him and silently insisted his command be honored. Bear complied, rather reluctantly, Cat observed, and soon the boat touched the shore of the mainland.

Cat grew fearful. This was not Seneca's island. This was possibly close to her father's camp. "Why . . . are we stopping here? Are you making Aunt Maddie get out and leave me?"

Seneca turned toward her. His jaw and gaze softened. He spoke very quietly. "No, of course not. It's important that I show you both something very dear to me, something I want you to know about. And I must do it today."

Cat frowned. He stood and assisted her and Madeline out of the boat, then motioned for them to follow.

Bear stayed at the shore, his eyes nervously shifting around the forest. "It is too dangerous now, *mon ami*," he whispered to Seneca. Seneca dismissed the admonishment with a slight wave of his hand. The tenseness between the two men was almost palpable.

Cat followed her husband up into the forest, turning to help Madeline over tree roots and boulders. It bothered her that Seneca did not assist them, but she was rapidly beginning to understand that was his way. She was glimpsing his belief that each person makes his or her own way through life on their own steam, in the very way they were climbing up the gentle side of a mountain.

They reached a summit, having had to stop often to allow Madeline to rest. Cat, too, was breathless from the exertion. She felt a vague sense of having been here before. And she knew why immediately when she saw the stone mounds topped by the chunks of pink granite. She'd rested here right before Harrison had attacked her.

Seneca stopped.

Cat's gaze swept the clearing. "What . . . what is this place? Why did you bring us here?"

Seneca touched the pink granite rock nearest him. "This is the burial ground of my mother and sister and my grandparents."

Cat let out a quiet "Oh," and Madeline tipped her head reverently as if in prayer.

"I wanted them to meet my wife and her beloved aunt," Seneca said, holding his gaze on the stone mounds. Then he turned and looked directly at Cat. "And I wanted you to know that my family is as much a part of these mountains as are the forests and lakes and animals."

Cat nodded. "I think I am beginning to understand," she whispered.

"I wish that to be so," he returned. He shifted his gaze back to the graves, reaching out and placing one hand gently on the granite stone atop his mother's grave.

Madeline stepped close to Cat and touched her arm. Cat leaned her head against the top of the old lady's hair. "I want to understand," she said to no one in particular. "I want to learn."

She stepped away from her aunt then and, with a great deal of soul-wrenching decision, reached out and placed her hand over Seneca's on his mother's grave. He flinched under her touch but did not withdraw his hand. Neither did he look at her.

Overcome with emotion, Cat walked slowly away from the graves and from the others. She needed to think more clearly than she ever had before, think on the consequences of her actions. For whatever the surface reasons, she'd taken a husband. She'd broken one vow to herself to voice new vows to another. So much for her vocal conviction to Evalina and Aunt Maddie that she'd never take a husband. For her underlying personal reasons, she was frightened. She could never let Seneca know he was the man of her dreams—he was the man she knew with whom she would fall deeply, irrevocably in love. Her love for this man would break her heart someday. She knew it. But she wouldn't let him know it. He was doing her a favor, that was all. She couldn't let him feel trapped.

Yet he'd taken her to the graves of his family. She must mean something to him if he could do that. She wished she could believe that she did mean something to him but knew she must not entertain those thoughts if she were to remain coolheaded for the next few days.

She wandered toward a grassy hummock at the edge of a bright green meadow, her thoughts heading straight toward her wedding night. Would he expect his conjugal rights? Or would he remain the gentleman he'd been up to now? With a blinding thought Cat knew she wanted him to exercise his conjugal rights.

"Oh, dear," she wailed to herself. "I am shameless. Perhaps I do want him to feel trapped."

She stepped out onto the grassy meadow, needing to see the expanse of sky, feel the wind. Without any warning she sank into mud over her ankles. "Oh!" she cried out. She tried to turn back, but with every step she sank deeper. She lifted one foot and the mud sucked off the moccasin. Seneca's mother's moccasin! She couldn't lose it. She bent over and, grimacing, plunged her hand down into the muck and retrieved the moccasin. She tried to move again and lost her balance. Down she went into the water and mud. The other moccasin came off.

"Help! Help me!" she called out. Desperately she fought

to find the other moccasin. For the moment she thought of nothing else except to retrieve it. She was relieved when her fingers closed over it.

The more she flailed, the deeper she seemed to go. How could this be? Was she locked in a nightmare? All she'd done was walk onto a cool green meadow. Was it all a dream's symbolism? She'd walked down the aisle of an island church to become Seneca Pierce's wife, and now she would sink in the quagmire of sham. Was that it?

"Cat?" Seneca's voice came to her. She saw him over the muddy wake of her entrance into this meadow. He stood on the dry hummock. "Don't move."

She watched him step carefully around the edge of bright green grasses. He moved quickly, stepping on unseen firm ground. Cat marveled at his agility, his knowing sense of where to step. Soon he was close enough to reach out to her.

"I . . . I saved your mother's moccasins," she said weakly, holding them up for him to see.

He took them from her hand and flung them onto dry land, then reached back for her. "Take my hand and hold on." She grasped tightly and he pulled hard. "Give me your other hand," he instructed.

With great effort she dragged her arm out of the mud and reached for him. Pain shot through her shoulder where the arrow wound was still healing, but she hung on to him with all the strength she could muster. Firmly, smoothly, he pulled her toward him. As the mud on her face dried, she could see the concern in his eyes. He was actually worried about her!

As she neared the edge, she raised to her knees. He leaned down and slipped his arms under hers and lifted her to her feet.

"Are you hurt?" He tried to wipe mud and grass from her face.

"My pride more than anything, I think," she managed. "I don't know how I could have done such a stupid thing."

"Don't berate yourself. You probably couldn't have known about the bog."

"Bog?" Cat turned around and looked at the lovely grassy meadow that had turned into an oozing wet trap. She saw the surge of mud and weeds where she'd struggled to get out. "I must have been daydreaming. I never saw it."

"It's not your fault. You never would have expected it. See? It looks just like a field. You're not the first to have fallen into one of these. It's nature's way of keeping humans humble."

"You didn't fall in." She looked down at his moccasins. "In fact, you're almost completely dry." She swayed.

He caught and steadied her. "I know where to walk. Only Indians and trappers who've spent years on these mountains know how to get around these things." He pulled her close to lean on him. "Can you walk?"

"I think so."

"Mon ami!" Bear's harsh whisper came from below the trees. "Someone comes! Hurry!"

Seneca whirled and grabbed up his moccasins from where they'd dropped. They hurried back through the trees to the grave site. He stood in front of Madeline, urging her to climb up onto his back. With Cat's assistance, she did so without question. He sent a sharply commanding look to Cat to follow and started down the summit as easily and swiftly as a deer. Cat tried to negotiate the crevices, boulders, and tree roots, but the soles of her feet were tender, the ground slippery, and her knowledge of mountain navigation naught. And she was frightened out of her wits. She turned her ankle, slipped, and started to fall down the mountainside.

In a flash, Seneca, barefoot now and without Aunt Maddie, was helping her up and silently commanding her to climb onto his back. Cat winced as a pain shot through her shoulder when he pulled her up over him. He bore her down the mountain to the shore as if she were no more than the weight of his ash pack basket. Aunt Maddie was crouched down in the bow of the boat, holding Seneca's moccasins. Bear had shoved off. Seneca entered the water as soundlessly as possible. Bear reached out and grabbed Cat and pulled her into the boat, indicating she was to sit on the floor. Cat did not look up, fearing she would see her father or Harrison crash through the trees.

In the next instant Seneca was beside her, had grabbed another paddle, and he and Bear propelled them swiftly and soundlessly away from the mainland.

They took a silent cursory trail around the lake, among small islands, past a stand of swamp ghosts, flooded trees bare of bark and bleached by the sun. They said nothing until a sense of safety permeated the air around them. Once they alighted on Seneca's island and Bear had pulled the boat into a hiding place of thick trees and brush, a certain measure of relief could be felt among all of them.

Inside the cabin Seneca busied himself making coffee.

Madeline sipped the hot brew thoughtfully. Seneca admired her way of thinking through her thoughts before voicing them. His mother would have liked Cat's aunt, he knew that instinctively.

"I think it's time for me to go back to camp," Madeline said, a slight frown pleating the bridge of her nose.

"I will take you," Bear announced.

"I don't think you should," Madeline told him. "You

will be questioned. They will demand that you tell them where Seneca is, and hence where Cat is."

"Do not worry, madame. I have never told before, and I have ways of avoiding truth when necessary. And this is necessary."

"What will you tell Father, Aunt Maddie?" Cat's worried voice put words to her anguished face. "What are you going to tell him about me?"

"I will do as you ask, dear. But in the interest of your safety, and Seneca's, I think it's best he doesn't know about the marriage for some time."

Cat nodded, understanding the value in her aunt's words. She slumped with an attitude of defeat. Seneca waited for her response, struck more strongly than ever by how much he did not know about the woman he'd married. How would she react to this? Would she give in to her father? How much time would they have before Garrett Stockdale found them and exacted his own revenge? Seneca knew the intensity of the impact this marriage would have upon Stockdale. And he also knew Stockdale was powerful enough to find a means to destroy him and all that he'd vowed to defend.

"Remember the time," Cat started suddenly, thoughtfully, "when Evalina and I took the train all by ourselves to Miss Bolton's School the summer we were sixteen? Evalina's mother wanted to send us both to that strict boarding school in Connecticut. We hated the idea. We loved Miss Bolton and the school. We thought if we went to Miss Bolton's on our own, they'd see that it was important to us, and we'd show that we were mature enough to make our own decisions."

"Yes, dear, but I don't see how that has any bearing on any of this, and—"

"We just took it into our heads to do it, remember?

Father was furious that I'd done such a rash thing, but later he said he thought it was good for me. Miss Bolton's was quiet and a safe place for me to think about what he'd planned for my life."

Madeline leaned across the table and took Cat's hand. "Dear, I have to leave. It's getting late. What do you want me to tell your father? Or should I just let him go on searching?"

"No, you can't do that. It wouldn't be fair to him. I'm certain he's worried sick right now. But don't you see, Aunt Maddie? If you tell Father I decided to go to Miss Bolton's again to think, he won't worry anymore and he'll give up the search. I hate to ask you to lie for me, but could you, just this once?"

Madeline laughed lightly. "You know very well my little lies for you have been many more times than 'just this once,' and some of them were not so little. I see the merit in what you're saying. But will he possibly believe you could get yourself from here down to North Creek to the train station and then on to Miss Bolton's? You know how treacherous the journey was coming up here."

"*Oui,* madame, that is easy." Bear thumped his coffee mug on the table. "I will take you back to the camp and say that I took you both to North Creek and then brought you back."

"Splendid, yes," Madeline responded. "Of course, you must say we paid you to transport us. Garrett would never believe anyone does anything without payment."

"*Oui,* and handsomely, I'll say!" Bear laughed heartily.

"Not too handsomely," Madeline warned. "Garrett believes I have no real funds of my own." She turned toward Cat. "He will ask when you plan to return to camp."

Cat sucked in her bottom lip in thought. "Of course he

will. Tell him . . . tell him I won't return to camp. I will see him when he returns to the city."

"All right," Madeline agreed.

"Now, whatever will you do about Harrison? I think you should avoid him as much as possible."

"I'd prefer it that way, anyway. I do think I shall let him know merely by look that I am aware of what he did to you. Perhaps that might keep him in line long enough for you to find a way to convince Garrett that you will not marry Harrison and why."

Lila leaned over and hugged her tightly. "Father will be very angry with you, Aunt Maddie." She caught sight of the big woodsman standing apart from them. "And I shudder to think what he might do to you, Bear. You will have to be very careful."

"Don't worry about us," Madeline told her resolutely, breaking gently from the circle of Cat's arms. "I can handle Garrett for me *and* for Bear. I'm stronger than I look when it comes to the people I love." She rose. "Shall we be off then, Bear?"

"Adieu it is!" Bear was up and out the door before anyone could say another word. He was back inside a second later, swiping his cap from his head and bowing low. "Much happiness to you, Monsieur and Madame Pierce. I shall return in a week to see what you're doing . . . ah, to see if you need anything, that is." His ruddy face grew ruddier, and he slapped his cap back on his head and banged out the door.

Seneca remained silent throughout the entire exchange except for the cheerful "Adieu!" he sent toward Bear's retreating back. This would be a difficult moment for Cat and Madeline, and he wanted to afford them some time alone. He strolled quietly to the door.

"I'll go down to the shore to help Bear with the boat. Whenever you're ready, Miss Madeline, we'll shove off."

"Thank you, Seneca. Wait." Madeline moved quickly to his side. She leaned up on tiptoes to try to kiss him. Seneca was obliged to bend down to meet her petite frame. "I trust you with my precious niece's life, Seneca. I know you won't fail either of us."

Seneca gave her a strong hug and felt the sweat of instant remorse dot his brow. He wished only for Madeline's happiness and safety, whatever would ensue in the coming weeks, possibly months. But he knew he might have a hand in causing her sadness and distress. He gazed deeply into her expressive eyes for a long time. Then he turned and went out to catch up with Bear.

Cat and Madeline stood facing one another, hands clasped. The old lady's eyes shone with tears. "I shall miss you so very much, darling Cat."

Cat held back a sob. "Oh, Aunt Maddie, how can I ever live without you?"

"You will get along quite well, my dear. Don't forget you are made of as much Christopher stuff as you are Stockdale. Be proud of who you are, and be happy over this marriage."

"I feel as if I will never see you again." Cat felt and sounded like the child she was when her mother died.

"Now don't say that. We will find a way to be together from time to time." Madeline clasped her into her thin arms.

"It won't be the same." Cat swallowed heart-wrenching sobs.

"No, I'm afraid it won't," Aunt Maddie said wistfully, "but it would have happened sooner or later."

Cat was wracked by profound sadness. Aunt Maddie was old, frail. She couldn't live in the harsh and loveless environment of her father's home. She would wither away and . . . die. Oh, God! She couldn't lose Aunt Maddie! She leaned back.

"Maybe we could have Bear tell Father you went with me to Miss Bolton's. That way you could stay here, you'd never have to go back to him. We could still be together. What do you say, Aunt Maddie? Stay here with me. It won't be so bad in a mountain cabin. And it might not have to be for very long, just long enough to—"

"No, dear, that's not possible. You have a new husband now. You must be together . . . alone."

Cat peered into her aunt's now weary eyes. "You know we're not . . . you know this isn't a conventional marriage."

"Yes, I do, and I'm most grateful for that knowledge."

Cat frowned. "I don't know what you mean."

Madeline bustled about, gathering up her bag and other belongings. "Never mind, dear. Now say no more. Garrett would not believe anything Bear said anyway without me there to back it up. You know that. With luck we will see each other again. Perhaps sooner than you think. I will do my best to get your father to relent. And I will get messages to you as often as possible. Soon it will be safe to return home—with your husband." Madeline leaned up and kissed Cat's cheek. "And now I must go. Bear will be anxious to have me back to camp before dusk."

The two women walked with arms around each other's waists to the door. They stepped out into the sun-warmed air. Around them leaves rustled and tall pines groaned, swaying in the breeze.

"Take extra good care, Aunt Maddie."

"And you, dearest Cat."

The two parted. Cat sucked in a shaky breath. "Oh,

dear, what about Evalina? I forgot. What will you tell her?"

"The same thing I tell your father. Evalina's a dear, but she cannot hold her tongue on important matters."

"I know. I'm sorry for that. She's my closest friend in all the world, except for you."

"It is safer this way," Aunt Maddie said. "I must go."

Cat embraced Madeline as if it were the last time they would ever touch one another. She had a foreboding sense that it might be, and she wanted to hold the dear old lady and the moment for as long as she could. Aunt Maddie pushed gently away, then headed down the path toward the shore.

Cat sensed Seneca's return to the cabin even though she did not hear his footfalls. When the door opened, her pulse pounded erratically. He stepped inside, still in his wedding garb.

"They got off all right," he told her.

"That's good." She stood at the far end of the room, still clad in her wedding dress.

He cleared the table of the coffee mugs and set them by a wooden water bucket on the sideboard.

"We'll be getting a storm in a day or two."

"Oh."

She picked up the wedding bouquet Bear had fashioned for her. It was drooping sadly. "I'd better get these in water."

"Yes." He found a jar on a bottom shelf and gave it to her.

"Will they get back to camp before dark?"

"They should."

"That's good."

Seneca walked to a bench by the fireplace and sat down. Cat watched as he removed the moccasins, picked up a soft cloth near the wood box, and began to clean them with a meticulous hand. He carefully went over the beads with one finger wrapped in the cloth. He brushed lightly on the bottoms until all traces of dirt were gone. Then he wrapped them in a different cloth and placed them in a low cupboard at the end of the cabin.

"If you'll give me your moccasins, I'll clean them and put them away," he said as he stood and turned around.

Cat caught a glimpse of his astonished expression when he saw that she was doing the same thing, seated on the balsam and blanket bed with his mother's wedding moccasins. When she was finished she handed them to him.

Their fingers brushed. Lingered. Parted. She flashed a look up at him once. He averted his eyes. She watched him take the moccasins, wrap them in a matching cloth, and set them beside the others in the cupboard. When he'd finished he turned slowly. She shifted her gaze quickly to the small window over the sideboard.

"It gets dark early," she observed.

"Yes." He ascended the ladder to the sleeping loft.

Cat sat motionless until she heard him return to the ladder. She observed him as he descended. He'd changed into canvas trousers, and a cream rough-napped shirt that moved over his shoulders and back with the rhythm of his lowering body. She felt a sudden urge to place both hands upon that back and feel the power of his muscle and sinew beneath them. Restless in her lap, her fingers twitched with desire. When he turned around to face her, she felt the heat of color spread over her chest and up her throat to burn her cheeks. She lowered her eyes and studiously brushed at the wedding skirt she still wore, fussed with and unnecessarily smoothed the finely sewn lace.

There was a need to plunge into something and get it over with. She felt a stab of pain the moment the words left her lips.

"I can't cook."

"I'm not hungry."

"I thought you might be. There was no wedding feast."

He inclined his head. "You sound disappointed."

"Maybe a little."

"Don't worry. I'm certain you'll have one for your next wedding, your real one. Probably a big white sticky cake, too."

It wasn't a cutting remark, Cat was certain of that. It bothered her nevertheless. "I doubt that. Divorced women don't have big weddings the second time. Even if there were to be a second time."

"Perhaps society would make an exception in your case."

"Perhaps."

He pulled on a canvas coat. "I'm going out hunting for a little while. Is there anything I can do for you before I go?"

"No, I don't think so." Her gaze locked with his.

He stood for a long moment, then averted his eyes, grabbed the door latch and didn't look at her. "You'll probably be asleep when I return. I . . . I won't disturb you. I'll go to the loft." He pulled open the door, stepped outside, and gently closed it after him.

Cat lay back on the bed. *My wedding night.* There were things a new husband and wife did on their wedding night. But this wasn't the usual kind of wedding night. It hadn't been the usual kind of wedding. And this would not be the usual kind of marriage.

There would be another wedding night for her someday. Maybe.

A real wedding night.
A real marriage.
If she wanted one. Maybe she did. Maybe she didn't.
Maybe.
Maybe not.

Twelve

Cat opened her eyes. An eerie gray-white light illuminated one corner of the cabin. Morning. Early morning. She lifted her shoulders off the bed and leaned back on her elbows. Quiet. So quiet. And cold. She felt dampness over her skin and on the blanket. Where was Seneca? Perhaps he was still sleeping. She couldn't hear anything, and it was certainly quiet enough to hear him breathing, just as she'd heard Aunt Maddie's breathing several hours before. So much had happened in those last hours.

She sat up and shivered as the cold air swept over her naked back. Her shoulder still ached, but less so, and she could feel a tingling around the wound. Under the blankets she rubbed her ankle, which was tender from her slide down the mountainside after the wedding. Her bare feet felt cold under her hands.

The gray-white light was slowly beginning to turn a rosy gold as the sun broke through the tree cover. Cat felt groggy, fuzzy-headed, as if she'd consumed too much champagne. But there'd been no wedding champagne. It must be the mountains, she decided. At night the air was cold and crisp and brought on a quick deep sleep. By day the sun was warm, then hot, and brought on the memory of dreams from the night before.

She hadn't slept very deeply the night before. She knew

when Seneca returned, heard him walk through the cabin, climb the ladder, and lay down on something. And she remembered the sound of a drenching rain banging the roof. She must have slept after that, but this morning she didn't feel as if she had. She should get dressed. It was too cold. There was too much to think about. She slid back under the blankets and pulled them up around her, then rolled to her side and drew her knees up. Something about the balsam and cedar in the mattress soothed her. The aroma was somehow satisfying. She closed her eyes.

The cabin door burst open. Lila went rigid under the blankets, eyes wide.

"Good morning, Mrs. Pierce."

Mrs. Pierce. His calling her that was as if he'd thrown a pail of cold water into her face, and it stunned her so she couldn't answer.

"Sleep well?" Seneca's voice was overly cheery as he strode into the cabin with an armload of short logs and branches and a burlap bag. He dropped the bag first, then set the logs down in front of the fireplace. He stood and brushed his palms together to rid them of bark chunks.

He'd pulled his hair back, and it hung over his shoulder in a thick braid tied with a rawhide lace. Cat marveled that he wasn't wearing a coat over the shirt he'd changed into the night before. Didn't he ever feel the cold and dampness?

He turned a bright face upon her, then slid his gaze around the room. "What, no breakfast ready?"

Cat narrowed her eyes. What in the world was he doing? He was so different from the way he was up until yesterday. Their wedding day. Their sham wedding day. He was not behaving in the manner of the man she'd married—the still, serene man on the surface who possessed controlled power on the inside.

"I told you last night, I can't cook," she said warily from under the blanket.

"I wasn't hungry then, so it didn't matter. I'm hungry now. No time like the present for you to learn. Up, woman! You can't lie abed all morning. This is the best time of the day. There's a wife's work to do."

Cat sucked in a breath. *Wife? Oh, God, wife!* "I . . . my shoulder hurts, and my ankle is swollen."

"They'll get better with use. If you don't move them, they'll stiffen up and it will be a long time before they heal."

"I don't have anything to wear."

"Right there." Seneca pointed to a pile of clothes on the floor at the foot of the bed.

Cat peered over the top of the blanket. "Those? I can't wear those." She stared at the trousers and shirt.

"You wore them the other night when your aunt and Bear cooked supper. They were all right then."

"They were all I had then."

"They're all you have now. Think of them as your trousseau."

"My trou—" She sighed and dropped her head back. No point in fighting about the clothing. She knew her other things were in no shape to wear. And he was going to insist upon her getting up now, wasn't he? "Is the coffee ready?" she asked sweetly.

"Did you put it on?" Seneca asked just as sweetly and looked over his shoulder toward the cookstove.

"Me?"

"There's no one else here."

"What about you?"

"I had to go out and get us something for supper. Worked up a big appetite. It's a great morning!" He pounded his chest like a zoo gorilla.

"Did you go over to the mainland?"

"What for?"

"Why, to buy something for dinner, of course."

Seneca laughed. *"Buy* something. I don't know what happened overnight to you, but you're not in the city, wifey dear, you're in the mountains. We don't buy dinner. We hunt it and bag it." He gestured toward the burlap sack on the floor. "There it is."

Cat leaned up and peered around him at the sack. "There what is?"

"Supper. Or dinner, if you prefer. Rabbits."

"Rabbits!" Cat fell back against the mattress, horrified. "How awful!"

"What do you mean . . . awful? I took great pains to get young ones for you so they'd be very tender. You don't sound at all grateful."

"Grateful! You killed baby rabbits and you expect me to eat them?" she shrieked.

"They're not babies. I wouldn't do that. I just avoided the old rabbits. They're very tough. I did this for you. We have to eat, you know."

Cat suddenly remembered the incident on the train journey north. Along the railroad track she'd seen a huge black crow devouring a rabbit. She remembered Evalina's shock and disgust, and the cool way she herself had talked about it being dinner for the bird. Now as she stared horrified at the bag filled with dead rabbits—then darted her gaze up to Seneca, who stood like a mighty hunter with crow-black hair—a sense of primal existence rolled over her like a mountain boulder in the force of a glacial melt.

"Eat," she said dully. At least he didn't sound as if he expected her to eat rabbits for breakfast.

"Think of it as hasenpfeffer from Delmonico's."

"Hasenpfeffer?"

"Rabbit stew. Same thing."

"No!"

"Yes. Don't tell me you didn't know they serve rabbit stew at Delmonico's?"

"They wouldn't. How—?"

"You don't really want me to tell you how Delmonico's gets rabbits and cooks them, now do you?"

Cat didn't say anything. She saw him watching her silent struggle, felt inadequate and vulnerable. "I'll get dressed now," she said at last.

"Good. I'll make the coffee this time, but it's up to you next time."

"Aren't you going to go back outside . . . or something?"

"What for?"

"So I can dress."

"I'm not stopping you from dressing."

"The privacy curtain is gone."

"I needed a blanket last night."

"Then you'll have to go outside so I can dress."

"No need for that. Did you forget I'm your husband?"

Cat's face burned. What was he doing to her? "How could I forget that? I remember very well."

"Oh, I see now," Seneca said as if he'd come to a new revelation. "You're inviting me to our marriage bed at last." He started toward her.

Her stomach clutched. "I—I didn't mean that at all."

Seneca stopped. "All right." He turned and began preparing coffee.

Cat's ego was burning more than her face. He certainly gave up rather easily. Didn't he find her desirable now that she was his wife? What had it meant to him when he'd kissed her so passionately the night before their wedding? Yes, it was true, this was a marriage of protection for her, but she'd expected she'd have to fend off his advances. After all, he was a man. She watched him moving about the table and cookstove. Oh, yes, he was a man, the most completely primitive masculine man she'd ever seen. Being near him unnerved her. She should be glad he didn't make advances toward her. That way she wouldn't have to defend her honor in so base a way as she'd had to with Harrison. She should be glad of that. Shouldn't she?

"I have to fetch water," Seneca said abruptly. He picked up a pail and left the cabin.

Cat watched his departure. Hastily she pushed out from under the blankets into the chilled air and snatched up the pile of clothes.

Seneca took his time getting water. He knew Cat would be up and dressed and have taken care of morning personal activities by the time he returned. It was a good thing. If he'd had to stand there any longer, knowing she was naked under his blankets, he'd have stripped off his clothes and dove into the bed with her. She wouldn't have escaped the immediacy of his desire for her, and he knew he wouldn't have stopped until he'd spent himself inside her. He longed for her to want him. He longed to give her physical pleasure, longed to watch her exquisite features lose their controlled perfection as her senses became lost in total abandonment to his playing over her body.

He had to stop thinking about it. This was not part of his life's plan, this marriage, this woman. He had greater visions to keep clear in his mind, had to control the breadth of complication this temporary marriage could evoke. Besides he was not part of her life's plan either—he knew that and he should be thankful. They both knew why Cat had married him. Strictly to prevent her father from forcing her marriage to Harrison Mayne. But only he knew why he married Cat. Strictly for business and protection of the mountains. At least that was what he kept reminding himself over and over.

Yet he couldn't help challenging her. He knew she'd never lifted a finger at home when it came to taking care of basic necessities like food, clothing, shelter. All of that had been performed by her parents or hired servants. He hated that about the wealthy. They turned women into helpless creatures who had to be taken care of, pampered, decorated, catered to. There was nothing self-sufficient about them.

He looked up into the morning sky. It was bright, but he sensed a building summer rainstorm in the air. He'd have to be certain that one loose spot in the roof was secure and bring in some dry firewood. Cat wouldn't know how to keep the place dry and warm. And she was probably afraid of thunder and lightning.

He thought of his mother then and his young sister. There was nothing they couldn't do for themselves. They could take care of a house, that was true, but they could also build it first. They could cook a rabbit or deer or fish, but they could hunt and kill and dress it first. When a man took such a woman for a wife, he had a partner. She might depend upon him for some things once they were married, she should even expect that. But a man could depend on her as well, and he could expect that. Not so with a woman like Lila Cat Stockdale.

Cat Pierce. His wife.

He couldn't stop himself from teasing her and watching her squirm. Yet if she were to survive in this world without the protection of a real husband or her father, there were things she had to know whether she wanted to learn them or not. But that wasn't any reason for him to take on the role of her teacher. They wouldn't be together very long anyway. The most they could do was learn to live together without too much difficulty.

He could stay away from the cabin for long stretches at a time. Maybe move in with Bear for a while. Oh, he'd have to check on Cat from time to time, just to make certain she was all right. But there was no reason they had to spend every hour of every day in one another's presence. None at all. The arrangement was temporary, and Seneca knew he could get through any experience easily, knowing it was temporary.

When he returned to the cabin, he found her dressed and sitting at the table. Waiting. She wasn't waiting for him, exactly. She was waiting for him to serve breakfast. The idea annoyed him. He guessed he was going to have to play teacher after all, at least for one day, if he was going to maintain his equilibrium in this arrangement. He couldn't leave her here defenseless. Tomorrow he'd go to Bear's place.

After four days of playing teacher to Cat's unwilling student, Seneca began to feel a new kind of weariness. He'd patiently taught her how to start a fire in the fireplace. She'd set the sleeve of his shirt she was wearing to smoldering and he'd plunged her arm into a bucket of water. He'd learned something himself. Always keep water handy if Cat was anywhere near the slightest flame.

He'd taught her to kindle the cookstove as well, but she hadn't quite mastered the art of controlling the fire. A few overcooked stews and soups, with piles of burnt sludge fixed firmly in the bottoms of the pots that she'd had to scrub was a better teacher than he was. The morning coffee was a special project all by itself. First she made it too weak, then she made it too strong. When he complained of either result, he could count on it being the opposite the next morning.

Cat tired easily at first, but after a while she'd seemed more agreeable to grasping his teachings and even stoically sustained cuts, bruises, and scrapes. He'd plied her with herbs and ointments and explained the properties of each. She'd been eager to learn about that and took to it easily.

They'd worked through a heavy rain and kept dry and then fought a fierce thunder and lightning storm and held the cabin secure. He observed she wasn't frightened of lightning at all.

"Isn't it glorious?" she said, leaning against the doorframe, her arms crossed over her chest as she stared off across the jagged Adirondack peaks. Lightning sliced through the gray-indigo sky in sharp angles, making a last show of its power.

From the back of the cabin, Seneca walked up behind her. "It is that," he said thickly. The storm was passing and, as they stood together and waited out its last heaving breath, he saw how flushed with exhilaration she appeared.

"I don't think I've ever experienced the power of nature quite so profoundly as I have these last few days in the mountains." Her voice held a note of awe. "Have you always understood it, felt that way?"

"Probably not as a very young child. I learned very much from my mother and grandparents and from my father."

"Then I think it must be that we are taught to appreciate the gifts and wonder of the natural world around us. If we have nothing to compare our daily life to, then we take it all for granted, don't we?" Cat rushed her words as if a revelation had overtaken her, and she had to get it out into the air around her so she could hold on to it. "We have to be taught. To think that so many intelligent people go through life not knowing about all of this. I mean, it's not exactly that they haven't heard the mountains exist, is it? It's just that they don't *know* how they exist, what they are, what a human being is among them." She turned back to him. "Am I making any sense, or has this perfect air made me a bit daft?"

Her smile was as bright as the retreating flash of lightning. Her features were soft, free of any artificial enhancement. Her eyes were alive with life. Seneca appreciated the beautiful change in her. He knew he would remember this time later as the very moment he fell in love with his wife.

After that stormy day Cat's willingness to learn knew no bounds. Each new thing he taught her she took to like a duckling to water. He had to smile to himself about it. He actually enjoyed teaching her, but more he loved the way she reveled in learning.

Never once did she mention her father or her fiancé.

At the close of each day, Seneca thought on when was the best time for him to start over to Bear's place. Short of hunting small game, Cat had learned enough to sustain herself for a while. Her patience with fishing would have to be cultivated, but she'd grasped enough about edible plants and cooking the meat he brought in to keep from starving. Just as he was close to moving to Bear's cabin as he'd vowed he would do, he'd think of something else Cat should know in order to keep herself safe, and he'd stay to show her how. He'd spent long hours in the early night outside of the cabin. He walked the shore, gazed at the moon, listened to the thunder rolling through the distant mountains, watched the lights across the lake at Prospect House fade out one by one. Anything to stay away while Cat prepared for bed.

Early in the morning he took care of his other business—anything to stay away when Cat awoke and dressed. He fought to keep his mind off her. That's when he did his best work on his own plans.

His latest survey drawings were almost complete. He'd contact Garrett Stockdale within the month. By that time several miles of track would be laid, and the crew would be waiting for the next set of instructions. And by the time Stockdale got back to New York, he'd know Cat had lied to him. Then when Seneca told Stockdale he'd married his daughter, he knew the old man would go into a rage. That's when Seneca would say he'd leave her if Stockdale's company complied with Seneca's directives on the laying of train track. That finished, he'd have achieved what he set out to do—save his family land, save that part of the Adirondacks and keep it wild. The winning of that war would taste sweet.

And the personal battle over his escalating feelings for Cat would come to a bitter end. He knew that, too. Not necessarily the way he wanted them to end. But he had no choice.

Cat was dressed in an ill-matched combination of Seneca's blue shirt and her green skirt which he'd mended and washed the bloodstains from until they were dark shadows. She wore a pair of his thick socks on her feet. There was no mirror in the cabin, so she could only imagine how her hair must look. Aunt Maddie had left a small comb for her to use, but it was too flimsy to get through her thick hair. And she must be pale as a ghost without her pomades, powder, and rouge. She wondered what Seneca thought of her looks now. He probably didn't even notice.

She'd straightened her bed and the coffee bubbled on the stove when Seneca came through the door.

"Good morning," she greeted him brightly.

"Good morning." He sniffed the air. "The coffee smells right." He set a basket of vegetables and berries on the sideboard, then went to the back of the room to change his shirt.

"Thank you," Cat said shyly, secretly glad for the compliment.

Her heart never failed to slam against her chest when he entered the room. He filled the space with his massive defined frame, his chiseled features, thick black hair. The moment she saw him she sought out his eyes, attempting to read in their sky-blue depths what he was feeling.

She could see something weary in them this morning. No doubt he was growing tired of teaching her everything about basic survival. She had to admit she'd hated the whole idea at first. Her hands had grown rough, her nails broken, her muscles ached. But her ankle had lost its tenderness, and her shoulder had healed so well that she hardly felt it anymore, even if she did wish Seneca would massage it again with wintergreen oil.

It was her thoughts which were still sensitive. She thought of Aunt Maddie constantly—wondered how she handled Father and if he believed her. And she wondered what Harrison was doing and saying, only as it applied to Seneca.

"There's a big storm coming this way," Seneca told her as he walked toward the table, buttoning his shirt.

"Oh," she said with disappointment. "I was hoping to get out and go for a walk today. I feel so cooped up. I'd like to learn more about the plants and herbs you use for medicine, and I'd like to see more of the island."

"I think you'll have time to go out if you do it this

morning right after breakfast. I've brought some bacon from the smokehouse." He searched in the bottom of the basket and retrieved a chunk of dark red pork and proceeded to slice it thickly.

"Do . . . do you think you could come with me? I don't want to get lost or something." She rubbed her hands nervously up and down the flour sack she had tied around her middle for an apron.

She heard him let out a breath through his nostrils before speaking. "I guess so. I was going to try to get us some fish for supper."

"I'll have to stay away from the shore, or I'll scare them away. I know I must look a fright."

He laughed. "You won't scare them."

She tilted her head. Was that a compliment? "I won't?"

"No."

"Why not?" She knew she was fishing herself.

"They're too busy looking for food."

Cat burned. "Well, thank fortune for that. I wouldn't want them to swim frantically away because of the great monster I'd seem looming over the water." She picked up the heavy iron skillet and slammed it onto the cookstove.

Seneca dropped the knife on the sideboard. "What happened? Did you drop the skillet?"

"No, I didn't drop the skillet." Cat slapped some preserved bacon grease into the skillet and watched it melt. She dragged over a large heavy bowl of pancake batter, scraping it loudly across the side of the stove.

"What's wrong? Are you angry at me?"

Cat slapped a ladle of batter into the sizzling grease. "Now what could I possibly be angry at you about?"

"I don't know, but ever since I mentioned going fishing you've—"

"Don't worry, I won't go fishing with you. Wouldn't

want to terrorize the wildlife. I'd probably have to fend off the crows, however, who'll find me as attractive as railroad bed carrion."

"What?" He lifted a griddle onto the stove and laid out the bacon strips.

"You heard me."

He looked over at her. "What's this all about?"

"As if you didn't know!" She slapped another ladle of batter into the grease, then jumped back as it splattered.

"Well, I don't know. You'd better flip that first pancake. It's getting dry and black around the edges."

"Just like me," she snapped. "Worse than fish bait."

The bacon started snapping, too. Seneca took a long fork and spread the pieces with obvious escalating aggravation. "The fire's too hot again. You've got to—oh, never mind." He opened the stove and shook the cook fire. "What is all this nonsense about fish bait?"

"Nonsense, is it? So that's what you think."

"About what?" He ran a frustrated hand through the top of his hair.

Cat flipped over both pancakes. They were burnt to a char. She threw down the flipper and burst into tears. Then she ran to the bed and threw herself facedown on the blankets.

"What's wrong?" he said from the stove. "Don't worry about the pancakes. I don't mind them burnt. Gives them a different taste."

"Be quiet!" Cat yelled into the blankets. She felt like a child who'd overreacted to something trivial, and she hated that returning feeling. During these last few days in the cabin with Seneca, she'd transformed herself into the woman she knew she could be. Now, flinging herself onto the bed with flowing tears, it was as if his lack of a simple compliment shrank all the growing she'd accomplished.

She was embarrassed, and she was as angry at herself for needing a compliment as she was at him for not offering one. She wished he'd go outside and do whatever it was he did out there. Go fishing. Something.

But he didn't. She heard him scraping the griddle and skillet over the stove. Then she felt him kneel down on the mattress.

"Cat, whatever is my fault here, I'm sorry. Tell me what I can do to help." His voice was soothing, gentle.

"You can't help this," she sobbed.

"What? I know, you miss your family. You want to go home. I'll take you whenever you want to go."

"No!"

"Tell me what it is. I'll do what I can to fix it."

Cat rolled over. She didn't care anymore how disgusting she looked. She was miserable, and her feelings were all jumbled, confusing her. She bawled like a baby. "You can't fix me. I'm a wre-heck. I look horrible, frightening," she sobbed aloud, "even to the fish-hi-hish!"

Seneca laughed heartily. "That's what you're upset about?"

"It's not fu-hunny! I can't even untangle my hair. I can't wash it myself. I don't have my rouge. You don't have any idea how I feel about that."

"No, and I'm thankful I don't." He stifled another laugh. "What are you worried about? No one's going to see you. You look just fine."

Cat bawled harder. "Well, you see me, don't you? You said I was hu-ugly." She rolled back and buried her face in the blankets.

"What? I never said you were ugly."

"Did, too," she muffled.

"I did not. When did I say that?"

"You said I wouldn't scare the fish away."

"Yes, I did, but—"

"See?"

"No, I don't see. I wanted to assure you that your presence wouldn't bother the fish. They'd be too busy—" Cat sobbed more. "Ah, I think it's coming to me now. Forgive me, but I didn't realize that what I thought was a compliment could be taken as an insult. I'm guessing that when I said you wouldn't scare the fish away, you took it that I meant you were ugly. Is that possible?"

Cat's sobs ebbed. Quite suddenly she realized there were some things even Seneca—the man she'd deemed knowledgeable about everything—didn't know and had to learn. Perhaps she would soon become his teacher. She nodded her head.

"Well, there's a start." He touched her shoulder where he'd wounded her days before. His voice gentled. "I don't think you're ugly at all. I think you're—" She didn't move, waiting for him to say more. "I'll take you someplace where you can see for yourself."

His words weren't exactly what she had in mind for him to say, but nevertheless she was intrigued. She rolled over and looked up at him. "Where?" she asked suspiciously.

"I promise you'll love it. You can even wash your hair there. There aren't any fish. Do you want to go?"

"Yes."

"All right, then. We'll have to make haste before the storm gets here. We need to eat that bacon. I'll cook up some eggs to go with it. Dry your eyes, and let's get going."

"All right."

Cat watched as Seneca stood up and went back to the stove to resume preparation of the lost breakfast. He broke the egg shells and sliced some bread with practiced ease.

She wasn't as good as he was, but she took pride in knowing how to break into an egg without smashing it and getting shell fragments into the pan. He didn't know how good a teacher he was, so knowledgeable, so capable, so able to express himself with words and his fascinating hands. And she was determined to show him someday just how good a teacher she could be, too.

As she straightened her clothes and washed her face, Cat realized she'd had a good time learning from him.

Learning about him was something else entirely.

He'd told her little about his family, about his father's work. He seemed so guarded about that. She perused his books. Mostly they told her of what he'd studied in college in architecture, science, surveying. She was surprised by his collection of English literature and wondered if he enjoyed those books outside of college. There were papers and reports by the Adirondack naturalists, writers, and surveyors. She recognized the names of Stoddard and Colvin from her father's library. But still she was able to glean nothing more of the man himself.

What she could tell him about her life took no time at all. When she reflected upon it, she could say her life held no surprises. Her most devastating moment was when her mother died, but Aunt Maddie had been there to ease her grief and fill the void. Other than that, she realized how single-layered her life was, just like every other wealthy girl she knew. They knew only how to embroider, serve tea, go to dances, attend dinners with their parents. How to be beautiful. She felt useless in comparison to Seneca's mother and sister, whose accomplishments he was openly proud of. He'd responded to descriptions of her life simply by nodding. And he'd asked no questions, delved into none of her secrets.

They ate Seneca's breakfast while he told her about the

island. The food tasted delicious to her, and his descriptions sounded beautiful. She loved these moments with him. They were bittersweet. She wanted to keep them, but she knew she'd have to let them go eventually. He was an enigma to her, and yet she felt connected to him more and more every day they were together.

Cat could admit she didn't like it when he left at night and stayed out a long time. She'd try staying awake, but she was so weary from the work that she'd fall asleep deeply and only barely be aware of his return. It disturbed her that he was already up and out of the cabin early in the morning before she awoke. They spent a great amount of time keeping out of each other's way, avoiding the possibility of physical contact. When such a thing occurred, she'd find herself tongue-tied and awkward. She thought she'd noticed him with similar actions, although that couldn't be true, of course. Seneca Pierce was completely certain of himself. Nothing bothered him.

She wished she bothered him. He bothered her. Night after night she dreamed of their kiss. Night after night she wanted more of them, more of him. She knew she shouldn't, but she couldn't help herself.

"You'll need your boots," he said, rising and clearing away their breakfast dishes when they'd finished. "And put on that canvas vest hanging by the door."

She did as he suggested and pulled on her boots. He shrugged into a jacket and picked up two large squares of toweling and a bar of soap wrapped in a piece of cloth. She followed him outside.

In the woods Seneca led Cat among trees and thickets down to the pebbled shoreline. He pointed out large dark orange and black butterflies flitting from weed blossom to tree limb, and pale white and yellow small butterflies that floated along the shore among water plants and grasses. He placed a finger over his lips to caution her to be quiet as a female mallard swam by with eight fuzzy brown ducklings trailing, their happy peeping blending with the throaty chugs of bullfrogs and the trill of redwing blackbirds.

He showed her wildflowers and jack-in-the-pulpit plants, tree fungus that resembled hand-hewn shelves, and globe-shaped orange toadstools. In a small clearing a flock of butterflies took off in a cloudburst of milkweed fluff carried on a breeze. Seneca took pleasure in watching Cat romp through their midst trying to catch them, her laughter like the sound of bells. She plopped down into the tall grasses breathlessly. The sun caught the copper of her hair, making her look golden all over. Floating white milkweed puffs drifted down and caught in some of the errant strands, crowning her with tiny stars. She giggled happily when a butterfly landed on her finger and flexed its wings as if showing off to her, and then didn't move a muscle until it took off on its own accord.

Seneca crept up soundlessly behind her and tapped her on the shoulder. When she jumped and turned around to him, he blew the morning moisture off a long fern frond he'd picked, dotting her face with dewdrops. She laughed and grabbed a handful of tiny pinecones and meant to pelt him with them. But he sprang up and took off on a run, with her bounding through the grasses into the trees after him. He hid behind a thick stand of paper birch trees and watched her search for him, laughing one minute, frowning the next, then calling sweetly to him in an effort to trick him out of his hiding place.

He let her see him then, and took off through the trees. He slowed to let her almost catch up to him, then ducked into a thicket. She ran right past him to the spot he knew well. When she stopped, he heard the audible intake of breath.

"Oh, how beautiful!" she exclaimed, dropping the pinecones.

He came up behind her. "Yes."

They stood in a protected inlet between his island and a tiny one connected by a tree-thick spit of land. In the curve of the land was a natural pool, clear and wide open to the sun. The patch of blue sky rimmed with thick clouds over them was reflected in the pool's serene water. He dropped the towels at her feet and set the soap on top.

Cat bent down and dipped her fingers into the water. "It's warm!"

He enjoyed the surprise in her voice. "It's warmer at the edge than it is in the middle, but it's still tolerable for a bath."

Cat looked up at him, eyes wide. "Oh, that would be heavenly! Is it proper?" She frowned a moment, and let her eyes skim over the cove and the pool. "I don't care if it's proper or not. You will be a gentleman and move discreetly away, won't you? And I would so adore a bath. Perhaps my hair, too . . . I'm certain you will laugh at this, but I've never washed my own hair. There's always been someone . . . I know, I know, I should learn how. No time like the present, as you said."

"If you need help, I can do it," he offered, then wished he could retract it.

Cat averted her eyes and dropped to her knees, and he knew she was as surprised at his words as he was. She almost pitched over into the water, but caught herself. And then she caught her reflection as well.

"Oh, dear, look at me. I am frightening!"

"No, you're not. You're a bit disheveled is all." They were having too good a time. He didn't want to let her become upset again. He raised his eyes overhead and scanned the sky. "Better start your bath. You'll run out of sunlight soon."

She picked up the towels and soap and stepped into a thick clump of bushes. He wandered back into the forest. Soon he heard her splashing in the pool, heard her squeals as the cold water surrounded her, then her utterances of pleasure.

He came out of the forest and sat on a rock out of her sight but where he could see her. She dipped her head and darted around in the pool like a playful otter. She rubbed the soap over her arms, and he saw her take the bar under the water and knew she was rubbing it over her legs, her stomach, her hips, her breasts and feminine places. He heard her singing contentedly. She dipped her head back to soak her hair, then rubbed the soap into it. No real lather formed, but soap-laden water ran down into her eyes, and then she wasn't singing anymore.

"Ow, it stings my eyes!"

She splashed water into them. He saw her pant for breath in fear, stand up, and blindly head toward shore where she knew the towels lay. She was going in the wrong direction and would soon walk into boulders strewn near the edge where the inlet fell off into the lake. Seneca jumped up and ran toward the pool, stripping off his clothes as he went. He splashed in and caught up to her, grasped her flailing arm, and extracted the soap from her hand.

"Calm down, calm down," he told her gently. "I've got you. You're all right." He lowered her into the pool once more and dropped down on his knees. The water rocked around them. "Rinse your hands and splash more water in your eyes."

She did as she was bidden. When she opened her eyes,

droplets of water clung to her lashes, and streams ran down her neck and shoulders where her hair clung.

"Oh, you shouldn't be here—"

"Hush," he whispered. "Don't think about anything outside this pool right now. Just let your mind fly away. Let your senses take over. Feel the water, smell the air, hear the birds. Close your eyes. All you see is what you sense."

"But I think—"

"Don't think," he said. He moved around behind her, sat down in the water, his legs stretched out on either side of her. Gently he lifted her heavy hair and spread it in the water. "Drop your head back," he instructed.

It took her a moment, but she did as he instructed. He cupped water and poured it over her hair, being careful not to let it run over her forehead toward her eyes. Then he rubbed the bar of soap over the strands. He placed the soap in her hand to hold while he washed her hair.

Seneca's fingers worked through her hair, separating the strands, massaging her skull. She let out small groans of delight. He pleasured in the soapy softness of her hair, the sun on his own body, and the water lapping gently over them both. He dipped her hair to rinse it. She arched her back and leaned on her elbows to drop her head farther into the water. He could see the roundness of her breasts and the dusky peaks just under the rippling water. She had bent her knees, and the sun through the water illuminated her legs, making them appear as golden as the rest of her body.

Despite the chill of the water below the surface, Seneca felt the heat of his own desire coursing low in his body, felt its burgeoning expansion. He listened to his own instructive words to Cat. He put his mind to rest and let his senses take over.

Finished with her hair, he massaged her neck, her shoulders, taking care around her wound which was healing well. He moved up her neck again and massaged her temples, her forehead, along her jaw, then ran his hands down her shoulders again to her upper arms. He felt her stiffen a moment, then release her tenseness.

And then he slowly slipped his hands under her arms, along her ribcage, and over her waist until he cradled her hips. Lifting her off the pool's finely pebbled bottom, he shifted his legs and brought her buttocks back to rest upon his thighs.

Cat let out a long breathy "Ooh."

Silently Seneca buried his face in her hair along her ear and nuzzled her neck. Then he opened his eyes and watched as he slipped his hands through the water and cupped her breasts, kneading them, tugging them, lifting them until her nipple peaks broke the water's surface. Desperately he wanted to take them into his mouth. With a firm lift, he thrust her stomach and hips out of the water until her feet were flat under her legs—sliding her up and over his shoulder until her head and hair hung down his back. Gently he played his fingers over the thatched mound at the vee of her thighs until she moaned. Swiftly he shifted his legs around and lowered her onto them so she lay across him and took first one nipple into his mouth, licked and tasted the water from it, then moved to the other.

She floated in the water across him, her eyes closed, her lips parted. She was lost in the totality of her senses and was giving herself over to him. He buried his finger deep inside her and, like a starving man, suckled her nipples, squeezing her breasts to bring more into his mouth.

Seneca lost himself in the feel of Cat's body under his

hands and mouth and to the totality of his own senses. Thunder rolled between the mountains and reverberated between them.

Thirteen

Cat's sensually drugged mind spun into the center of a cyclone, luring her into the eye of her internal storm with a force greater than her physical and mental strength. Thunder and her pulse roared in her ears. She heard her own moaning inside herself. Water and Seneca's mouth laved her skin, making exquisite responses in her nipples and nerve endings so extraordinary she thought she could not bear another moment of it.

And then the rains came, pelting her skin with icy drops. Seneca erupted up and out of the water, bearing her in his arms, his mouth consuming hers violently, earth-shatteringly. She was vaguely aware that he carried her to a protected area and dropped to his knees. Still possessing her mouth, he stretched her body out on the thick cushion of Adirondack duff. And then he wrenched his mouth from hers.

"Open your eyes, Cat," he commanded over the maelstrom of rolling thunder and rain pelting tree branches and the skin over her exploding heart.

She didn't want to open her eyes, wanted only what she was seeing in her mind to be her reality. Silently Cat screamed, *"I love you, Seneca!"* She craved to be Cat Pierce inside herself. If she opened her eyes, she'd know she was Lila Stockdale, properly brought-up young lady who would never, ever feel the way she was feeling, let a man do what she desperately wanted him to do to stop the raging in her loins. With every roll of thunder, a fierce tide of longing swept over her with a force that reverberated through her.

"Open your eyes, Cat!" he commanded once more.

She forced her eyes open. He was above her, supporting her raised shoulders. Rain and pool water ran from his hair down his face and dripped onto her breasts. His bronze skin glistened with it, his full, perfectly defined lips carried it like nectar.

"I want you to see me, know it's me," he growled.

He dropped his head sharply as if to kiss her. But he didn't. She focused on his lips, willing them to capture her mouth once more, willing them to say the words she longed to hear from only Seneca. Then her gaze lifted and found his. His eyes were as stormy as the mountain sky— wild, flashing with lightning-hot promise of tides of abandoned pleasure. He slipped his hand over the sleekness of the wet skin below her abdomen, over the wet curls, throbbing mound, his fingers pointing the way. He spread his fingers flat under her bottom and pressed the mound with his palm. Squeezing, kneading, rubbing, causing an erotic friction outside that rivaled her pressing need inside.

He claimed her mouth and slid his hand from under her to gently spread her lifted thighs. Rain pelted her and felt like a constant drumming of his fingers. He parted those private lips, and she jumped as raindrops splashed against her tender skin like tiny shards of ice that instantly turned to drops of molten lava.

And then his fingers were inside her: fast, hot, caressing. His open mouth claimed hers completely. His tongue performed the same rhythm as his fingers.

He mesmerized her, tantalized her, seduced her whole

being to the wild, primitive soul that yearned to be un-
leashed. This man was more than any dream Cat could
create. He was beyond real, larger than life, greater than
her universe. She knew now she'd been waiting for him
all her life. Fiercely her hand slid up his drenched arm.
He delved deeper inside her, tongue and fingers. She
clutched his shoulder. And then an intense quivering
wracked her insides where his fingers relentlessly probed,
caressed. She arched her back and dragged her mouth
from his.

"Oh, please, please, no—"

"Yes," he said huskily, "yes. That's what you really
mean, don't you?"

"Yes," she whimpered.

He claimed her mouth again.

Cat hung on to the thread of sensibility inside her mind
until it snapped. And then she lost all reason and what
little was left of her strength. She was catapulted into the
storm, up where the thunder began, then plunged over the
top to fall into the deep well of roiling heat his fingers
led her to. Her insides pulsed against him. Still he drew
her, vibrating his fingers against her, pulling her deeper,
deeper still.

The wind whirled leaves and fragile tree branches
around them. Seneca withdrew his fingers. Then he lifted
her effortlessly into his arms and bore her through the
rain-dripping forest to the cabin. Inside he kicked the door
closed and gently lowered her onto the bed of balsam and
blankets.

"Oh, God . . . oh, God," she said over and over, rolling
her head back and forth on the blankets, her eyes clamped
shut.

Seneca pulled a blanket over her and quickly rekindled
the fire in the fireplace. Cat opened her eyes and saw him

standing with his back to her, leaning against the mantel, breathing raggedly and staring into the fire. She saw the strength of the back of his neck where it met the broad shoulders. Rivulets of water flowed down his back to his buttocks. Cat closed her eyes, then had not the strength to keep them closed. She felt a need to see him naked, all of him.

His buttocks were a paler bronze than his back and legs. She let her gaze travel the long lean length of him, trailing it over his calves, bare feet, then back up over his buttocks and the line of bronze that flowed up over the expanse of his back. He turned then and walked back to the bed. She sucked in her breath and shut her eyes.

"Cat." His voice was husky.

Cat opened her eyes and saw him looming above her like a fantastical bronze god. Long black strands of hair hung over his face, clung to his jaw, sending rivulets of water down over his massive chest. His braid hung over his shoulder, glistening in the rising firelight. His abdomen was flat, waist narrow. His muscular thighs were streaked with water that ran down to a dark vee below which she could not bring herself to look.

He leaned over, dripping water on her, and slowly pulled the blanket down the length of her.

"Look at me, Cat," he commanded.

With a wild shudder she opened her eyes and stared up into his face.

"Look at all of me," he commanded again.

It took great strength for her to drop her eyes hesitantly down the length of the front of his body. They stopped at the sight of his long firm erection. Its length glistened in the firelight. He stepped over her, straddled her on the bed. Her mind whirled with questions, but she felt no fear—only a wild longing for what his fascinating fingers and tantalizing tongue would do next. His eyes glittered with primal desire, and once again she was mesmerized by his total command of her.

"I'm going to show you what I want you to do for me." His voice crackled with the burning logs.

He dropped to his knees, raised hers and spread them wide. He lifted her buttocks and braced them against his thighs. Then he leaned over and kissed her mouth deeply— demanding, probing, sucking the breath out of her. He left a burning kiss at the hollow of her throat, then trailed his lips over each breast, pulling the nipples, teasing them into hard nubs. He left a path of moist kisses from her breasts to the crisp nest of curls between her thighs. She gasped.

Holding her gaze with his fiery own, he caressed the opening to her intimate cavern with the fingers of both hands until she thought she could stand no more of it. He drove her to a frenzy of emotions she desired yet had no experience in controlling. He lowered his great dark head. The strands of his hair brushed against her abdomen, mingled with her feminine curls. And then he kissed her softly.

Cat let out a breathy "Ooh," and instinctively shifted her hips away.

He moved them back and slipped both hands under her buttocks and squeezed slowly on each side. The warmth of his hands permeated her skin, and the rhythm of his manipulation was a most erotic sensation as he lifted her intimate opening closer and closer to his lips.

He kissed her again, this time lingering, holding his lips against her. He squeezed her buttocks more, pressing her against his mouth. Again he kissed, lowering his lips, then kissing, nuzzling, pulling her flesh, kneading her buttocks. Cat rolled her head side to side, moaning, pleading no, then begging for more.

He slid his tongue in and out of her with lightning speed, and she cried out. He did it again, then kissed her, slid it in again, kissed and tongued her until she was writhing in his hands. She tried to pull away, wanted to push him away, clutched his shoulders—but nothing she did deterred him. His tongue was relentless until she could stand no more.

She arched her back and slammed against his lips as the feverish roiling of an internal tide cast her over the sharp shore of his relentless, compelling tongue and mouth. When the explosions came, Cat grabbed the sides of the bed, clutching the blanket in her fists. He lifted his lips lightly, and then her fingers were in his hair pushing him, grinding against his mouth, unable to get as close to him, as deeply inside of him as he was in her. She let out a cry on a crack of thunder that took her to the ends of the earth.

And then the tide receded. He held her buttocks, still kissing her gently, raining the insides of her thighs with kisses and returning always to the throbbing center of her body. She lay panting, spent, yet her hands and feet tingled with coursing power. Behind her closed eyes she saw them together in such a way as she had never in her wildest dreams imagined. But she knew there was more. Seneca had yet to penetrate her with that beautiful shaft of his manhood he'd commanded her to look at. What was he waiting for?

And then his words echoed in her mind. "I'm going to show you what I want you to do for me." Her body went rigid. She couldn't do that! Ladies weren't supposed to do that! As quickly as the thought flashed in her mind, she extinguished it. For the first time in her life, she was behaving like a woman who'd been buried under piles of suffocating silks. Every inch of her was on fire with desire, and she didn't want that feeling to escape. She breathed deeply of the scent of damp balsam, burning cedar, male body, and human lovemaking.

He lowered her hips back to the blankets, then leaned over her, brushing her breasts with his chest. He kissed her, and she could taste herself on his lips. In her state of erotic abandonment, the taste stimulated her more. She felt his hardness against her open legs, and the touch startled her. Was he going to?

Seneca rolled over onto his back, Cat's soft flesh in his hands as he pulled her with him until she lay atop him stretched out head to foot. Again he kneaded her buttocks, grinding her against his middle, kissing her thoroughly. He couldn't get enough of her. It was as if there would be only one time when they could be together like this, as if life would starkly intervene and these moments would never come again. They were moving yet suspended in their own time. He was insatiable, his hunger growing, gnawing at his insides. The more he took from her, the more he wanted, needed. He burned with the need, ached with it.

Then he drew his lips away from hers, slid his hands along her arms, and gently pushed her up. She stared down at him with questioning eyes. There was no stopping him now. He knew what he wanted from her.

"Give to me," he commanded, gently but firmly pushing her shoulders. "Give to me as I gave to you."

He knew he must have numbed her sensibilities, but he no longer cared. For this day, this night, he would give all of himself to her and take all of her. She was drugged with their lovemaking, he could see it in her swollen lips, feel it in her throbbing thighs and the wholly feminine part of her. He couldn't let her stop now. Yet looking at the woman lying atop him now, he believed she didn't want to stop either. They were borne on a savage wind that hurled them through the storm, and they had no control over it. They had no choice but to go with it and let it whirl them where it would.

"Kiss me." He closed his eyes. "Kiss me."

She lowered her sweet lips to his and kissed him tentatively at first, then more demandingly. Seneca felt his mind and the vision from his soul rise above to look at them together. He saw her exquisite pale body over his dark one, saw her legs separate to straddle his hips. The rush of desire within him flowed down to pool in the center of his body. He fought to control the urge to plunge himself into her glorious depths.

She opened her eyes, and they burned over him with the feral glitter of a lynx. She'd given herself over to her most basic desires, her hunger. He read her eyes with the instinct of ancient soul-keepers. She knew her prey, knew how to trap him and suck him into her silken web. She leaned back, and her eyes swept over him with a ferocity he'd never seen in them before.

And then she was running her tongue over his skin, tracing every plane of him. He plunged his hands in the wet tangles of her hair and pushed her lower as his throbbing excitement built like an encroaching thunderhead. He felt her shaking but knew she wasn't cold. The heat of the fire licked over their skin, causing a further fever pitch in both. She generated an unbearable desire in him, an anticipation for what she would do. He knew she'd had no real experience in making love, but her instincts were wide open, raw, rubbing against him with friction that ignited his insides and became a raging forest fire in his mind.

And then he stopped guiding her. Mindlessly his fingers played in her hair, lifting it from her head, letting it fall, spreading it over his stomach and chest, pulling it up from the nape of her neck. He hung on to the ends of her tresses as she lowered more and more until her lips were at the triangle of his thighs. He spread his legs wide and offered himself up to her as if he were a burning sacrifice to the great goddess of the spirit world.

He shuddered when her hands closed around him. He raised his shoulders and braced his torso on his bent arms and watched her. Her eyes devoured him first. Then she slipped her knees between his thighs and bent her head over him until her hair fell like a curtain around him. He watched as her head moved up and down slowly. As her lips caressed the tip of him, he felt it vibrate in the circle of her hands. Timidly she took him into her mouth, then let him go. His mind screamed for more. Again she kissed the tip, then took him inside her mouth. He felt the slick warmth, the edges of her teeth. Again she let him go, took him again, let him go. He wanted to be gentle, but it was all he could do to keep from plunging into her adoring mouth. She kissed along the length of him, then nestled her lips in the thatch at his base, nibbling toward his thighs and down one and then the other. He dropped his head back and groaned in the ecstasy of her ministrations.

Cat sat up, breathing heavily, her chest rising and falling. Seneca sat up to meet her, taking her full breasts into his hands and kissing her hungrily. Roughly he pulled away from her lips and splayed his fingers over her ribs. He lowered his hands to her hips and around to her buttocks, then lifted her up on her knees.

"Open for me," he commanded her gently. While the heat of desire stormed in him, he would not let the power of it hurt her. He would make the moment as beautiful for her as he could.

She spread her knees apart and he slipped his long legs

between them. His hands sought her soft hot insides and felt the slick wetness of her anticipation. Slipping his fingers out of her, he lifted her high then settled her over him and slipped his pulsing tip inside her. His mind shifted into control. He had to keep himself in check to give her the most pleasure and the least pain.

Gently he rotated her hips with his hands until she was doing it herself in sweet rhythm. He lifted both breasts and suckled one nipple and then the other while she rode against him gently. His ardor escalated. His sweat mingled with the dewy moistness that covered her skin. He slipped his hands around her ribs until his fingers met at her spine. With his lips he pulled her nipple into his mouth and swept his tongue over it with swift hot licks. She groaned and dropped her head back, pushing her breast farther into him until his mouth was filled with her soft flesh.

He dropped his hands to her writhing buttocks, grasped them, and pulled her down harder onto him. She stiffened as he thrust firmly against her internal barrier. She cried out when he broke through. And then his control shattered. His hands tightened over her buttocks squeezing the soft flesh, grinding her against him as he thrust harder and harder. His mouth hungrily sucked and laved one breast and then the other. Her hands tore at his hair, her nails scraped his shoulders. She cried out over and over, but not in pain—he knew that. The cries came from deep in her throat in the throes of wild ecstasy.

Seneca held her tight against him and rolled them both over so she was on her back and he was over her. Cat opened her eyes and watched him rocking against her, thrusting in and out of her. His face was bathed in firelight, his eyes were wild, his mouth open, lips bared against straight white teeth as he lost himself inside her.

He seemed to be on another plane without her, and she didn't want him to leave her.

"Take me with you, take me with you!" she whispered raggedly.

And then he was over her, his mouth buried in the hollow of her shoulder. He reached around and lifted her hips until she knew to wrap her legs over his back. And then his glorious hands found her buttocks once more, kneaded them, slipped his fingers along the base of her opening where the hard heart of him thrust against her, and played over her as the raindrops had as they lay in the forest during the storm. Again she felt the deep quivering in her loins. At the moment she was hit with the full impact of her own storm, Seneca thrust into her and let out a long groan. He dragged his hands out from under her and braced his torso on either side of her body and raised above her. His body went rigid and then shuddered deeply as he pumped his seed into her. Then he fell over her, kissing her lips, her eyes, her cheeks, her throat, her ears, and returning finally to her mouth.

For a long time he rocked and shuddered against her. She felt the still pulsing shaft within her subside.

She couldn't breathe, but his lungs heaved as he pressed his chest to hers. She closed her heavy eyes and gave over to deep sleep, awoke for several moments, then fell asleep again.

Cat couldn't tell how long she'd been asleep, but when she opened her eyes she could see a hint of daylight in the window. As she rose to consciousness and the memory of their fierce lovemaking of the night before flooded back, she felt the length of Seneca behind her as they lay on their sides. He was pressed against her, warm and sticky. One arm was crooked under his head, the other was thrown across her stomach, and his hand lay over her lower thigh.

Cat sighed. Her imagination and fantasies could never have conjured such an event as she'd experienced with Seneca the night before. Her thighs ached, her back throbbed, and she was moist and sensitive between her legs. She'd never known what could happen between a man and a woman. She shivered at the thought.

Seneca's mind started to sharpen when he felt Cat shudder against him. Slowly his sleep fell away and his consciousness rose to the surface. His body became aware of how her curves were fit against it, shoulder to bent knees to toes. Her lovely buttocks were pressed against his rising manhood. His hunger of the night before had been sated, yet feeling her against him now set the gnawing again in his depths.

He kissed her between her shoulder blades and heard the little moan she gave. His hand began to move sensuously over her thigh, then up her stomach to caress her breast. She moaned and pushed against his palm until he held the fullness in his hand. Then he trailed his hand from her breast up over her throat to her lips. She kissed his fingertips, and then he played with her full bottom lip, pulling it down until her mouth opened and he could slip a finger inside. She suckled his finger as he'd suckled her nipples, and the sensation pulled him completely out of his slumber. He ran his tongue over her shoulders and down her spine, tasting the salt from her skin.

She pressed her buttocks against him harder. He took his hand from her mouth, slid it over her breasts, down her middle and between her legs where he rested his fingers in her warm nest. With his hips and hands he lifted her and slid under her until she lay with her back on his chest, her head dropped back on his shoulder. He turned her head and began to kiss her deeply. Then he situated his hips under her buttocks and spread her legs wide. His shaft came up to rest against her opening. She moaned and meant to pull her lips from his, but he captured and held them.

One hand rested between her legs. The other caressed her breasts, rolled her nipples between his fingers, until she strained against them for more. He teased them, wouldn't give her the intensity she desired and she began to squirm over him. She pressed her mound against his fingers, rubbed them, urged him to caress her. He moved them only slightly, playing over her private lips so lightly, he could barely stand it himself. And with both hands she grabbed his hand and forced his fingers inside her. Holding his hand against her, she moved her other one up to force his other hand to give her breasts what they longed for. She squeezed his hand and fingers, moved them over one breast and then the other until her chest heaved and she was gasping for breath against his mouth.

She writhed against his fingers inside her and then slipped her hand lower to clasp his shaft. He shuddered at her heated touch, and she proceeded to drive him as crazy as he knew he was driving her. She fingered and squeezed him and writhed against his fingers. Her other hand left his at her breasts and dropped back around his head to clutch his hair and grind his mouth and tongue deeper into hers.

She was in complete control of him, and he gave over to her. Whatever her hands instructed he did. If she pressed against him, he plunged his fingers more deeply into her wetness. If she squeezed his manhood and teased the end of it, he writhed against her. A long guttural moan vibrated against his mouth, and she began to rub his shaft with an exquisite friction.

They moved together in mutual rhythm until the all-consuming waves of climax overtook them both. He bucked under her and she rode above him long and hard until they both lay lifeless in the engulfing aroma of the cedar and balsam bed.

After an exhausted nap, Seneca awoke. He slipped out of the bed, then leaned down and picked her up in his arms.

"What are you doing?" she asked groggily.

"We both need a bath," he said and swung her around, heading for the door.

"No! You can't mean—"

"Yes! Grab that towel. We're going down to the pool."

"Oh, God—no. It will be freezing!"

"I think we could both use some cooling down, don't you?"

She struggled in his arms all the way through the forest path, through the open field where the butterflies had flocked, and into the water. She had the wherewithal to drop the towel on dry land. He lowered them both into the water. She was right. It was freezing against her raw and feverish skin.

"Ow!" she yelped.

He laughed. "It feels good, doesn't it?"

"No, it doesn't!" She splashed as if to get out, but he caught her and dragged her to him.

"Yes, it does. It feels good. You know it does," he said huskily. "It feels good over your breasts." He touched them lightly. "Over your back." He ran his fingers down her spine. She relaxed against him. He trailed his fingers over her buttocks, then around to touch the mound at her thighs. "And the water especially feels good right here, doesn't it?" He lapped his fingers against her. She groaned as if in submission.

And then she pushed him back. He lost his balance and went under the water to the sound of her pealing laughter. She tried to get away, but he was up and caught her. He dove under the water, slithered between her legs, and left a fleeting kiss there on his way through. She jumped and dove into the water. It no longer felt cold, just refreshing.

They splashed in the pool, catching each other, eluding, tantalizing, enticing. Above them birds sang and squirrels chattered. The water sprays sent up by their splashing turned to instant rainbows before returning to the pool.

"This must be what Adam and Eve felt like in the Garden of Eden," she breathed when they'd stopped splashing.

He lifted her in his arms, and she floated out straight in front of him, feeling the sun warming her face and the water lapping over her nipples.

"Perhaps," he said. "But Eve would pale in your beauty in this Eden."

Cat's eyes snapped open. That was the first time he'd complimented her. "Do . . . do you mean that?"

He nodded. "You are beautiful, Cat, exquisite. Your beauty rivals the sunrise."

His words were as poetic as his actions. Holding her buoyantly in the water, he kissed her lips tenderly, lingeringly. Then her breasts, her stomach, her thighs, and one last kiss between them.

"You play like a child, and you make love like a woman," he said against her throat. "You're a child of nature and a woman of sensual passions."

She stopped floating, bent her knees to rest in his arms while hers encircled his neck. "I had only a hidden sense that wildness existed in me," she whispered, "but I never had the opportunity to test it—until you."

"You'll never forget these last hours," he said quietly. "Nor will I."

His voice carried a note of regret, Cat thought. Not regret for having engaged in so completely primal and intimate an interaction between a man and woman. Even in the embryo state of her own feminine emotions and responses, she believed in her heart he did not regret their lovemaking, just as she had not. It was regret for something else.

She nodded thoughtfully at his words. She needed nothing spoken to express the suffused truth in her heart. She would never be the same woman she'd been before these last few days. When the moments came for this business association to come to an end, Cat knew she would be consumed by regret that the marriage hadn't been real.

In her mind another question gained clarity. Was she feeling more honest during this time with Seneca, more honest with herself than she'd ever been in her life? If that were so, how would she ever conduct her life later when he was no longer a part of it?

And then in her heart she gave her own answer. The unearthing of her own truth and honesty would sustain her more than anything else ever would. Knowing what she'd learned about herself, what Seneca had taught her, what she'd taught herself, she would never again be the dependent girl she'd been born to be. From this moment on, she vowed to be the mistress of her own life.

Cat and Seneca filled the ensuing days with discovery of one another—each new thing treasured—holding time momentarily suspended in the protective forest of his island. They played hard like children in a new park, made love furiously like the new lovers they were, then languidly like longtime lovers who reveled in the responses one another's touch could elicit from the other.

Cat reveled in the freedom of her days spent working around the cabin or walking in the island forest, her evenings spent by the fire reading from his vast selection of books. And her nights spent locked in his arms, her body entwined with his. When she watched with fascination the way he swept his hair into a braid, he combed out her hair and fashioned two braids tied with rawhide thongs and strung beads. Then he bade her put braids in his hair every morning after their baths. She wore pieces of his clothing and some of what could be salvaged of her own and went barefoot most of the time. He fashioned a necklace of seed pods and beads strung on thin rawhide and presented it to her. And she felt as if he'd given her a piece of priceless jewelry.

Cat wished her mother could know what it was like to be a man's partner as well as his wife, while becoming and maintaining her individual self. While she believed she and Seneca did not own each other, right now they belonged to each other.

Neither of them spoke of the inevitable day when their idyllic interlude would come to an end.

Cat knew she was coming to the point when she would have to leave her flight of fantasy into freedom on Seneca's island. Her dreams had been filled with visions of Aunt Maddie rocking alone in her bedroom. Her father's face appeared often—sometimes his silent features seemed sad, questioning; other times he was stern, demanding. She'd thought of him in brief flashes when her mind wasn't sensually saturated, wondered about his reaction to her impetuous disappearance. A more than reasonable time had passed for her to be visiting Miss Bolton's School, and if he hadn't inquired already, Cat knew her father would soon send a driver on the mission to retrieve her.

The longer Cat lived with him in the cabin, the more she wondered about Seneca's chosen way of life. She marveled how it was he would choose to live the solitary life his island afforded when he was educated and capable of greater achievements in a civilized society. At times he carried a note of bitterness in his voice when he spoke of the speed with which the country was developing.

"But isn't that the way it's supposed to be?" Cat asked him one evening over a supper of partridge stuffed with wild onions and field garlic.

"Why?" Seneca returned offhandedly.

"Progress, of course. Cities, trade with exotic countries of the world. Father says—"

Seneca's gaze darted to hers, and a dark look passed briefly over his face. It was the first she'd spoken of Garrett. Now the word stung her lips and hung in the air between them.

"What about your father?" His voice was low, intentionally unemotional she surmised.

She swallowed and moved uncomfortably in her chair. "Nothing, really. Just that I remember him saying that progress was inevitable, and the sooner some people accepted that fact, the easier it would be for them."

"Easier? How?" Now Seneca's voice sharpened. "How can anyone accept the leveling of the land, the destruction of a way of life?"

Cat didn't know how to answer that question. Up until these last few days, she wouldn't have known that question existed. "Well, because they have no choice, I suppose."

"No choice?" Seneca slammed his fist on the table.

Cat jumped, and he instantly regretted his outburst. His own thinking had been blurred by these last few days with her. Their sham marriage had turned into something he hadn't bargained for, and he was struggling with his own demons because of it.

"I'm sorry," he said. "I didn't mean to frighten you."

"I . . . I just don't understand everything about it—the land development, I mean." Her voice was low and quiet. "You and Father are in such opposition, and what I thought I knew before no longer seems the one way. I'm sorry I upset you."

Seneca let out a long sigh. "It's not your fault." He meant that. He may have been disdainful of her way of life, but he knew she hadn't chosen it. She was born to it, knew nothing else.

"Do you believe you have choices, too?"

"In what way?"

"Oh, choices like where to live and what to do?"

"I've made them," he said firmly.

"But there are so many other opportunities open to you. I mean, you're educated, and you seemed very comfortable in my home last spring when you came to dinner. And you're equally comfortable here."

He felt her probing him for some reason, and he didn't enjoy the unsettled feeling that lumped in the pit of his stomach. "I can live wherever I choose and be glad. This is where I choose."

"But don't you ever want to go out, see people, eat meals on real plates?" Cat pressed.

"Not particularly. I've found the experience rather unsatisfying most of the time." He frowned. "What are you trying to say, Cat?"

She fidgeted with her mug. "Aren't you ever bored? That's what I wonder. With all you can do, wouldn't you want to work at something meaningful?"

Seneca grew tight-lipped. "I am."

"What?"

"It's my business. I think you're putting words into what you think I should want, when what you really are talking about is what you want, isn't it? You are the one missing the social life. I do understand that, you know."

She sighed, and her eyes grew teary. "All right, I admit that I'm missing Aunt Maddie very much. And Evalina. And I wonder about what Father's thinking. If he's worrying."

"And Harrison? Are you worried about him, too?"

"No!" Cat clutched the mug with both hands. "I do miss my home. And look at my hands! I've ruined them with work here."

"I haven't forced you to work. I do expect you to take care of your own personal survival. I thought you'd been doing very well."

"I know. I believe I have learned a great deal, and I've actually felt satisfied with my accomplishments. But at times I've thought about the way Martin presents a meal, and how Mrs. VanSchyler cooks it, and how breakfast is always there the moment I would awake. I miss having clean clothes, going to the shops, the theater."

"Parties?"

She nodded slowly. "Sometimes. I miss the people. Don't you?"

"I have Bear."

"He's wonderful, but how can he be enough? Oh, Seneca, couldn't you try to live in the city? You've done it before, temporarily, but couldn't you try it again? We could do so many things together. I do have an obligation to my family, and it's time I considered them."

Seneca rose abruptly and went to the window. He felt suddenly suffocated, in need of a restorative deep breath of fresh mountain air. He took several, but they didn't assuage the tightening in his chest.

The unthinkable had happened. He and Cat had made love as if two people had never ever made love before them. They were the most mind-, body-, and soul-shattering experiences he'd ever spent with a woman. The dimly lit memory of those before her went out as if he'd blown a hard breath on the mantles of a lantern, snuffing out all light. And he knew she'd experienced the same. There wasn't any possibility that she could pretend the way her body had reacted to him. That made his experience even more profound.

He knew why now. She had feelings for him as deeply as he had for her.

Seneca stared out into the pitch-dark sky. They were more than just feelings. He knew that, too. But he wouldn't put it into words. He'd be strong enough not to do that. To put his feelings into words would give her power over him, power to deter what he meant to do.

The clarity of his plan had blurred up to now. The time had come to end this marriage and this unrealistic time he'd spent with Cat. And the sooner the better.

"Seneca?" Her voice was gentle from close behind him. "There's something I want to tell you. I love you, Seneca. I didn't mean to, but I do."

He clamped his eyes shut briefly, then opened them and turned to face her.

"It's time for you to go home, Cat."

Fourteen

"Madeline!"

Garrett's voice resounding from his study startled Madeline as she walked slowly along the hallway toward the stairs leading up to her room. The stay in the mountain camp which, thank fortune, had been abbreviated by two weeks, and the last several days at home in the Stockdale mansion had been tense ones for her. She'd been feeling poorly, and owed it to the strain surrounding Cat's fabricated flight to her old girls' school and the fib she'd been sustaining concerning it.

She'd been tense as a spring holding the knowledge inside. Even Martin, the Stockdale houseman, had questioned her rather intently upon her return. On more than one occasion, she'd tried to talk to Garrett about Harrison and what Cat had told her about him. Garrett would hear nothing of it. Madeline wondered if he simply was refusing to hear anything that might sway him from his conviction that the Mayne and Stockdale families, and their resources, should be joined by his daughter's marriage to Mayne's son. She'd finally given up trying to talk to him about so delicate a subject as Harrison's assault of Cat, believing that her niece's powers of persuasion would be much greater upon her return.

Madeline knew she had to continue to act as if she

didn't know Cat's whereabouts, but she hoped it wouldn't go on too long. Much as she wanted her precious niece to spend a glorious few weeks in the mountains in the company of so equally glorious a man as Seneca Pierce, she was rapidly losing the strength to continue with the lie.

Reluctantly Madeline stepped around the study door that stood ajar and obeyed her brother-in-law's summons. "Did you call me, Garrett?"

"Where is she?" he demanded, standing imperiously behind his desk. A stoic Martin stood by the heavily draped window.

"Where is who?" she returned in a timid, confused voice.

"Don't play innocent with me, woman! Lila, of course. Where is she? I know you know, and you'd best not withhold the information if you know what's good for you both."

Madeline reached out for the back of a chair to steady herself. The very moment she'd dreaded was upon her. Silently she implored the good Lord to give her strength to get through the next hours. Garrett must have found out that Cat wasn't at Miss Bolton's.

"Well? Don't just stand there. I know she isn't at Miss Bolton's School and so do you."

"What?" Madeline urged surprise into her shaky voice. "Of course she's at Miss Bolton's. She said that was where she was going. Oh, dear." She managed a tear and a quivering lower lip. "You don't suppose something terrible has happened to her?"

"Don't give me that. I can see right through your ruse. Apparently before you and my daughter fabricated this story, you didn't bother to check with the school to see if Miss Bolton could take her in. It seems Miss Bolton died several months ago, and the school has been closed since the end of the last semester." Garrett planted both hands on his hips and set his chin in that haughty angle Madeline had never liked.

She moved slowly and sat down as heavily into the chair as her petite body allowed. "Surely this news is some mistake. Perhaps the newspapers—"

"I didn't read the item in the newspapers!" Garrett shouted. "I sent Martin after Harrison when he decided to go up there to fetch Lila home. Harrison convinced me I'd indulged her whim as you'd requested, but it had been long enough. She's had plenty of time to come to her senses."

"I see," Madeline said as knowingly as she could. "And then Harrison made up the story that—"

"They learned of Miss Bolton's passing through the groundskeeper."

"But of course there was still my dear friend, Miss Skiles, the nurse, and the other two teachers. They reside at the school. Surely they can attest to—"

"It was your Miss Skiles who further informed him that no guests had come to stay at the school because it was officially closed while the trustees deliberated its future." Garrett glared at Madeline.

"How very tragic," Madeline said in a tiny voice, and she didn't mean merely the closing of the school.

"Indeed. I trusted Lila. I've never known my daughter to lie to me so deliberately." Garrett sat down in his huge desk chair and changed his tone. "I know she confides in you. Surely you understand how terribly worried I am about her. If any danger were to befall her . . . I couldn't bear it if I lost her . . . too."

Madeline didn't believe that ploy for a moment. Garrett was good at playing on her sympathies, or anyone else's, to get what he wanted. In this case he wanted private information that Madeline continued to refuse to give.

"Now, Garrett, I understand your concern. Danger could befall her, as you say, right in her own home. I'm certain Cat is all right. She can take care of herself."

"She can *not* take care of herself!" Garrett's softened tone disappeared. "She makes stupid mistakes. And stop referring to her with that disgusting nickname. She has disappointed me, not to mention Harrison."

Yes, let's not mention Harrison at all, Madeline thought.

"She lost all sense of her duty, has done her best to thwart our plans for her future. And all since she met Pierce," Garrett went on.

"Mr. Pierce?" Madeline asked with profound innocence in her voice. "Why, whatever could he have to do with Lila's lack of arrival at Miss Bolton's?"

"You know very well what. You heard Harrison's story. He saw Pierce attacking her. He has a vendetta. The savage attacked him as well."

"And as I told you at the time, Garrett," Madeline returned more strongly, "Harrison's story was just that, a story. I think Cat . . . Lila . . . rebuffed his advances. His pride was wounded. I thought you believed that."

"I did wonder about it after you told me you'd seen her, and that she was distraught and took it upon herself to go to Miss Bolton's to think things through. I believed that was good for her—she'd been acting strangely for months. I'm certain Harrison could have been frustrated at the way she's been keeping her distance from him, putting off the wedding, moping listlessly around the place. She brightened only when we were preparing for our holiday at camp. I thought getting out of the city would be good for her, thought the air would clear her head."

"And you were completely right, Garrett."

"Don't patronize me, woman! Lila never went to Miss Bolton's and you knew it when you lied to me with a straight face and told me she had. You and she connived this story. Now unless you'd like me to commit you to Dr. Raymond's Communal Home for the Infirm and Insane, and ensure that you never see Lila again, I suggest you tell me this instant where she is."

Madeline's hands shook as she gripped the arms of the chair. "Garrett, please—don't threaten me like that. Don't react this way. Why don't you let Lila make her own decisions? She's old enough. You know she doesn't want to marry Harrison, and—"

"She does not know her own mind. Harrison is the correct husband for her. I've protected her all her life. I . . . I won't be around forever to continue doing so. I've appointed him to carry on in my stead." Garrett ran a hand through his wiry white hair. "I will take no more argument from you, Madeline," he said wearily. "I know you know where she is. If you don't tell me this minute, I warn you you will be in the Raymond home before bedtime."

"Don't do this to me, Garrett," Madeline pleaded. "Don't make me betray Lila."

"Martin, take a message to Dr. Raymond immediately," Garrett said.

"That won't be necessary, Father."

Madeline spun around at the sound of Cat's voice. She pushed out of the chair and ran sobbing to embrace her.

Garrett rose sharply to his feet. "Stop blubbering, Madeline, and sit back down." He waited until she'd complied before speaking to his daughter. "You have a lot of explaining to do, young lady. I suggest you go to your room and prepare for dinner. The Maynes are our guests. Following that, your fiancé and I will have a long talk with you right here in my study. You may go."

"Thank you for that warm welcome, Father," Cat responded evenly, a hardness in her voice. She made no move to obey his orders. "But I have no intention of going upstairs just yet. I've only just returned from an unplanned trip, and you greet me as usual by issuing orders without even inquiring about my welfare. Whatever made me think I'd worried you or suppose you might possibly have missed me?"

Garrett swayed almost imperceptibly, then swallowed hard. "Of course, I was concerned for your whereabouts and your safety, Lila, once I learned Miss Bolton was deceased."

"Miss Bolton is dead?"

"Yes," Garrett said smugly. "And you would have known that if you'd gone to the school as your aunt told me you had. What have you got to say for yourself?"

She removed a colorful woven shawl from her shoulders and set it with a small pouch on the reading table near the door. "How tragic about Miss Bolton." Cat felt genuinely sorry to hear that news. She'd loved the ramrod-straight old woman, despite her rigid rules. And she'd had no compunction about lying about where she'd been, regardless of what her father knew. Her whereabouts no longer mattered.

"Yes, well. . . . You may go now. You, too, Martin. Madeline." Garrett dismissed them all. "We'll speak after dinner, Lila."

"No, Father, we'll speak now. I have something to say to you, and it cannot wait until after dinner." Cat kissed Madeline's cheek as the older woman, smiling gratefully at her return, passed by. "Do not close the door on your way out, Martin. Thank you."

"Now just a minute, young lady—"

"If that's all the time you'll give me, then so be it. You are right, I did not go to Miss Bolton's School."

"I'm glad you admit it."

"I went to Seneca Pierce's cabin." Cat admitted that none too easily. Her emotions were a mixture of relief to have said the truth and trepidation at her father's reaction.

Garrett blanched for the merest of seconds, then set his mouth in a grim line before he sputtered, "I knew it! I knew Pierce had something to do with it. How could you do that to your betrothed? And to me? I daresay you'll be hard-pressed now to keep Harrison's devotion."

"I don't want Harrison's devotion, Father! I never did. And all I wanted from you was understanding and support. I gave up long ago wanting your love. I never wanted to marry Harrison. It was all your idea." Cat's voice took on a note of desperation, which she fought to control. "You should know he is not the man you think he is."

"Nevertheless, you know very well what's expected of you."

Cat took a step forward. Her hands clenched and opened nervously. "I know what was expected of me in the past, that's true. I never questioned your authority, your right to make my decisions for me. But I'm not the same daughter I was when I went away. And so now I will question *you*. Why was I expected to marry Harrison? Why does such ancient history have any bearing on my life today?"

"Let's talk about this when he is here." Garrett came around from behind his desk. "It's time to prepare for dinner."

"All right, if you won't answer, then you'll listen to me." Cat folded her arms across her chest. "I want to tell you something very important. I would like your support

but if you do not offer it, then I'm afraid our ties as father
and daughter will be broken forever."

"Now you listen to me, young lady! Just who do you
think you are? You've been with that Indian, and he's
turned you against me, hasn't he?" Garrett glared at her,
his face reddening quickly.

Cat stepped back, tilting her head questioningly. "Why
would you think he would turn me against you? He hardly
knows you. If you'd give him a chance, I'm certain you
would—"

"I won't give him the time of day. If you want to call
his your home, you stay away from him, do you hear me?
You stay away before—"

"Before what, Father? Before I'm ruined?"

Garrett narrowed his eyes. "You are ruined already,
aren't you?"

Cat's laugh was almost crazed. "Ruined, Father? Just
what do you mean by that? Has my thinking been awakened? Is that what you mean? Have I finally realized that
you can't force me to live your way if I choose not to? In
that sense, then yes, I'm ruined by your definition."

"You know very well what I mean. Stop playing cagey
with me." Garrett's breaths were coming in short spurts,
and his voice was shredded.

Cat threw her hands into the air. "Yes, I do know what
you mean. You're asking if I'm no longer a virgin, aren't
you Father?"

"Don't speak in that disgusting manner to me."

"If your precious Harrison had managed to finish what
he started, I'd have lost my virginity in the forest on the
ground, where he managed to trap me."

"He wouldn't—"

"He did! I managed to get away, to hit him. If I hadn't,
he'd succeeded in his attempt, Father, would you still

be asking me if I'd been ruined? I'm beginning to think that it wouldn't matter to you as long as Harrison had done the ruining." She choked on a suppressed sob. "You'd think nothing of it, would you, as long as Harrison and I would marry and fulfill your insatiable need to build your damned railroad!"

"That is enough!" Garrett leaned heavily against his desk. "You've said just about enough. We won't speak of this again. I'm warning you, Lila, if you ever so much as speak the name of Seneca Pierce again, if you ever go near him, I'll—"

"I'm afraid it's too late for that, Mr. Stockdale." Seneca came around the open study door. "Your daughter and I are married."

Garrett rose with a start, then stepped back sharply as if hit with a falling tree. He would have stumbled if not for grabbing his desk for support. "Pierce, how did you get in here? You and your lies are not welcome."

Cat tilted her head defiantly and stepped back, linking her arm through Seneca's. "If you still want me to call this my home, Father, then I hope you will be gracious enough to properly welcome me . . . *and* my husband."

"Husband? This is absurd!" Garrett shouted. He gripped the edge of his desk so hard his knuckles turned white. "You wouldn't dare be married without the church, without your family present," he choked.

"There was a church, Father. We were married in it." Cat softened her tone. "And I want you to know I missed your presence at my wedding."

"I would never attend a wedding between you and this . . . barbarian. I'll have it annulled, and you will marry Harrison before the year is over."

"I will never marry Harrison, no matter how much you threaten me. *He* is the barbarian, Father. You must listen to me," Cat pleaded. She started toward her father intending to make him understand.

"I'll have it annulled," Garrett repeated darkly.

Cat stopped and raised her chin. What she was about to say to her father now, only a few weeks ago she couldn't have imagined she'd do. But she'd said so much in the last few minutes, that say it, she would. "An annulment cannot be arranged, Father. This marriage has been consummated. I will swear to that loudly and clearly."

Garrett grunted loudly. "And I will swear he forced you to lie! What hold does he have over you?" he shouted. A harsh cough immediately followed, and he clutched his chest.

Cat ran to him, Seneca beside her. "Father, what is it? Are you all right?"

"Mr. Stockdale, let me help you to your chair." Seneca took Garrett's arm.

"Get away from me!" Garrett shrieked. "I know what you're doing! I know exactly what you're doing!"

"Father, what is the matter? Seneca is only trying to help you—"

"Mr. Stockdale, Martin said I could find—" Harrison came into the study. He stopped and turned ashen. "Lila! Pierce? What in hell is going on?" He stepped swiftly back into the hallway and sent a young servant scurrying for Martin, then went around by Garrett's side and hovered over him.

"I'm all right, I'm all right," Garrett said impatiently, pushing him away. "Just a little indigestion."

Martin arrived then. Seeing the pale look on his employer's face, he took water from a pitcher on the sideboard and, using his own handkerchief, bathed Garrett's forehead and nape of his neck. He released his collar buttons and tie, and soon Garrett relaxed and his breathing came more smoothly.

Harrison straightened. Cat saw the way his demeanor changed in less than a breath.

"Lila, darling, we've all been beside ourselves with worry." He came around the desk as if to embrace her, all the while glaring at Seneca.

Cat stepped back and took Seneca's arm. "Just exactly what have you been worrying about, Harrison? That I might tell the truth about what happened in the mountains?" She was feeling stronger than she'd ever felt in her life. Standing up to Harrison and her father was something she'd wanted to do for years. And now she could do it. Yet as her knees buckled beneath her skirts and she tightened her grip on her husband's arm, she believed that in her father's house she might be strong only as long as Seneca stood by her. If only she could count on him to stay in the charade long enough for her to be rid of Harrison once and for all. If only her marriage were not a charade at all.

"I . . . I don't know what you mean . . . dearest," Harrison said with a venomous edge. "In any event I think we should discuss our private affairs at another time. Your father isn't feeling well, and dinner is about to be served. That is, once Pierce is ushered out of the house. Isn't that right, sir?" He turned toward Garrett.

"Yes, yes it is," Garrett bit out.

Martin left Garrett's side and approached Seneca, meaning to escort him out firmly.

Cat held fast to her husband's arm. "If Seneca goes, I go, too, Father. Is that what you really want?"

Garrett looked up wanly. "Lila, I will not allow you to manipulate me. This whole affair is unacceptable. You know it. Please don't make me force you—"

"And please don't make me force you, Father. I want peace between us."

"Yes, Mr. Stockdale, we have something to settle," Seneca said, his gaze level with Garrett's. "Shall we talk privately? Or would you rather wait until Stewart Mayne arrives?"

Before Garrett could respond, Harrison crossed the room to stand over Cat.

"Lila, your father wants him out of here," he said sternly. He took on the look of one who fancied himself in control of a difficult situation. "Martin, do what you are told. Mr. Pierce is unwelcome."

"I mean it, Father," Cat said, looking at him past Harrison. "If Seneca is unwelcome in my home, then this is no longer my home."

Martin looked back at Stockdale. Seneca stood firm. Cat held his arm. Harrison glared at Lila, then looked questioningly at Garrett.

"All right. He can stay until I come to a decision. Your aunt Madeline's heart will be broken if you leave here." Garrett ran a hand over his perspiring forehead. "You drive a hard bargain, Lila. I never would have thought you'd turn so hard."

"Mr. Stockdale, sir, I must protest this arrangement." Harrison's fury was causing him to rock back and forth erratically on his feet. "Why are you giving in to this unreasonable demand of hers? She's being fooled by Pierce. You know how she is, how easily she is swayed. You must take a sterner hand with her. Believe me, when I'm her husband she won't get away with such displays of spoiled tantrums."

"Shut up, Harrison. You've no say in this for the time being. Lila says she's married him." Garrett dropped his head wearily into his palm.

"What?" Harrison's face turned brick red, and Cat thought from the sound of his voice that he might be choking. "Where? When? How could you?"

Cat lifted her left hand to display the ring Seneca had given her. She could have imagined it—she wasn't certain—but she thought she saw a glimmer of satisfaction cross Martin's features.

Madeline hurried into the study. "Oh, my dear Cat, did I just hear that you and Mr. Pierce are married? I'm so happy for you!" She ran to hug them both, and Cat saw the merry fibbing twinkle in her eyes.

"Madeline, for God's sake, will you stop eavesdropping?" Garrett admonished her in his most annoyed tone.

"Dinner is served, upon your presence in the dining room," the houseman said a little too brightly. He took Garrett's arm and helped him leave the study.

"Come along with me, dear." Madeline took Cat's arm and drew her away.

"What do you think you're doing, Pierce?" Harrison growled when they were all out of earshot.

"I'm not certain what you mean, Mayne," Seneca said calmly, holding his gaze steady on his opponent.

"You'll never get away with this. This marriage is a lie. I'll get the truth out in the open, and I'll make you pay."

"I'd be careful about your threats, Mayne. We all have some truths we'd just as soon remained hidden. You have something to pay for yourself where my wife is concerned, and I mean to see you pay it."

Seneca watched the nervous faces of those gathered around the dinner table. Madeline was fluttery effusive, until Garrett hushed her with a low command. Harrison was artificially garrulous, causing his mother to silence him with a look that sent daggers. Stewart Mayne was unnaturally polite, making small talk and attempting to include Seneca and Cat in the conversation. Seneca responded easily, if only with clipped sentences, trying to set the man at ease. He'd never had real quarrel with Stewart, except in a peripheral way. Mayne had been and still was, after all, Stockdale's partner. He didn't much like his choice in a wife and understood where heredity factored in when it came to their son—but Stewart was all right. Weak, but all right.

Cat fairly glowed in a deep blue dinner dress that set off the healthy new blush to her cheeks. Light danced in her eyes, a smile played around her full lips as she and her aunt exchanged glances. Seneca was fully aware of how easily she slipped back into her ways of a wealthy young member of New York society. Observing her selecting the correct fork, sipping wine from elegant crystal, he tried to fit the picture of her in his clothes—barefoot in his cabin, naked with him in a mountain pool, or in his bed giving over to her passions—against this picture in her father's mansion. The contrast was so acute, it unnerved him for a few moments. His own picture of himself took on a new light as well, and he didn't altogether like what he was seeing.

For all her look of elegance and self-assurance, Cat seemed reticent to converse. Seneca knew she was still too upset with their arrival and subsequent scene with her father to relax, too disturbed in seeing Garrett's angry reaction to their marriage, even though she'd known he would abhor it. His only indication of her newfound sense of herself was when she softly refused a serving of brussels sprouts offered by a servant and ignored her father's silent admonishment.

Seneca was feeling the most comfortable of them all,

and he knew it. Seated next to him, Cat found ways to secretly touch her arm to his as they ate, her leg to his under the table. Seneca gave her subtle pressure in return. He knew she needed that assuring touch, that connection to him to hold her own among this group—and regardless of their marital arrangement, he wanted to give her the reassurance she sought. Her father looked at her only surreptitiously, and when he did, his gaze carried a venomous glare. Seneca could not understand a father treating his own child in this manner, no matter what she'd done to displease him.

As the conversation escalated and floated around him, he thought back to his young years and his father, and how they were with each other whenever they were together. Seneca adored Eli Pierce, thought him to be the greatest teacher in the world. From him, and from his mother, Tahli, Seneca had learned how to care for the earth and for people. They had loved him and his sister, Janey, with a nurturing protective embrace that was open enough to let them run free to explore—to discover what it was that would make them the intelligent productive adults they would become, the eventual strong parents they hoped their children would be, and the caretakers of the earth and life they expected them to be. For Seneca's family, the preservation of life above all else was of the utmost importance.

Seneca felt darkness cloud his mind as he remembered his family's death. His mother and sister had died of a fever. He'd survived it himself, barely, but he wasn't strong enough to bring them through it. He'd failed them through no fault of his own.

But his father's death was another matter altogether. He'd settled it inside himself deeply enough so that the pain had subsided to a dull ache, but he'd never pushed it entirely from his mind. Since his first invitation to dinner at the Stockdale mansion, the ache had throbbed with a new pulse—and he knew he'd been unconsciously plotting his revenge. Events had presented themselves, and he'd seized upon them, manipulating them to his own advantage. Watching a scowling Garrett Stockdale consuming food with a predator's voraciousness, Seneca felt justified in his actions. Garrett was the reason his own father was dead, and Seneca wanted to make him to feel the pain he'd been feeling all these years.

Cat slipped a hand over to rest on his thigh. It was at once a touch of reassurance for herself as well as possessiveness. Seneca felt the tingling heat her touch generated spread up into his groin. He slipped his hand down to cover hers and squeeze it gently. Lila Stockdale was his wife. *His wife.* He hadn't manipulated that, exactly. The idea had presented itself in a rather offhand manner over bear stew. He'd offered to marry her, and she'd accepted.

Seneca recalled his mother's teachings: Consider the best good for all, decide the best good for himself. He wondered about that now in the wake of his marriage to Cat. Perhaps it was too soon to answer. In any case he found himself thinking of her as his wife, his real wife. He couldn't have that. Not and bring the whole episode to a close in a few months. While he had business to take care of, and take care of it he would, he was beginning to know what it would feel like when he and Cat would part. Even in the moments he was feeling protective of her, and knew she was feeling possessive of him, he felt the differences between them were as wide as the Hudson River.

"You were wonderful at dinner," Cat told him as they walked slowly along the upstairs hallway.

"Was I?" Seneca replied unemotionally.

"Yes." She tilted her head to look up at him. "Is something wrong?"

"No."

"You seem preoccupied. I'm sorry if it was difficult for you to be in this setting."

"It wasn't."

"But you miss the mountains, your cabin."

"I do, yes."

They came to the tall oak door of her bedroom, and Cat stopped. Would he come in with her? Should she invite him inside? Or would he simply expect to share her bed? He was, after all, her husband, and so it was perfectly natural that he should. Yet they were in her father's house now, and Garrett barely tolerated Seneca's presence in it. And this marriage was supposed to be a business arrangement, entered into to keep her father from forcing her into a liaison with Harrison Mayne. In that case Seneca should take one of the guest rooms down the hall, shouldn't he? She wished he'd make his own decision and act upon it, taking the matter out of her hands entirely.

"Well," Cat said, searching for words to bridge the moments from that one until she was settled in bed.

"Well?" Seneca asked, taking no initiative whatever to decide.

Cat sensed he'd done that purposely. Just then Aunt Maddie appeared at the top of the stairs and started down the hallway toward them.

"Oh, good night, darlings. I'm so happy you're home and safe and that your marriage is out in the open." She leaned on tiptoe and kissed them both on the cheek, then opened the door to Cat's bedroom. "I'll turn down your bed for you, as usual."

She scurried into the room and lit a candle lamp, leaving Cat and Seneca standing at the door. Cat stepped just inside and saw that Martin had brought in the modest canvas traveling bag she'd shared with Seneca for their trip to New York. She felt her face grow warm. The houseman had simply assumed they'd be sharing her bedroom. Why shouldn't she, then?

Aunt Maddie climbed up the two wooden steps next to the four-poster bed and turned down the lacy crocheted coverlet, thick patched quilt she'd made herself in the wedding ring pattern, and creamy ecru sheets. The matching elaborately crocheted ecru tester overhead fluttered as Maddie's energetic movements shook the bed lightly. Then she scurried out as fast as she had entered, smiling and patting each of them on the cheek as she passed.

Cat hadn't remembered how romantic her bedroom looked under the evening lamplight, all buttery soft as it was now. Or was it only romantic now that Seneca stood at the door with her? No matter. Her mind was made up. She went to her bureau and opened the second drawer. She took out a pile of her things and set them in her cream satin boudoir chair.

"Here is space for your things." She indicated the open drawer.

"That won't be necessary," Seneca said quietly.

"Oh, but, please use it. Your clothes will be unwearable if they stay in that bag." Cat felt shaky. Did he mean to leave her that night and go back to the mountains?

He stepped into the room and seemed to fill the space with his height and presence. Cat thrilled at the flickering candlelight dancing over the planes of his bronze face and over the width of his shoulders and breadth of his chest. He wore the same dinner jacket he'd had on that first evening last winter when he'd startled them all with his tardy arrival. Her senses reeled even more this night than they had then—for now she knew the feel of him, the power of him under those clothes, when before she could only wonder.

"Do you want me to stay with you, Cat?" Seneca's voice was low, smoky, throaty.

She stood at the end of the bed, rocking slightly in her garnet satin high-heeled slippers. Her shoulders were so stiff from holding them erect all evening, she could barely nod her head. She wanted him to stay. Desperately desired him.

Seneca shut the door behind him. He loosened his jacket and shrugged out of it, then opened his shirt revealing his naked chest. He passed her and stepped to the side of the bed, leaned against it. Cat turned and watched him remove his boots. When he slipped out of his shirt and then lowered his pants, she was shocked to discover he'd been wearing nothing under them. She was glad in retrospect that she hadn't known that fact at dinner. She never could have sat through it visualizing his body naked under his formal—at least for Seneca—dinner clothes.

He walked toward her with deliberate steps. Cat suddenly felt embarrassed, or was it something else? Her mind reeled, and she couldn't make sense of it. She'd seen him without clothes in the mountain forest, in his cabin, and had reveled in the sight and scent and feel of his body. Yet now, in her own bedroom, she was feeling awkward, wary, as if she should exercise restraint.

Why was that? He was her husband, after all, was he not?

Seneca stood over her. He placed both hands on her shoulders. "You're used to having someone undo all those buttons down your back, aren't you?" He ran his finger over the high neck of her dress. "That's my job this evening. Turn around," he whispered and gently urged her with the pressure of his fingers.

She turned slowly, and he felt the trembling in her shoulders. There was a shyness about her tonight, he could feel it. Perhaps it was the tension of being in her father's home and bringing a man to her bedroom. Seneca managed the fabric loops and buttons with some difficulty. There must be two dozen of them running from her nape to below the small of her back. Undressing her had been so much easier in the cabin. He'd simply pulled the shirt from her and buried himself in the soft flesh of her breasts, for she'd been free of underpinnings while they'd lived in the mountains. She seemed to be a different woman here in the mansion—a woman he'd forgotten he'd met months earlier.

His hands trembled a little. He was feeling different himself. He managed the last button and pushed the gown forward off her shoulders, revealing the creamy expanse of her back. He leaned over and placed a soft kiss at her nape below the upswept curls of her hair. He felt her shiver under his touch. She turned slowly to face him. Her eyes were large, luminous pools of deep green, radiating caution rather than the lust he'd witnessed in them in the mountains.

"What's the matter, Cat?" he asked gently. "Are you sorry we're together?"

"No," she responded almost inaudibly.

"Is there something else?"

She nodded. "I feel . . . *married.*"

He gave a light laugh. "You *are* married."

"I know. But it's different here. In the mountains I felt . . . not married, somehow. I know that's wrong, to do . . . what we did and not feel married. But here I feel really married."

"And does that somehow mean to you that married people don't make love?"

"I—I don't know, exactly."

"Are you uncomfortable thinking of making love under your father's roof?"

"I guess so. It's just that I've always heard that married woman simply endure . . . it . . . for the sake of their marriage. But our marriage is different. And, oh, I don't know. I'm so confused."

"We don't have to." Seneca pulled her into his arms.

Cat slipped her arms around him. He shuddered under her cool touch, surprised at his own burgeoning need to have her.

She leaned back in his arms to look up into his face. "I want to," she whispered. "I want to so much."

Seneca needed no more encouragement. Carefully he slipped her gown over her body to pool at her feet where she'd stepped out of her slippers. He untied her petticoats and let them follow. She was dressed in all the undertrappings of a lady of society, from the laced corset to white lace-trimmed pantaloons and stockings. He marveled at how quickly she'd reverted back to being the Stockdale daughter but dismissed the thought readily. Instead he took his time and his pleasure in removing each layer with great gentleness.

When she stood before him with only the lamplight shadowing her curves, he lifted her in his arms and carried her around the side of the bed and set her down. She sat on the edge, her spread legs dropped below. He cupped her buttocks and slid her forward toward his rising need. He pressed against her warmth. His hands slid up her arms and shoulders, over her throat, and settled in her hair, removing each comb and tossing it on the pillow until the long curls tumbled around her.

With a sharp intake of breath, she clasped his head roughly and drew his mouth down on hers, thrusting her tongue between his teeth. Seneca's control dissolved. He dropped his hands and lifted her legs to encircle his waist. Then he pushed his palms under her buttocks and lifted her, burying himself deep inside her. She clung to him with a fiercer strength than he'd felt from her before.

With her thus impaled, Seneca carried Cat toward the full-length oval oak-framed mirror which stood in the corner. Their feverish kiss broke, and breathlessly they watched husband and wife making love, truly consummating the real marriage they both thought they'd entered into in name only.

Fifteen

Garrett took to his bed during the next week. The family's physician, Elias Merriweather, made vague allusions to a heart condition brought on by recent disturbing events. Dr. Merriweather cautioned all members of the household to maintain a calm atmosphere, to appease Garrett's every desire, and under no circumstances to cause him any anxiety.

Cat was emotionally shaken. She'd never seen her father in such a weakened condition. He was the strong one, the powerful one. When her mother died, he wouldn't allow tears in public from any of them. She and Madeline had grieved in private together, never where anyone might see and perceive a weakness in the Stockdale family. While he'd never allowed it before, Garrett seemed to welcome Cat's hovering over him now, bringing tea and hearty soups from the kitchen, urging him to eat, reading to him. When he summoned, she responded dutifully, gladly.

Seneca surmised at least some of her father's debilitation was fabrication between Garrett and the doctor in order to maintain control over the Stockdale family by using the guilt he knew Cat and Madeline would feel. In many ways Garrett still controlled them. Seneca observed father and daughter together, and what he sensed disturbed him. For all her declarations of independence, for all her expressed bravado in marrying him knowing full well her father would be livid about it, Cat still appeared to cater to Garrett, to be under his influence. They spent a lot of time alone behind his study's closed door.

Perhaps she truly was concerned about his health, but Seneca commenced wondering if Cat were more of a schemer than he perceived her to be. He didn't like the unsettling feelings filling his mind about her—and about himself and his reasons for staying in the city. But most difficult for him to understand was his overwhelming sense that Cat was betraying him. He had no genuine right to think that, but think it he did.

The activity of Stockdale Transportation and Development Enterprises interested Seneca a great deal. Track into the North Woods had been laid at an average of two miles a day, sometimes more, depending on the intensity of the games tracklayers played to best each other. The *New York Times* reported that construction of Stockdale's own camp—as the unique architecture of the rustic mountain mansions was called—progressed rapidly and rivaled the Durant family's famous Camp Pine Knot.

Seneca wondered where all the funds were coming from to support Stockdale's private venture. Did Garrett have a hidden personal reserve? Very unlikely, given the extent to which the man was driven to use every penny he could get his hands on to forward his railroad. That left the possibility of his dipping into the corporate account and writing off the expenditures against the railroad construction.

One evening at dinner Stewart Mayne mentioned that there would be a meeting of the principal officers and a leader of the tracklaying crews at the corporation's offices, two days hence. Garrett said he was too ill to attend and, to everyone's surprise, suggested Seneca attend in his stead. Seneca wondered what Stockdale's motive for that might be. In any case he meant to be present for his own devices.

Prior to the noonday meal on the day of the board meeting, Seneca pored over his own notes and the latest construction plans which Stewart had given him, at the writing desk in the bedroom he shared with Cat. He tapped his fingers over several folded pages filled with crude handwriting. The ever-resourceful Bear had managed to get a private message to him by way of a city sportsman for whom he'd served as guide.

Bear's news was most disturbing. The woodsman had seen men walking around Seneca's family's grave site, taking measurements and making notes, and it worried him. How had they known where that plot of land was situated? Seneca had purposely omitted it from construction drawings he'd provided the company. Nevertheless, tracklaying had been advancing at a remarkable speed, Bear reported, and he urged Seneca to return to Blue Mountain Lake as soon as possible.

Torn by his friend's urgency and his own need to remain in the city, Seneca delayed departure, believing he could do more good right where he was for the time being. At least that was his convincing internal argument.

"Look what I've just purchased for you!" Cat burst into the room followed by a young male servant barely visible behind the stack of boxes he staggered under, and the ones which dangled off his arms by their strings.

Seneca looked up at the lovely woman whom he'd been thinking of more and more as his wife, first with escalating warmth and more recently with a chilling understanding of the reality of his actions.

"What have you bought for me today? I don't wear any

of the dozen shirts you bought three days ago, Cat. You've got to stop this shopping spree you're on."

Cat directed the servant to place her packages on the bed, then dismissed him. She stripped off her long black gloves, then lifted from her perfectly coiled hair the snug woolen hat, a deep shade of russet that matched her fitted coat, and dropped them on the bureau.

"Why should I?" she asked brightly. "I've the funds to do it, and it gives me great pleasure to shop for you. Oh, and it is ever-glorious outside! Autumn is nipping the air with a vengeance. I do love autumn in the city." She shrugged out of her coat and dropped it over the boudoir chair.

Seneca rubbed the bridge of his nose with two fingers. "Autumn is particularly spectacular in the Adirondacks. The woods and mountains will be ablaze with color. I think you would enjoy it." He wished with all his heart he was there right now.

"Ooh," Cat shuddered. "I'm certain it's very cold up there now. Evalina and I had tea at the fabulous tea room by the park. They served a wonderfully sweet Greek pastry. And can you imagine—Evalina produced a secret message from Bear! Isn't that precious?"

Normally uninterested in the frivolous gossip of society women, Seneca's interest was piqued at Cat's words. "Bear wrote to Evalina?" His gaze drifted toward an empty space in the air. "He must have fallen harder for her than I thought."

Cat set about organizing her packages on the bed. "Well, let me tell you, Evalina's simply giddy with the idea. This is his second note to her. She's written him as well, and just adores the notion of a secret admirer."

"I hope she's careful with Bear's feelings. This is brand

new to him, a city woman encouraging his advances. I hope she's not toying with him."

"Oh, I don't think so. She seems quite taken with him. She's invited him to visit this weekend. Won't her parents simply die when he comes to call?" Cat clapped her hands together like a gleeful child.

Seneca frowned. "I'm not certain he'll come to call, as you say."

"He will when he learns Harrison has been seeking Evalina's favors as well."

"Harrison?"

Cat clicked her tongue "Can you imagine? I've warned her about him, with discretion, of course. He was never interested in her before. Suddenly he's lavishing all manner of flattery on her now. If he thinks I'll be jealous of his attentions toward my best friend, he's sadly mistaken."

Seneca pondered a moment. "I doubt he cares whether you're jealous or not. I have a feeling he may have other ideas in mind in his pursuit of Evalina. Joseph Madison has come into some money recently, and perhaps Harrison has designs on its future. Or . . ." he let his idea percolate in his mind before speaking, " . . . Evalina is valuable to him in a much more secretive way."

"Evalina keep a secret?" Cat laughed. "Not possible. She's the most guileless person I know."

Seneca looked at her thoughtfully. "That's exactly what I mean. But I'm more concerned right now with Bear than anything else. You must caution Evalina to be very careful with his feelings."

"Don't worry. She won't hurt him. She's too giddy about him." Cat began snipping the strings on her packages with a small pair of scissors. "Anyway, Bear told her there would be snow falling in the mountains soon. Snow

It stays so late up there, why does it have to come so early?"

Seneca mulled over this latest bit of news—Bear's communication with Evalina, disregarding the prediction of snowfall. He decided to share with Cat the fact that Bear had contacted him as well, choosing which of his friend's messages to impart. "I've had a message from Bear, too. He's taken care of his shanty and is now readying my cabin for winter. It's quiet and utterly beautiful there once the snow has fallen. And the hunting is superb. I should be getting meat in for the winter right now."

Cat ignored his words. She excitedly tore into her purchases, rustling tissue paper, tossing box covers right and left. "Look at this! Isn't it stunning?" She held up to one shoulder a man's tailcoat in a soft dove-gray fabric. Draped over the other arm was a pair of coal black trousers with a narrow gray stripe and a matching vest. "Perfect for the club dinner and dance this Saturday. Don't forget to wear the gold watch fob I bought for you yesterday." She spread out the clothing over the array of boxes which contained handkerchiefs, cravats and neckties, and gold shirt studs.

"I'll not wear any of those fancy accessories—ever. You can return them and ask for your money back. You're being much too extravagant."

"Seneca, really. Don't be difficult. You have to be dressed properly for the club. Now that Father seems to be coming around and accepting you into the family, you don't want to embarrass us, do you?" Without looking at him, she tore into another long box. "And look what I've bought for myself. You'll be so proud to be with me when I wear this." She held up a stunning gown of velvet in a deep red and fluttered her left hand over the bodice. "See how perfect it is with my ring?"

Seneca didn't agree with Cat's words regarding her father's acceptance of him, but he said nothing. He could not dispute that the expensive gown's hue rivaled that of the garnets in his mother's ring. A ring given with love by his father. He wondered now whatever made him give Cat that ring, reminding himself of the reasons why they both entered into this so-called marriage. Yet at the moment Maurice Sender pronounced them husband and wife, offering that particular ring to this particular woman had felt very right.

"Shall I model it for you?" Cat asked with an enticing note in her voice.

"If you wish." Seneca went back to his drawings and his extensive notes.

He reminded himself for at least the tenth time that morning that this wasn't a real marriage. Cat seemed to be forgetting as well. It felt to Seneca as if she were molding him into the kind of husband she was expected to have—the businessman and society member Harrison was.

As Seneca observed Cat back in the world in which she'd been raised, he knew she'd fallen back into her old ways of behavior.

Seneca didn't yet know his own reasons for this business arrangement. In fact, he was not as clear about them as he thought he'd be when his opportunity arose to settle things with Garrett Stockdale and end the turmoil he'd lived with since he was a boy. But his exploding feelings for Cat had nothing to do with business, and he didn't want to fight those with as much fire as he knew he'd have to summon. He needed every ounce of strength to get through the next few days. He had to do his best to complete that business before too long. He'd been complicating his own reasoning the longer he lived with Cat.

Cat cleared the bed of her packages and carefully hung up the suit she'd purchased for Seneca. He'd been so busy the last few days with his papers, so preoccupied over meals, that he'd seemed to forget she was present until they retired for the evening. Then he acknowledged her presence by exquisitely filling her with his own. She'd felt a greater physical and emotional strength in herself as her muscles and limbs and senses awakened to their wild lovemaking.

She loved to look at him, to watch him move. It thrilled her to know that beneath the perfectly fitted city clothes was the naked bronze Iroquois warrior with whom she'd fallen hopelessly in love. She loved to see his blue-black hair glisten in the flickering candlelight, the way his skin shone in the glow. Her fascination with his hands grew stronger than ever. She could not get her fill of watching them work over his drawings, fuss with coat buttons and shirt fasteners—and most especially trailing over her, touching her and caressing her intimately until she was crying out, begging to stop, begging him never to stop.

Ever since the first night they'd spent together in the Stockdale mansion following the announcement of their marriage, Seneca had seemed more ardent than ever, almost rough. She was at once thrilled by his ardor and almost frightened of the power of him. But the last two nights were decidedly different. He'd been in private conversation with Stewart Mayne after Garrett had retired. Soon after, Martin presented him with an envelope that had been brought over by messenger. Now she knew it to be from Bear. Seneca had hardly said a word to her when they were preparing for bed. And when she'd stretched down beside him, snuggling into the hard contours of his long body, he hadn't responded with his usual awakening. Instead he'd arisen abruptly and set to work over his drawings with a new fervor. She'd fallen asleep wondering if he was just like her father and the others, utterly consumed with railroad construction and the development of the Adirondacks to the exclusion of all pleasurable pursuits.

Cat smiled to herself. Perhaps she had a way to interest him now, draw him away from those infernal surveyor's maps and drawings.

Seneca ran his fingers over Bear's scrawl. In a few days he would have to cut the ties to Cat and get out of the city and back to the mountains. Tracklayers were on a definite route toward Blue Mountain Lake and the village that was growing quickly. Sportsmen found the hunting and fishing superb. Prospect House was becoming famous as an elegant mountain resort, and more and more people were arriving every day. The grueling trip by stagecoach was being challenged daily. Steamboat traffic was picking up. Stockdale had interests in that, too. Seneca didn't mind that so much, but he was consumed with knowledge of the rate and direction of the tracklaying.

Being with Cat—helping her through her initial confrontation with her father and Harrison—had been his first duty to the promise he'd made to her. Staying with her, making love to her night after night in her plush bedroom had not been his duty. But it had been his desire. And in the process he'd let his focus slip.

No more, Seneca vowed. Not since that morning when he'd learned a vital piece of information that was exactly the element he needed to put his final plan into action. His question about where the money was coming from to back Stockdale's personal construction had been answered when he overheard the servants gossiping, and heard Martin corroborate that Garrett Stockdale was mortgaged to the hilt, including the mansion, to back his North Woods camp and his development company.

New York State was about to enter into litigation over Stockdale's illegal acquisition of land upon which already more than forty miles of track had been laid. In addition, the land Stockdale had acquired cheaply was now subject to taxation. That information—in conjunction with stock certificates held by other backers, certificates that would become worthless if Stockdale and the company went bankrupt—offered Seneca the opening he needed to bring Stockdale down. He'd do what he could do with the business end of it while he was in the city, but then he'd have to get back to the mountains and physically stop the encroaching tracks.

"Well, how do you like it?" Cat asked throatily from behind him.

He turned in his chair, draping his arm over the back of it. She stood at the end of the bed with her arms in the garnet gown, holding it up around her neck. The contrast with her honey-amber hair and creamy skin was breathtaking.

"It is beautiful," Seneca replied quietly. "And you are beautiful in it."

"Perhaps you'd like this better," she whispered. She dropped the gown to a swirl at her feet and stood before him in naked splendor.

He liked it all right. But Seneca was determined now to stop the physical part of their relationship, to keep his mind on his work, and to make his break from her easier to take. For both of them.

"Cat . . ." He shook his head slightly.

She stepped out of the gown and walked slowly toward him through the golden light, long legs gliding as if on water, full breasts swaying lightly.

"Perhaps you should feel the fabric. It always makes a difference to me when I'm considering taking something

I admire." She leaned over and brushed her breasts across his lips. "Any comments?"

Seneca let out a long breath through his nostrils. He could comment, all right, and he was fast losing control of himself. He felt the heaviness gathering below his abdomen, his blood heating.

Cat buried her hands in his hair and pressed his face between her breasts. "Kiss me," she commanded.

He pushed his head back. "Cat, this is not the right time to—"

Her voice was rasping, commanding. "When isn't it the right time for us, Seneca? *Any* time has been the right time for us. Make love to me. Now."

Unable to resist her further, he slipped his hands around her hips and caught the soft flesh of her buttocks in each palm. Groaning in surrender, he buried his lips between her breasts, then covered them with kisses. She dropped her head back and moaned deep in her throat.

Seneca paused for the briefest of seconds, just long enough to consider this might be the last time he would ever make love to Cat. He knew it would be more electrifying than ever between them. He swept her up over his shoulder like a sack of flour and dropped her down on the bed. He stripped out of his clothes and threw them over her gown on the floor. And then he was over her, pressing the naked length of him down her soft skin, burying his tongue in her mouth, her ear, the hollow of her throat, her navel, and then spreading her legs and tasting of her until he brought her to the explosion of pleasure they both craved.

Her small cries incited him beyond reason, and he was inside her with a fury, plunging again and again, until his seed poured out and he filled her with all the essence of himself.

Somewhere in the back of her mind, Cat heard the bell sounding for the midday meal. She pictured the servant tugging the bell ribbon in rhythm with the pulsating of her insides. She matched Seneca's thrusting with wild abandon, over and over, until the meal bell insisted over and over that they could not be late to the dining room. Father expected them to be there. Cat was torn between her own consuming desire for the lovemaking she shared with Seneca and the conditioned part of her that responded always to her father's demands.

Seneca lay over her, engulfing her, breathing deeply and softly caressing her breast. She moaned with pleasure, almost giving over to the magnetism burning in his expressive hand. But the other influence, the old influence of obeisance to her father, won out over her own desire.

"Seneca," she whispered hoarsely. "Luncheon is being served." She pushed at him, trying to lift his shoulder from where it pressed hers into the deep bed quilts. "We have to go. Now."

He stiffened and raised above her. His eyes, always a soft sky-blue, now glittered glass hard and bored through her with acuity. "Of course. It wouldn't do to be late for a meal with Garrett Stockdale for any reason, would it?"

"I'm glad you understand," she whispered, a tiny bit fearful of the angry look on his face. "They would wonder about us, you know."

He got up quickly. "And we couldn't have your father and the servants wondering, could we? Fortunately for us both I've come to a new understanding." He went to the washstand and cleansed himself, then shrugged quickly into his clothes as she took care of her own toilette. "I'll see you in the dining room."

Cat watched him leave the bedroom. What had she done to make him react so? He knew what was expected in her home. Father had been reasonable about her surprise marriage to Seneca, even though she knew he didn't like it one bit. Now, in his illness especially, she would not upset him in other ways. Perhaps Father would come to understand her more now. Perhaps he would accept Seneca and take him into the company as a partner. That would make everything perfect. Perhaps now that he was feeling weak, Father would see the merit of having Seneca and his intelligence working for him. Surely Seneca would see the value in that arrangement as well.

She decided she'd speak to Seneca about that. And she would also gently suggest he cut his hair. City businessmen did not go around with hair hanging below their shoulders or pulled back into a long switch. Much as she'd loved it on him while they were in the mountains, and she'd miss running her hands through it, his manner of wearing his hair like a wild mountain man was simply not appropriate for him in his future position with Stockdale Enterprises.

Cat speeded up her dressing. Smiling and feeling quite sure of herself, she went downstairs to luncheon wondering only vaguely what Seneca meant when he'd said he'd come to a new understanding.

"It's all turning out simply perfectly, Evie."

Cat and Evalina were seated in the parlor working on their needlepoint. Luncheon had passed rather smoothly, with Seneca being even-tempered to whatever her father commented on. As usual, business was the dominating topic of conversation, but since there had been only the three of them, she noted with some measure of curiosity that the subjects were circumspect, not focused on the Adirondacks.

Madeline sat on a nearby sofa, reading. Even in the daylight hours Cat noticed Aunt Maddie was forced to read with her book close to lamplight. She seemed to be aging rapidly right before her eyes. An uneasy loneliness swept over Cat. She made a mental note to have Dr. Merriweather examine Aunt Maddie during his next weekly visit to their home.

"And I couldn't be more surprised." Evalina giggled. "Who would have thought that Seneca Pierce would become, well, one of us?"

"Well, I don't think I have him completely changed over quite yet, but I'm working on it."

Aunt Maddie looked up from her book and removed her tiny spectacles. "Dear Cat, you must think about what you're doing. You shouldn't take a man like Seneca and try to remold him more to your requirements. He's quite wonderful just the way he is. Any woman would be proud to—"

"Nonsense, Aunt Maddie," Cat cut in. "I'm not trying to remold him. He seems to enjoy my guidance. See how different he is here? He talks more and is as articulate as anybody we know, too. He's extremely intelligent, he's educated, and he has a good head for business. I think it's what he secretly wants, anyway. And I'm happy to be with him."

Evalina nodded vigorously, setting her tightly coiled ringlets to bouncing. "If it weren't for the way he lets his hair fall loose and persists in wearing those deerskin leggings and shirt around the house, no one would ever know he was an Indian."

"It's true," Cat agreed. "But it thrills me to know he can be both the earthbound Indian and the lofty businessman. Remember how he looked the first moment we saw him last winter? At the beginning I was stunned by the impact of his sheer wildness. But then I allowed myself to scrutinize him when he wasn't looking. Except for his hair tied back and the beaded neckpiece he wore, he looked like every other associate of Father's or like the university professor he was then."

Madeline folded her spectacles and set them on her book on the side table. "He admitted then that was a temporary position. I heard he taught the course as a favor to one of his own professors who was taken ill. Really, dear, I urge you to reflect upon the possible results of your actions." Madeline's voice told Cat she was feeling disappointed in her niece. "I thought you were drawn to him because of the man he is in his own right. I thought you loved him."

Cat set down her needle. "I do, Aunt Maddie, I do love him. Completely. But he has not spoken of love for me," she said quietly.

"Truly?" Evalina sounded shocked. "That's not the way you always dreamed it would be with your husband."

"No, it's not the way I always dreamed. But this marriage isn't what I always dreamed of either."

"What do you mean? It's so deliciously romantic, of course, your running off into the forest to marry a wild savage. Everyone, simply everyone, is going on and on about it. Why you're the talk on everyone's lips."

"He's not a wild savage, Evie. I wish you wouldn't say things like that. And I wish other people wouldn't say them either."

"Well, I'll stop saying them, but you'll never get anyone else to stop. The girls are positively green with envy. Why do you think he hasn't told you he loves you? He does don't you think?"

Cat sent a pleading glance to Madeline.

"Perhaps it's not his way to put his feelings into words

dear," Madeline responded. "I remember well those days spent in the cabin with you and Seneca, and how he was then. He might not say it in the words you expect, but he showed his feelings more than either of you were aware."

"You were in the cabin with Lila and Seneca?" Evalina fairly burst with this newfound knowledge. "I had no idea, Mrs. Allgood. Then you knew about Lila and Seneca? You were there when they were married, weren't you—and Mr. Stockdale doesn't know, does he?"

"No, he does not know, Evie, and I caution you to keep this to yourself," Cat warned.

"Oh, it is delicious, simply delicious!" Evalina prattled. "But I'm not certain yet if I'll forgive you for leaving me out of it." She sighed. "How I wish I had a dear old aunt who would tiptoe around with me behind my father's back. We'd have such delicious adventures. Perhaps I'd even be married to Bear by now!"

"I'm sorry, dear," Madeline said wearily to Cat. "If I'd been thinking more clearly, I wouldn't have let that slip out. Your father would probably make good on his threats to have me committed to that insane asylum if he knew I'd helped you to marry Seneca to avoid marriage to Harrison."

"Don't worry, Aunt Maddie. It won't go farther than this room." Cat leveled a strong admonishing gaze on her friend. "Will it, Evie?"

"Oh, no—of course not. It's too delicious a secret. Harrison's pride was wounded you know, but he seems to have rallied. Just imagine—Mr. Stockdale has never found out! But he finds out everything. I think he has spies everywhere." Evalina leaned over and whispered to Madeline, "Did he really threaten you with an insane asylum, Mrs. Allgood?"

"Evalina, you are to forget you've heard any of this,

do you understand me?" Cat spoke harshly. Then she rose and went over to sit down beside her aunt and give her a warm hug. "Don't worry, Aunt Maddie, I won't let Father do anything to you. He's so weak right now anyway, he couldn't. And we mustn't let anything upset him."

"Do not underestimate the power of your father, Cat," Madeline said, dropping her head onto her niece's shoulder. "He is a very powerful man. He lets nothing stand in his way."

"Oh, I think he's changing," Cat said gently. "I can tell. He would never have let anything prevent him from attending a meeting of Stockdale Enterprises. Yet today he said he would rather stay home and rest. The meeting wasn't that important anyway. I think it's only a matter of time before he understands that he can give up some of his hold on the company. And when he does, I expect Seneca will take control."

"A leopard doesn't change his spots," Madeline said evenly. "If your father told you the meeting wasn't important enough for him to attend, he's either dying and doesn't care, or he has implemented another devious plan."

"Aunt Maddie, how can you say such a thing?"

"Because I know him much more than you do. He's done terrible things in his lifetime, dear. It's time you faced up to that."

"But he'd never do anything to hurt my husband. Especially now that he sees how valuable Seneca is to the company. And he has to see how much he means to me." Cat patted her aunt's hand.

"Don't be so certain he doesn't have something else in mind. You should be aware of that. Especially because you know what his company means to him. I overheard some disturbing news that I hope is merely gossip among the servants."

Cat tilted her head toward her aunt. "What kind of news?"

Madeline laced her fingers in her lap, contemplating whether or not to speak of what she'd heard. After a heavy moment, she relayed it. "I overheard Martin tell Mrs. Van-Schyler that Garrett has put everything he owns into backing this Adirondack railroad, this house, and has put into jeopardy the funds of the stockholders. I don't quite understand it all, but it seems serious enough to worry the servants and make them anxious about their future in this house. They believe that the bank will foreclose on your father, and they will be out in the streets penniless before long, and we'll be begging right along with them."

"I don't believe that," Cat breathed. "It's just idle talk among the servants."

"I don't want to believe it, either, dear, but you know how they manage to learn the truth. And you know how consumed your father is with this scheme to best the Durant family in developing the mountains. And we've always sensed there was something in your father's and Seneca's past that has caused bad blood between them." Madeline sat up and looked Cat directly in the eyes.

"I did wonder about it once, but I don't really think that anymore, Aunt Maddie. Really. I think it was our vivid imaginations at work. And now the servants have taken up with it—"

Evalina cut in with a tone in her voice that suggested she was about to weave one of her tales. "Maybe they did know each other once and were in love with the same woman."

"Evalina! Stop being ridiculous!" Cat didn't want to

admit that Aunt Maddie had planted too many seeds of doubt in her own mind right now.

"It could happen, you know. Or maybe your father knew Seneca's father once, and they had a fight and your father won and sent Seneca's father off in disgrace."

Cat stared off into space.

"Or . . ." Evalina tapped her index finger against her lips. "Or maybe your father knew Seneca's mother and he loved her, and if he hadn't deserted her they'd be married and Seneca would be your brother—in which case it would be scandalous that you'd married him, and your father would be worried sick you'll produce some absolutely abominable children and—"

"Evalina, that's enough!" Cat stood up quickly.

"What? I was just doing what we've always done, making up delicious stories." Evalina dropped her eyes dejectedly. "I didn't mean any harm. As usual."

"It's time we stopped fabricating stories, Evie," Cat told her gently. "It's time we both grew up."

"Oh, I suppose. But it's so boring to be grown up, don't you think?"

Cat rose and let out a long sigh. "I'm afraid I won't be continuing my needlepoint this afternoon. I've developed a headache. And Aunt Maddie is tired, too."

Evalina turned a skeptical glance on Cat. "Really? Or are you just going upstairs for an afternoon tryst with your handsome husband?"

"Evalina, really!" Cat said with exasperation. "Seneca has gone out this afternoon. He had business to attend to. Now we'll say our good afternoons for today."

Unabashed, Evalina gathered up her needlework, preceded Cat out of the parlor, took her cloak from the hall clothes rack, and shrugged into it. "Don't worry, Lila, if you are thrown out into the streets, you can come and live with us. You, too, Mrs. Allgood." Humming, she left the Stockdale mansion.

Madeline rose and walked out of the parlor, catching up with Cat at the foot of the stairway. Cat linked her arm through her aunt's, and together they started up the stairs. Near the top, Cat felt a wave of dizziness sweep over her. She gripped the banister tighter and managed to get to the landing without Aunt Maddie noticing her distress. In a moment the wave passed. She was just tired, that must be it. She hadn't had a moment's peace since she left Seneca's mountain cabin. The tension with her father and Harrison surrounding announcement of her marriage, the profound excitement she'd been experiencing as Seneca's wife, and now her father's illness had all been too much. She'd ask Dr. Merriweather for a bracing tonic and perhaps something to settle her fluttering stomach. On second thought, she preferred to manage her indigestion, or whatever it was, for herself. She'd brought some burdock roots from the mountains and would steep her own tonic from them.

In the meantime she'd try to rest more often. The pace of her life had certainly quickened since she and Seneca had returned to the city.

"Gentlemen, gentlemen," Stewart Mayne shouted, rapping a gavel against a wood block on the long oak table in the conference room of Stockdale Enterprises. "Quiet, please."

"Father, get hold of yourself," Harrison spat. "We can't have this savage in this meeting. It's your duty to throw him out."

The other five men around the table, including Clyde Brigham and Joseph Madison, fixed their gazes first on

Seneca, who had entered the room in his fringed deerskin leggings and overshirt, his dark hair flowing free around his shoulders. Several rolls of drawings rested through the crook of his arm. Next the men focused on Stewart Mayne, clearly ready to accept whatever decision at which he arrived. Harrison was so angry, his face had turned a vivid red and his eyes shifted about sharply.

Seneca stood at the end of the table next to Garrett Stockdale's empty chair. "You know I have a right to be here now, Stewart," he said without emotion.

"Yes, I do," Stewart replied. "Gentlemen, as you have no doubt heard, Mr. Pierce here is Garrett Stockdale's son-in-law."

The others didn't utter a word.

"Father, have you lost your mind?" Harrison stood up and came around the table to face Stewart. "He has no business being at this meeting, and you know it."

"Harrison," Stewart said with decided aggravation in his voice, "as Garrett's son-in-law, Mr. Pierce has a definite right to be here, just as you would have been had you married Lila. It is only because you're my son and have been involved with the company for so long that you are still here."

"You know damned well he prefers me to be his son-in-law."

"This is not the place to discuss this, Harrison. Regardless of what you or he prefers, the fact remains that Lila married Pierce. He's taking his rightful place. Now sit down." Stewart faced his son with a steady glare until Harrison retreated.

"It's not over yet, Pierce," Harrison threatened and headed for the door.

Seneca said nothing. He noted a rolled set of drawings on a long side table, the kind tracklaying crews used. He smiled, remembering when he'd drawn them months ago, and seated himself in Garrett's chair.

Harrison stormed out of the meeting, presumably to head straight back to Garrett with a report, Seneca figured. He wasn't worried about his hasty exit whatever. By the time Harrison could get back to the meeting with any messages from Stockdale, Seneca would have laid down his concept in such a way as to have turned the tide of Stockdale Enterprises' direction in the Adirondacks.

"As I was saying before the interruption," Daniel Bray, Stockdale's chief tracklaying foreman began, gesturing toward the set of drawings on the side table, "we need more comprehensive surveys than the ones we've been using." Bray, a burly man with wiry gray hair and a furrowed face, was a soft-spoken Westerner and experienced railroad builder brought east by Stockdale for the express purpose of building the Adirondack Mountain Railroad.

"What's wrong with them?" Stewart asked.

Bray ran a frustrated hand through his shaggy hair. "Why, at times we're not even certain we're in the same mountains these drawings say we're supposed to be in. The weather has been takin' some bad turns. We're at a standstill. Stockdale is fit to be tied, so Harrison tells me. Threatening to fire the lot of us unless we make some progress. I don't mind telling you if my crew didn't need the work, I'd walk off this job. No offense to you, Stewart, but your son is a belligerent kid who stomps around spouting off what he says are Stockdale's wishes. Well, some of 'em are darn near impossible. And dangerous. The men are getting hurt too often, and they're getting unruly."

Stewart Mayne sighed. "I understand what you're saying, Daniel. I wish we could do something about it."

"You can do something about it," Bray insisted. "Haven't you got as much right? You've got money in this venture, too, haven't you? Make some right decisions while Stock-dale's ailing before you haven't got a tracklayer left worth his salt."

Mayne looked around at the others. They shrugged or looked away. "We do have money in this venture—you're right about that, Daniel—but Garrett has the majority and the controlling interest. Some of our group here have never been involved in such a monumental undertaking. They bow to Garrett's experience and expertise. And I act in the best interests of the whole group, as best I can, and to guard my own investments as well. I don't know what else to tell you right now."

"Well, then don't expect anything to happen from now on," Bray said. "When I go back and tell the crews this, they'll steal what's left and be gone before the week is out."

The company officers buzzed among themselves, then shouted demands at Stewart and at Bray, who stoically stood his ground in the face of their anger. Seneca observed the whole proceeding without offering a word. At the peak of their argument, he saw the perfect opportunity to set his own plan in motion.

"Gentlemen, gentlemen," Seneca called out firmly above the din. They quieted and he continued. "Gentlemen—and with your permission, Stewart—I believe I can solve at least some of your problems."

He stood up. The others calmed but sent him looks of skepticism.

Seneca unrolled one of his drawings and spun it around so Daniel Bray could study it. "What do you think of that?"

Bray frowned and looked it over first in a manner suggesting he wouldn't put credence in it. Then his frown smoothed. Seneca unrolled the other drawings, and Bray studied those more closely. The others stood and acted as if they were studying them also, but Seneca knew they hadn't much notion of what they were looking at. Except perhaps Stewart Mayne, but he showed no evidence one way or the other.

"This is the east side of Blue Mountain Lake, right?" Bray asked Seneca.

"Right."

"You're saying we can route the track from the southern Racquette Lake extension over this terrain, take it right down into the town?"

"Right to Prospect House if you want," Seneca concurred.

Bray studied the survey drawings and maps. "It looks like it could work."

"Well then, you'd better hop to it," Clyde Brigham said, nodding his head.

"And the sooner the better," Joseph Madison agreed.

Stewart Mayne stroked his chin and turned a questioning glance on Seneca. "Do you really think your idea will take care of these terrain problems once and for all, Seneca?"

Seneca turned his gaze on the drawings. "I know it will, once and for all."

"I'll get these up to the site right away," Daniel said, rolling the drawings and grabbing his dirty hat from a row of pegs near the door.

"If this doesn't work this time," Madison said, "I'm getting out of the railroad business while I still have anything left. You'd be wise to do the same, Stewart."

"Gentlemen, whatever happens, I wish you the best," Seneca said. "Incidentally, I'm certain you know there are other things you could put your money into that will do good for others and reap profit for yourselves." He moved toward the side table and gathered up the original drawings Bray had brought with him. "If I can help you with anything else, do let me know."

He stepped out into the hallway and shut the door to the conference room firmly. He stood still for a moment and considered the best time for him to leave for the mountains himself. Leave New York City.

Leave Cat.

Sixteen

One afternoon a week later, Cat left Aunt Maddie's room, thoughts heavy upon her mind. Their private talk had both elated and frightened her. She hadn't expected to feel this way, so set adrift from one place, so anchored to another. She'd sought her aunt's advice about the barrage of physical and emotional feelings she'd been experiencing since she'd returned to the mansion in Gramercy Park with Seneca as her husband.

"It's perfectly understandable, Cat, darling," Aunt Maddie had said. "You're a woman now."

"But why do I still feel like a child when I'm around Father?" Tears threatened to break loose, and Cat had difficulty swallowing them back.

"That happens to every woman, I think. And remember, dear, he prefers you to remain his little girl always. That's how some fathers are."

"I can't be that," Cat sniffed, "especially not now."

"I know. Perhaps when you talk to him, explain things to him, he'll understand."

"I wish. Yet I don't understand him. At first, he was so resistant to Seneca's presence in our lives. Then he seemed to accept him as his son-in-law. He did let Seneca go to a board meeting in his place, remember?"

"Yes, I remember."

"But lately he's been telling me things about Seneca's past, saying we should be wary of trusting him. It upsets me, but I try not to let it. He says he's plotting something behind our backs. I don't want to believe that. Seneca works hard for Father's company. Night and day he works on his maps and drawings and figures. He knows and understands those mountains like no one else. Seneca could be such a great asset to the company, if Father would let him be."

"Now dear, you mustn't count on that," Aunt Maddie warned. "I don't think either one of them wants that."

"Well, what do they want? I'm certain I don't know. I do wish they could be friends. Especially now."

"Yes, especially now," Aunt Maddie said sadly. Then she brightened. "Perhaps you can talk to each of them separately and then bring the two together. After all, through you they have a common bond now."

"Do you think? Oh, Aunt Maddie, I don't know if I have the strength to complete such a monumental task. They are both such strong men. I wish they could be on the same side. I wish they both could be on my side, but I don't always feel that from them. It's as if I'm a bone between two starving dogs which despise each other. What am I to do?" Cat despaired.

"Well, dear, I have no experience in these matters, I'm sorry to say. My father adored my David, and it was mutual. Although I suspect their political views might have someday caused a rift." Aunt Maddie settled back against her pillows. "Do let me know how you fare, dear. I'm afraid I must nap now."

As Cat walked slowly down the hallway, she wished her mother could be with her now. If only for a little while. She passed her father's study and peeked in. Her father was seated in an easy chair at the side of his desk, going over a spread of papers.

Garrett drank from a cup of herbal tea laced with brandy as he did every afternoon. He did not look up. It was as if he'd sensed her presence. "Lila, we must speak seriously about your future now."

Cat observed as the weeks of recuperation passed, he did not show a marked improvement in health under Dr. Merriweather's care. Yet every day he managed to go to his study, to receive one or two of his associates and discuss business. This afternoon a black leather-bound ledger lay closed in his lap.

Cat tucked her father's silk dressing robe more closely around his throat. "Can't it wait until you're stronger, Father?" She didn't want to talk about the future for a while. The present was—while complicated and fraught with tension—enjoyable for the most part just as it was, and she was not ready to relinquish it for more depressing subjects.

"I may never be stronger. In fact, I may not last the year."

"Now, Father, you know I don't like it when you talk that way."

Regardless of all the rebelliousness she'd felt because of Garrett's determination to control her life, he was still her father, after all, and Cat believed she must love him if only because of that. Aunt Maddie may have taken her deceased mother's place, but there was never anyone to take her father's place. She wished, now that she was married, he would look upon her as grown up, possessing a mind of her own with ideas and thoughts that mattered. Perhaps he would soon. She hoped he'd be strong enough to listen to her as the adult she was now, instead of a little girl.

"Nevertheless," Garrett returned in a firmer voice, "I must prepare for your future, even if you avoid thinking about it. There are things I wish to accomplish before I leave this world, and your security and situation are of great importance to me."

"I'm very secure now, Father. You don't have to worry about that." Cat dropped to the ottoman in front of his chair. "My life is growing more wonderful every day."

"If you're referring to Pierce, there is nothing secure about your situation."

"Oh, Father, if you'd only give Seneca a chance, you'd see that he's perfect for me, for us."

"It's you who do not see, Lila. You defied me, and I've been the one to pay for it."

"What do you mean, you're paying for it? Hasn't it been going well with the business? Surely you can see what a help Seneca has been since you've taken ill."

Garrett raised his hand to silence his daughter. Much as he loved Lila in his own way, she did not understand the ways of business. Her immature blundering into this marriage with Pierce was costing him too much, and he meant to put a stop to it in whatever manner he could.

"I'm afraid I have very bad news for you, Lila. Unfortunately Pierce knows about this as well."

"Bad news? What bad news does Seneca know about?"

Lila's curiosity was obviously piqued. He could tell she'd become worried, and in the past he could always capitalize on that.

Garrett sighed and flipped open the ledger. "We must complete trackage to Blue Mountain Lake and beyond by next spring or we'll be ruined."

Lila stared at him. "Ruined? What do you mean? Why is it so important that the track reach Blue Mountain

Lake? Can't it run in another direction and be just as valuable to you?"

"No, it cannot. Try to understand this, Lila, please. Passage to Prospect House and points beyond is what will attract guests and businessmen. They, in turn, will see the value in opening the Adirondacks for sport and development, and for track to the Saint Lawrence River and Lake Ontario. They'll invest heavily. We stand to make a great deal of money. Do you understand now?"

"I only understand your obsession with it. Why can't you listen to Seneca? He can guide you—"

"Hush up about Pierce!" Garrett shouted. Startled at the sudden change in his tone of voice, Lila jumped. "He knows how critical my situation is, and he's using it against me."

"What are you talking about?"

"Everything, *everything* I own is tied up in the railroad." Garrett feebly shoved the ledger toward his daughter and pointed at the figures.

Lila stared at the rows and columns of numbers. Garrett started to retrieve the ledger, but she held on to it tightly. She turned the pages slowly and worked to absorb all that she was reading.

"What does any of this have to do with Seneca?"

"I have learned that Pierce knows my capital, both in stocks and cash, is tied up in the railroad. That's why he thwarted my plans with his own surveys and directed the track into worthless land."

Cat's heart pounded in her ears. "There must be some mistake. Perhaps the men couldn't read the surveys properly and simply took it upon themselves to redirect—"

"Don't be so naive, Lila. I've been informed the last seven miles of track laid, with Pierce's drawings as guides, end at a bog. There's no firm land foundation to lay more in that direction. What's there has already begun to sink and will have to be torn up if it's to be salvaged. I can't afford another setback like that or I'll lose the railroad, the land, my camp, everything. Including this house. Pierce is to blame."

Lila stared off into space, recognition slowly lighting her face. "Yes, I do see now. The bog."

Garrett snapped his eyes up to hers, and his anger deepened. "You knew about this?"

"Calm yourself, Father. I knew about the bog, yes. I can understand now why the tracks are sinking. I was almost lost myself there. I came upon it and stepped right into it without any sense whatsoever that the earth would change so drastically."

"Then you can understand that he knew exactly what he was doing with those drawings."

Lila thought for a moment. "I'm certain it's all a mistake, Father. You see, I believe Seneca was only doing what you are doing—trying to save his own property, protecting his family. So you see how much alike you are?"

"Alike?" Garrett sputtered. "The last thing I am is anything like Pierce!" His daughter was more addle-brained than he would have liked to even suspect. He could no more be like that Indian than he was like Seneca's father. Eli Pierce was just as simpleminded about things. He thought big, but when it came to putting the plans into action, he became overly concerned with land inhabited by savages. He would always let his altruistic nature get in the way of progress, and ultimately in the way of their own accumulation of assets.

Suddenly Garrett's mind sharpened. She'd said something about. . . . "What did you mean about Pierce and family property?"

Lila brightened. "It's very simple. Seneca's mother and

sister and grandparents are buried not far from that bog. It's sacred ground for his people."

"You say these graves are near the bog?" Garrett asked.

"Yes, that's why it makes sense that he would attempt to steer the work crews away from them. They must have taken a wrong turn or something. That's why—"

"Are the graves marked?" he probed further.

"Not like Mother's, with an engraved headstone, if that's what you mean. I didn't know what they were when I first saw them. But Seneca understands the meaning of the stones he has piled in mounds. Pink granite. They're quite lovely, really. There are trees protecting them all around like a glen."

"Pink granite, in mounds you say?" Garrett stroked his chin.

"Yes. You must be very certain the crews know where those graves are so they will leave them undisturbed. They mean everything to Seneca."

Garrett nodded, deep in thought. "I understand. Yes." He definitely would make the crews know exactly where those graves were. Harrison could handle it for him—and be grateful to him for the chance to exact retribution against Pierce. At last . . . the breakthrough he'd been seeking.

Lila grew excited in her belief that everything was going to be all right. "Don't you see? You would do the same thing if our home was threatened. I'm certain if you explain to Seneca the difficulty with his drawings he'll make them right. It was all a mistake, I just know it."

Garrett thought long before his frustration grew too much for him to contain. "Lila, will you get hold of yourself? Pierce is smart, I'll grant that. He doesn't make mistakes with his drawings. He knew exactly what he was doing by routing the tracks that way. He knew they'd sink and would cost me even more money and time to replace. He is trying to destroy me . . . destroy *us*."

"But why would he do that, Father? What is the reason? Is there something in your past that would make you think he would do such a thing? I don't understand it. I don't understand why you can even think this way or why you seem to hate him so."

"Lila, the past is dead. I've done nothing to him, nothing. You must understand the full meaning of this latest event. I think you do but are unwilling to accept it yet. Pierce wants to destroy me. He will use any means. First he used you, and now he has in mind to destroy my very existence."

"Me? Father, what do you mean, me?" Lila's voice shook.

She grasped the folds of her skirts in her fingers. He'd planted some real seeds of doubt in her mind. Garrett knew that would upset her. Her conviction to be Pierce's wife was not as solid as she liked it to appear.

"He married you knowing full well I would be against it. But it was a way for him to move into my house, gain access to my private papers."

"He married me to save me from marrying Harrison. I didn't want to marry Harrison, Father, but you were forcing me. I was desperate. Seneca did it for me. He wasn't trying to do anything to you. He wouldn't . . . I think he wouldn't do that."

"Oh, but he has, hasn't he? Now, don't worry, I can make this right for you. I have my attorneys looking into an annulment right now. People will simply believe you were duped into the marriage. He forced you during his kidnapping, hoping to get money from me."

Lila jumped up, holding her hand over her heart. "Father, what are you saying? He didn't kidnap me. He saved my life."

"How do you know that? You said yourself you woke up in his cabin and you were wounded and in pain. He shot you, then kidnapped you to get to me." He grasped his daughter's hands and held them tightly. "I know it's difficult for you to understand, but believe me, when this is all over you'll thank me for acquiring a speedy annulment for you. You can go away for a while. Perhaps an ocean voyage to Europe. You can take Madeline as your chaperone and even Evalina if you wish. What do you say to that? And when you come back, you and Harrison can be married as originally planned. You will have overcome this unfortunate incident, and you will be helping me and the future of Stockdale Enterprises as well. This is exactly what you've been groomed for."

Garrett believed he knew his daughter well. She would not be able to refuse his plea for help nor his offer of a holiday. He would sell some of his stock to afford to send her off to Europe. It was best she was out of the way when he took care of Seneca Pierce. If it was the last thing he would achieve on earth, he would see Pierce dead if need be, and his railroad empire thriving. Lila's marriage to Harrison, and the additional funds Stewart Mayne had pledged to the company upon their wedding day, would keep it solvent until his Adirondack ventures were thriving and producing abundant wealth. He would beat the Durants at their own game and show the world that Garrett Stockdale was a man to be reckoned with. That would settle his part in the Union Pacific scandal once and for all. Perhaps even a town could be named for him. Then he would leave an extensive estate and legacy for his only child and her heirs. Everyone would know what a great man he was.

Yes, Garrett Stockdale believed he knew his daughter well.

And so it came as a great shock when Lila pulled her hands from his grasp and ran toward the study door, shouting at him.

"There will be no ocean voyage to Europe, Father. And there will be no annulment. There will never be a marriage to Harrison. Seneca and I are married. We've consummated it, and nothing you can do can ever change that!"

She ran from the room, slamming the door behind her.

Cat's flight from her father's study had ended outside her bedroom door, behind which she knew Seneca was working. She stood there for a long time pondering his words, thinking over the last few months, recalling some of Seneca's actions. In her heart she understood her father might be right about Seneca's motives. He wanted to bring Garrett Stockdale down, and there was more to it than saving the mountains. And her father wanted to bring Seneca down, and she knew there was more to it than just the railroad at stake. Still, she would not give Seneca up. She held the solution to all their problems, and through it she would find the means to stave off this mutual destruction her husband and father seemed bent on.

As she waited outside her closed bedroom door collecting her thoughts and settling her raging emotions, Cat realized she was without tears. On the contrary, a new strength consumed her, an emotion that she understood now had been kindled in Seneca's cabin some months ago and had accumulated a heat fanned by self-confidence and security. Allowing herself a few more moments, she wondered how it was she'd never taken charge of her own life, why it was the women she knew all lived in the shadows of their men.

With a deep breath, she entered the bedroom, slowly closing the door behind her.

"I know what you've been doing, Seneca, and I want to talk about it."

From his seat at the writing desk, Seneca momentarily raised his eyes from the papers he'd been reading before going back to his work. "And just what do you think it is that I've been doing?" he replied calmly.

Cat stood halfway between the door and the desk. "My father tells me you're trying to ruin him, and I want to know why."

"It appears you believe him. We've talked about this many times. I'm saving the mountains from ruin by men who would plunder them for their own gain and nothing more." He rubbed the pleated space between his eyes. "Men like—"

"Like my father, is that what you were going to say?"

Seneca knew what his answer would mean to the two of them. Their fate was inevitable, and there was no turning back now.

"Yes."

Cat's green eyes grew glassy with unshed tears. Her hands shook, and she started to pace the length of the room. "I didn't believe him before. I didn't believe *you* before. I know neither of you have revealed to me all of the facts as you see them, but I've begun to understand that you are both single-minded."

Seneca continued to concentrate on his papers, but the words blurred in front of him.

Cat stood at the edge of the bed. "If he knows why you want to destroy him, he won't tell me. You're my husband. You tell me, Seneca. Why do you want to do this to him?

He's mortgaged everything, including this house. You knew that, didn't you? He'll lose everything that means anything to him. And that's what you want, isn't it? What you set out to do. Why, Seneca, why?" There were no tears in her voice.

Seneca stood then. She deserved to know the truth. He considered whether or not she was ready to take it. There was something different about her right now. She wasn't behaving like the spoiled rich girl he believed she still was, even after those weeks in the cabin.

"Because he destroyed everything that ever meant anything to me," he said thickly.

"What . . . what are you talking about?"

Seneca ran his hand through his hair and strode to the window. Below, the New York street bustled with carriages and pedestrians. Couples. Children. Families. "I think it's best you don't know," he said huskily.

"Don't use that with me," Cat choked. "Tell me. I'm your wife, remember?"

He spun around toward her. "You're not my wife."

"What do you mean? We're married. You know we're married!"

Seneca went to her, grabbed her shoulders and forced her to sit on the bed. "Here is the cold, hard truth of everything. I wanted that wedding ceremony because needed Garrett Stockdale's daughter to be my wife."

At the sight of her eyes turning hard and dry, he dropped his hands from her shoulders. He turned his face away and fixed his gaze on the closed door. For the second time in his life he felt like running away, as far and as fast a he could. If he had any sense, he'd get up right now and leave her and not look back. But for reasons he was only beginning to comprehend, he knew he couldn't run this time, had to stay long enough to give Cat an explanation

He was at a point of no return, and he wouldn't stop now. He owed her that much.

He breathed deeply and let it out slowly.

"You've been a spoiled child all your life. I thought it was possible to teach you the value of land and resources. You seemed to like living in the mountains for a time, but I think you didn't feel their power inside the way I do. We came back to the city together and I could see that even though you'd taken me as your husband, your life hadn't changed all that much. You reverted back to the willful little rich girl you always were, and you brought me into the life your father had created for you. I went along with it. I thought I could . . ."

Cat's shoulders dropped. She stared down at her hands folded in her lap. "You thought you could use me to get at my father."

"At first, yes, I did. And then I thought if you loved the mountains the way I do, saw what their preservation meant to me and to others, you'd convince your father to stop his plans for timber removal, development, and for the railroad. But you didn't, and after a while I regretted what I'd done."

"Regretted marrying me?" His silence forced Cat to go on. "But why?" she breathed. "What did we do to you that was so horrible? How could you use people like that?"

Seneca turned on her then. He stood in front of her, close and menacing. His suppressed rage gathered momentum and exploded. "I'm amazed you can ask such a question. You used me to save yourself from your father's intent to marry you off to Harrison Mayne."

"That wasn't the only reason," Cat blurted out. "I . . . I had feelings . . . *have* feelings for you, and you know it. And there's more now."

Her words ripped into Seneca's heart. He steeled himself against the pain and rushed on. "Then you tried to turn me into the perfect son-in-law for your father. You learned your wiles at the knee of your crafty father, my dear. He used my father and their partnership in the building of the transcontinental railroad to further his own personal interests. He used him, and then he used him up, physically, emotionally. And then he purposely bankrupted him.

"I don't care if you believe me or not. It's true. Garrett Stockdale, Stewart Mayne, and Eli Pierce were partners in the Union Pacific construction back then. Your father bled my father dry of the money he had. He couldn't get back to my mother and sister, who were sick. And he'd vowed to them he would do right in business, make something of himself, make them proud of him. But he became a broken man. My father committed suicide, and it was your father who drove him to it!"

Cat shrank back from him, folding in the middle. "I don't believe you. Father couldn't—Oh, God, that's horrible. I'm so sorry, Seneca, so sorry for you." Cat slipped her arms around his waist and tried to hold him.

Seneca pushed her arms away. "Don't feel sorry for me." He moved slowly and sat down on the bed next to her.

Cat sucked in her lower lip. She didn't want to believe what he was telling her, yet she knew in her heart he wasn't lying. She felt his pain profoundly. She wanted to comfort him. He wouldn't let her. She wanted to understand everything, understand what was really happening between him and her father, between him and herself. Her mind reeled with all that her father had told her and now all that Seneca had said. She didn't want to believe either one of them, yet she sensed they'd both told her their own truths.

She needed to be comforted right now, by him, the man she loved. But he was cold as granite.

She tried again, attempting to make some sense of all that he was saying. "Why do you think it was my father who drove yours to suicide?"

Seneca stared straight ahead. "My father joined the railroad company to do something big with his life, make a new life for our family," he said dully. "When he arrived on the plains he saw how the crews—crews who were in his employ since he was a partner—were working on the trackage for so little money they could barely live. People who'd sunk their hard-earned cash into what turned out to be worthless stock because of the greed of others like your father who took from it, lost everything. Some even lost their families over it. And the worst thing for my father was seeing how Indians were dying and being driven out of their lands by the building of the railroad. That was not my father's vision. He saw the value in the railroad, wanted it to make people's lives better, offer prosperity, not destroy them. And when he realized how much he'd allowed his own desires to take over and cloud his thinking, he could not face the part he knew he'd unwittingly played in it. Nor could he face my mother. He felt the shame of the credit scandal."

Seneca sobbed then. "He was out of his mind with the brutal destruction of a people, people he felt akin to, and he just snapped. By the time I could get to him, he . . . he was desperate. When he saw me he ran to the trestle bridge and jumped. I tried to stop him, but I wasn't fast enough or strong enough. I grabbed his coat, but he got out of it." Seneca choked. "He was crying so hard. And I couldn't stop him. He jumped from a railroad trestle into a ravine. I guess seeing me at that moment was too much. Your father drove him to despair, and seeing me was the trigger that pushed him to the breaking point."

He dropped his face into his hands, and his shoulders shook. He knew then he hadn't grieved over the loss of his father—the great loss to him as a boy growing up, the great loss he knew his mother and sister had suffered. But he cursed himself for his weakness in letting his emotions overtake him in the presence of Garrett Stockdale's daughter.

He felt her hand on his back, felt it rubbing his shoulders. He knew she wanted to comfort him, but he wouldn't let her. If he did, he knew he might cling to her and never let her go. To do that would be to let go of himself. He would never let that happen. He straightened his back sharply, raised his head, and set his jaw firmly. Cat removed her hand from his shoulders. He rose and went to the window.

"I ran away as fast as I could. It took me a month to get home, and when I arrived I found my mother and sister sick and dying. I buried them myself in my grandparents' burial ground on the mountain. I blame your father for all of it."

"But what about Stewart Mayne? Why aren't you placing as much blame on him? He was as much a part of everything." Cat's voice was desperate.

"He was duped as much as my father was. In fact, he was trying to help my father get out of it and get back to us. Stewart said his own family didn't care much for him. He wanted to be loved as much as he knew my father was by us. He wanted that kind of family for himself. I never blamed Stewart. I think he's been trying to make it up to me in recent years."

Cat's desire to comfort him left her. Her desire to be

comforted by him ached within her. She knew that was not about to happen now. Her mind focused, and her constricted voice took on a hard edge. "So the two of you have been plotting to take my father down, haven't you?"

"Not the two of us. Just me. Stewart had nothing to do with this. He merely thought he was helping me regain some sense of direction. And he felt by employing me he could build this Adirondack railway with little destruction to the mountains and to the people who live in them. Under normal circumstances that would have been right thinking. He was, in his own way, trying to pay back a personal debt. And I wanted to save what was left of my family, just a mound of graves on a mountain."

"Didn't you realize the tracklayers would figure out eventually that you'd given them survey maps that would lead them right into that bog?"

"Of course. But by then your father would be out of money, and no one would back him again. He'd be finished." Seneca voiced the finality of his plan simply.

Cat sighed with new understanding. "And so you married me to add insult to my father's impending injury by your hands. You knew he'd be livid when he found out I married the son of Eli Pierce, knew he'd think you were plotting against him. You wanted him to feel threatened, desperate. But he didn't, did he? Instead, he allowed you to address the company board in his absence." Her voice scaled. "He wanted to trust you because you are my husband now."

He whirled on her. "He wanted to set me up for the fall! He wanted to suck me in like he had my father. He thought I'd fall for it because I'd married you. And he wanted to ruin me once and for all. He didn't need another Pierce throwing honesty in his face. I think it was sweet irony for him to have Eli's son working for him. I'm not entirely certain how he'd bring it all about, but I knew he would, and I've beaten him to it."

Cat clamped her hands over her ears. "I won't listen to this! He's strong-minded, but I won't believe my father is as evil as you say."

Seneca went to her and took her hands from her ears, trapping her wrists in his fingers. "You'd better listen to it. You said yourself he's controlled you all your life. He controlled your mother. He has your aunt cowering. And beyond that he wants to control everything he touches. You have no power against him!"

Every fiber in Cat's body strained with anger and frustration. She shook her wrists free. "You don't know me at all, do you?" Her voice was dangerously low. "You've never taken the time to know me. He doesn't control me any longer. He's trying to force an annulment, but I won't let it happen. He wanted me to marry Harrison. But look what I did. I disappointed him terribly when I married you."

"Yes, just look!" Seneca shouted. "You're just like him. You did it to save your own pretty little behind."

"I did it for more than that and you know it!" she shouted back. "I love you! Are you satisfied? I love you! I think I've loved you from the first moment I saw you. But maybe I only loved the dream of you. I don't know. I don't know." She forced calm then. "And I love my father. All I want to do is be happy. And I want you to be happy. And I want him to be happy. And I wanted to be a part of making you both happy. But now nobody's happy!" She flung herself down on the bed and caught herself before she sobbed into the quilts. Instead, she sat up and set her jaw, holding old emotions in check.

Seneca ran his hands through his hair, then walked back to the window. "Maybe we deserve each other after all.

We used each other. It would serve us both right if we were tied to each other for the rest of our lives. But the other irony of it is that the marriage isn't real. We aren't married."

Cat rose from the bed and leaned against the bedpost. She felt weaker than she had when she'd lain wounded in Seneca's cabin. These moments with him were far more painful than she ever could have expected.

"That's the second time you've said that. What do you mean we're not married, that I'm not your wife?" Her voice cracked. "We have to be married."

"Maurice Sender is or was a monk," Seneca said wearily. "No one knows where this was or even if it was so. It's doubtful whether or not he can perform a legal marriage ceremony, but it didn't seem to matter at the time."

"But we signed something. We repeated vows. Bear said he was real."

"Bear believes he is real. I don't."

"But you went along with it, you allowed the ceremony to go on. All that, just for revenge on my father?"

Seneca turned back toward her. "I wasn't thinking of revenge then."

Cat didn't look at him. "What were you thinking of then?"

"It's not important now."

"It's more important than ever."

Seneca turned back to the window. As he watched the people below, he knew with a stab of renewed pain how much he'd lost. He'd lost so many he loved. His father, his mother, his sister. He hadn't wanted to love anyone again, more to save himself from loss than anything else. The last person in the world he would have chosen to love was Lila Cat Stockdale, daughter of Garrett Stockdale, the man who destroyed his family.

But he'd fallen in love with Cat in spite of his fight against it. And now he had to let her go, and the fight against that was just as strong. He couldn't weaken now, had to keep up a stream of hurtful words. They would make his running away from her so much easier.

"It will be easy for you now, won't it?" he said acidly. "There doesn't have to be the inconvenience of an annulment. And you can give up your crusade to change me into something I'm not. Your father will find a way to cover up your little indiscretion. And I'm certain Harrison will want to pick up where he left off with you. This time you will be eternally grateful that he has saved you from a life of poverty. You can live just as your father wanted you to live. Just as you really wanted to live all along. There is no need for you to give up anything to go to the mountains and live in a cabin with a wild Indian, is there?" He started for the door.

"Seneca! Where are you going? Don't leave! Don't do this to us!" she pleaded.

"There is no us, Cat. There never could be."

"Yes, there is. What about up in the mountains? What about at the cabin? We made love. I never knew what that could mean, really mean." She held onto the bedpost for support. "We made love everywhere. It was more than I ever dreamed in my fantasies, more exquisite, more thrilling, more engulfing than I could have ever imagined. What about that?"

Seneca stopped at the door. He didn't turn to face her. "It was nothing more than a man getting what he needed from a woman. Even you know about men and lust."

"I don't believe that! Neither do you. I wanted you as much as you wanted me. I still do! What about bathing together? Making love in the pool? In the forest? In your balsam pine bed? In my bedroom here in this house? Even on the train coming back here? What about all that? Can you honestly say to me it was only lust?"

Seneca clenched his fists. "It was what it was."

"Oh, God, please don't mean that, please!" Cat's voice broke. "You don't want to admit it, but you love me. You know you do. You *know* you do. I know you do. You can't mean that all we've been to each other has meant nothing to you."

Seneca clenched his fists, then whirled around. "I do mean that. If you think about it someday, you'll remember exactly what it was. When you're the perfect society matron—as Mrs. Harrison Mayne presiding over some tea party in your own mansion—you'll have forgotten all about it."

"Never, never. Seneca . . ." She faltered but managed to reach out and grasp his arm. "Please, listen to me. Please talk to me. I'll understand. I know how to make everything right. Father will understand, and you will, too. Stay with me, please."

Seneca couldn't stand to see Cat pleading and crying. His insides were on fire with the pain and wrenching apart of the two of them. But it had to be. The past would always loom like a specter over their present.

He could not live in her world. She could not live in his.

There was nothing that could bring them together to overcome that. Nothing.

He looked into the emerald-green eyes now glistening with tears. Her alabaster skin was now blotched with red patches and tear tracks. Pain turned her ready smile to profound sadness.

She would get over it. She would get over him. It was in her nature. He knew that.

It was not in his nature.

He couldn't help himself. He grabbed her and pulled her roughly into his arms. With passionate strength he kissed her face, her throat, tasted the salt of her tears, took in the subtle perfume of her hair. He pushed his hands over her hips, her waist, up toward her breasts. Her slender form had filled out some. Her curves seemed more accentuated. She was almost voluptuous now.

He was hungry for her, wanted her more now than ever before.

He drove his lips into hers like a madman, slipping his hand up her throat and cupping her chin and jaws, forcing her to kiss him. She didn't resist.

His fury subsided and he kissed her sweetly, tenderly, with a controlled fire. He stepped back from her, gazed longingly into her eyes, then closed his own. His whisper was almost inaudible. "You're right. I do love you. Goodbye, Cat . . . Pierce."

And then he left the room.

Cat stood stunned. What had he said? Goodbye? He had said he loved her. Then how could he say goodbye?

"Seneca!" She rushed into the hallway. He stopped at the top of the stairs. "We haven't finished."

"There's nothing left for either of us to say." He didn't turn around.

Cat stayed calm. She would not plead this time. He had a choice. And at last she knew she had a choice as well.

"Perhaps you've nothing left to say, but I have much more," she told him evenly. "If you don't want the servants and other members of the household to hear what I have to say, you'll come back into the bedroom. I won't keep you long. When I'm finished, you can decide to leave or to stay."

Seneca stood strong and impervious for several moments. Then he turned and walked slowly toward her and went back into the room they'd been sharing. Cat closed the door and walked to the window.

"I don't know everything," she began, stopped, and began again. "I don't know everything that went on between my father and yours. And Seneca, you don't either. You weren't there with them." He started to protest, but she raised her hand. "Wait. I will say what I want to say. You cannot blame my father for your father's death, regardless of anything he might have done. They were in business together. Your father took his own life because he couldn't cope with everything. *He* took his own life. He wasn't thinking about his responsibilities, his family. He was thinking only of himself. I think when you arrived he was afraid to see disappointment in your eyes, afraid you'd accuse him of not taking care of his family. And, Seneca, he knew you'd be right."

Seneca stood silently in the center of the room, arms hanging down at his sides. His hands balled into fists. "You don't know anything about my father," he growled.

"No, that's true. You don't know anything about mine either, only what you built in your mind to help you and your family over your grief at losing Eli."

Seneca let out a hard breath. "My father wouldn't leave us, he wouldn't desert us unless he was forced to. Your father forced him to do it."

Cat remained more calm than she ever had in her life. She wasn't certain where her strength was coming from, but it was as if some deep force within her was at last free to support her.

"Your father could not have been forced to desert you and your family. Could you have done that?"

"Of course not! I went back to them—I was with them through their sickness. He wasn't! I did it all. I saw their pain! *I* buried them!"

"And *nothing* could have forced you away from them during that time," she said gently. "It's time you gave your father his own responsibility. He did it, Seneca. He took his own life. I know it's horribly painful to admit your father deserted you, but I think you know he did."

Seneca turned his back on her, and she saw his shoulders shake. "Are you quite finished with your speech now?"

"No. I have one more thing I want you to hear." She took a deep breath. "For whatever reasons you did so, you married me. Now you want to run out on your responsibility to me as well. I married you, and yes, I know the reasons I had then weren't as honorable as I would have liked. Nonetheless, we did marry. We made a commitment to each other, and we believed the ceremony was real even if the marriage was not. At first. I took our vows seriously. Maybe not right away, but when we came back here I believed in our vows. I believed I was your wife and you were my husband, and there were certain understandings between us . . ."

"You know I was a convenience for you," he uttered low.

"In my spoiled little girl way, that was most likely so in the beginning. But in case you haven't noticed, Seneca, I'm a woman now. Nothing is a convenience for me anymore. You especially. But perhaps that's all I've been to you. Am I, Seneca? Have I been merely a convenience for you, a means to an end? A way to justify your father's suicide in your own mind?"

Seneca said nothing.

Cat waited interminable minutes.

Seneca did not turn around before striding to the door and leaving the room.

Cat's strength left her. She dropped to the floor, her silk skirts pooling around her. She sobbed quietly into them.

"He's left me," she sobbed over and over. Then she sat up straight and dropped her head back, letting her tears fall freely. She hugged the middle of her body tenderly.

"He's left *us*."

Seventeen

Winter fast encroached upon the Adirondack Mountains. Seneca spent his long days cutting and stacking wood for his cabin, hunting and storing meat, fishing, and tracking the presence of the railroad builders until heavy snowfall and plunging temperatures drove them away.

He spent his even longer nights in the cabin brooding about Cat, about her last hurtful words, and about the foolishness of his actions by marrying her, no matter how temporary the situation was to be. But more, he lamented what might have been, and it eroded his insides. When he wasn't languishing in dark moods, he entertained anger and frustration over the shallowness of Cat and society women like her and berated himself for expecting more.

No matter how hard he worked, how much and how often he railed against her and himself, he could not escape the truth that pelted him in icy slashes as stinging as the sleet and snow that battered the mountains. He loved Cat, loved her with a magnitude as powerful as any emotion he'd ever experienced for family and land. The self-knowledge rocked him at his very core—the means to live with it unreachable.

He visited his family's graves only once. He couldn't bring himself to talk to his mother's spirit the way he always had. His consuming sense of shame built a barrier between them. He could not bring himself to speak out loud, talk about his father, talk about his vow to protect everything that had always meant so much to him. He believed himself a failure, but could not name his successes—so his inability to acknowledge them underscored that failure. He questioned everything he'd done in his life and saw nothing as a real accomplishment or a return to the earth that had given him life.

The days and nights stretched into weeks, the weeks into months, but even the promise of an early spring did not shake him from his melancholy.

Bear burst into Seneca's cabin early one morning. "You come, *mon ami*," he beckoned. "They are among your family." He stepped back outside in the early spring snowfall.

Grimly Seneca donned thick moccasins and wool coat and snapped up his rifle from a rack near the door. Silently he followed Bear through the frosted forest to a secluded vantage point in which to observe the grave sites. They saw three men walking around the area, murmuring low. One of them turned around and Seneca caught full view of his face. Harrison Mayne.

Seneca stepped out of his hiding place, rifle leveled on the three men. Bear emerged to stand by his side, large, imposing.

"You're on private property, Mayne. Get out now," Seneca growled.

"Well, well, fancy meeting you out here, Pierce. We all wondered where you'd run off to, leaving your lovely bride all alone."

Seneca swallowed the knot of remorse that threatened to break through the hard shell of defense he effected. "You're trespassing, Mayne. Take your men and get out."

A fourth man came up the incline, puffing when he

reached the others. He lifted his head, startled to see Seneca.

"Seneca! Well, it's good to see you, son." Stewart Mayne shot out his right hand in greeting.

Seneca's hard gaze glanced off the offered hand and froze on Harrison and the others. "Stewart. I didn't expect . . . I hoped you were different from the rest of them. You're still Stockdale's partner through and through, aren't you?"

Stewart slowly dropped his hand. "You don't understand, son. Give me a chance to explain."

"I don't want your explanations," Seneca bit out.

Harrison planted his hands on his bulging hips and leveled a surly glare on his father. "Easy for you to call him 'son,' isn't it, Father? If ever there was a weak link in Garrett's chain of command, it's you."

"Shut up, Harrison," Stewart commanded. "I've known Seneca since he was a boy. He and Eli Pierce had a special father and son relationship, and I was honored to know them both and count them as friends." He looked back at Seneca. "I still feel that way."

"Do not misplace your honor, Stewart. Take these men and leave. This property is off limits to Stockdale Enterprises and any other Stockdale affiliation." Seneca held the gaze of the older Mayne and wanted to believe he saw understanding in an old friend's eyes.

"Now, now," Harrison drawled insolently, "no need to disparage your wife that never was. Lila's little deviation with you has been forgiven by Garrett and by me. She knows her obligations." He sent a disdainful glance over his shoulder toward the graves.

Seneca watched the malevolent Harrison. A brief urge to wipe the smug smile off his sagging jowls stabbed at him. He curbed it. Harrison knew only to act on orders.

So the loyal daughter had informed her father and former fiancé of his private and beloved place that cradled his memories and the remnants of his family. There was no other way Harrison could have found it.

"Harrison, leave it alone." Stewart stepped between his son and Seneca.

"Leave, Stewart," Seneca said. "Please."

Stewart stood still. His features told a thousand sentiments silently: sorrow, regret, care. But he had a job to do, and Seneca knew it. "Can we talk about all of this?" he asked gently.

"No, sir, we cannot. It's best you leave now." Seneca moved a step closer to stand his ground.

The next few minutes were a blur of confusion. Harrison knocked his father to the ground. The two railroad workers jumped Bear, while Harrison—in what Seneca thought in a flash was a pure act of infantile insanity—challenged him by drawing a pistol and aiming it at him. Seneca reversed the rifle in his hands and swung, connecting the butt of it with Harrison's jaw. Mayne's pistol went off and the erratic bullet caught Seneca in the upper arm. The two men fell backward, away from each other. Bear handily took care of the other two, snatched the pistol from the ground near the grave mound, and attended to Seneca who'd forced himself up to his feet and moved toward Stewart.

Seneca lifted the older Mayne's shoulders and took the bandanna Bear handed him to wipe away the blood at his temple. Stewart came around and opened his eyes.

"You'll be all right," Seneca told him. "Go back home."

"Seneca," Stewart whispered, "give up the fight. I beg you to do this before anything worse happens."

"Go back home, Stewart." He helped him to his feet,

then turned toward Harrison. "Get your father and these men out of here, Mayne."

Harrison staggered to his feet, wiping blood away and nursing the ugly welt that had swollen on the side of his face. "You've lost, Pierce. Face it. You've lost everything. We'll be back, and next time there'll be more of us. By summer there'll be trains running right through this spot." He leaned over and spat upon Seneca's mother's grave.

Seneca lunged for him, stopped by Bear's mighty grip around his shoulders and Stewart's physical intervention of Harrison. Silently then the intruders retreated.

Ignoring his bleeding gunshot wound, Seneca leaned down and wiped Harrison's spittle from his mother's grave with the sleeve of his coat. He did not stem the flow of tears that overtook him.

Cat left the dining room following breakfast intent on making her morning visit to her father's bedside, where he'd been confined the last several weeks. Her thoughts hung about her like a burdensome cloak, heavy with the loss of Seneca in her life and the reality of the severity of her father's declining health. Not a daylight hour passed without thoughts of Seneca, not a fitful night passed without dreams of him by her side.

She'd spent the first few weeks of winter in a cloud of gloom over their denouement. But then the secret she carried inside grew with warmth and wonder, lifting her gloom. She was going to have a baby! With spring would come new life, just as the season had promised since time began. Her strength grew with each week, and she spent hours in apprehensive wonder about the life she was carrying in her womb—a life she and Seneca had created out of what she'd believed in her heart was love.

She wasn't certain what she would do once her condition became blatantly apparent, but she had decided not to let Seneca know about the baby. Even her father did not know yet. Aunt Maddie understood her decision but did not agree with it. And Cat had sworn Evalina to secrecy. If Seneca were to come back for her, she had to know it was because he loved and wanted her first. Without him, the baby was hers and hers alone, blood and spirit of Seneca, flesh and soul of Cat.

As she laboriously climbed the stairs to her father's room, Cat was startled to meet Harrison descending.

"What are you doing here?" she snapped, possessing no mood and energy to sidestep his caustic remarks, nor to suffer his leering innuendos.

"And a warm good morning to you, too, my dearly betrothed." Harrison's upper lip curled into a sneer as he reached for her hand and kissed it before she was quick enough to evade his grasp. She snatched it away and wiped the back of it on her apron.

Cat glared at him. "You are not my betrothed. In case you've forgotten, let me remind you I am already married."

Harrison dropped his head back and laughed loudly. "Must be you haven't spoken to your father this morning. He has interesting news for you."

"I don't know what you're talking about." She started to pass him, then thought to ask him something she'd been concerned with for a while. "What about your intentions with Evalina? Are they honorable?"

"As honorable as ever I can be. My attention to her served its purpose. Her father came forth with more money once he considered I might be taking his little twit of a daughter off his hands. I couldn't wait to be rid of her. Besides, it seems she has a secret admirer, a very interesting secret admirer."

Cat was certain Evalina had let it slip that she was corresponding with Bear. She wondered just how much more her friend had slipped. She tried then to pass Harrison, but he blocked her way.

"Why are you here, Harrison? If your wish was to annoy me this morning, it won't happen. I have better things to think about than your petty aggravation."

"That won't last, my dear. Soon you will have much more important things to think about. As for my presence, I was simply reporting to my boss . . . as always."

"Stay away from my father, do you hear me? He's too sick to listen to your ramblings." Cat did not look at him, willing his loathsome visage away from her sight.

Harrison straightened, blocking her last step to the upper landing. "As usual, my dear Lila, you go about in a fog, oblivious to reality. Your father, sick or no, is fully in charge of Stockdale Enterprises and all that concerns it. It was my duty to inform him of the altercation my father and I and Garrett's crew had with Pierce in the mountains."

Cat's gaze snapped up to meet Harrison's sneer. "Seneca? You saw Seneca?"

"Let's just say we saw each other. My father and I and two of our crew were paying our respects to his family grave. For some reason he didn't take kindly to it. In fact, he was downright inhospitable."

Cat felt her pulse race. "You . . . you were at the grave site?" She knew what the family graves meant to Seneca. He would look upon Harrison's presence as a desecration of all that he believed sacred. "How did you find out about it?"

"Funny you should ask that. Your dear friend, Evalina,

shared the contents of her love letter from that Frenchman with me."

Cat narrowed her eyes, trying to discern if Harrison was lying to her. If Evalina had learned of the graves through Bear, and had passed the information on to Harrison, Cat would end their friendship in a trice.

"But," Harrison paused, making certain, she thought, his next words would have the impact he sought, "we couldn't have found the graves without your help."

Cat's insides turned over. "What . . . whatever do you mean, my help?"

Harrison's caustic voice softened to a sarcastic complicitous whisper. "You were dutiful, for once, when you told Garrett just where the graves could be found."

Cat blanched, remembering the conversation with her father. "I was only trying to protect them. I didn't mean for you to go to them."

Harrison's chuckle was sinister. "When you think about it, it was the polite thing to do. After all, it wouldn't be right to simply drive a locomotive over that spot without first showing Pierce how sorry we are he'll have to lose it, now would it?"

Tears welled at the back of Cat's eyes, but she bit them back. "Is . . . is he all right?"

Harrison leaned close to her, setting her off balance until she was obliged to grip the banister to keep from falling down the stairs. "Well, now listen to this. The whore wants to hear about the condition of her savage lover while her betrothed stands before her with an injury she hasn't even noticed."

Cat did her best to ignore his insult. She took brief notice of the ugly dark bruise on his fleshy face and chose to keep silent about that. One thing was blindingly clear to her more than ever. Harrison Mayne was dangerous, and she in danger being near him. She set her jaw. "Is Seneca all right?" she demanded with as much aplomb as she could muster.

"He'll survive." Harrison seemed loath to tell her that. "The wound will heal, I'm sorry to say."

"Wound? What wound?"

"Simply a little gunshot wound to the arm. If it hadn't been for that big French oaf who shadows Pierce, I'd have killed him."

Cat sucked in a sharp breath.

"Surprised? Don't be. I'm made of much more than my future wife has ever given me credit for."

"Stop calling me that!"

"Oh, but don't you see? I must call you that. I know your marriage to Pierce was a sham." He bent down and breathed so close to her she was obliged to avert her face. "And you're about to become very undesirable to other eligible suitors of your station. After all, you're plumping out with unattractive fat, aren't you?" His eyes narrowed and his voice grew hard. "And no one will want a fat spinster with a bastard savage brat!" he hissed.

Cat's whole being was stricken at the onslaught of Harrison's words. He knew her secret, and on his lips the whole beautifully clean essence of it was made dirty.

"Now I've surprised you again, haven't I? You're wondering how I know. Well, Martin is quite loyal, you know. And the servants do whisper. And they talk rather loudly when they are paid to do so. But don't worry, my dear. I'll be happy to be its father. I know what it needs. Discipline. You'll see. Unless, of course, you got rid of it. No one would be the wiser. And I would never tell a soul."

She tried to push past Harrison. "You are disgusting and hateful. I won't hear another word of this. I'm going to see my father now."

"Good, good," Harrison snarled. "When he's through with you, I'm certain you will see the value in your continuing loyalty to Garrett . . . and to me."

Cat frowned in confusion but did not lessen the intensity of her loathing glare. She tried to step around Harrison, but he continued to block her, laughing in his mocking way.

"Let me pass," she demanded.

"Anxious to learn your fate, my dear?" He swept his arm wide, ushering toward the hallway that led to her father's room. "Do hurry. Garrett's not long for this world, and I know you would believe no one but him as regards your future and mine. And Pierce's."

Cat gave him as wide a berth as she could, given the small space at the top of the landing, preferring not to have one inch of her body or clothing come in contact with him. He descended the stairs, laughing with self-pleasure, calling out, "Be sure to give the happy grandfather my congratulations."

Tears blinding her vision, Cat was almost to her father's door when Aunt Maddie rushed from her own bedroom. "Cat, darling, what is it? I thought I heard you and Harrison arguing. Are you all right?"

With a harsh swipe across her face, Cat brushed away her tears. "Oh, Aunt Maddie, he was horrible. He said he shot Seneca."

Aunt Maddie's breath caught. "Oh, dear God—it wasn't fatal, was it?"

"No, but I can't bear it. I can't stand all this. I will have to go to Seneca, tell him everything. That's right, isn't it, Aunt Maddie? I should swallow my pride and let him know about the baby. I'm so tired, I can't bear up under all this."

"Shh, dear. Yes, I think you should tell Seneca. He deserves to know about your condition. He'll take care of you. I know he will. He loves you, my precious girl."

Cat looked deeply into her aunt's eyes. "I wish I could believe you. I don't want him to take care of me. I want him to love me for me, not just for the baby."

"He does, dear. Now, we must make haste to prepare for the journey to the mountains. You must not delay a moment longer."

"But what about Father? He's so very ill. How could I leave him?"

Aunt Maddie drew her diminutive frame up as straight as her weakened condition would allow. "You cannot think about him. You have much more at stake than a bitter old man."

Cat sucked in a sharp breath. "Aunt Maddie! How can you say such a thing?"

"Lila?" Garrett's frail voice came from his bedroom. "Lila, is that you? Come."

"Father, what is it?" Cat rushed into Garrett's bedroom and saw Dr. Merriweather bending over his bed.

The doctor looked up at her and shook his head.

"No! It can't be. He's not—"

"No, no, dear. Calm down," Dr. Merriweather whispered. "He's weakened considerably. You must prepare yourself, Lila. He will not last much longer."

Cat bit back stinging tears. She stepped around the doctor and gazed down at the shell of the man who had once been a powerful force in business. Regardless of the scandal that surrounded his involvement in the construction of the Union Pacific, her father's contribution to its completion was well known and respected. And he'd raised her without her mother for almost the whole of her life. She believed she loved him—even when she'd believed she'd hated him for his unreasonable expectations of her and his seeming disregard for the rights and welfare of others. He was her father, after all.

"Lila? Is that you, daughter?" Garrett's voice was a feeble whisper.

Cat dropped to her knees next to his bed. "Yes, Father, I'm here. Don't talk." She took his cool hand in both her warm ones.

Garrett shook his head slowly. "I must. Leave us alone, Doctor." When Merriweather left the room, he turned importuning eyes on her. "Promise me, Lila."

"Anything, Father. Promise you what?"

"The company will be yours . . . soon. You must finish what I started."

"Father, no. You will get stronger. You will see everything to completion. I know nothing about business." She rubbed the back of his hand vigorously as if willing strength to enter it.

"Don't worry, Lila. Stewart has pledged his support. And Harrison will be the one in control. As your husband, he can handle everything."

Cat swallowed. "Husband? Father, you know I'm married to Seneca."

"No need to keep up pretense," Garrett said, his voice a bit stronger. "I know everything. The marriage was not real. You are free to marry Harrison. A proper explanation will be made to everyone."

"I don't want a proper explanation, Father. I *am* married to Seneca."

"Nonsense. A ceremony performed by a hermit is invalid."

Cat's insides quivered. Evalina must have let out another secret. "Father, I believe he was a real cleric."

"You will no longer speak of it, Lila. It is a lie, and

you will not speak lies. You will be Harrison's wife and the head of my company. You will carry on as I wish."

"No! Father, please do not order me to do such a thing. It is wrong." Tears fell down her cheeks with increasing intensity.

"Stop crying. It shows weakness." Garrett turned his face away from his daughter.

"Whether it does or not, I can't help it. Father, there is something I've been keeping from you."

Garrett sighed impatiently. "And what insignificant thing could that be?"

Cat bit her lip for one moment, hesitating to let out her precious secret. Maybe it would soften her father to know she was carrying his grandchild. Maybe he would see that she couldn't possibly marry Harrison. She gathered her courage.

"I am pregnant. Seneca and I are to be parents of your grandchild." Every fiber of Cat's being tightened to the breaking point.

Garrett said nothing. His only indication that he'd heard her was the clenching of his jaw, the flexing of it under his gaunt cheek.

"I know about your mistake. Very ill-advised of you," he said at length.

"Perhaps ill-advised but definitely not a mistake. Oh, Father, I'm so happy about it." Her voice hushed. "Isn't it wonderful? I'm to be a mother. You're to be a grandfather."

Garrett turned back to her. "It is a disgrace. You will do as I say, Lila. You will marry Harrison."

"Father, please. I can't do that. I don't love him. And Harrison wouldn't want the baby. He might do something terrible to—"

"You will do it first. Listen to me, Lila. I will have you

married to Harrison. I will have him carrying on my wishes. The railroad will be built."

"I won't marry him, Father. I'll leave—and you will never see me again."

"Do that and I'll destroy those precious graves of Pierce's!"

Cat looked at her father, perhaps seeing the real man for the first time. Her heated frenzy turned stone cold. She spoke at length. "I understand now. If I do as you wish, then you will spare Seneca's family's graves."

"I knew you would see reason. This is for the best, Lila. I know Pierce doesn't know about the baby, but he does care about that site."

Cat got to her feet. "I believe I finally understand you, Father. Everything is business to you, everyone has a function for you in business."

Garrett stared grimly ahead. Cat allowed her past suspicion to take form. A new realization took over in her mind. Her father was right in his own way. One achieved a rightful place in life by treating everything in it as business. It made perfect sense. Emotion should be cast out of her life. It had brought only pain and heartache. Cold hard business sense should direct her life from this moment on.

"You'll be pleased to know you've taught me well," Cat said coldly. "This is my decision. I will marry Harrison, but only when you order the redirection of the railway away from Pierce's family plot."

Garrett lifted his chin.

"Will you swear to that, and put it in writing?"

Garrett shrugged, then nodded.

"Further swear in writing that you will relinquish the land you've acquired and turn it over for state protection, so that no railroad and no development can occur in that acreage."

Garrett went rigid. "Will you get rid of the bastard you're carrying?"

Cat squared her shoulders. "No."

He turned toward her, as softened a look on his face as Cat knew he could arrange. "Be reasonable, Lila. It will be over quickly, although you should have done it much sooner than this. Dr. Merriweather will handle everything. No one will ever know. You will forget it all in due time."

"No."

Garrett went rigid once more. He stared into the ceiling, making his will abundantly apparent.

Cat grew into a hardened, mature woman in that moment. She clasped her arms over her middle, holding the innocent life growing inside her. At that moment the child moved as if to tell her it was getting ready for its last weeks before breaking into the world.

Her whole being cried out to protect her unborn child, and to protect what was important to the only man she would ever love. He did not want her, but that did not diminish the depth of her love for him. In the face of such erosive warfare inflicted by her own father and by the man she was forced to marry, she knew she was the only one who could save Seneca and the child of their love. Think of it as strictly business, she told herself. Strictly business. That would resolve the conflict once and for all.

"I will go away and have my baby—" she let out a long shaky breath, "—if you will make me the head of Stockdale Enterprises. Again, in writing. There is no longer the matter of trust."

"On your wedding day, when your last name is Mayne. Done."

"I assume everything is to your liking . . . Garrett."

Garrett shifted his gaze toward her. Cat read in the cold eyes that she was no longer his daughter. She was merely another playing piece in his game of accumulation and acquisition of power.

"Agreed . . . Mrs. Mayne."

Cat cringed. She now pitied the man she'd regarded her whole life as all-powerful—the man she'd wanted desperately to feel love from, wanted desperately to give her own love to, freely and gladly. And she felt sad for herself. But the fate of father and daughter was sealed in that moment of stark, brutal truth. She turned and walked from the room, head held high.

In the hallway Madeline leaned against the wall. Her heart palpitations had escalated. She feared she might faint before she could collect her thoughts, plan for the deed she must do. She closed her eyes and prayed for one more burst of strength.

Spring awoke the glen with fragrant wildflowers and the happy song of nesting birds. Cat rocked her baby in her arms beneath a sun-filtered canopy of tall white pines. A soft breeze rustled through her hair and lifted the fine dark strands on the baby's head. The child stirred in its soft rabbit fur bunting.

Seneca came on silent moccasined feet through the mountain duff. He stood smiling above his wife and child and rained blossoms of rose, golden, and cream over them until they both laughed. He dropped beside them and gathered the precious bundle in his arms. Then he stretched out and lay his head in Cat's lap, holding the baby against him.

"It's as perfect as we dreamed it would be, isn't it?"

Cat whispered, looking down at the two most important people in her life.

"More," he responded, lifting a finger and placing it lovingly over her lips.

She kissed his finger. "Remember when we swam in the pool and played beneath the waterfall and you told me how precious was the gift of children? How they are the carriers of our dreams, the builders of our future?"

Seneca caressed his wife's face before dropping his hand to touch the downy soft cheek of the child that snuggled against his stomach. "I don't think you understood then, but I know you do now."

"You are right, I didn't understand. Your Iroquois teachings were so different from my own. I didn't know about the dreams until you taught me."

"Your dreams were not the same as mine, but now our night spirits harmonize and teach us the same. This is our future, this child, the future of generations to come. Our child will be as free as the bear and wolf cub to live among the earth, the lakes, the mountains. And we must listen to the wisdom of the child."

A stab of pain sliced into Cat's heart. "It's not to be. The child must leave me to grow up among strangers. It must know life is made up of sacrifices." Roughly she pushed Seneca's head from her lap and rushed to her feet.

"Go, then!" Seneca sat up, cradling the now struggling infant in his arms. "You were never to be the mother of my future generation—you could never carry on as my mother did."

"I could have!" she shouted. Her voice echoed among the trees, and the birds flew off on a great flapping of wings.

Thunder from the gathering storm resounded through the mountains, and the skies opened sending pouring rain over her. Seneca stood in the shelter of the trees, dry, protected. The thunder evolved, clattered, and a huff of thick smoke rolled between them. A clang of brass and the grinding of metal on metal carried on the wind, then a whoosh of steam blasted against her hot and wet.

"Dearly beloved," came her father's voice as he emerged from the cloud of smoke, "it is time to move on to the next station."

Cat looked down at her dress for the first time. The white lace of her wedding gown was stained with blood. She raised her eyes to Seneca and the struggling baby in his arms. They were so far away now. The smoke engulfed her, choked her. Seneca stood in the clearing where the air was crisp and clean. His eyes bored into her, the blue of the cloudless sky in them turning hard as a glass wall.

"Wait!" she called to her father as he walked toward her, hand outstretched. Behind him someone laughed. Harrison in a black morning coat. "I want to stay a while longer."

"Time has run out, Lila," her father said, taking her arm.

Cat reached out with her other arm through the smoke. The child reached from its fur bunting and grasped her outstretched finger. It pulled with the strength of a creature greater than any human or animal. She saw its eyes, blue-green, deep, hypnotic. In them she saw sky and sea and herself soaring above life on the wings of an eagle.

"I want to stay here!" she cried out.

"You agreed to my terms," her father said, pulling on the sleeve of her wedding gown.

"I cannot. My heart. The pain."

"The pain will pass. You will forget. Her father pulled harder until the dress sleeve tore away from her shoulder. He grabbed her naked arm and dragged her back.

"I will never forget!" she screamed.

The baby gripped tighter and pulled her hand. The thunderous sound of a train engine burgeoned behind her. Her father hauled on her arm. The baby's grasp tightened on her hand. Her chest strained. She heard the sound of tearing. Her wedding gown split down the middle and fell away. With a mighty pull her father wrenched her toward Harrison. Her other hand tore away from her body, locked in the baby's grip. She saw her own blood staining the ground around her feet.

Her father dragged her. Harrison caught her and threw her into a train car. The engine roared. The gears engaged, the wheels moved forward. Seneca and the baby stood in the middle of the tracks. The locomotive lurched forward.

Cat screamed and screamed and screamed. "No! Seneca! Save us, save us!"

The baby cried. Its face turned red and ugly. Her hand fell from its grasp. The tiny mouth opened and a keen wail cut through the vapor.

The locomotive chuffed and sped forward. The smoke thickened. Seneca's face faded. The baby's cries sharpened. Cat's eyes burned. Tears and smoke blinded her. Seneca's face disappeared. Cat's body shuddered, then split apart in a heart-wrenching stab of searing hot pain.

The baby's anguished cries mingled with her own and gorged her head. Then all was quiet as blackness engulfed her. She knew total comprehension of the sensation of death. From a deep hole in space, she heard the voice of an angel calling.

"Cat. Lila Catherine."

Cat roused. "Yes," she whispered through parched lips.

"It's a girl, darling Cat, you have a daughter." Aunt Maddie's voice from far away and echoing in her mind became as soothing as the cool cloth that bathed her face

A tiny high-pitched cry caught the turbid thickness in her mind. She summoned her voice which seemed to be lost in a fire and forced it over swollen lips. "Seneca?"

"No, dear." Aunt Maddie stroked the back of her hand. "I'm here. And our friend Bear is here. And now your beautiful baby daughter is here."

Cat struggled with the exhaustion that threatened to pull her back down into the frightening gloom. "Baby?" she whispered. Then, with dawning understanding, "I've been in labor. It was all a dream, a dream. My baby's here? Is . . . she all right?"

"She's perfect, darling, just perfect." Aunt Maddie set the baby against her mother's stomach. "She has as strong a voice as you had when you were born. Your mother said then that you would exercise that voice all your life."

Cat slipped her hands to the wriggling bundle against her heart. "What . . . what is she wearing?"

"Rabbit fur. Isn't it wonderful? So warm and soft. Bear found it here. He wrapped her in it the moment she left your womb."

"Fur. I dreamed about fur."

"I think you dreamed about many things. Your labor was long and very difficult, darling. This little one gave you a hard time. But she's worth it, isn't she?" Aunt Maddie took a soft cloth and blotted the moisture on Cat's face. She helped her to sit up against several rolled blankets.

Cat smiled feebly and gathered her daughter close to her breast. "I had so many bad dreams. Father. And the rain. And . . ."

"And Seneca. You called his name over and over."

"Is . . . does he know?"

"No, dear, he doesn't know. You said you didn't want him to know. He is back in the city."

Cat looked down toward her sleeping baby and bit back tears. She'd made a bargain with her father and she'd kept it. Holding the tiny form, the child so dependent upon her for her very life, Cat despaired silently how she would ever go through with her decision.

She could not bring the child into a marriage with Harrison. He would be cruel, she knew that. He would never let Cat forget about the months she'd spent with Seneca. She would never forget them either, but she knew Harrison would make them seem soiled, sordid, and he would make certain the child was taught the same. She could not have her daughter grow up in such a destructive environment. Everything was her own fault, and she'd made a pact that she hoped would amend it. Regardless of how right-thinking it had seemed at the time to save the mountain forests, and especially Seneca's family's sacred ground she'd agreed to sentence herself to a life in a prison constructed by Garrett. She saw no way out of it, no other way to return to Seneca all he had given her.

"Where are we, Aunt Maddie?" she asked at last when her mind could no longer stand the careening thoughts that wounded her senses.

Aunt Maddie lit more lamps. "We're in Seneca's cabin on the island in Blue Mountain Lake."

Cat snapped her pounding head around. "How—?"

"I thought it was best, dear. You needed to get away from everyone. I got in touch with Bear. When he told me Seneca was coming back to the city, I decided it was best to come here. Bear helped me with you."

"I don't understand. We boarded the train for the seclusion of my old school, didn't we? You spoke of a new hospital or a midwife—I don't really remember. How did we get here?"

Aunt Maddie folded her hands contritely over the crud

apron she wore. "Do forgive me, Cat, but I lied to you. I planned to come here all the time. I didn't know what I was going to do once you realized we were heading into the mountains. But then, you went into labor, and oh, my dear, you were so sick. I was frantic with worry I'd lose you. If it hadn't been for Bear, I don't know what I'd have done."

Cat smiled warmly at the dear old lady whom she'd loved all her life and knew loved her as well. "Thank you, Aunt Maddie, for taking such good care of me and my baby. But Bear, will he tell Seneca about . . . everything?"

"No, dear. I told him you didn't want Seneca to know about the agreement you made with Garrett and Harrison. He understood, but he was insistent upon telling Seneca about the baby. He said the Iroquois believe that children are a gift from the Creator and that no one can deny acceptance or care of that gift. I persuaded him not to tell Seneca. But dear, you must think about the consequences. It isn't right that you keep knowledge of the baby from him."

Cat clamped her eyes shut. "I must. I will lose my baby forever if I don't protect her from everyone. Father and Harrison would use her, I fear, to control Seneca even more. I don't trust them not to go back on their word. If Seneca knows nothing about this baby, he will be fearless in defending his beliefs. He has to have that. And my baby has the right to grow up away from that conflict. I will give her the best life she can have. She deserves that."

"She deserves to be with her parents," Aunt Maddie said, "no matter the circumstance."

"Please don't make this any more difficult than it already is. I've already made the plans. My baby will live at Miss Bolton's School. She'll be safe there. Miss Skiles assures me she has a lifetime arrangement for living quarters. I've committed funds to her and the school will be reopened. I will hire more teachers and another nurse for the baby."

"She needs her mother," Aunt Maddie said as firmly as her weary voice could manage.

"I will visit her whenever I can without Harrison being the wiser. She will be safe there. I've made all the arrangements."

"You've become like Garrett, Cat. You've even made a business of your infant's life."

"Yes, I have, Aunt Maddie. I've learned that's how others live and succeed." Cat drew the baby to her breast for her first taste of mother's milk. She reveled in their connection, she and her daughter, their bond. And she bit back any tears she might have succumbed to in her former life.

Madeline turned back to finish cleaning up the basins and cloths from the birth. She felt weary to the bone, as if she'd experienced the physical birth herself of this precious baby from this precious child of her heart. Cat had changed in the process, and Maddie's heart was heavy with knowledge. She could think clearly no longer. Her plans to see Cat through a private peaceful labor and birth were fulfilled.

Now the rest of their future was in the hands of Seneca's Creator.

Eighteen

"I'm sorry you don't wish to wear your mother's wedding dress, dear." On the bed in her own room, Aunt Maddie laid out the new dress Rosamund Mayne had sent over for the wedding.

"I couldn't do that, Aunt Maddie." Cat sighed wearily. "You understand, don't you?" She gathered her petticoats around her and stepped into the hideous gown with its high neck and voluminous sleeves. There was no telling where Rosamund had picked up this dress, but it was safe to say that it was old enough for the white satin to have turned a sickly yellow. The garment was as unflattering as anything could be, and was weighty enough to be a burden in its own right beyond the burden of this marriage.

Aunt Maddie nodded. The two women fell silent as a look passed between them which spoke volumes of what each was thinking.

As she pulled the dress up around her, Cat's fingers passed over the scar on her shoulder where Seneca's arrow had struck her. She could almost smell the aroma of wintergreen from his collection of herbs and oils that he'd rubbed over the area to relieve soreness. She bit back the hot tears that threatened to weaken her resolve and shrugged into the heavy garment.

Her thoughts drifted back to a morning in the Adiron
dacks when she'd stepped into a mountain guideboat wear
ing Aunt Maddie's white petticoats and Seneca's blu
cotton shirt—and the way he'd presented her with hi
mother's wedding slippers. They'd all floated across th
lake to a fairy-tale island and a wedding the memory o
which had grown more precious and lovely to her ove
the last few months.

A knock came to the door and Evalina, more sombe
than she'd ever been in her life, entered in a simple gow
of rose satin. "Here you are. I thought you'd be in you
bedroom."

"I chose not to be," Cat said dully. The last thing sh
could have done was to dress for her wedding with Har
rison in the bedroom she'd shared with Seneca. His pres
ence still permeated the walls and especially the bed. Sh
could still see their reflection in the mirror as their tw
bodies were entwined in exquisite lovemaking.

"Everything is quite lovely, Lila," Evalina said gentl
"The church is decorated with flowers and tall white car
dles in silver candelabra. And Mrs. Daggett has practice
on the organ for so long as to make certain the music
just perfect. I think she might need to bind her old knee
to keep them from falling apart when she starts pumpir
for the real ceremony. I think she'll miss it when the ne
pipe organ arrives. Reverend Daggett is complacent ;
always—as if he officiates in this kind of wedding ever
week." She clasped and unclasped her fingers as sh
paced the length of the room, stepping over Cat's sho
and bits of wedding paraphernalia.

"I doubt he has ever officiated in a ceremony quite lil
this one," Cat opined.

"I'm not so certain about that. People who don't lo*
each other get married all the time. Just ask Mother. (

Mrs. Mayne. She'll give you an earful." Evalina went about fluffing Cat's veil and inspecting the headpiece.

"I just want it over quickly. No sentimental drivel about loving and cherishing."

"I do wish it could be different for you, dear, just as I know you've always dreamed." Aunt Maddie began the laborious chore of fastening the thirty-seven buttons at the back of the wedding gown.

"I've grown up, Aunt Maddie. No more childish dreams. I will have enough to do just to live through each day." Cat took the yellowed lace veil from Evalina, swirled it over her head, and set it down onto her high coiled hair.

Evalina secured the veil with combs and then straightened it out to its full length in back. "Did you know there are holes in this? I mean bigger ones other than the usual."

"Yes, I saw them. I believe they were made by mice."

"Yeeks!" Evalina stepped back. "How can you even touch it? And why would anyone give you such a disgusting thing to wear on your wedding day?"

"I believe it's a statement about how my future mother-in-law regards me. But I really don't care." Cat avoided inspecting herself in her mirror, leaving that chore for Aunt Maddie.

Evalina leaned in closely to the two women and whispered, "And where is darling little Janey Catherine?"

Cat caught her bottom lip and said nothing.

"My precious little grandniece is safe with her nurse," Aunt Maddie said.

"I do wish you'd let me see her, Lila," Evalina returned, pouting. "I promise I will tell no one where she is."

Cat turned to look at her dear friend. "I know you promise, Evie, but I can take no chances with anyone discovering the whereabouts of my daughter. If Harrison or my

father knew, I fear they would conjure worse things tha
they had with their railroad plans."

Evalina dropped down on the bed. "I feel so responsibl
for that. I had no idea they would do such a thing."

"It's done, Evie. Don't worry about it now. I'm certai
you thought telling Harrison about the graves was inno
cent conversation."

Evalina's head snapped up. "Oh, but I didn't tell hin
You must know I wouldn't do such a thing, Lila. I ar
your true friend, even if I do seem the scattered twit. Ha
rison intercepted a note from Bear to me. Isn't that ju
abominable? I mean, reading other people's mail and the
using it against you."

Cat watched her friend's childlike eyes. She'd been to
occupied with her own dilemmas to notice that Evalin
had matured as well. It was gratifying to know that sl
hadn't divulged the location of Seneca's family's grave

Cat's shoulders sagged slightly before she caught he
self and straightened them. Seneca believed she'd to
Garrett and Harrison exactly where the site was. She w
guilty only of telling her father about their existence
the hope that she could prevent their destruction in t
course of the railroad construction.

The innocence of all three of them—Bear, Evie, a
herself—had been used to great advantage by Garrett ar
Harrison. Cat vowed she would never succumb to su
calculating deception again.

A soft knock came to the door. Aunt Maddie opened
to Martin, who stood erect as a post in his black suit.

"It's time, Miss Lila. Mr. Stockdale has been safe
deposited at the church. He seems weaker today th
usual. Perhaps it's all the excitement of the wedding."

Cat did not respond. She turned toward the door a
started to follow Martin.

"Perhaps," Aunt Maddie said.

In an unusual act of intervention, Evalina stepped between Cat and the door. "It's not too late, Lila. You don't have to go through with this wedding. I'll help you get away. I mean it." Her face was earnest, her hands tight on Cat's arms. "Just because loveless marriages occur every day doesn't mean you have to be in one of them. Just say it and we'll get out of here now."

Cat hugged Evalina, then leaned back and looked into her friend's worried face. "You are my honest and true friend, Evie. I'm sorry I ever doubted you. Thank you for offering to help me escape. You know what your family would say about that. You would never be free if you did such a thing. In any case I can't leave. I've made a business arrangement, and I will honor it."

"Oh, Lila, I know the truth of why you're doing this. You're saving Seneca's land, preserving his family's graves. If he knew about this, I know he wouldn't let you go through with it. Please, it's not too late."

"It *is* too late." Cat left her friend's embrace. "Seneca has made his choice regarding me. I'm making mine regarding all of us. If you don't want to be a part of this wedding, I understand. It's not too late for you to change your mind either."

Evalina sighed in surrender. "Well, this is it, then. I stand by your decision, and I'll be your friend forever. No matter what happens, I hope you'll remember that." She embraced Lila then and reverted into her usual cheery self. "I'm proud to be in your wedding, just as we always planned. And I hope someday you will be in my wedding. Should I ever have one. The specter of spinsterhood looms on my horizon, I fear."

"Nonsense, Evie, you will have a wedding of your own one day. And I promise I will be in it just as we've always dreamed. I can only wish for you that it is a happier occasion than this one."

"If I had the courage to marry the man of my dreams, my parents would be mortified. In which case it would not be a happy occasion." Evalina gathered up her bag and wrap, intent on preceding Lila from the room. She sighed wistfully. "But since that will never happen, I will most likely marry someone they feel is appropriate for them and for my station. Then everyone will be happy."

Cat smiled with understanding as Evalina passed her. She watched her shared girlhood dreams flounce out of the room on the waves of her friend's curls and gown. Perhaps if they'd never put those dreams into words, she'd be satisfied now with the fate of her future. She embraced her brief reminiscence, then let it go. Taking in a deep breath, she accepted the finality of what the impending wedding ceremony would mean to the rest of her life, then let the breath out and departed from Aunt Maddie's room, closing the door on her old life forever.

Seneca sat behind the desk in his office at the university, cleaning out drawers and going over course materials he meant to leave for the next person who would occupy this position. He'd accepted reappointment to the faculty for one semester, telling himself he needed the added mental challenge of teaching to keep his mind off Cat and the life they'd shared. He was relieved that the semester was over, yet at the same time wished it was not.

He knew somewhere deep inside himself he'd hoped to catch a glimpse of her. He was torn between knowing he should stay away from her and wanting to see her, wanting to tell her she'd been right in everything she'd told him about his father . . . and about himself. The understanding of her words at last had thrown him into a long period of reexamination of everything he'd known in his life. He hadn't yet found his grounding again—had yet to learn what his life should mean before it was over.

He'd sworn he would not seek her out, and he believed that was best for her. But his vow had left him frustrated and irritated with himself every time he walked by the Stockdale mansion after dark. On numerous evenings he'd stopped on the street—opposite the bedroom they'd shared—and watched the lighted window until the lamp was extinguished. He knew it was Cat who extinguished the light, but she couldn't know she'd been fading her window into the black of night that was as deep as the darkness in his soul.

For the last few weeks, he noticed that Cat's bedroom light did not come on in the evenings. He wondered if she'd taken a holiday. Then, grimly, he decided she'd married Harrison Mayne and had gone to live with him. The idea had tormented him for days until he'd put himself directly in the path of Martin as he made his way from church one Sunday morning. The houseman gave a tight-lipped answer to his query, offering only that Miss Lila and Miss Madeline had taken a trip away for health reasons. Seneca assumed that Madeline's weak constitution had taken a downward turn, and he felt sorry for that. He'd come to love Cat's dear old aunt.

A knock came to his door.

"Come in," he called with no enthusiasm.

"*Regarde, mon ami.* The Frenchman is loose in the big city!"

"Bear!"

Seneca leapt to his feet, came around the desk, and embraced his friend with gusto. The two slapped each

other on the back and laughed amid the genuine joy of
their reunion.

"Whatever enticed you out of the North Woods? I would
think the oncoming days of early summer and the great
hunting would have held you there more secure than one
of your own traps. Come in, come in!" Seneca closed the
door behind the big man who looked grossly out of place
in his red plaid wool shirt, canvas pants, and heavy boots.

"Thought I should see to your welfare, *mon ami.* Don't
want big city to dull your powers of perception." Bear
swiped the knitted cap from his head and dropped heavily
into the oak chair placed opposite Seneca's desk.

"I'm fine as you can see." Seneca circled him warily,
scrutinizing his friend's visage. "What's different about
you?" he asked thoughtfully.

Bear shifted self-consciously in the chair. *"Moi?* Deef
er-ant? Only that I seem to be tourist attraction here. No
one even notices me up home."

"Hmm," Seneca said, retracing his steps. "Could that
be because they've never seen your hair cut above your
shoulders and your beard trimmed neatly? Ah, I know
what the real difference is now!"

"What?" Bear eyed him suspiciously.

"You've taken a bath!"

"Aw, *mon ami,* you make it sound like it never
happens."

"Well, let's say we both know it's a rare occurrence."

"You don't change, except for teacher suit." Bear swept
a keen gaze over Seneca's dark gray coat and trousers,
then back to his face. "You never cut hair. It's real long."

Seneca strode around behind his desk and sat down.
"You ever hear of Samson and Delilah, my friend?"

"Oui, once. His hair was long, too, right?"

"Right. And when Delilah insisted he cut it, his whole

vorld crashed around him. She almost had me considering
t."

"Delilah?"

Seneca laughed lightly. "Someone as beautiful and
owerful in her own way. As you can see, I did not
veaken."

"Ah." Bear vigorously nodded his head. "Mademoi-
elle Cat, no?"

Seneca held his gaze level with Bear's for a protracted
noment. "Even though I know you've missed me terribly,
know your loss couldn't have dragged you here. So
/hat's going on? Has Evalina managed to trap you?"

Bear's grin was lopsided at first, then turned to a serious
ne for a moment. "It is Mademoiselle Evalina who calls
ie here, *oui*. I come more for you."

"Me? Why?"

"Mademoiselle Cat is to be married to Monsieur Mayne
oday."

Seneca took that news stoically. But he felt as if he'd
een kicked in the stomach by an irate mule. He expelled
r from his lungs in one hard column. He turned in his
hair and looked out the window.

"I'm not surprised. And it's no concern of mine."

"Should be."

"No reason."

"She already has husband. You."

Seneca turned back to Bear. "That old geezer Sender
in't be a real priest. And you know that sham ceremony
ccurred only so Cat could keep her father from forcing
r to marry Mayne months ago. Obviously the pretense
dn't work for very long. She got over it and did what
ie was supposed to do."

"What about you, *mon ami?*" Bear said low.

"I did what I was supposed to do. And I guess it worked,

didn't it? They stopped the railroad from driving over the mountains, and I preserved my family's graves. End of story."

"Don't think so, *mon ami*. You didn't stop the railroad by yourself."

Seneca leaned both forearms on his desk. "I know Bear. I'm sorry I didn't say so. I owe you my deepest gratitude for what you did to help me."

"No, no, not me. Mademoiselle Cat." Bear jumped up.

"Cat? What do you mean? She didn't help. She almost brought about the ruin of those mountains."

"Ah, *mon ami,* you thick as stump." When Seneca glared at him, Bear settled down. "Or Mademoiselle Cat smarter than mountain cat. She make new deal with father and future husband. They run railroad, no wedding. They stop railroad, she marry Mayne. *Voila!* No railroad. Wedding." He brushed his thick palms together.

Seneca went rigid. "What—what are you talking about? You're saying Cat agreed to marry Mayne so her father would stop building the railroad through the mountains?"

"Oui. Save graves, save mountains. See?"

"No, I don't see. Stockdale was adamant about track going through that area to Blue Mountain. He didn't care a whit about my family's grave. Why would he just quit construction?"

"Mademoiselle force him to go other direction. He needs money. She marries Mayne, he gets money, he can still build railroad. But she make him agree to build away from your land, away from family."

Seneca rose and walked to the other side of the room. "What's to keep him from going back on his word once she's married to Mayne? A promise doesn't mean much to a man like Stockdale."

"Mademoiselle Cat make him sign papers with lawyer

She will control company. He can't break word. If he does, he can get out of marriage, take money. See?"

Seneca eyed him skeptically. "How do you know all this, anyway?"

Bear grinned widely. "My little grizzly bear tells me everything."

"Evalina?" Seneca grinned in spite of the serious news he'd just heard. "You really did fall for her, didn't you, you old fox skinner?"

"My heart, she breaks for her." Bear crossed his fists over his chest. "Mademoiselle Evalina writes me much. She said father signed papers. Mademoiselle Cat make him do it. He's sick. He signed."

"Well, those papers are probably as worthless as what she and I signed when we went through with that wedding." Seneca paced the length of the office. "Nothing will change. She'll marry Mayne, and Stockdale will have more money to put behind his schemes." He turned toward Bear. "And you're to be a wedding guest once again. Isn't that ironic?"

"Don't have to. Not too late, *mon ami*. You can stop "

"No, Bear, I can't stop it."

Bear's face expressed his sadness. Seneca turned toward the window. So it was finally going to happen. Cat was going to marry Mayne. It was best. He and Cat didn't belong together. She couldn't live in his world forever, and he wouldn't live in hers forever either. There was nothing to hold them together, no matter how much he'd ached for her over the last months, no matter how many times he'd thrown himself into a bank of deep snow just to cool his physical lust and freeze his frustrations.

Yet, if he made an appearance at the wedding, it would certainly make Stockdale nervous, wouldn't it? No, he couldn't do that to Cat. He didn't want to ruin her wedding day. And if he saw her in a wedding gown, walking down the aisle to marry someone else, he knew he wouldn't be able to bear it. Why put himself through that agony?

But it would be a test of his masculine strength if he did go. Wasn't it customary for the powerful and proud Iroquois to test themselves at every opportunity in order to prove their mental and physical strength? He could find a hidden place in the church and watch her be married. That would finalize everything in his mind. He had to do it. It was the only way to preserve pride, the only way to force himself to get on with his life as it was before.

"Where is this wedding to be?"

Bear brightened. "Church near her house."

Seneca opened a storage closet, went inside, and closed the door. When he emerged he was dressed in his mountain garb, fringed doeskin shirt and leggings and moccasins.

"Let's go, my friend," Seneca said, slapping him on the shoulder. "You're taking another wedding guest from the mountains." He hurried to the door and strode down the hallway.

"Wait!" Bear called, hurrying behind him. "There's more you must know before—"

"I don't need to know another thing," Seneca replied from several strides ahead. "I know all there is to know to bring this to an end for us both."

At the strains of the pump organ—albeit hesitant chords owing no doubt to Mrs. Daggett's tired knees—Cat waited at the back of the church for her cue to start down the aisle. She could see Harrison grinning, no, leering, from his place at the altar. She shuddered, understanding the meaning in his leer. He was telling her their wedding night was not something she would very soon forget.

Garrett sat in a front pew wrapped in a blanket, hovered over by the ever-loyal Martin. Even in his obvious physical weakness, Cat felt the power of his will. His close presence to her and Harrison at the moment the wedding vows were uttered, and the finality of the reverend's pronouncement, were exactly what he'd been living for over the last several weeks. Even in illness he would see his grand plan at least to the beginning of the next phase.

Cat let her gaze linger on her father for a long moment. How different he was, how different she was from the golden-curled child who'd climbed on his knee to sit for a family portrait with the beautiful Catherine, her adored mother.

That was the real dream.

This was the real life.

At the church with Bear, Seneca stood on the steps and listened to the faint organ music emanating from inside.

"You go ahead," he told Bear. "Evalina will be giddier than usual if she doesn't see you before the ceremony. I want to sit outside until it has started."

Bear nodded compliance. "Go to the back of church. There is sun there. Good place to think." He opened the door and started to go in. Seneca caught a glimpse of the bride's back before the door swung closed. His insides clutched.

"Steady now," he whispered to himself.

Perhaps Bear was right. Sitting in the waning sun for a few minutes before going inside might do him some good. He looked up into the sky. Clouds were gathering. The air was growing decidedly cool. It would rain before this day was over. Seneca started around toward the side of the building. He could always count on the weather to reflect his moods exactly. If he needed any corroboration, this was it. He was truly a creature of nature. Nothing would ever change that. Nothing.

He was almost to the rear corner of the church when he heard a voice. He stopped. It was a woman. She was crying. No. She seemed to be crooning. He moved quietly until he reached a place where he could observe without being seen.

Miss Madeline!

What was she doing outside? She should be inside witnessing the wedding of her niece. Was she all right? Perhaps she took sick again and, knowing the dear old lady as he believed he did, she wouldn't want to cause a scene that would spoil the event. Seneca frowned. How could anything spoil this already stained event?

He waited to see if she would compose herself. She was holding something. A bag? A blanket? He took one step closer.

"It's all right, Seneca," she called out to him. "No one will see you. You can come out."

Seneca's heart jumped in his chest. The sly old lynx had known he was there! He'd misjudged her powers of perception. Or had Bear sent him back there on purpose? He stepped out of the shadows and walked toward her.

"Miss Madeline, I'm happy to see you again. But why aren't you inside the church? Are you feeling ill?"

Madeline raised her gray head and smiled at him warmly. "Actually I'm feeling quite strong really. In fact I know I'm about to feel better than I have in years."

Seneca cocked his head. "You mean you're happy Ca is marrying Mayne?"

From behind the church wall, the organ struck up the chords of the song, signaling the bride to begin her walk down the aisle.

"Absolutely not. She'll never marry him, anyway."

Had the woman gone daft? "Dear Miss Madeline, she's in the church right now doing that very thing. What do you have there?" He indicated toward the bundle.

"I have here the most powerful gift in the world. This precious gift will change all our lives in a single moment."

She *was* daft. Seneca drew nearer. He'd have to find a doctor to help her.

"May I see it?" he asked gently.

"Of course. Then you won't be such a skeptic and think this nothing but the ramblings of a crazy old coot."

"I think nothing of the kind."

"My dear Seneca, your eyes have always given away your true feelings."

So she was sly as well as perceptive. And maybe daft. Madeline turned toward him and uncovered her bundle. Seneca took a step back. "A baby?"

"Oh yes, but what a baby." Madeline smiled and caressed the infant's cheek.

"Whose—?"

Madeline lifted the child, who yawned before thrusting a tiny fist into its tiny mouth. "This is Janey Catherine . . . Pierce. She's your daughter, and Cat's."

The rainstorm's thunder hadn't yet begun, but Seneca felt its impact in his chest and legs. It knocked him off balance, forcing him to reach out and touch the church wall to steady himself.

The organ music swelled into its crescendo, signaling that the bride was almost to the altar.

"My . . . Cat's . . . ?"

Madeline looked down at the baby. "You'd never know it, Janey Cat, but your father is a university professor. I guess living in the mountains for so long has affected his speech." She lifted her eyes to Seneca, then stood with some effort. She held the bundle out to him. "Why don't you hold her and see for yourself?"

Seneca was frozen. If he let go of his attachment to the church building, he knew his legs would give out and he'd be reduced to a heap. He closed his eyes and breathed deeply, gathering strength from his own spirit and from the spirits of his mother and sister. And then he held out his arms to receive his daughter.

The organ music stopped.

Madeline placed the baby gently in her father's arms and pulled away the quilt so he could see her in full view.

Seneca's breath caught in his throat. He gazed down at the beautiful tiny life in his arms. His deeply understanding Iroquois spirit told him why Cat hadn't let him know about the baby. A tear rolled down his cheek and fell upon her forehead like a natural baptism. He leaned down and kissed it away. When his vision cleared, he looked at his child fully for the first time.

"See her dark hair? And look how much she has. Just like yours," Madeline said softly.

"Yes, but see the golden glints through it," he whispered back. "Just like her mother's."

"And her skin is lovely, isn't it. Like coffee."

"Perfect. Coffee with cream."

"Like her mother and father. When she wakes, you will see her eyes are blue with a touch of emerald." Madeline touched Seneca's arm. "She has the best of both of you."

Seneca blinked back his tears and gazed into Madeline's eyes. "Does she?"

"Oh, yes. She wails like her mother, but she's stubborn like her father."

The organ music began again, and a high-pitched soprano voice sang words of devotion and everlasting love.

"Now Miss Madeline," Seneca said, smiling lovingly

at her and then adoringly at his daughter, "just what do you mean by that?"

"Just that her mother despairs over the loss of you, and you are too stubborn to admit your own despair and do something about it."

Seneca shook his head. "What . . . what do you mean?"

"You know exactly what I mean. You both want each other. You both have a child who needs her parents. Cat thinks she's saving you and your land. She's become cold and hard, has made a business of everything. You think she's a spoiled little rich girl who's getting her way, and so you retreat to your North Woods like a hermit."

The soprano stopped.

The child in Seneca's arms stirred and opened her eyes. She stared up at her father with a challenging blue-green gaze.

"Say it straight, Miss Madeline. What do you think?"

"I think a lot. What I know is, papers have been signed that have to do with the direction of the railroad around the Adirondacks. Garrett is dying. There was no annulment because he believed your priest wasn't real. Evalina and I are very resourceful women. We have another powerful tool for you to use if you both are strong enough to take it. No one expects us to have brains in our heads. Except for Bear." She reached out to take the baby from Seneca's arms. "We are also smart enough to know that if the wedding going on inside that church is not stopped at this moment, it may be legal and binding. It would behoove a certain Iroquois warrior to get in there and rescue the mother of his baby, and the love of his life."

Seneca relinquished his daughter to Madeline's arms as if in a trance. Cat would be lost to him forever if he didn't move. Why did it feel as if his moccasins had taken root?

And then out of the corner of his eye, he saw the back

door to the church. He embraced Madeline and Janey Catherine and kissed them both. Then he uprooted his moccasins and ran for that door. Behind him he heard an old lady's whoop followed by a strong baby's wail.

"For as much as Lila and Harrison have pledged their vows," Seneca heard the minister say as he burst through the back door, "I pronounce that they are husband and—"

"Stop! This woman cannot marry this man!" he shouted.

Cat clutched her bosom in shock. Evalina dropped the bouquet at her feet and threw her arms around her friend. Harrison lunged, and Bear leapt out of a pew up onto the altar and gripped him around the stomach before he could carry out his intention to strike Seneca.

Garrett let out an anguished cry. The crowd stiffened and then a noisy chatter escalated among them.

"Who is this . . . this strange man?" Reverend Daggett shouted. "Get out."

"I'm not leaving." Seneca saw Garrett trying to rise from his place in the front pew. Martin was restraining him. "I have something to say. This marriage cannot go on."

"You had the chance during the ceremony to speak your piece," Reverend Daggett said, his eyes shifting to Garrett to Cat, to Harrison, and then back to Seneca. "You didn't This hulk of a mountain man set to a coughing spell for so long we were obliged to hold the ceremony until he composed himself."

Bear laughed loudly. "Good trick, eh, *mon ami?*" he whispered. "What took you so long to get in here?"

"I was detained by a couple of very lovely ladies," Seneca whispered with a smile. "And something tells me you knew about them, *mon ami.*"

Bear clamped his lips tightly.

Seneca reached out and grabbed Cat's arm. Her eyes were wide with confusion and terror.

"What do you think you're doing? Get away from me. This wedding will go on! Reverend Daggett?" Cat stifled a sob. What made Seneca come here? He would ruin everything. More than he could ever know. She had to get him out of here. Now.

"This wedding has ended," Seneca shouted over the crowd. "You can all go home now. You missed the real wedding. I'm taking *my wife* home now."

"I'm not your wife, remember?" Cat bit out and wrenched from his grip. "Sender wasn't a real priest. You said so yourself, remember? The marriage was all a sham from the first moment the idea fell out of my mouth. You agreed to the pretense, remember?"

"I remember everything. I was wrong. I was wrong about everything, including the pretense." He took both her arms in his hands. "This is the truth, my dearest love, and I've only just understood it myself. I want to believe in Maurice Sender's authenticity, in that wedding, real or not. I have to believe in my own integrity, my own honesty. All along I wanted to believe in my heart that if we'd truly been married, I never would have gone to the lengths I had to try to ruin your father. And my pride and my sense of myself would never have allowed you to mold me into the perfect husband just to make your father happy either. I know now that wouldn't have had to happen if we'd believed in each other, believed in our love right from the start."

Behind Seneca, Cat could see Harrison struggling against Bear's powerful grip. He said something incoherent until Bear silenced him with a firm hand over his mouth. Behind her she heard Evalina's gleeful giggle.

Cat swayed for a brief moment, then steadied herself. "It's too late for any of this, Seneca. Please go away. You don't understand everything. This wedding must go on as planned."

"No, Lila," Evalina said, drawing closer. "There can't be a real wedding. You *are* already married to Seneca."

Cat whirled around in anguish. "Will you stop saying that? We aren't married?"

"Yes, you are." Bear produced a folded paper and handed it to her. "See?"

Lila unfolded the paper and read the contents, all the while running her finger over the embossed seal of the state of New York at the bottom. Seneca moved to her side and read the document along with her. The full impact of what he read was almost incomprehensible to him. He read the document three times before the truth hit him.

"This says we *are* married. Sender *is* a real priest. What we signed in his shack of a church held up. How did you get this, Bear?"

"Mademoiselle Evalina do it. I give her page from Sender's book. She take it to lawyer. He says it's real. You Cat can't marry *stupide* Mayne. See?"

Cat looked up, scanning the faces around her with a confusion that wracked every nerve. "This can't be. I have an agreement with my father—"

"Forget that, Cat. We'll fight it together. You were right. Everything you told me was right. I've been so blind. Wanted to be blind then—but no more." He took her arm and began pulling her toward the back of the church.

"What . . . do you want from me?" Cat managed through a constricted throat. Excitement, fear, anticipation, anxiety, deep and longing love for Seneca—every emotion she'd ever known coursed through her, setting her nerves pulsing erratically.

Madeline appeared at the altar with the crying baby in her arms.

"I want you . . . and our precious daughter . . . to get out of here *now*. We have to talk, we have to think, and we can't do it in the midst of this chaos. Will you come with me?"

There was a struggle in the congregation.

"Miss Lila, please come!" Martin pleaded. "Your father, I think he's . . . dying."

Cat's terror froze her. She turned and stared beyond Seneca's shoulder toward Garrett, saw her father slumped forward, saw Martin and Stewart Mayne lower him to the floor. She dragged her gaze back to Seneca, to her baby, back to her father, then Seneca once more, her mind spinning with confusion.

Seneca released her and gently stepped away from her.

"Go to him," he said quietly. "When it's over, come to me. I'll be waiting in the mountains for you and our daughter."

Seneca ran to Madeline, kissed his child on the forehead, and sent one last look over his shoulder to Cat.

And then he disappeared beyond the altar.

Nineteen

Cat floated in Bear's guideboat across the summer calm of Blue Mountain Lake. Janey Catherine slept peacefully in her arms, wrapped in a woven rainbow-striped blanket.

"Oh, Lila, this is just delicious, just so simply delicious," Evalina breathed from behind her.

"I never thought I'd hear you say that about the Adirondack Mountains, Evie," Cat said with a light laugh.

"It's more than the mountains," Evalina replied seriously, "and you know it."

"Regarde, ma chérie," Bear said at Evalina's back, where he stood and dipped the oar smoothly into the glassy lake. "This is the best time, after the blackflies have flown."

"Ooh, don't remind me." Evalina shivered. "I remember our last holiday up here. Wearing those hateful netting hats and trying to take tea or sip sherry through them was terrible."

"Don't worry, *chérie,* you shall sip sherry without bother from now on. I will protect you." Bear's chivalrous instinct showed as large as his massive frame.

"Isn't Robert just marvelously delicious, Lila?"

Cat chuckled. "Yes, Evie, I can absolutely agree that Bear is the second most marvelously delicious man in the world." She bent over her baby daughter. "Janey Cat" father is the most delicious, isn't he, darling girl? Yes, he is," she crooned.

"Regarde," Bear said, pointing ahead. "The church and Maurice." He raised his oar in salute.

"Oh," Evalina breathed, "it's as quaint as you said."

"Wait until you see inside." Cat sent a wave to the priest, who was still draped in his burlap robes. Her breath caught in her throat when she sighted Seneca on the steps of the church. "There he is," she whispered to her daughter. "Your father is beautiful. Wait until you see him."

He was a glorious sight in his fringed doeskin shirt and leggings. His hair was loose over his shoulders, the sun glinting off the ebony strands and colorful beaded thongs that decorated the narrow braid down one side of his face.

Behind Maurice Sender on the shore, Seneca waited at the door of the little church. He caught a glimpse of the guideboat as it rounded the island point, and his pulse raced and his palms grew moist.

"I'm jumpy as a spring frog, Aunt Maddie," he said to the old lady who sat in the doorway in a chair constructed of shaggy-barked Adirondack cedar logs. His shaky voice turned to awe. "My wife and daughter are coming to me. The Creator has blessed me twofold."

"All three of you are blessed, but I the most," Madeline said.

Seneca turned back and pulled the knitted shawl more closely around her shoulders. "Are you feeling all right?"

"Yes, my dear nephew, I will be strong enough, long enough." She smiled up at him and patted his cheek. Then she peered around him. "Look, here they come."

Seneca stood straight and slowly turned around. With Maurice in the lead, Cat was climbing the hill toward him, their baby in her arms, Evalina and Bear close behind. His breath caught in his throat. The whole group looked beautiful, but his wife and daughter were an exquisite sight coming to his open arms.

Cat wore his blue shirt and Madeline's white lace petticoats as she had at their first wedding. Adorning her hair were delicate sprays of wildflowers in rose, yellow, and white tied with narrow blue satin ribbons. She came to him and held out her right hand.

"I feel as if this is the very first time we've come together," she whispered.

"It is the most honest time," he said, kissing her palm. He raised his hand and touched her cheek. "I'm sorry about your father, and more sorry he did not feel it in his heart to forgive you before he died. I know that must hurt you deeply."

Cat mouthed a silent thank you. "I loved him because he was my father. But I've learned that life is ever-evolving—something you knew all along. Our fathers lived their lives their own way. Now we must live our own. am looking forward to loving my life with my husband and child."

"Children," he amended gently.

"Yes," she whispered.

Seneca lifted his daughter from her mother's arms and placed her in the waiting embrace of her grand aunt Maddie. He motioned for Cat to be seated in another log chair opposite the door. She tilted her head questioningly but complied. Seneca turned back to Aunt Maddie and opened the ballooning brocade bag at her feet. He extracted familiar bundle.

"My mother's wedding moccasins," he said, turning back to Cat.

Emotion welled in Cat, and her eyes filled with happy tears. "Oh, I am so happy to wear them again."

Seneca knelt down in front of her and lifted her foot

esting it against his thigh. He removed her boot and
lipped the wedding moccasin on, then kissed the toe of
t. He repeated the same ceremony with her other foot.
'hen he rose, took her hand, and brought her to her feet.

"Come, come." Maurice beckoned them toward the al-
ır. "It is time once more."

"Wait," Aunt Maddie said. "Cat, look in the little room
ı the back. There is something more for you."

A question in her mind but not on her lips, Cat retreated
) the back of the church. When she stepped inside, tears
f joy spilled down her cheeks. Aunt Maddie had brought
er mother's wedding gown.

Seneca, his daughter nestled in his arms, walked down
ıe aisle with Madeline on his arm. Evalina, in the colorful
own she'd worn at the Prospect House masquerade ball,
ıe one Bear admired, walked slowly down the aisle ex-
laiming over the beams of sunlight making intricate pat-
ırns on the floor as they were received through the glass
anes. Bringing up the rear was Bear in his canvas pants
ıd an eggshell open-necked cotton shirt.

Once they were all standing at the altar, Cat emerged
om the little room. In the dazzling sunlight she walked
ɔwn the aisle to her waiting family and friends, the
armth of her body and the sun making her mother's
hite satin gown float around her in a soft aura. Seneca
ıcked in his breath at the beauty of the woman who was
 be his forever.

At the front of the church sat a guest who surprised
at.

"Stewart?" A confused smile touched her lips.

Stewart Mayne stood and came to them. "Yes, my dear.
hope you don't mind. I had to be here with you. You've
ways meant so much to me, and Seneca is the son of
ı old friend."

Cat leaned forward and kissed Stewart's cheek. "You'r looking fitter than I've seen you in a long time. I'm gla you're here. I . . . *we* will look to you for guidance as w change the course of Stockdale Enterprises."

"I am proud to be with you both. Incidentally, I thinl you'll be happy to know that Harrison and his mothe have gone off on a round-the-world cruise. They won't b back for months. Perhaps never, if my luck holds out." Stewart chuckled. "And I have your new home ready fc you to move into at any time."

"Thank you." Cat smiled.

Garrett hadn't lived to see the completion of his grea camp. Seneca had modified the design so as to eliminat its ostentatiousness and make it one with the natural lak and woods in which it stood. Cat knew the new home wa a perfect haven for a growing family and, happily, it ir cluded two rooms for Aunt Maddie.

"Shall we?" Maurice urged.

The wedding party stood before the wizened old pries who closed his eyes and raised his arms and bony hanc in an arc over his hunched shoulders. Sweet birdson drifted through the open window on the scent of balsar and cedar. Silently Maurice stood thus for a long momer while the others waited for him to speak. At last Jane Cat gave a baby squeal.

Maurice opened his eyes. "Now that approval has bee granted, the rest of you may speak your words."

Cat turned toward Seneca. "I come to you now, my tru and only love, with all my heart and with all the rig reasons for us to marry. I step into your world and brir to you part of my own. I love you, Seneca, with everythir that I am and will ever be, and I will give my all to yc forever in our world."

Seneca beamed down at Cat. He transferred his wid

wake daughter to Bear's massive arms and swept his em-
race around the frail shoulders of Aunt Maddie.

"I come to you now, Lila Catherine Pierce, with open
nd embracing heart, soul, and mind. I love you with the
epth and breadth of the eternal life of these mountains.
step into your world and bring you part of my own. The
reator gave us first the gift of love between us—and
econd the greater gift of a child made from that love. We
re supremely blessed in our world."

Tears spilled down over Cat's face, but her smile was
adiant as she gazed up at her husband.

"Are there rings . . . again?" Maurice asked.

Aunt Maddie reached for a small pouch hidden in Janey
at's blanket. She grinned. "Most precious place I knew
 keep a precious symbol." She withdrew the original
ng Seneca had given Cat in their first wedding.

"Oh, Aunt Maddie," Cat cried, "you've been the very
ainstay of my life."

Seneca took the ring from Madeline and, smiling with
ve, slipped it over Cat's finger.

Cat bit her lower lip and looked up at Seneca. "I . . .
don't have the ring for you."

Seneca lifted his left hand, showing the wedding ring
ladeline had produced at their first wedding. "No need.
never took it off."

"I see there is no silk or bear grease to consider this
ne," Maurice observed. He held out the dusty ledger.
Sign here, then."

"And here," Evalina said, producing the official docu-
ent printed with the Great Seal of the state of New York.
We're not taking any chances with this ceremony!"

Cat and Seneca signed both documents, and Maurice
ised his arms once more. "Has anyone else anything to
ntribute?"

All was silent.

"Then with the power vested in the air around us, pronounce you are husband and wife," Maurice said in scratchy voice.

Janey Cat Pierce let out a little cry to let her parent know she was getting hungry.

"And daughter," Maurice added.

Madeline let out a little sob of happiness.

"And aunt."

Bear grabbed up Evalina and swung her around so tha her colorful skirt ballooned out around her. *"Regarde, m little grizzly, we are next!"*

Evalina's giggle trailed around them. "Oh, it's deliciou simply delicious!"

Maurice dropped to the floor amid his burlap robe "Done! Once and for all!"

As loving celebration swirled around them, Cat an Seneca kissed deeply. When they parted and gazed int each other's eyes, they knew that, like the Adirondack there dwelled in them both—and in their child and futur children—an extraordinary magic and hearts that woul remain . . . forever wild.

Dear Reader:

It was pleasurable hard work for me to write this book. Travel and research into the Adirondack Mountains, one of my favorite places on the planet, is always a journey of love. As an author, I am always interested in people and information on the Adirondacks and enjoy hearing from others who feel the same way.

A few things I thought you'd like to know: There really was a Durant family, and their history is part of the building of the Union Pacific transcontinental railroad as well as the development of the Adirondacks. There really was a Prospect House overlooking Blue Mountain Lake, and Thomas Edison did pull the switch that lit up the first hotel in the world outfitted with his electric lights. Following a colorful and exciting history, the deteriorating building was demolished in 1915. There are a few remaining Adirondack Great Camps, remnants of a unique period of history and architecture in New York State. While Native Americans did not reside in that area of the mountains, they did hunt and trap throughout the region and were known to the early residents.

Whether because of the spirits of Cat and Seneca, other living and departed Adirondackers, progress and the invention of the automobile, or perhaps the indomitable force of the mountains themselves, railroad companies and tracks came and went throughout the Adirondacks, but never survived in that area of the mountains depicted in this book of fiction.

The Adirondack Park was established by law in 1892. It is the largest state park in the contiguous United States—larger than both Yosemite and Yellowstone National Parks—six million acres of mountains, lakes, forests, streams, and towns. For more information on this fascinating region, read *Township 34* by Harold K. Hochschild (or any of the seven volumes taken from it and published separately by the Adirondack Museum); *The Adirondacks Illustrated,* a narrative guidebook by the great photographer and illustrator Seneca Ray Stoddard, first published in 1874; *Fairy Tale Railroad* by Henry Harter; Alfred L. Donaldson's *A History of the Adirondacks* (two volumes); and *Great Camps of the Adirondacks* by Harvey H. Kaiser.

The Adirondack Museum at Blue Mountain Lake takes at least a full day to experience and offers a great many volumes, maps, and photographs of the area. Sagamore Institute at Racquette Lake (a great camp built as Sagamore Lodge by the Durant family and later sold to the Vanderbilts) provides several resident educational programs from spring through fall. And the Adirondack Railway from its station and museum at Thendara offers a historic ride into the past on original cars. Those are only a few suggestions among vast resources available.

Finally . . . Article XIV of the New York State Constitution deems Adirondack Park . . . forever wild.

Garda Parker
Bouckville, NY
November 1993

About the Author

Garda Parker is the author of five previous novels: SCARLET LADY, TEMPTATION'S FLAME, ARIZONA TEMPTATION, OUT OF THE BLUE, and LOVE AT LAST; and two novellas: SNOW ANGELS and BERMUDA QUADRANGLE.

Garda is the campaign writer at Colgate University. With her partner, Bob Milner, she lives near a small lake in Bouckville, New York, the antiques capital of the state. She has a grown daughter, Tamara.

Taylor—made Romance From Zebra Books

WHISPERED KISSES (3830, $4.99/$5.99)
Beautiful Texas heiress Laura Leigh Webster never imagined that her biggest worry on her African safari would be the handsome Jace Elliot, her tour guide. Laura's guardian, Lord Chadwick Hamilton, warns her of Jace's dangerous past; she simply cannot resist the lure of his strong arms and the passion of his *Whispered Kisses*.

KISS OF THE NIGHT WIND (3831, $4.99/$5.99)
Carrie Sue Strover thought she was leaving trouble behind her when she deserted her brother's outlaw gang to live her life as schoolmarm Carolyn Starns. On her journey, her stagecoach was attacked and she was rescued by handsome T.J. Rogue. T.J. plots to have Carrie lead him to her brother's cohorts who murdered his family. T.J., however, soon succumbs to the beautiful runaway's charms and loving caresses.

FORTUNE'S FLAMES (3825, $4.99/$5.99)
Impatient to begin her journey back home to New Orleans, beautiful Maren James was furious when Captain Hawk delayed the voyage by searching for stowaways. Impatience gave way to uncontrollable desire once the handsome captain searched *her* cabin. He was looking for illegal passengers; what he found was wild passion with a woman he knew was unlike all those he had known before!

PASSIONS WILD AND FREE (3828, $4.99/$5.99)
After seeing her family and home destroyed by the cruel and hateful Epson gang, Randee Hollis swore revenge. She knew she found the perfect man to help her—gunslinger Marsh Logan. Not only strong and brave, Marsh had the ebony hair and light blue eyes to make Randee forget her hate and seek the love and passion that only he could give her.

WHAT'S LOVE GOT TO DO WITH IT?

Everything . . . Just ask Kathleen Drymon . . . and Zebra Books

CASTAWAY ANGEL	*(3569-1, $4.50/$5.50)*
GENTLE SAVAGE	*(3888-7, $4.50/$5.50)*
MIDNIGHT BRIDE	*(3265-X, $4.50/$5.50)*
VELVET SAVAGE	*(3886-0, $4.50/$5.50)*
TEXAS BLOSSOM	*(3887-9, $4.50/$5.50)*
WARRIOR OF THE SUN	*(3924-7, $4.99/$5.99)*

EVERY DAY WILL FEEL LIKE FEBRUARY 14TH!

Zebra Historical Romances
by Terri Valentine

vailable wherever paperbacks are sold, or order direct from the ublisher. Send cover price plus 50¢ per copy for mailing and andling to Penguin USA, P.O. Box 999, c/o Dept. 17109, ergenfield, NJ 07621. Residents of New York and Tennessee ust include sales tax. DO NOT SEND CASH.